RESISTING HER ARMY DOC RIVAL

BY
SUE MacKAY

A MONTH TO MARRY THE MIDWIFE

BY
FIONA McARTHUR

MILLS & BOON

Sue MacKay lives with her husband in New Zealand's beautiful Marlborough Sounds, with the water at her doorstep and the birds and the trees at her back door. It is the perfect setting to indulge her passions of entertaining friends by cooking them sumptuous meals, drinking fabulous wine, going for hill walks or kayaking around the bay—and, of course, writing stories.

Fiona McArthur is an Australian midwife who lives in the country and loves to dream. Writing Medical Romance gives Fiona the scope to write about all the wonderful aspects of romance, adventure, medicine and the midwifery she feels so passionate about. When she's not catching babies, Fiona and her husband Ian are off to meet new people, see new places and have wonderful adventures. Drop in and say hi at Fiona's website: FionaMcArthurAuthor.com.

RESISTING HER ARMY DOC RIVAL

BY
SUE MacKAY

Published in Great Britain 2017
By Mills & Boon, an imprint of HarperCollins*Publishers*
1 London Bridge Street, London, SE1 9GF

© 2017 Sue MacKay

ISBN: 978-0-263-92638-5

Printed and bound in Spain
by CPI, Barcelona

Dear Reader,

Almost everyone has scars—mental and/or physical. Some are minor, others serious, but all affect the person carrying them. These scars and how they're coped with are what make people interesting.

In *Resisting Her Army Doc Rival* Captain Madison Hunter has had more than her share of bad luck, which has left her unable to show anyone her body and thus keeps her away from getting close to men. Captain Sam Lowe isn't bothered by that— he's got his own guilt to deal with, and he finds Maddy fascinating and beautiful. But she's no longer the bright, bubbly personality he vaguely remembers from school. And the sadness lurking in her eyes and her fear of smoke has him pulling up the barriers around his soul so fast it's bewildering. But there's something about this woman he can't ignore. If he was ever to put his heart on the line and get close to someone it would be Maddy who'd make him do it.

This story didn't come easily for me. There's a lot of pain in my hero and my heroine, and I really wanted them to have their moment—to learn to live freely again and know what it's like not to be on guard all the time. But they didn't make it simple for me. Oh, no. Every word and emotion was dragged out onto the page, and I'm relieved they finally got their happy ending.

I hope you root for these two as you read their story.

Drop by and let me know if they affected you as they did me: sue.mackay56@yahoo.com. Or visit my website: suemackay.co.nz.

Cheers,

Sue MacKay

To the most gorgeous and precious wee people in my life. Grandies Austin and Taylor. I love you to bits and can't believe how lucky I am to get Austin hugs and Taylor smiles.

And to Laura McCallen for your unfailing patience to see me through this story. (At least you appeared patient from my end.) :)

Books by Sue MacKay

Mills & Boon Medical Romance

Midwife...to Mum!
Reunited...in Paris!
A December to Remember
Breaking All Their Rules
Dr White's Baby Wish
The Army Doc's Baby Bombshell

Visit the Author Profile page
at millsandboon.co.uk for more titles.

Praise for
Sue MacKay

'I highly recommend this story to all lovers of romance: it is moving, emotional, a joy to read!'
—*Goodreads* on
A December to Remember

CHAPTER ONE

CAPTAIN MADISON HUNTER stepped out of the New Zealand Air Force freight plane and onto the tarmac, relieved to be on terra firma at last, flying being her least favourite of the things she had to do. Then the searing heat of the Sinai Peninsula slammed into her, ramping up the discomfort level and making her gasp.

'Who needs this?'

'Beats Waiouru in winter any day,' quipped the communications major striding alongside her. His energy was embarrassing after all those hours crammed between cargo crates, doing nothing more intelligent than playing endless rounds of poker.

'Guess that's because you've been here before. Right now I'd be happy marching through snow and sleet,' Madison retorted, thinking longingly of the isolated army base where she'd done her basic training, hell hole of the North Island that it was.

'At least your boots will be dry.'

'True.' Sodden boots were the bane of army exercises back home. They never dried out before the next foray. Looking at the dusty ground in front of her, she finally smiled. 'This couldn't be more different. Exciting even.' If she could ignore the heat.

Heaving the thirty-kilogram pack higher on her back, Madison rolled her shoulders to ease the tightness. Didn't work. Sweat streamed over her shoulder blades, down her face, between her breasts. *Must have been out of my mind when I signed up.* 'Did I miss the clause in my contract saying beware of sun, sand, dirt, and sweat enough to drown a small creature?'

'Page three,' quipped Major Crooks.

'I take it the high temperature is relentless.' Dry heat shimmered against the white block buildings, while the air was almost cracking. Off-duty soldiers lounged in what little shade they could find.

'I never got used to it on my last tour.' He pointed across the dusty parade ground. 'See that building to the right? It's the medical unit.'

Madison scoped the basic structure with a faded red cross painted above the door. Less than what she'd worked in on base at home, more than she'd been led to believe she'd find here. Had to be a positive. 'I might drop in after a shower.' If she didn't fall asleep standing under the water. Her body ached with fatigue. There hadn't been a lot of sleeping going on during the flight. She probably stank like a piece of roadkill about now.

A man stepped through the medical unit's entrance, and paused. Tall and broad shouldered, his body tapered down to the narrow hips his hands settled on. Looking in their direction, his gaze finally settled on her.

Sam Lowe? As in the guy every girl from high school had fallen in love with Sam Lowe?

Her knees sagged, and not from the load on her back.

Seriously? Someone she knew from home when home had been Christchurch? Now, there was a surprise that lightened her mood a notch. Not that they'd been friends in any way but she'd grab at any familiar face in an alien environment; until she'd settled in, any rate. Unless she'd got it wrong, and that wasn't Sam.

'Are you all right?' Major Crooks asked.

'Fine. Where're our barracks, do you know?'

He pointed. 'Over to the right, behind the mess block are the officers' quarters.'

'Thanks, I'll catch up with you later.' Right now Madison wanted to check out the man she thought she recognised, but was probably so far off the mark she'd sound stupid uttering his name.

She squinted through the heat. No doubting the vision that reminded her of standing on the side of the rugby field, barracking for their high school team as he led them to yet another win. It was definitely Sam Lowe striding towards her, those long legs eating up the ground like nothing bothered him. It probably didn't. Those shoulders and the cocky tip of his head backed up what her eyes were seeing, but there was little else she knew about him, she realised.

'Captain Hunter, Madison.' The man had the nerve to snap to attention in front of her. And grin. *He still does that.* Smiled and grinned his way into and out of every situation he faced. An expert, no less, she now recalled. *Still arrogant?* Well, she wasn't a spoilt brat any more—if she'd ever been—so possibly he'd changed, too.

'Sam,' she replied, at a loss for words. She didn't trust unexpected surprises. They tended to backfire on her.

He said, 'Welcome to the Sinai.'

Her voice returned, spilling out more than was necessary. 'I can't believe this. We're both in the army, posted to the same region, on the same base?' What were the odds? They even had rank in common. Her teeth ground back and forth. Slim to zilch. Showed how wrong she got things these days, despite the harsh lessons she'd endured already. A medical insignia told her more. 'You're a doctor, too.'

He nodded. 'We've been expecting you.'

'As in me personally?' Of course her name would've been on the staff list that'd have come through days ago. But, 'I doubt you realised who I was,' she retorted, suddenly on edge in front of that dazzling smile, and needing to shield herself from its dangerous intensity. So? Relax. She knew how to cope with men, had learned the hard way to always be careful and cautious. Just ignore them. Easy-peasy.

'As in a new medic, fresh from home and not worn down by the day-to-day grind of living in camp.' He widened his grin. 'And, yes, as in Madison Hunter, high school prefect and science genius.'

Oh, yeah, it would be too easy to fall into that grin, and forget the pain of being betrayed after trusting a man with her heart once already. Reining in the bewilderment overtaking her faster than a speeding bullet, she stood to attention. 'So we'll be working together?'

'I'll be out of your hair next week.'

He wasn't getting anywhere near her hair. But was he admiring it? Yeah, he was. Something like shock diluted that brazen glare he'd been delivering.

Fair cop. She did look very different these days. Her

waist-length hair had fallen prey to the hairdresser's scissors the day after she'd joined the army. Crawling under barbed wire through mud and snow while dressed in full army kit had made the thick locks she'd considered her best feature very unattractive and in need of constant attention. What had Sam been talking about? Apart from hair? 'So you're one of the medics I'm replacing.'

'Afraid so.' His shoulder moved, oh so nonchalantly.

That grin was now crooked. Instead of loosening the hold it held over her, she was drawn in deeper. It was beguiling and threatening in an I-can't-afford-to-check-this-out kind of way. Desperate for a distraction—no, Sam already had that role—Madison glanced around the compound. She checked out the perimeter fence and saw women, men and children sitting in a huddle, resignation on their faces.

'Why are there civilians waiting outside the camp?'

'They're hoping to see a doctor or nurse.'

Her heart tightened for the sad-looking bunch of people. They appeared helpless, lost even. It took all her willpower not to drop her pack and race across to ask what she could do for them. That was one of the reasons she'd joined the army after all. 'I want to help them.'

'It's not that easy, Madison.'

'Why not?' She flung the words at him. 'It's why I became a doctor. Isn't it the same for you?'

He took her question on the chin. 'I understand, but out here you're a soldier first, doctor second.'

'So you're saying we ignore those people?' Her hand flapped through the air in the direction of the perimeter. 'Seriously?'

'No, I'm not.' Sam's mouth tightened as his gaze stopped on the people she'd noted. 'We do see some of the locals under a strict system involving body searches and metal detectors before bringing them in.'

'We don't hold regular clinics?' She'd been told she would be attending to outsiders, and had been keen to get amongst them.

'More than enough,' he grunted, 'but so many people require medical attention it'd be a never-ending stream if we allowed it.' Sam locked his now fierce eyes on her. 'We do our share. Remember why you're here, Captain.'

'But there are children out there.' She couldn't help wanting to help each and every person in that crowd waiting quietly as though they had nothing better to do, but especially the children. They were pulling at her heartstrings already. It would be a struggle not being allowed to put her medical skills to good use as she wanted when there were people needing them. That was why she'd trained in the first place, to make life better for others, especially children now that she likely wouldn't be having any herself.

'Yes, there are. Cute as buttons some of them, too.' His face softened briefly.

'They look so desperate.'

Sam shook himself and growled, 'Don't be fooled. They're not all what they seem.' He started walking again.

'They're not?' But he didn't, or chose not to, hear her.

On a sigh she changed the subject. For now. 'I'll see you around. I need to find my quarters.'

'I'll—'

'I don't think so. Major Crooks gave me directions.'

Then she added lamely, just in case Sam didn't get the point, 'He's been here before.' Having this man escort her through the camp was not happening. She required a few minutes to put her left-field reaction to him into perspective. He might be a sight to behold, and a face from the past, but she had to learn to stand strong and inviolate. Vulnerability might've become her norm lately, but it was one of the things she was working hard to overcome. So when her danger sonar said be aware of this man, she was going to push him away.

'I was about to say I'll see you later in the medical unit, where I can introduce you to everyone.' He stared at her, annoyance vying with interest in those eyes that appeared to notice far too much, his mouth flat at last.

While *her* mouth ached with the tight smile she was trying to keep in place. Her eyes had better be fierce, not showing her true concerns about this exchange. Having anyone know her inner turmoil would see her back on that plane, heading home. 'Yes, Captain.'

His face instantly became inscrutable, every last thought and emotion snapped off with the flick of a switch. Her tense muscles tightened further. She'd gone too far. He didn't deserve her attitude, but a woman had to look out for herself. Especially in a place she did not understand. In a fit of pique for coming second to her in an exam result Sam had once told her she was a spoilt little rich brat, and right now she was proving him correct. He'd also said she knew nothing about the real world. *If only he knew.* Back up. She didn't want him to know about the disaster that flipped her life upside down.

Suddenly she was tired of it all; exhausted from the

trip, from the heat, from the short but stupid conversation with Sam. She wanted to get on with him, maybe get to know him a little—without falling into that grin. 'I look forward to learning the ropes from you.'

'I'll see you later.' Sam's boots clicked together, then he spun around to stride away, his back ramrod straight, his hands clenched at his sides.

He's better looking than ever. Shut up. But it was true. The boyishly handsome and beguiling face had become chiselled, mature, and worthy of more than a glance. As was that muscular bod. Her traitorous body was reacting to the thought of what his army fatigues covered. Only because there'd been a sex drought in her life for so long, surely? Not that Sam would be the rain that broke it, even if her body was thinking otherwise.

Heatstroke. Had to be. But she'd been out in the sun less than half an hour. Admitting things about a man she'd met minutes earlier would have more to do with her wobbly state of mind. Things that weren't conducive to working alongside him. Captain Lowe. Remember that and forget his looks, his muscles, and that open face she'd managed to shut down. But she was female after all and did enjoy being around a good-looking guy. She wasn't immune to physical attributes that would send any breathing, feeling woman into orbit. Despite the fact that letting down the barriers so that a man could get close would take more guts than she possessed, she could still appreciate perfection when she saw it.

Maddy shook her head abruptly. *You came here to do a job, not to fire up your hormones.* Experience had taught her that she couldn't do casual sex; she had to have some connection with a lover. When she'd fallen

in love she'd known it had been worth the wait. Until
that man, who had become her husband, had pulverised
her heart along with her confidence, and she was back
to square one. She was unlikely to ever forget Jason's
appalled reaction to her disfigured body. She'd believed
in his love. Now she knew not to expect any different
from any man, so knew keeping safe was entirely up
to herself.

'Captain? Your room is number three in that block
behind the mess hall.' A soldier appeared in her line of
vision, a clipboard in his hand, thankfully blotting out
that irritating sight of long legs and tight backside that
had her in a spin.

'Thank you, Private,' she acknowledged as she
turned in the right direction.

One step and Madison froze.

Thick smoke billowed above a hut on the far perimeter.

A chill slithered down her spine, lifted the hairs on
her arms. Her heart leapt into her throat. She forgot to
breathe. 'No.' The word crawled out of her mouth as fear
swamped her. 'No-o.' Smoke meant fire. No, please, no.
She couldn't deal with that. Not today. Not ever. Not
again. Anything else, yes. *Move. Run.* Someone could
be trapped inside the hut. *Move.* She remained trans-
fixed, staring at that murky column rising into the air,
twisting, spiralling out of control.

'Move, damn it.' *Do something.* But her boots were
filled with concrete. 'I can't.' Her fingers touched her
midriff, not feeling the scars through her uniform, but
they were there, as familiar to her touch as her face in
a mirror was to her sight.

'Madison?' Sam stood in front of her.

She tried to look away from that smoke. She really did. But her eyes had a mind of their own, were fixated with the swirling, growing cloud. As the smoke darkened, horror darkened her soul. Knots cramped her stomach. Bile spewed into her mouth, soured her tongue. Finally her lungs moved, expanded slowly against her chest.

Strong hands caught her upper arms, shook her. 'Captain Hunter, what's the problem?'

The air stalled in her lungs again. *Breathe out slowly; one, two, three. Now in, one, two.* 'There's a fire.' She jerked her chin in the right direction as her lungs contracted, forcing hot air through her mouth.

Sam glanced where she'd indicated. 'That's not smoke. It's a dust whirl. Get used to it. We get plenty around here.' That intense stare returned to her face. What was he seeing? Apart from someone who should be behaving like a soldier? And clearly wasn't.

'You're sure? You haven't gone to check it out.'

'I'm sure.'

Her knees sagged, and her shoulders drooped further into his strong grip. Air escaped her lungs again. 'D-dust I can cope with.' Phew. She was safe; she didn't have to rush into roaring flames to rescue Granddad, pull him free of burning timbers. Except she hadn't managed to save him. A blazing beam had seen to that. The sweat on her back chilled, her damaged skin prickled. Granddad.

Someone was shaking her. Sam. Of course. 'Madison, look at me.'

I can't do that. He'd see right inside, would know

she was a screw-up. Nothing like the confident girl who used to cope with everything and had always been a success. She certainly didn't used to do vulnerable. Digging deep, she tried to find that Madison, but she was long gone. Burned in the midst of a fire. 'I'm all right. I don't mind dust.' That scratchy sound coming across her tongue was not her usual voice; instead, it sounded like a cat when its tail was stomped on.

'You won't be saying that for long. It never goes away, coats every damned surface, and gets into places you won't believe.'

But it won't kill me, or scar my body, or terrify me. Or take someone I love. Or change my life for ever. Shaking in her boots, she continued staring at the thinning cloud as it changed direction to head away from the buildings. A grenade had been lobbed at her within minutes of arriving. This place was not good for her.

Just as well Sam still held her. To hit the ground with thirty kilos on her back would hurt, and write her off as a loser in everyone's eyes.

Did he know he was rubbing her arms with his thumbs? Couldn't, or he'd stop immediately. She didn't want that. Not yet. She needed the contact, the comfort, which showed how messed up she was. She was an officer in the New Zealand army, for pity's sake. 'It's truly only dust?'

'Yes, Madison, not smoke.'

The unexpected gentleness in his voice nearly undid her. She wasn't used to that tone from men any more, and it reached inside to tear at her heart, slashed at the barricades she kept wound tight. She tilted forward, drawn by an invisible thread, needing to get closer. Her brain was begging Sam to wrap his arms around her.

Her chin flipped up. Under pressure from her pack she straightened her spine and locked her eyes on his. He'd have her back on that plane heading home quick smart if he knew what she wanted of him. Good idea. That'd get her away from here and everything she suspected was going to test her over the coming weeks and months. Something at the back of her mind was pushing forward. *I am not a coward.* Not even a little one? *No. Not even a tiny one.* Messed up? *Yes.* But she would not add coward to her CV. Twisting her head away from that all-seeing gaze, she locked her eyes on the dust that had ripped her equilibrium apart.

'Dust can be a nuisance. Dirty and scratchy.' Slowly, one shallow breath at a time, her lungs relaxed, returned to doing their job properly. There *was* little resemblance to smoke in that whirl. She'd made an idiot of herself. 'Thanks for rectifying my mistake,' she whispered.

'Any time.' Sam stepped back, his hands dropping to his hips in his apparent favourite stance, taking that strength and safety with him, leaving her swaying until she found her balance, but like he was ready to catch her if necessary. That she could cope with; the intensity he was watching her with she could not.

Madison slowly looked around, taking time to get her body back under control. She was a soldier, and a doctor. No one need know she lost her cool at the sight of smoke. Or the smell of it. Or the roar of flames. Except Sam had already witnessed her near breakdown. She could only hope he wasn't going to be like a dog with a bone until he found out what that had been about.

She risked a glance at him, and gasped at the worry filling his steady summer-sky eyes.

'Are you all right?' he demanded.

'Yes.' The thudding in her chest had spread to take up residence in her skull—beat, beat, beat. She needed to get indoors, away from dust clouds—and compelling eyes that had already seen too much. 'I've never seen dust like that, and naturally…' Would he fall for this? 'Naturally I thought there was a fire. I won't make that mistake again.'

'You'd better not. It would be a hindrance on patrol. You could endanger others.' His worry didn't diminish, suggesting he was concerned she wouldn't be competent enough to do her job as a soldier.

'I think you'll find I know what I'm doing.' But reality was sinking in fast. This was nothing like practising back home, however seriously the officers had taken every manoeuvre in which they partook. If she did freak out at the sight of smoke again she might not get away with it. But as long as the camp commander didn't see fit to lock her up in a padded cell she'd be all right.

'You'd better.' His worry might be abating but he was still studying her with the intensity of a microbiologist looking down a microscope.

Which rattled her nearly as much as the dust had. Her vulnerability was rearing up again, pushing out from the corner she worked hard at keeping it tucked into. Sam—or anyone on base—must not find her lacking. Neither could he learn how insecure she could be.

'Are you sure you're okay?' he asked in a less autocratic tone.

'How long have you served on the Peninsula?' Suddenly her time here stretched before her, filled with uncertainties. Would she be strong enough to lead troops outside the camp? There'd be no respect from them if she turned into a blithering idiot because of dust. Or smoke.

'Twelve months, give or take a day.'

She'd do less. Thank goodness for something. 'Have you enjoyed your tour here?' Anything to avoid the chasm she was looking into right now.

His nod was sharp. 'This has been one of the better ones.'

'So there've been others.' Others that hadn't been as comfortable, the edgy tone of his voice suggested.

'Yes.'

'Guess I've a lot to learn.'

'Definitely, but we all have to deal with things we're not at ease with when we first arrive. You'll be fine.' The grin was back, a little forced, but she'd accept it as it made her relax a teeny bit more. For now the danger of falling into that compelling look was far less risky than exposing the vulnerability that haunted her. This was Sam Lowe, a man she could relate to because they came from the same city, had been to the same school, and right now someone familiar was like balm on feverish skin.

Bet he's a fantastic doctor. And a good soldier. He'd always done well at everything he did. Yes, she remembered that much about him. The pounding behind her eyes intensified. There was too much to deal with right now. 'I need to settle into my room.' She *needed* to look forward and not back, something she couldn't manage while in Sam's presence.

'I'll see you later in the medical centre.'

She nodded. 'I'll be there as soon as possible.' And get started on her new job, even if she only got to meet her colleagues and learn the layout of the unit.

Sam turned away, spun back as though trying to catch her out. The intensity in his gaze had not backed off. Whatever he was looking for, she doubted he found it because finally he shrugged, said almost kindly, 'Welcome to the Peninsula, Maddy.' This time he strode away without a backward glance.

He remembered her friends called her Maddy? Or was it a natural abbreviation of Madison? That was more likely. He wouldn't remember much about her. Why should he? They hadn't mixed in the same crowd or been in the same classes. But… A sigh escaped her lips. The way her name sounded in his gravelly voice was something to hold onto. It warmed her when she was already hot, flattened the goose bumps that dust had raised, gave her hope. Hope for what? No idea, but it was so rare she'd hold onto it anyway.

The pack still weighed her down, pulling so her spine curved backwards, but it was the head stuff that kept her rooted to the spot. That and the man whose long legs were eating up the parade ground as he put distance between them. She felt as though she had too many balls in the air and wasn't about to catch any of them.

Trudging towards her barracks, she tried to drag up memories of Sam. He'd been head boy in their last year, captain of his sports teams, a natural leader if the devotion from others wasn't a figment of her imagination. Officer material for sure. Which said he'd want to be in charge here in the medical unit. Probably was anyway, given he'd been here for a year.

Too much to think about right now. Exhaustion gnawed at her. Her body ached and her head was full of wool. The heat pelted her from every direction. She was in way over her depth and had no idea how to get out. But she would find a way: after a shower and a full night's sleep in a bed, and after time to reflect on how she could move forward without blotting her copybook.

Now, there was a first.

Could be quite exciting really.

CHAPTER TWO

'MADISON HUNTER SURE grew up beautiful,' Sam muttered. But, then, she'd had a good start, had always been cute and pretty, and had kept the guys on the lookout for her around the school grounds.

Slamming the outside door behind him, he cut off the heat—and the sight of Captain Hunter. He recalled the pert nose, the sweet mouth, and the thick, dark blonde hair that had swished back and forth across her back whenever she'd worn it free of the ties that the school had insisted on most of the time. That mouth wasn't so sweet any more; tightened quickly as a lightning flash at times. But not in a sulky, spoilt manner. More as if something had hurt her in the past and she was desperate to hold herself together. There'd been a load of fear in her eyes, her face, her stance. What had that been about? Something horrendous that had changed her for ever? That'd be an explanation he could understand all too well. As for the short bob—who'd known how curly her hair was? Must've been the weight of it all that had kept it nearly straight back then.

'What had I been thinking when I rushed out to welcome her on base?' Had he wanted a taste of home?

From someone who knew next to nothing about him? They were virtually strangers, had barely acknowledged each other eighteen years ago, mainly because they'd had nothing in common. These days his cocky confidence had been replaced with caution and a blinding awareness of how life could implode in an instant. Drawing everyone close to him no longer happened. Instead, he used the guilt he carried to keep everyone distant. How could he be happy when other people weren't able to be because of him?

Drawn to the window like a lad to the candy shop, he stared out at Madison dragging herself towards the officers' quarters. Tall, slim and, from the muscles tightening under his palms when he'd caught her, very fit. Enough to make a man put his heart on the line. If he had a heart. Which meant she was safe from him. He'd put that particular organ in lockdown two years ago to protect anyone from being hurt by him.

But he couldn't deny the blood in his veins. It was heating him, hardening him, reminding him how long it had been since he'd been with a woman. Too long. An oath ripped out of his mouth as the truth slam-dunked him. Unbelievable. He wanted Madison. Minutes after saying hello to someone he barely knew and he was reacting with none of the usual hesitations that instantly sprang up to protect him, and her. Unbelievable.

He was going to have to pull tight on those bands around the pit that held all his emotions. In a very short time Madison was proving to be a challenge to everything he held close and accepted as his way of life now. He'd have to dig deep to keep her off limits. But he'd had plenty of practice over the last two years, so what was one week of hardship? An impossibility? No. Definitely doable.

The window was warm against his forehead as he tracked Maddy's slow movements. Exhaustion folded her in on herself as she hauled one shapely leg after the other. He should've taken her pack and dumped it in the barracks regardless of the fact she'd been in a hurry to get away from him. How hard would it have been to do something kind instead of walking away to save his own sanity? There was no answer. Only minutes in her company and she'd begun scrambling his brain like the eggs he'd had for breakfast.

'What's the great attraction out there?' Jock called across the room.

'Nothing,' he muttered.

'So you're going to stand there all day gaping at *nothing*?' Jock was supposedly going through patient records, removing the ones of those staff heading back to New Zealand next week.

Grabbing the interruption with both hands, he turned around. 'What's up? That stack of files doesn't appear any lower than it did an hour ago.'

Jock had probably been texting his family and pals at home. Now that they both only had a few days remaining it was getting harder to focus entirely on this tour of duty. Home was beckoning. For him that meant another army base, another round of training as well as working in a local hospital surgical unit until the next posting. More time to contemplate the empty years ahead.

'I hear the new medic's arrived. Guess we'll meet her shortly.'

'She's unpacking.' *You're going to fall under her*

spell in a snap. She was everything a red-blooded male could ask for.

'You've met her?'

'Long time back.' Yikes. He hadn't mentioned recognising her name in the email from headquarters. Now Jock would go for his throat. Sam tried to deflect him. 'Just passed her on the field, said hello.' Had seen her become as still as a rock, colourless as marble, staring at something he'd been unable to figure out as though it was going to attack her. He'd caught her before she'd face planted. What had that been about? Smoke, she'd said. Dust, he'd told her. The fear that had blitzed him from the shadows lurking in her eyes had dampened her spark into a dark brown bog filled with hidden torments. Genuine, don't-hurt-me fear. He hated that. There'd been signs that spoke of pain and anguish, signs she'd desperately tried to hide. And failed.

What happened to you, Madison?

No, he didn't want to know. Knowing would lead to wanting to learn even more and before he knew it he'd be getting close to her. He'd seen that fearful look before—in William's eyes as he'd lain dying. Sam's head tipped back as pain stabbed him. William. His best friend. They'd clicked the moment they'd met on the first day of training at Papakura Military Camp. The friend who'd never returned home after following him to Afghanistan.

'Sam,' Jock called, loud enough to break into his maudlin thoughts. 'You got the hots for this woman? Or is there some juicy history?' Jock's expression was full of expectation.

Go away, man. But that wasn't going to happen any

time soon, so Sam went for the obvious. 'I guess Madison will come visiting when she's ready,' he told the man who'd refused to back off from becoming a friend, no matter how often he'd been pushed aside.

Jock's head tipped sideways. 'Something you're not telling me?'

The guy was too shrewd for his own good. 'Can't think of anything.'

He got laughed at for his efforts. 'You've fallen for her.'

'In thirty seconds? Give me a break.' He shuddered at the thought. And that wasn't because Madison was a horror.

'I've heard that's all it takes.'

'Shouldn't you be sorting those files?'

Wrong thing to say.

'So I'm right.'

He had to shut Jock up fast. 'You couldn't be further from the mark. I cannot, will not, fall for a woman, no matter how much she interests me.'

'You ever think it time to let that go, mate?' One of Jock's eyebrows lifted nonchalantly, as if he didn't know the boundaries he was stepping over. But he did, and wasn't afraid to show it.

Heat hit Sam's cheeks as he snapped, 'Knock it off, Jock. You know the story. Nothing's changed.' Anger tightened his gut. He would never let it go. He didn't deserve happiness when William had died because of him.

Jock started to say something and Sam was instantly defensive, cutting him off. 'Don't go there,' he repeated, the warning loud and harsh in his voice. Back in New Zealand there was a woman hurting because of her fiancé's death, a lovely woman who'd never have William's children or share her life with the man she loved.

But across the room his pal merely shrugged as if this wasn't important. 'No problem. So where did you know Captain Hunter?'

'Madison. We weren't friends, just attended the same school. But there was no not knowing who she was.' Sam dragged his hand over his face. Maddy's career moves had been unbelievably similar to his. 'And don't even say we should play catch up on people we might both have known at school. I'm not interested so I'm staying out of her way as much as possible for the time I've got left here.' As the words were spilling regret flicked through his jaded psyche. He wanted to spend time with her despite the restrictions he'd imposed upon himself. But he'd stay away. One week wasn't too long to hold out on this strange need to touch base with her sneaking through him. One week.

'You seen the roster for tomorrow's patrol?' There was a mischievous sparkle in Jock's eyes that didn't bode well for his vow to stay clear of trouble.

Dread he didn't understand floored him. One look at the notice board partially explained. 'Swap with me.' Maddy had problems. He'd seen them in her eyes, in that fear, and for him to get involved, maybe help her, would endanger both of them. Ultimately he'd let her down, one way or another. He did that to people who mattered to him. Never again. 'Please,' he grunted. Not quite begging, but damned close.

'No can do. I'm rostered to take my crew into town and check out the hot spots there.'

'So swap.'

'Nope.' Jock shook his craggy head. 'Captain Hunter's all yours.'

Sam's crew would be patrolling beyond the town's perimeters. 'That sucks. She'd better be up to scratch,' was all he could come up with, though he didn't understand his concerns. Neither did he understand why his fingertips tingled and his groin ached just thinking about her.

Like he was eighteen all over again, working hard to be Mr Popularity at school, to show it didn't matter he was being raised by a family that was unrelated to him because his own had left him. A wonderful, kind and caring family, but not his.

Jock clapped a hand on his shoulder. 'These next few days could prove interesting. Time I witnessed you being brought to your knees over a woman.'

'You going to let up on this any time soon?' The guy knew what had gone down in Sam's past so why all this bull dust?

A low cry came from the treatment room, cutting through his gloom. He raised an eyebrow at Jock. 'One of ours?'

Jock shook his head. 'That's the mother of a three-year-old boy with five rotten teeth and inflamed gums. They were brought in while you were out filling the gas tanks.'

So he hadn't been texting. 'You never mentioned them when I came back.' Or when he'd started out to welcome Madison.

Jock shrugged. 'You want to swap anything, you can take this one for me.'

'Where are you up to with the boy?' Sam held out a hand for the notes being extended in his direction.

'Waiting on bloods before putting him out so as we can extract what's left of his teeth.' Jock fidgeted with other files on his table. Everyone knew he hated working with children, found it too stressful since losing a child in an emergency operation under extreme conditions in Afghanistan two years ago. He'd been on a hiding to nothing before he'd even picked up the scalpel but no one had been able to make him see that then or afterwards.

Sam could've asked to change places on patrol in return for taking over the boy's case and Jock probably would've obliged but, damn it, he wouldn't do that to his pal. All right, Jock was a pal, was getting closer all the time, but not so close Sam would hurt him. Good to have him at his back, though.

'Would you look at that?' Jock's eyes were so wide he appeared blinded by bright lights.

Sam didn't have to turn in the direction his mate was staring to know Maddy had entered the room, way earlier than he'd expected. 'She's quite something, isn't she?'

'Can see why you were mooning at the window.'

'I wasn't mooning.'

Jock's head bobbed like a balloon on the water. 'You sure you don't want to stay on for the next six months?' he cracked.

Sam laughed, if that's what the strangled sound that burst from his mouth was. Bitter, dry and full of despair. 'I'm no good for her.' But he had to face up to her—now and again and again over the coming days—

without becoming mesmerised by her. He turned to nod abruptly at Madison. 'That was quick.' Some colour had returned to her cheeks, but the exhaustion remained.

'The shower was cold.' Her shrug was defensive.

'That happens around here.' Relief softened him. Her fear had backed off. He doubted it was gone, but right now she wasn't being crippled by it. Wariness now met his gaze. Was she worried he'd told everyone she'd freaked out over a dust cloud? Not a chance. 'Cold water's just another thing to get used to. Come and meet the crew. Jock, Madison Hunter.'

Jock was on his feet in an instant, his hand extended in greeting. 'Hey, great to have you on board. Sam says you two know each other from school.'

Her mouth twisted into something resembling a smile. Not her old full-on, love-me-or-get-out-of-my-space smile, but something softer and more cautious that inexplicably settled over Sam's heart, loosened some of the tension he wore twenty-four seven. She said, 'That's an exaggeration.' She might've been talking to Jock but those weary eyes were on him. 'I didn't play rugby and Sam wasn't into debating.'

'You still do that? Belong to a debating team, I mean.' Damned if he could turn away. It felt as though he was falling into a pit, a deep one filled with the scent of home, the warmth of people he'd grown up with, the lure of a future he'd denied himself too long. And would continue to deny himself. But he would not hide from Madison for the next week. Decision made, he closed the gap between them. 'You used to be very good.'

'At arguing a point?' Her mouth softened. 'I still

argue about most things, but no longer under the guise of representing a team.'

'You sure Sam wasn't in your team?' Jock filled the sudden silence developing between Madison and Sam and halting the prickly sensation tripping down Sam's spine. 'He's always disputing everything around here.'

'Really?' Those brown eyes widened, lightened into the colour of his favourite milk chocolate. 'So you know better than the army?' she teased.

'Don't tell the commander.' He grinned.

'As if he doesn't know,' Jock quipped, before heading towards the room where his young patient waited.

'I said I'd take that case,' Sam called after him. He needed to get out of here anyway. 'You give Maddy the rundown on how the clinic works.'

'No, you do that.' Damn the guy but he'd shut the door on anything else Sam had to say.

'What case?' Maddy asked. 'Can I do something to help?'

'No, everything's under control. Anyway, you're not fit for duty until you've had some sleep.'

'I guess. One of the troops unwell?' She didn't let a subject drop easily.

'A child was brought in to have teeth removed.' Now she'd really crank up the questions.

'One of those waiting outside earlier? I thought you said they weren't allowed in very often.'

'There are exceptions. Especially with children.'

'I'm glad.' Her hand hovered over her stomach. 'Kids shouldn't be denied treatment because of the adult world around them.'

'Agreed.' He took a long breath, pushed aside

thoughts of children and babies, especially those he'd once hoped he might have with a special woman he could give his heart to. When Maddy opened her mouth he rushed to close her down before she said something that might have him saying things he told no one. 'You like kids?'

That hand flattened hard against her belly. The fingers whitened they were so tense. 'Adore them.' Her voice quivered.

Why? What was going on? Things weren't adding up. Earlier she'd been terrified of smoke that hadn't been smoke, now there was a distinct hint of sadness in her expression. 'So do I,' Sam commented, still wondering if Madison had problems at home. There were no rings on her fingers. Her surname hadn't changed. 'You haven't married or got into a full-time relationship?' he asked, oh, so casually, so as not to wind her up.

'Divorced and single,' she muttered after a long minute contemplating the wall behind him.

He hadn't realised he'd been holding his breath until he heard those words. Would've been better if she was hooked up with someone. Then he'd be able to laugh at this annoying sense of wanting to get closer to her. He'd never step on another man's patch. What did that matter when he had no intention of having a relationship at all? 'I'm sorry to hear that. About the divorce, I mean,' he added quickly, in case she misinterpreted his comment.

'So was I. At the time.' Then she winced. No doubt thinking she'd said far too much about herself. 'Shall we go and see if we can help Jock?'

'Sure.' The boy did not need three doctors but Sam

needed to get back on track with keeping away from Maddy, and she, he suspected, needed a diversion after revealing something so painful. The divorce must've been something she hadn't wanted. Had she got over it? For her sake, he hoped so. Wasting life pining for what might've been would be a shame, thought the expert at it.

CHAPTER THREE

'NEED SOME BLOOD HERE,' Sam called from the other side of the treatment room six hours later.

At the sound of the deep voice that brought images of pebbles rolling up the beach on a wave Madison looked up to find Sam watching her. 'You want me to get it?' When she already had her hands full?

His headshake was abrupt. 'You carry on extracting that bullet.'

'I'm on to it.' Literally. The forceps she held tapped against metal deep in her patient's thigh right on cue. Maddy grimaced. Talk about being thrown in at the deep end. Removing a bullet from this man's thigh wasn't difficult, but it was different from anything she'd dealt with in emergency departments back home. Which could explain why Sam had given her this patient when they'd been called in from the barracks. Getting her up to speed ASAP. Bullets and the army went hand in hand, she just hadn't thought she'd be facing any this soon. She'd wanted something outside her comfort zone, and now it looked like she'd got it.

He seemed to have to pull his gaze away from her to call out, 'Cassy, a bag of O neg wouldn't go amiss here.'

'Coming right up,' replied the nurse she'd met half an hour ago when she'd raced in dressed in a hurriedly pulled on long T and shorts.

One wide-eyed stare from Sam and she'd also hauled on scrubs quick smart. He had no idea of the hideous sight her garments covered, and the scrubs would make doubly sure neither he nor anyone else did find out. 'What's up?' she'd asked at the time to nudge his attention away from her. Just in case Sam had X-ray vision and could see through her clothes.

He'd brought her up to speed fast. 'Three locals were brought to the main entrance with injuries sustained when a man in the market went berserk with a gun. You've got the thigh wound.'

'Not a problem,' she'd replied, and had ignored his muttered comment that had gone something like 'nor should it be'.

'We have stocks of blood on hand?' Maddy asked now. 'Seriously?' This wasn't a fully equipped hospital with all the bells and whistles. Neither was there a blood bank to draw from.

'We keep a small supply on hand. The troops donate as it's required.'

'I guess we're lucky the gunman wasn't a very good shot or there'd have been more casualties,' she said, dropping the bullet into a stainless steel dish with a clang.

'The hospital in town will be busy with other victims,' Sam explained. 'We get those who're prepared to make the uncomfortable trip out here.' He paused cleansing the gaping wound on his patient's head and watched as she sutured her patient's laceration. 'Very tidy.'

Her hackles rose. Did he think she wouldn't do a good job? Of course he wouldn't know she was a perfectionist. Lifting her eyes, she drew a quick breath. The face looking at her was devoid of rancour, filled only with admiration. 'Thank you,' she muttered, bewildered, and waited for the axe to fall.

'So sewing's one of your talents.' His smile was soft, not egotistic or antagonistic. Apparently genuine. Even friendly.

Which worried her more than an abrasive style would've. 'It wasn't until I went to med school.'

'You wouldn't have had to make your own clothes when you were growing up.' Now he grinned in what was becoming a familiar way.

'Nope. Does anyone these days?' she asked. She was softening more and more towards him, and she hadn't been here twenty-four hours yet. Hard not to when he was playing nice, when her arms still had memories of those strong hands keeping her from dropping to the ground earlier. So much for remaining aloof to safeguard herself from rejection. The first rejection had decimated her. She'd never get up from a second blow. Come on, Sam was only being friendly, nothing else.

'Not me, for one. I let the army choose my clothes.'

She aimed for light. 'Not Paris fashion, are they?'

'Now, that's something I know nothing about,' he drawled.

'Me either.' But her mother dressed superbly from high end shops. Madison came from money and that had caused grief at school from some of the small-minded sorts. Shame none of those imbeciles had bothered to learn how hard she'd worked during out-of-school hours before mouthing off about her family. 'But I admit to having an interesting wardrobe back home.' A fantastic collection of outfits her mother had bought her and which were totally impractical in her day-to-day life. Something to do with getting back out amongst the city folk and finding a new man apparently.

Maddy shuddered. Not happening. This time because she'd learned how fickle love truly was. One glimpse of her scars and Jason had come up with every excuse in the book to bail on their marriage. Sure, he'd taken a few months—long, dark, lonely months—but in the end he'd gone. And he'd supposedly loved her. What she'd never got around to telling him was that her chances of having children had been severely compromised as well. What had been the point? She hadn't wanted him staying because he'd felt sorry for her.

Focus, Maddy. That's history.

Continuing to suture the wound in front of her, she stifled a yawn. So much for getting some sleep before her tour got fully under way. Who was she kidding? Her head had been full of Sam Lowe, dust and smoke, Sam, burns, and more Sam. Digging for a bullet had been a welcome reprieve.

Sam was staring at her, lifting goose bumps on her skin and unexpected, unneeded hope in her belly. 'You okay?' he asked.

'Yes.' She stared right back, her breath hitched somewhere between her lungs and her nostrils. The deeper she looked into that well the harder it was to find the strength to ignore him. The same concern she'd seen in the midst of her meltdown over the smoke blinked at her. Which was plain scary. Could she manage to work alongside him without falling into the trap of wanting him? *You don't already?* That's why she had to keep him at arm's length. This yearning for Sam was growing, not in great dollops but it was there, moving in under her skin, raising her temperature degree by agonising degree, shaking her need to remain immune to men until cracks were beginning to appear.

Cassy nudged Sam. 'One bag of cells for your man.'

His gaze appeared to drag across Maddy's face, a soft caress, as though loth to leave, then he flicked his head sideways to eyeball the nurse. The syringe in his left hand was in danger of snapping as he stepped back from the bed. 'Get a line in, will you?'

'No problem.'

Maddy dropped her eyes to her patient, focusing on his wound but unable to push Sam out of her mind. That need he'd brought to her expanded around her determination to ignore it, swamped all ideas of staying immune to him in particular, frightening *and* exciting her. Forget the excitement. How? Remember the horror in Jason's eyes the first time he'd seen her burned abdomen. That particular image could always toughen her resolve like nothing else could.

'How's the third victim doing?' she heard Sam ask through the mess in her head.

Cassy answered, 'Went into cardiac arrest but Jock got him back. You think your man needed blood. Not even close.'

'We need a volunteer to give a pint?'

Maddy looked up at Sam's question. 'I'm O neg, if you need it.'

'We're good to go at the moment.' The nurse slid

a needle into Sam's patient's arm. 'Righto, my man, let's get you hooked up and these little red cells doing their job.'

Madison let the words wash over her. Operating rooms were the same wherever she went, and as close to home as she knew these days. Listening to the banter, suturing a shredded muscle was soothing in an odd kind of way.

Sam had gone quiet. A flick of her eyes showed him working on his patient's scalp where the man had taken a pounding from an unknown object. His attention was so focused on the job that he had to be trying very hard to ignore something. It wouldn't be her, surely? Hopefully not. Yet a shaft of disappointment jabbed. Disappointment she refused to delve into. Instead, she hunted for a bland question and came up with, 'Where are you headed next week, Sam?'

'Burwood.'

The military base near Christchurch. 'Really going home, then, huh?'

'Until the brass find some other place to send me.'

'When was the last time you spent any time there?'

At first she didn't think he was going to answer but finally he managed, 'Ages ago. I haven't seen Ma and Pa Creighton for far too long.' Guilt lined his words and filled his eyes.

'Who are they?'

'They took me in to live with them when I was fourteen. The kindest folk you'd ever want to know.'

And he hadn't been to see them for a while. She knew not to ask about that, and for once managed to keep quiet. Not that she stopped wondering what had happened that he'd needed a home back then. Where had his parents been? Had he been a welfare kid? She knew about them as when she'd been young her parents had fostered two boys slightly older than her whom she'd adored and had been devastated when they'd left to return to their families.

Then Sam interrupted her fruitless machinations. 'Why did you join up?'

'I was looking for something different to the usual track of building a big, fancy career in a private practice.' She'd wanted out of her life as it had become. At least until she could face a future without the husband and children she'd always dreamed of.

'That had been your initial goal?'

'Yes. Then I had a change of mind.' A near death experience could do that.

'Going to tell me why?'

'No.' Then she added, before she could overthink it, 'Not now.' Explaining about the fire and the ensuing disaster would be hard. But hard didn't begin to explain the consequences that had followed that terrifying night. 'I guess eventually I'll go back to that idea but not yet.' But would she?

The army had taken her away from home and the hideous memories, from her concerned family with their endless suggestions of how to get back on track. There were awful memories ground so deep she'd never expunge them, but they were slightly easier to ignore when she wasn't living and working in her home town. Something she owed her sister for. She wouldn't have chosen the army as a cure if not for Maggie's suggestion—nagging, more like—that it could be a way to reinvent herself. She'd grabbed that thought and signed up without thinking too hard about what she was letting herself in for. Desperation made people do strange things.

On the plus side, her body was fitter, more muscular and in the best shape it had ever been. Her smart mind was faster, sharper, and yet only now was it dawning on her what she had landed herself in.

So much for being intelligent. Hope I haven't messed up big time.

Too bad if she had. The only way out of here was by court-martial or in a wooden box. Not options worthy of consideration. Yet she was supposed to be getting over horrors, not facing new ones. By the end of her tour, far from the comfort of home and her well-meaning but over-protective family, she fully intended knowing what she wanted to do with the rest of her life, and the past would be exactly that. The past. That was the plan anyway. Except plans had a way of going off track.

'I hear uncertainty in that answer.' No challenge sparked in the eyes now locked on her. Instead curiosity ruled.

Her natural instinct was to pull down the shutters. Habit was a strong taskmaster. Since the fire, she was done with showing anything but the truth, even a watered-down version, so she usually kept quiet. But now she was starting over? Straightening her already straight spine, she said, 'I haven't got any long-term plans at the moment. I'm taking everything one day at a time. Or one tour anyway.' Now she'd said too much.

He nodded, said quietly, 'You and I have something in common.'

Hideous memories? Pain? Fear? She hoped not. She didn't wish bad things on him. 'You aren't going to be a soldier for ever?'

'No idea. I had planned on it, but now who knows?'

That sounded lame, but before she could ask Sam to expand on what he'd said Jock appeared in their cramped area.

Sam looked down at his patient. 'Think we're about done. You?'

'The guy didn't make it.'

Madison's head flicked back and forth between the two men, then she locked on Sam. 'This isn't uncommon, is it?'

'Losing a patient? No.' That get-me-anything smile was back in place, but his serious voice didn't match it. Could be Sam was hiding his own despair at what they dealt with.

Hairs lifted on her neck. 'Sam?' His name fell out of her mouth.

'You're in a brutal environment now, Madison.'

Phew. He thought she was thinking about the medical work. Better than him knowing the truth. 'I get that,' she replied.

He went on. 'It takes time to get used to the injuries we see here, especially what causes them, but if you don't you'll sink.'

'I'm hardly likely to do that.' She could feel her muscles tightening. Stop it. New approach, remember? No more getting uptight over everything. Forcing the tension aside, she tried for normal. 'But thanks for the warning. I'll be on guard.'

'You'd better be. For all our sakes.' His words were

sharp, but the smile that accompanied them lessened any suspected blow. It was genuine, not full of I'm-so-cool attitude.

'You'll have to trust me on this, Sam.' Huh? That was a big ask. There wasn't room for trust in manoeuvres with an unproven soldier. That's how people died, or so the training officers back home had hammered home.

Sam's smile faltered, slid away. 'I will.' Forceps clanged against the steel of a kidney dish, loud in the sudden silence. 'But if you find you're struggling I'm not bad at listening.'

Now, there was an offer she'd have to decline. Talking one on one with Sam with no one else around about personal concerns would be taking things way too far. Shame. It could be good to sit over a coffee and chat about life in general, learn a few snippets about what made him tick. There was a depth to him that drew her in, intrigued her. 'Strange how real life is way different from those lofty ideas I had at school. Nothing turns out as sweet and easy as it looked then.'

Grief shot through his eyes, darkening them to a dull, wintry day. There was a storm in there, swirling emotions moving too fast to catch. 'Time we talked about something else, Madison.' There was no force behind his words, just a low, please-stop-this tone.

'Fair enough,' she answered equally quietly, more than happy to oblige. But what sore had she scratched?

'You caved too easily.' He stepped away from the bed, rolling his shoulders, pulling up a grin that didn't fit quite right.

Aha. He definitely hid behind that mouth, those grins. 'Lack of sleep catching up.'

'That explains why you've also gone quiet,' Sam gulped around another grin. 'You sure you're who I think you are?'

'Probably not.' She wasn't recognising herself at the moment.

He came around the bed to stand directly in front of her. His finger tilted her chin so she had to meet his gaze. The intimacy of the gesture shocked her, but she didn't want to pull away. Waiting for him to say whatever was on his mind made her nervous. Her jaws locked, while her brain spilled words she struggled not to utter.

His finger slid over her jaw before he removed his hand and stepped back. 'I like having someone from my time at Christchurch High School turn up here. That was a good place in my life and you've brought back memories even if you weren't involved.'

Her head spun. 'You haven't kept in touch with guys from school?'

'Not really. I couldn't wait to get out of town at the time, not realising how lucky I was to live there.'

'So visiting Christchurch doesn't happen often?'

Sam shook his head at her. 'Unfortunately not. Life has a tendency to throw curve balls just when I think I'm ready to go back there and maybe look into setting up a practice.' Those summer-blue eyes quickly darkened back to winter.

'Well, well. I sure hit the nail on the head earlier.' Jock stood beside them, looking from her to Sam and back.

'Can it,' Sam snapped. His shoulders were back to

tight, and straighter than a ruler. His jaw pushed forward, and the winter in his gaze kicked up an ice storm.

'If you're done, let's grab a coffee,' Jock said as though nothing out of the ordinary had gone down.

The glove Sam was removing tore as he tugged it. 'Nah. You entertain our new medic. I've got things to do.'

Contrition caught Madison. She didn't know if she'd contributed to upsetting him, but she regretted it if she had. 'Sam, I don't understand what's going on but, whatever it is, I am sorry.'

'You haven't put a foot wrong.' He stared at her, a war going on in his face. 'The thing is, Madison, I'm at the end of my tour of duty, you're at the beginning.' He swallowed hard. 'So good luck. You're going to need it.' He turned and stormed out of the room.

Madison stared after him, regret at his abrupt departure swamping her. 'What just happened?'

Jock shrugged. 'Welcome to the Peninsula. It does strange things to the sanest of us at times. Sam will be his usual self by sun-up.' But his gaze was worried as he stared after his friend.

Sam did three laps of the perimeter, walking hard and fast. His breathing was rapid, while his body dripped with sweat despite the cooler night air.

'Damn it, Madison, get out of my head.' He didn't want her lurking in there, reminding him of the future he'd once longed for. The future that had held a wife and family, people to shower with love, to protect and give himself to. The future that was no longer his to have.

He looked around, hoped no one had heard his outburst. Only went to show what a state Maddy's arrival had got him into if he was talking to himself out loud. Might get locked up if the wrong person overheard him. A week in the cells would keep him clear of Madison. Now, that could be a plus.

Why had the arrival of Maddy, someone he'd barely known so long ago, flipped up all the pain and anguish he kept hidden deep within himself?

Stopping his mad charge, he leaned a shoulder against the fence, drawing in deep gulps of sticky air. None of this ranting was helping. This was when he missed his pal the most, missed venting about things that stirred him up.

William had filled a gap in his life in a similar way to how Ma and Pa Creighton had filled in for his mother when she'd died. Sam's skin tightened. The guilt he'd carried over his friend's death stymied everything he thought he might do next with his life. Having fun when his friend was beyond it was not possible. Finding happiness with a woman was undeserved and to be avoided at all costs in case he ruined it for her.

Sam shoved away from the fence, began jogging, his shoes slapping the hard soil and raising dust.

Voices and laughter beckoned as he passed the open door of the officers' canteen where the rest of the crew, including Madison, would be drinking tea and eating cookies to replace the nervous energy they'd expended in Theatre. Operating on victims of gunfire or a bombing made everyone uneasy, reminding them why the army was there. Reminding them all that any one of them could be the next on the operating table. He should be in there, relaxing, cracking jokes, putting the day to bed, not out here, winding himself into a knot of apprehension.

He continued jogging.

Until his heart lurched, forcing his legs to slow then stop. A harsh laugh escaped him. He'd been so busy thinking about Madison he hadn't seen her in the shadows laid across the ground from the mess building. She shuffled across the parade ground, her arms hanging at her sides, her chin resting on her sternum. Close to lifeless.

'Hey,' he whispered softly, almost afraid she'd hear and straighten up, put strength back in her muscles and pretend she was fine. The picture before him was honest, and punched him in the gut. This was a new picture. One thing he did remember was that Maddy had always been energy personified. Not right at this moment, though. Neither had she been earlier when she'd come off that plane.

Oh, Maddy, what has happened to you?

A shaft of pain sliced into him. For her. He didn't want her suffering, hurting, crying on the inside.

Madison paused her slow progress, glanced around. Had she heard his footfalls on the dirt? Was she aware of him? She took a couple of steps. Guess not. Then she stopped again, leaned back and stared up at the sky where a myriad of stars sparkled. Her hands lifted to her hips as she gazed upwards. The outline of her breasts aiming skyward forced the air out of his lungs.

Beautiful. Even in her overtired state she was the most alluring woman he'd come across, from that attractive short hair right down to the tips of her boots.

Sam spun away, trying to fling the ache she'd created from his body. Another circuit of the camp might fix what ailed him, though running in his current state would be a novelty. He turned back to look at Maddy again. *Call her Madison. Maddy's too intimate, too friendly.* Yet it was all he wanted to call her.

'You done beating yourself up?' Jock strolled into his line of vision, hands shoved into his pockets and a sympathetic smile on his face. 'Feel like a beer?'

'Thought you'd never ask.' Two in the morning and they were talking about having a beer. How messed up were they? 'We've got patrol at zero eight hundred hours.'

'Then we'd better get on with it.'

The beer wasn't going to happen. They'd settle for a mug of tea followed by a few hours' kip, and he'd wake to a new day that didn't include X-rated pictures of Madison Hunter. Wouldn't he?

A shiver rattled Sam as she continued strolling away towards the barracks. His body was giving him messages he had to knock down. He was not getting close to her. Not now. Not ever. So he'd treat her as he did everyone else around here, as a fellow soldier and doctor, and see where that led. Hopefully out of the she's-so-sexy-I-could-cry slot and into the just-another-medic category.

Slam. There it was—a mental picture of Madison standing in the middle of the medical unit, looking good enough to eat.

And he was hungry. Starved, in fact.

But the past went wherever he went, haunting in its persistence, preventing him moving on and grabbing life's chances. Painful when he thought about all he could've had, and would never obtain. He was not en-titled to love and happiness ever after. He'd thrown that away with William's life.

Why the surprise? It wasn't as though he didn't know better. His mother had told him never to trust anyone with his heart after his dad had ditched them in an old shack by the river in one of Christchurch's less than savoury districts.

Sam knew how these things worked, had always known, yet he'd still carried a thread of hope in his heart. Ma and Pa Creighton had shown love and happi-ness were possible when they'd taken him, a sulky kid with no credentials except how to shoplift with impu-nity, into their home and family and given him a chance. He'd believed them, in them.

Until his friend had died. That had been reality kick-ing him in the gut, reminding him he'd been wrong to think he could have it all.

CHAPTER FOUR

'IF THAT FLY doesn't go away quick smart I'm going to smash it with the back of my hand,' Madison muttered under her breath. But she didn't move, not a hair. The blasted fly kept crawling across her face.

She scoped the landscape for anomalies, her back to the dilapidated concrete block building her patrol was inspecting from a hundred metres. Her hands gripped the weapon she held hard against her body. The silence was excruciating. The lack of movement was scary, and a warning in itself. The air hummed with tension as soldiers waited, watching and analysing everything around them. They'd just received info of insurgents hiding out in what used to be a police station and was now a ruin after being bombed last year.

'Cop, Porky, move in.' Sam spoke in a low voice that didn't carry beyond the troops. 'You three…' he pointed to the soldiers beside Madison '…take the left. Captain Hunter, you're with me and Jerry on the right.'

Sam was checking her out, otherwise it would've made more sense for her to go left with the others. He'd been observing her all day and it bugged her. Of course he wanted to know if she was up to speed on a mission, but did he have to be so obvious? She wouldn't have been sent here if she couldn't do her job.

Madison scanned the landscape once more before following Sam and Jerry. Movement caught her attention. 'Wait,' she called softly. 'Five o'clock, inbound, one person, on his belly.'

Every soldier paused. Sam was instantly beside her, moving fast without appearing to. He followed the direction of her gaze and nodded once, abruptly. 'Well spotted, Captain.'

She ignored the glow of satisfaction warming her. She was only doing her job, and proving she was capable of it, but there'd been a hint of respect in Sam's voice that she couldn't ignore. It touched her when she didn't want to be touched by him. If words could do that, what damage would physical connection do to her stability?

'Ah!' She stifled a cry. No one put a hand on her these days without having it swiped away. Imagine Sam spreading his hand, palm down, on her stomach, on the warped skin. Nausea swarmed up her throat.

'Captain?' Sam growled softly.

Gulp. 'We still going inside?' she asked.

'After we've checked out that crawling body, established whether they're friend or foe, we'll reconnoitre.' He nodded at the two men beside him, pointed where he wanted them to go. 'Cop, Porky, hold your positions and keep watch over the police block.'

What was it with all these nicknames? Porky was thinner than a broom handle. Madison scanned the ground all the way up to that small person they were targeting. Nothing else stood out. She checked to the left, the right. 'All clear.'

'We'll run opposite Porky and Cop,' Sam told her, and immediately was on his feet, running in a crouch, his weapon ready.

Madison followed, matching him step for step, her eyes constantly scanning for anything out of the ordinary. Nothing was remarkable, and yet nothing was normal when compared to what she knew back home. 'I think it's a child.'

Sam stopped, took in what she'd observed through binoculars. 'A lad. Don't be fooled. He could be as dangerous as any adult you'll come across.' He flicked his hand at his side to get the attention of the soldiers on their left flank, pointed to the boy.

Cop raised a thumb, and they all moved forward slowly, expectantly, until Sam and Madison reached the boy, who immediately spread his arms and legs starfish style in the dirt.

Madison dropped to her knees, reached out a hand.

'Don't touch him,' Sam growled. 'He could be carrying.'

The boy cried out a torrent of words that Madison couldn't comprehend. A glance at Sam told her he was none the wiser.

'Now what?'

Sam didn't get a chance to reply. The boy flipped his clothes up to expose bare skin underneath. He wasn't carrying. Could be he was just a normal kid doing what kids everywhere did, playing in the dirt. A very dangerous place for games, if the warnings she'd heard were true. And why wouldn't they be? The soldiers who'd been stationed on base for the previous year knew first-hand what went on out here.

The air whistled across Madison's lips. 'Thank goodness.'

'Stay with him, soldier. Be alert,' Sam commanded Jerry before moving away.

Thump. A low explosive sound broke through the silence from behind the building, followed by a gut-twisting cry.

After checking they were safe, Sam raced around the corner, Madison on his heels.

'Man down.' She stated the obvious the moment she saw past Sam.

'Cover us,' Sam ordered, and fell to his knees. 'Porky, you okay?'

'It's his foot. Something exploded under him,' Cop told them.

'Take Captain Hunter's place. Don't forget there could be more out there,' Sam ordered. 'Madison, give me a hand here.'

Instantly she knelt on the opposite side of Porky, glancing around before focusing on their patient. His left boot was shredded, as was his foot from what she could see. Tugging off her pack, she pulled out the emergency first aid kit, tugged on gloves and found thick gauze pads to help staunch the bleeding.

Sam helped himself to more gloves then began assessing Porky's injury. 'Hang in there, Sergeant. I'm going to have a look at the damage. Okay?'

'Figured as much.' The soldier bit down hard as Sam began probing his wound.

'We need the helicopter,' Madison said. 'I'll call it in.'

'Do that.' Sam leaned closer to her, said quietly, 'I suspect he's going to lose that foot unless he's very lucky.'

'His luck ran out when he got hit.' She called base and quickly explained the situation. 'They're on their way,' she told Sam and Porky.

'This damned dust doesn't help,' Sam muttered as he tried to protect the site of the wound.

'You warned me it got everywhere.' Porky needed to get to Theatre urgently, or be in sterile conditions at the very least.

Sam flicked her a warm glance. 'Yeah, and this would have to be a bad scenario.' He found the morphine in the kit and drew up a dose, glancing over at her before administering the drug into Porky's thigh. Then he spoilt her focus. 'You haven't been confused into thinking it's smoke today?'

'No.' She shuddered. Made to touch her belly where the scars were tingling, stopped just in time. Or had she? Sam's eyes were following her gesture. 'I only make any mistake once.' Or tried to. Making an idiot of herself on patrol was not an option. The soldiers would never trust her as their leader when Sam left. Yesterday had been a timely lesson. Dust, not smoke. She'd gone to sleep saying it. She'd come close to tripping up today when she'd seen thin lines of real smoke spiralling from dwellings, but with Sam keeping a close eye on her she'd managed not to lose her grip and to smother her unease. So far he had no cause for concern about her behaviour while on patrol that she knew of.

Porky's face turned grey. Sweat covered his pallid cheeks. Shock had set in. Madison lifted his eyelid. 'Pupils dilated.' She took his wrist in her hand, felt for a pulse. 'Weak and rapid.'

'Trying to clean this is hopeless.'

Madison swabbed at the ankle, cleaning away blood and sand, constantly aware of the broken bones, and the pain too much pressure could cause. 'We can't do a lot out here except keep him comfortable.'

'I need to bind the foot as tightly as possible,' Sam said. 'Hand me the gauze. It'll do the trick.'

She dug through the bag and came up with a large roll that would go round Porky's foot and lower leg several times. 'This'll work.'

The wonderful sound of rotors beating up the air reached them, and Madison relaxed back onto her heels. 'Thank goodness for the cavalry.'

'I second that.'

It took only moments to lift Porky onto the stretcher and into the belly of the helicopter.

'A well-oiled team,' she muttered.

Sam tossed her emergency kit in and turned to her. 'Up you get. Someone has to go with Porky and I've got a team to bring back to base after we've gone through the police block.'

'I could do that,' she retorted, then wished her words back. 'Sorry, you do know your way around far better than me.'

'Yes, Madison, I do. We also still have a boy to escort away from here.' Then his mouth tipped into a smile, a friendly one. She was getting used to those. Had started looking for them. 'Besides, you've had more than your share of drama since arriving less than twenty-four hours ago. Take the ride, and make the most of it. It doesn't happen often.'

'That's something to be grateful for.' She found herself returning his smile. 'Not needing one of our own to be cas-vaced out, I mean.'

'I knew exactly what you meant. Now go. The flight crew don't like hanging around, too dangerous. Especially when we don't know who might be loitering beyond the building.'

'Be careful.' Please. *I'd hate for something to happen to you.* She leapt on board, helped by the waiting hands of the co-pilot who then pointed to the bucket seat that was hers for the few minutes it would take to reach base. Looking out the gap where a door used to be, she saw Sam, hands on hips, staring after the helicopter as it rose, flinging sand and dirt at everyone on the ground. For a brief moment his gaze locked with hers, creating chaos in her stomach and beyond. Defrosting more of the ice that had been in her belly and the back of her mind for far too long.

Then the chopper was too high to see him and she shuffled her butt back in the uncomfortable seat to watch over their patient, who'd drifted into shock-induced unconsciousness. Reaching for Porky's wrist, she again took note of his rapid pulse rate and the pallor of his skin, all the while thinking about those fierce yet kind blue eyes that showed a side of Sam she didn't want to acknowledge for fear of where they might lead her.

I might find I like Sam Lowe too much.

Now, there was a worry. But what harm could liking the guy do? Plenty. For starters, there were those unwanted moments when her body reacted favourably to his. Favourably? What was this? A weather report? More like hungrily. She wanted Sam. There. She'd admitted it. No going back on her thoughts. Which kind of made becoming only friends difficult, if not impossible, unless she found a way to banish the intense physical yearning that had begun unfurling yesterday. They would not be getting close in any way. She simply didn't have the courage required to expose her body.

The day she'd seen those scars disfiguring her torso for the first time had altered her for ever. The pain from the burns had had nothing on the agony that new view had created. It'd taken nearly six weeks before she could look again, a sneaky peek at the ugliness that was the new her. It had been worse that time. Her shocked memory from her first viewing of the scars had not been honest. The horror and despair had floored her that day; while her strength had deserted her over the months spent fighting one infection after another in a cloud of pain. Sometimes she'd been conscious, at others she had been blissfully unaware of anything going on around her.

If she ever considered anything so stupid as to want to strip down naked with a man, she only had to bring Jason to the front of her mind. The revulsion in his eyes when he'd inadvertently seen her burns had scarred her more than the fire had. He'd tried to hide it, deny it, but, hey, she'd seen the same look in her own face the day before so had instantly recognised it for what it was.

Nowadays there were moments when she thought if only she had the guts to move on, not care what anyone thought, she might actually find a man who loved her enough not to give a damn about a bit of damaged skin. Looking through the helicopter's opening, she scanned the sky for a miracle. Nope. Nothing.

Thought so. You have to love yourself before you can ask anyone else to.

She stared outside again, looking for the source of that whacky idea. Nothing. No dragons slaying beasts, no witches on broomsticks chasing away black clouds.

The helicopter nudged onto the landing pad outside the hospital unit on base, jolting Madison back to reality, refocusing her attention to shifting Porky without causing him any more distress.

'You don't take time to settle in before everything turns belly up, do you?' Jock was clambering inside the aircraft.

'I'm hoping I've seen the worst for a while,' she tossed over her shoulder as she raised Porky's eyelid. 'No one home.'

'Probably for the best until we're inside. Fill me in on the details while we shift him.'

She did, leaving nothing out. 'Sam's still patrolling that area around the old police station. He wasn't convinced the area was clear of insurgents, and there's a boy to see clear of the site.'

'I'm surprised he didn't take the flight and leave you out there.' There was an irritating smile on Jock's face. 'He's always the first to put newbies under pressure, and there's no pressure like your first patrol when something goes wrong.'

So Sam had been kind to her. Her mouth lifted into a smile.

'What?' Jock asked.

'Maybe Sam thinks I'm more use to Porky than he might be.' Huh?

Jock spluttered with laughter. 'Tell me you're joking.'

'I'm joking. Why?'

'Because Sam is a brilliant surgeon and knows it. Believe me when I say he was doing you a favour.'

'Truly?' Gobsmacked just about described her. Damn it, Sam was starting a thaw deep inside her that she didn't want to end until all the frost had gone. One day after arriving here and he was inadvertently encouraging her to look outward, not inside all the time. Which only spelt danger. She might become enthralled with him, even go so far as to fall in love with him. In a week? Why not? There were a hundred reasons. Her heart wouldn't withstand another bludgeoning. It hadn't recovered from the first one.

'Truly.' Jock laughed at her.

It wasn't hard to find a return smile for Jock. He was one of the good guys. 'Hadn't we better get cracking with fixing Porky's foot? Though I have my doubts about whether we can save it.' She'd do everything within her power to keep from amputating if it was up to her. Everything and then some. Porky deserved that. And so did she. Here was an opportunity to fly, show what she was made of, and she wasn't going to blow it.

Having showered to remove the grit and now dressed in theatre scrubs, Sam entered the small, crowded operating room, desperate to know how his sergeant was getting on, fearful of the answer. That foot hadn't been in good shape. Porky was a professional soldier who prided himself on being the fittest, and was one of the best at what he did. Without his left foot he'd be relegated to an office out the back of nowhere for the rest of his army career. He'd hate that with a vengeance.

Jock looked up as the door shut behind him, and tilted his head in Madison's direction, his eyes wide. Was he telling Sam he was impressed with their new medic? Or things had gone badly for Porky? No, he knew Jock and didn't think he was telling him something was wrong.

Moving closer to the operating table, he saw Madison was leading the surgery. So Jock had handed the reins over. Interesting. That meant she knew her stuff. Jock was a perfectionist who let no one rain on his parade.

Maddy worked with infinite patience, putting that decimated foot back together. Out in the desert Porky's foot had looked done for. Now there was a strong chance it'd be hanging around for a long time to come. *Go, Maddy.*

'Watch an expert at work. Never seen anything like it, considering she's not an orthopaedic surgeon.' That was awe in Jock's voice.

'Seems Madison doesn't do anything by halves.'

'Worked out on patrol, then?' Jock hadn't taken his eyes off the surgery still going on.

'Couldn't fault her. Got a sharp pair of eyes on her, too.' She'd been the first to see that kid crawling towards them. She'd also kept her promise to not let dust whirls disturb her. There had been a couple of instances when her hand had touched her midriff but her focus had been fixed on their environment, observing everything around them.

'The guys okay about her?'

Sam nodded. Oh, yeah. They more than liked Captain Hunter. She could've asked them to crawl backwards all the way to camp and they'd have leapt at the chance to win her attention. 'She slipped into her role as easily as a cold beer could slide down my throat right about now.' Madison hadn't tried to show she knew what to do, had instead got on with the job as required. Not every officer arriving out here for the first time behaved like that.

When he stepped closer to the operating table Madison raised her eyes. 'Didn't hear you come in. Thought you'd be hours away still,' she murmured, before returning her attention to the job in hand.

He was already forgotten. Porky was in very good hands. His eyes dropped to the operation site. Her long, slim fingers moved deftly, gently, even though Porky wouldn't be feeling a thing. Ideas of what those fingers might feel like on his own feverish skin wound around Sam, teasing him, lifting goose bumps on his arms. Her movements were smooth, purposeful. The suture needle caught the light as she pulled and pushed it, reminding him of one of those spinning rides at the fair. Now you see it, now you don't. Now I touch you, now I don't. Damn it.

Jamming his hands on his hips, he stared down at the patch of floor between his feet. Nothing there to distract him or make him curl his toes.

Get me a cold drink, fast. I need to drown these crazy thoughts before they take hold and wreck my common sense for ever.

Except this was nothing new. He'd felt the same tightening, same need warming his blood whenever he was interested in an attractive woman. Often. But today—

today's longing was about more. As though the whole package was a possibility.

'You clear that police site?' Jock's sharp question interrupted his daydream.

'Without a hitch.' He risked watching Madison some more. 'Porky's got a good chance of a reasonable recovery, then?' he asked no one in particular. Singling out Maddy would make her more important in his eyes, and he so didn't want to do that. He'd gone too far along that track already.

Again she glanced up to him, like she was connected to him somehow. That could prove awkward considering where his mind had been headed. 'No guarantees on how well the foot will function but I think we can say he's going to keep it.' There was a challenge in her eyes, telling him not to argue the point.

He wouldn't. The sergeant needed all the positive vibes he could get. 'That's a better prognosis than I gave him two hours ago.'

'Me, too,' Madison conceded. 'I didn't think he stood a chance, especially when Jock asked me to take over.'

That hit him smack bang in the chest. She'd admitted she might not have been the best person to do the job without a thought to the consequences for her own reputation. Again that annoying question sprang into his mind. *What's happened to you?* She got spooked by dust whirls, admitted she wasn't perfect when it came to operating, had accepted he'd been in charge on that morning's patrol without a murmur. His gaze dropped to her midriff, or where it should be under the loose scrubs she wore.

I so don't know you. But I sure as hell want to.

'Sam, did you find what got Porky?' Jock asked as the operation was being finished. 'Madison thought he might've stepped on a landmine but I reckoned he'd have lost a lot more than his boot if he had.'

'There was nothing left of the explosive device to investigate but we found a homemade pressure bomb on the other side of the building that we're presuming was the same as what Porky trod on. Small, amateurish but still destructive.' It'd been pure luck the second incendiary device hadn't been completely buried so that the sun's rays had caught it enough for Cop to investigate. Someone else could've been badly injured if he hadn't.

'Porky, Cop. What's with all these nicknames?' Madison asked. 'How come you haven't got one, Jock?'

Sam and Jock laughed.

'You have? Jock's a nickname?'

'The man's a Scotsman from way back,' Sam told her.

'Three generations ago,' Jock growled. 'Nothing Scottish about me.'

'He likes haggis.' Sam shuddered. 'How anyone can eat that is beyond me.'

'You got a name, Sam?' Madison asked as she straightened up and dropped the suture needle into a dish. Her hands immediately went to rub her lower back.

Heat clawed up his cheeks. 'Ah, no.'

'Rooster.' Jock laughed.

Her eyebrows rose endearingly, a query blinking out of those large eyes. 'Do tell.'

'Cock of the roost,' Jock happily explained.

Madison laughed, a pure, tinkling sound that went

all the way down to his toes, heating bits of him on the way past.

He loved that laugh. It touched the chill inside him, taunted him, spoke of life and love. Swallow. No. Haul on the brakes. This had to stop. Now.

'What shall we call Madison?' Jock asked. 'You remember anything from your school days?'

As those dark blonde eyebrows rose in surprise, Sam shuddered. *I need to get out of here. Now.* 'Maddy,' Sam replied, careful to avoid anything contentious as he headed for the door. The muscles in his back tensed, his skin prickled. He could feel her eyes boring into the back of his skull.

'That's not a nickname.'

He had to stop his getaway and deal with this, otherwise Jock would keep at him. 'I can't think of anything else,' he lied. Inferno would get her more attention than she already had. Besides, he was the one feeling like an inferno, she was merely the match.

Jock asked, 'What about your family? Did they have a pet name for you?'

She was smiling when she said, 'Spark. As in bright spark.' Instantly the smile disappeared, replaced by anguish. 'But not now.' Her hand went to her stomach, rubbed lightly, left then right. Did she even know she did that? Did she realise the brown shade of her eyes turned muddy when she was disturbed? And how her forehead creased, bringing those shaped brows closer together?

'Maddy it is,' he said quietly, hoping to dispel her distress, hating to see Maddy terrified at unguarded moments. Looking around, he knew he wouldn't find the cause in this room, that it came from somewhere deep inside her, but he looked anyway. Preferring to think Madison was all right, that nothing bothered her so badly she went still and pale in an instant. Knew he was lying to himself, but what was a guy supposed to do? Go hug her? Whisper sweet nothings in her ear until she laughed? He'd get an elbow in the gut for sure.

Would she survive out here where nothing was guaranteed? Not her safety, her sanity or her privacy.

More than anything, he wished for that. He needed to know she'd be okay, would survive the coming months without another wound to her soul.

But only time would take care of her. Time, her colleagues and her own strength. He'd have to wait long, agonising months to be sure she made it safely back home.

And when she did, he couldn't be there to welcome her.

CHAPTER FIVE

'THAT QUEUE ISN'T getting any shorter,' Madison muttered as she wiped her forehead with the back of her hand for the umpteenth time.

'I wonder why.' Sam grinned.

'You think it's funny?' The line of soldiers waiting to see a doctor was ridiculous. 'Don't they have anything better to do? I mean, they're very fit. You can't tell me every one of those men is ailing from something.' None of the soldiers who'd presented to her had actually been sick or in need of any treatment, so what was going on here?

'I'd say there's nothing wrong with most of the men.' Sam's grin only widened. 'But there hasn't been a new, good-looking female come on the base for months now.'

These guys were lining up in the heat and dust to get a look at her? 'Get out of here.'

'No way,' he answered with a wink, apparently deliberately misinterpreting her. 'I deserve the break since I've been working my butt off dealing with non-existent aches and pains when not one patient…' he flicked fingers in the air '…actually wanted to see me. I don't have the right curves.'

No, but he had all the muscles any woman could wish for and they appeared to be in excellent working order. Of course, she couldn't comment on *all* of them. 'Right. I'll fix this.' She strode through the door. 'That's it, guys. Show's over. Get back to work and start being useful.' Or whatever they were supposed to do at the end of the day.

A private stepped up. 'I've got a pain in my belly.'

Madison read his name tag. 'How long have you had this pain, Private Johanson?'

'It started while we were out on patrol this morning. Thought I'd eaten something off for breakfast and it'd go away after a time, but it hasn't.'

'Where exactly in your abdomen is this pain?'

'All over the place.' The soldier ran his hand lightly over his belly.

Maddy wondered if she was being stitched up yet again, but something about the guy's demeanour suggested maybe not. 'Come in and get up on the bed.'

Relief lessened the stress in his face. 'Boots off?'

'No, but pull your shirt up.' As she gently felt his abdomen he lay dead still, not even breathing. She pressed deeper, feeling for any sign of a distressed appendix.

'That's not nice,' the private groaned. Sweat popped on his brow and upper lip. Impossible to fake that.

Her fingers continued gently probing his abdomen.

He sucked air through clenched teeth.

This man had a genuine complaint. 'That was worse when I lifted my hand away?'

He nodded.

Another indicator she was on the right track. 'Where did the pain start?'

With a groan he hovered his hand above his right side near where she'd applied light pressure. 'About here. Stayed there for hours then spread around.'

She checked his name badge again. 'Reece, I'm going to take your temperature and then a blood sample.'

'Thanks, Captain. What's my problem?'

'You might have appendicitis.'

'Great.' Reece closed his eyes.

Once she had an EDTA blood sample Madison made a smear to stain when it had dried, then ran the blood through a very basic haematology analyser. 'Slightly elevated WBC,' she told Sam when he came across to see what she had.

'Checked the smear for immature neutrophils?' he asked.

'Will as soon as the slide's stained.' Neutrophils were the white cells that reacted to infections and in this case if the numbers were increased and/or immature the result would back her diagnosis. 'Twelve percent band forms,' she told Sam ten minutes later. A textbook result for appendicitis.

'Our man's going to Theatre, then.' He headed for the exit. 'Back in a moment. Going to get our anaesthetist out of the mess. I'll assist you.'

Madison shook her head after him. Still checking up on her. It should irk her, but it didn't. Probably because she was exhausted and would be glad of another pair of eyes on the job. Hard to believe she'd arrived only thirty hours ago. So much had happened she'd believe anyone who told her it'd been a week.

'Private, I'm going to operate to remove your appendix. The good news is I don't believe it has perforated.'

'Glad you've got something terrific to tell me, Captain.'

'Hey, I'm sure it's scary, Reece, but this is a straightforward operation. You'll be sitting up drinking tea and eating a sandwich before you know it. Have you heard of keyhole surgery?'

'Sounds small.'

'Exactly. You won't even have a scar to show off.' Why some men liked to flaunt their wounds was beyond her. Guess a surgical one wasn't hideous like burns. Most scars didn't turn people into paranoid nutcases like she'd become. While explaining what she was going to do in basic terms without the ick factor, she undid the laces of Reece's boots and pulled them off. 'Might as well get you comfortable. When did you last eat?'

'At thirteen hundred hours. Didn't feel much like food so only had a snack bar.'

He hadn't been in her patrol so must've been with Jock. 'That's in your favour. Here's Cassy to help you get ready.'

The private blushed. 'Hi, Cassy.'

'Reece.' Cassy looked anywhere but at their patient.

'Let's get this happening.' Sam strolled into the room. 'Anders is on his way. Just finishing dinner.'

'Lucky guy,' Madison muttered. Lunch seemed days ago.

'Here.' Sam passed her a chocolate bar. 'Get that into you.'

'Thanks.' She tore off the wrapper and took a bite. Rolling her eyes, she said, 'Heaven.'

'It's not a good look when the surgeon faints halfway through an op.' Sam gave her one of those smiles she already treasured. They were warm and encompassing, aimed straight for her heart, whereas his grins were fun and wicked and she liked those, too.

'You have a point.' Crazy but she found herself constantly looking out for those smiles. They made her feel as though she wasn't on her own. Not that she was, being surrounded by military personnel, but there were times when she needed someone beside her that understood where she came from, who she was. *Hey, that's not Sam. He doesn't have a clue about me.* But they had walked the same streets, attended the same school, followed the same career paths.

Another bite of the treat he'd brought her. The chocolate gave her an instant boost. As did a glance at Sam. Or maybe the sudden energy rise was the result of his smile. Whichever, her shoulders lifted and her blood warmed, and the tiredness dogging her took a hike. A temporary fix but that was all she needed to get through the next thirty minutes.

'I see I'm not rostered on in here tomorrow morning.'

'Never say that.' Sam shook his head at her. 'You're only tempting fate. There's no such thing as not being on duty around here.'

'So I've noticed.' Madison didn't try to dampen the warmth cruising her body, waking her up.

Watch it. Don't let him do this. He'll be gone in less than a week and I don't want to be left wondering how well we could've got along.

'You going to stand there daydreaming all night?' the man winding through her veins asked. 'How about getting a move on so we can hit the canteen sooner than later.'

'Yes, sir.'

'Watch it,' he retorted, as he nudged open the door into the scrubs room. 'We're not on patrol now.'

'No, but you'll be keeping just as close an eye on me throughout the operation.' The warmth was cooling. She was no longer a registrar. Appendectomies were straightforward surgical procedures. Sure, things could, and occasionally did, go wrong, but she was more than competent.

'Don't panic, Madison. I'm not checking your operating abilities. You're a qualified surgeon with a ton of experience behind you. I'm sure you've done numerous appendectomies. I'm simply assisting as I'm on duty and ready for something more exciting than torn nails or pretend sore throats.'

She'd got that wrong, then. 'You know my medical career history?' She wasn't sure how she felt about that.

'Just supposing, having been there myself,' he muttered over his shoulder. 'Med school, specialty training, and then deciding what to do next. Except I'm still surprised you're not working to becoming established in private practice.'

'So am I,' Madison replied without thought. Yikes. Now he'd ask again why she'd changed her mind, and she wasn't about to talk about the year she'd had away from medicine while she'd got her health back. She needed a diversion and quickly, judging by the questions brewing in his eyes. 'I don't remember you being at our school in years nine and ten.'

He named a low decile establishment on the outskirts of the city. 'I moved across town from there to live with Ma and Pa Creighton in year eleven. It was a bit of a shock starting in with your lot. For one, my grades were appreciated, not poked fun at.'

'Are the Creightons relatives? Distant ones?' It wasn't usual for strangers to take a child into their lives like that.

'No.' Water splashed over the side of the basin when Sam shoved the tap on full. Whatever he said was lost in the noise of running water and the harsh scrubbing of his hands.

Now she'd gone and stirred up things apparently best left alone. Placing her hand lightly on his shoulder, she tried to ignore the ripple of muscles under her palm. 'I'm sorry if I've overstepped the mark.'

Under her palm Sam went rigid. The scrubbing stopped and he stared down at the floor, his arms braced each side of the basin. 'Ma Creighton and my mother were friends when they were kids. When Mum got a cleaning job at the same school Ma Creighton taught at they renewed their friendship.' Lifting his head, Sam locked his gaze on her. 'Mum died and the Creighton family didn't hesitate to take me in. I could've kept going across town to my old school but I'd hated it there, was glad of the opportunity to start afresh.' Hurt dripped off his words.

He'd started in a new school and a new family all at once. Lost his mother as well. That explained his take-me-or-leave-me grins. He wanted to be liked but was afraid to risk himself. 'Must've been hard for you. Did you have any close friends who knew?'

His headshake was abrupt. 'No. I liked it that way.'

'I get it.' She really did. Sharing her anguish was not happening. She didn't want sympathy, just honest friendship.

'See you in Theatre,' Sam muttered as he pushed past her.

'Sure.' Madison followed, her mind absorbing this information. He must've been so lonely at times.

Something he'd obviously been an expert at covering up.

'Glad that's over,' Madison commented around a yawn. 'Reece came through easily enough.' The top half of her scrubs hit the laundry basket. One hand firmly held her T-shirt in place to stop it riding up and revealing her scarring, something she'd become practised at when around other people. Using communal showers when she'd first joined the army had been awkward, and had seen her getting to the shower block very early or equally late in order to save her pride. A towel had always been on hand to wrap around her body if someone came in. Once a group of younger female officers had deliberately gatecrashed her ablutions but after seeing her fully naked they'd apologised and left her alone from then on. The real surprise from that experience had been that she'd never heard a word about it around camp. It was enough for her to forgive the women.

'No reason why he shouldn't have. He's fit and healthy.' Sam's scrubs followed hers. 'Let's see what the cook's got for us.'

'I'll give that a miss. I'm not hungry.' Who knew where her appetite had gone but the thought of food made her nauseous.

'That chocolate bar wasn't enough,' Sam muttered.

No, but spending any more time with you would be too much. 'Probably not.' Another yawn. 'But sleep's more important right now.' There was cotton wool in her skull and grit in her eyes, and tomorrow she had to be on her mettle for whatever came her way.

'You reckon you'll nod off now? Right after doing an op? On an empty stomach?' Disbelief radiated out at her from deceptively calm eyes.

Sam knew she wanted to avoid him.

He wouldn't understand she was doing this so she didn't get too invested in him. So that when he left her heart would be fine. Hearing that snippet about his mother's death and the Creightons' generosity had her wanting to dig deeper into who he was. Which was a slippery slide down into trouble. She'd stay clear of him as much as possible.

That's how it had to be. With Sam and any man who interested her. *Really?* Her heart slowed as sadness clogged her blood. Really. She was not exposing herself, her body, to be laughed at or, worse, turned away from with horror. Anyway, the fact she mightn't be able to have children would be another turn-off for most men, and one she wasn't strong enough to face.

'Hello, Maddy, anyone home?' Sam waved a hand in front of her eyes.

'No, I'm asleep on my feet,' she retorted. Slapping her hands on her hips, she took her confusion out on him by growling, 'Quit hassling me, Sam, before I do something I regret.'

'This I can't wait to see.'

She poked his chest with a finger, bounced on her toes. 'I'm exhausted, but I'm also feeling wired.' Energiser bunny in disguise.

'In other words, overtired.'

'Thank you, Doctor.' Throughout her body muscles tensed, ready for action of some kind. Any kind.

An annoyingly big smile hit her in slap bang in the stomach, winding her up so fast it wasn't funny. At the same time her insides resembled melted jelly and all her tension evaporated. How did he do that? She, of all people, knew better than to be taken in. Not just by Sam, but by anybody. Yet… Her thigh stung where her palm landed hard. Sam smiling at her just—just got to her in ways no one had for a long time. Make that in ways she hadn't allowed for a long time, ways she'd fought hard to remain immune to. And tonight she had no fight left, was exhausted beyond measure. Spinning around, she aimed for the door. 'See you tomorrow.'

Sam followed her outside as though nothing bothered him, like he wanted her company. 'Come for a walk around the perimeter.'

That's what she was about to do. Alone. 'You go and eat. You must be hungry.'

Get away from me, give me space to douse the warmth you've created so that jelly sensation can solidify back into concrete.

'You're jumping off the walls from an adrenalin rush brought on by operating.' His hand on her elbow did nothing to cool her down. Quite the opposite.

'As I already said, yes, Doctor.'

His hand remained on her elbow. He matched his strides to hers. 'Throw in exhaustion and you're more than hyper. A fast walk will help quieten you down. Followed by food, you'll then sleep the sleep of the dead.'

Madison jerked away from him. 'That's taking things too far.' The cooler night air was soothing on her flaming skin. Not enough to calm down and become rational again, but it was a start. Heading in the direction of the perimeter, she began striding out fast, her chest rising and falling rapidly.

Sam stuck by her side. 'Glad you're seeing things my way.'

'I don't need a chaperon.'

'I could do with stretching my legs, too.'

For the first few minutes Madison said nothing, her fists beating the air as she jabbed them up, jerked them down, up, down. Dust lifted at every step she stomped. Her skin was soon hot and sticky. 'This is stupid,' she huffed through a dry mouth.

'You don't like silence?' So light and chatty. Nothing was rattling the man.

So she tried a different tack. 'Did you always want to be a doctor?'

'No. That came after the fireman craze at six, a cop driving fast cars at ten. I finally thought being a doctor would be cool when I was fourteen.'

She huffed a lighter breath. So far so good. 'Find me a small boy who hasn't wanted to do those things.'

'Who said I was small?' he quipped. 'What about you? A princess, a dancing queen, then a doctor?'

Because there was no insult in his tone she let him

off with his quip about being a princess. 'Just as pre-
dictable. A vet, as many of the girls in our science class
wanted to be.'

'What happened? You'd have easily gotten into vet
school. Top girl of our year, and all that.'

He remembered? Wow. 'Vet school's hard to get into,
and the end of many students' dreams. When I told Dad
I wanted to be a vet he made me get a job at the SPCA
at the weekends and at a vet clinic cleaning cages after
school. Said I needed to learn vets weren't all about
cute puppies and kittens but dealing with their pain
and suffering.'

'A wise man, your dad.'

'Yep. I couldn't handle it when any dogs came in
injured. Their pain was my pain, in an over-the-top
teenage kind of way. As Dad had known, that made me
realise I couldn't do the job. Those dogs, and the cats,
at the SPCA would look at me with their big, trusting
eyes, as I got them ready to visit the vet. Sometimes
they didn't come back. I always felt as though it was
my fault if they were euthanased because I'd been the
one to prepare them for their visit.'

'You don't feel the same about humans?' Sympathetic amusement crackled between them.

'Of course I do, but it's different. Don't ask me how,
it just is.' She'd fallen to bits when her dog had had to
be put down after being hit by a car. She'd refused to
replace him. She could still drag up a mental picture
of Buster's big trustful eyes on her as she and her father had taken him to the vet. 'I don't have to put down
my patients.'

'No regrets?'

Madison shook her head. 'Not at all. I like helping people as much as I adored attending to those animals. Being a surgeon suits me, although it is quite intimate in a way.'

'The invasiveness of it?' Sam nodded. 'I'm always awestruck by how people who know nothing about me are willing to trust me enough to operate on them.' They'd reached the mess block. 'Ready for something to eat?'

'I'm still not hungry.' But that hyper feeling had quietened down. 'Think I'll head for my barracks.'

'Have a drink with me and we can share a plate of fries.' He held open the door leading inside the mess.

'Do you always boss everyone around like this?' she asked as she slipped past him into the bright light of the nearly empty mess, her stomach winning over the need to put distance between them.

'Only people who beat me at physics.'

'Did I?' Laughing, she sat down on a stool at the bar and said, 'Why did you go to Auckland to do your training? Were you running away from Christchurch?'

CHAPTER SIX

Yes, in one way Sam had been running away. 'I won a scholarship to Auckland University.' He still filled with pride at his achievement. 'I was determined to go to med school and a scholarship made it a lot easier.' The money he'd made filling shelves in the local supermarket after school hadn't exactly been overwhelming. Moving to Auckland hadn't been cheap but there had been no shadows lurking in dark corners, no memories of his mother at the local shops or in the library there.

'Why medicine?'

Ah. More back story coming up. He wasn't used to talking about his past, or anything close to him, come to that, but it seemed he couldn't help himself around this woman. At least he'd soon be out of there and not likely to bump into her again. 'Mum was chronically ill for as long back as I can remember. She was a diabetic, an asthmatic, and had Crohn's disease. Living in poverty didn't help her situation.'

'That's so unfair, copping all those illnesses.' The sympathy in Madison's voice could undo him if he wasn't careful.

Now he recalled why he never talked about this stuff.

But he'd started, couldn't seem to stop. 'When I was old enough to understand that Mum couldn't get out of bed some days because of her health and not because she was the lazy cow my father called her, I tried to do everything possible to help her. It wasn't much.'

'You were only a kid. It was your father's responsibility to care for her, surely?'

'You've got to be there to do that. He left when I was four. Just upped and walked away one day after the beer ran out and Mum couldn't find the energy to drag herself to the liquor outlet to get him some more.'

'Oh, Sam. You got a bad deal.'

He glugged down some of his water. 'Yes. And no. We were dirt poor but I was always sure of Mum's love. She struggled to hold down a job because of her health and that made me feel bad because I knew she only went to work to give me things.'

'She was a good mum.'

When Maddy's hand covered his, Sam struggled to hold back the sudden tears welling up. Damn her, he did not need this. He hadn't cried for his mother since her funeral. But seemed that now he'd started he wanted to talk about the rest. 'It wasn't until she went to work at that school and hooked up with Ma Creighton again that she stayed in the same job for more than a year. I suspect Ma Creighton stuck up for her whenever the school board talked of getting rid of her.'

'Friendships can be the best thing out.' Her hand tightened on his.

He didn't want friendship with Madison. She'd want more of him than he was prepared to give. Pulling his hand away, he continued, now in a hurry to finish his story. 'From the day Ma and Pa Creighton took me in and made their home mine I was determined never to give them any reason to regret their generosity. They were exceptional, kind and considerate, and at the same time they never went soft on me.'

Yet, except for a couple of brief phone calls, he hadn't spoken to them in a long time. All part of his withdrawal from being too near to anyone. People he got close to tended to desert him one way or another and he couldn't risk losing the two who'd stepped up for him when he'd been a confused and angry teen. Guilt waved at him again, cramped his gut. He missed them so much, thought of them most days. Next week, he knew, he should finally visit them.

'You want another of those?' Madison tapped his water bottle.

Letting him off the hook? Had she sensed his pain, known to back off? 'I'll get it.' He should walk away from her while he still could. But it was nigh on impossible when Maddy managed to wind him up and soften his stance all at the same time. During the past day and a bit he'd thought more about his future, and his past, and Madison, than he had in two years. It was as if she'd taken a chisel to those tight bands around his heart and created a gap through which his real emotions were escaping. Emotions such as need, want, love, and—dared he admit it?—excitement. He couldn't afford to give in to these feelings. Another shiver; deeper this time. It had been too long since he'd believed there might be someone special for him out there. The risk was huge, but right this moment it was hard to deny himself a glimmer of hope. Seesawing between two worlds, he swung towards Madison, went with keeping the conversation light and chatty. 'I did have a blast in Auckland.'

'Has the city recovered?' she asked with that cheeky glint he enjoyed more than a cold shower on a hot day.

Though a cold shower might soon be necessary to cool the heat banking up internally as he watched her shift her curvy backside on the stool, unconsciously letting off fireworks in his belly, further lightening the weight wedged there since she'd turned up on his patch. 'I hope so.'

Sam tilted forward, halving the gap between them. Her scent floated on the air, instantly transporting him back to the peach tree in the yard of the only home he'd had with his mother *and* father. Large, ripe, succulent peaches. It had been the year he'd turned four and he'd spent hours under that tree in summer, playing in the dirt, shaking the branches to bring down the fruit to shove in his mouth and feed his hungry belly, sticky juice sliding down his face. Dad used to sit there, reading the paper, smoking, drinking beer, pushing a toy truck around when he could be bothered. At the end of summer his dad was gone, out of his life for ever.

Sam jerked back. *Stop this nonsense.* He didn't do thinking about the man who'd fathered him and then discarded him easier than last week's bread.

When he next looked at Madison he found her deep gaze fixed on him, almost as if she was searching for something he wasn't sure he wanted found. She sure had him thinking about things he'd long buried. Another diversion was needed. 'What about you? You stayed on in Christchurch?'

'Yep. I'm close to my family and my girlfriends went to Christchurch University as well.'

'Why the army?' Never had he asked so many questions of someone. What was in the water?

'To get away for a while. Decide what to do with my career. And to do something for my country. I like that we can help other people less fortunate through the military.'

'Tell me to shut up if you don't want any more questions, but did your failed marriage have anything to do with leaving Christchurch?'

'Shut up, Sam.' It was said without anger. Without any emotion at all. She was hurting. He could see it in the white fingers gripping her bottle, in the flat line of her mouth, the dull eyes.

He backed off instantly. 'Fair enough.'

Then she paid him back with, 'You never married?'

'Not even close.' A shortage of women hadn't been the problem. Finding one he could fall in love with had been. Then William had happened and he'd understood he wasn't entitled to happiness.

Madison was eyeing him with caution. 'So no little Sam Lowes running around?'

'Nope. I wouldn't dream of having children if I wasn't in a happy, strong marriage.'

Her mouth twisted up in a wry smile. 'I have to agree.' Then she chuckled. 'My sister has four kids. She married an Italian and they live just down the road from our parents.' Maddy's face lit up. 'Those girls are gorgeous. Little minxes, every one of them.'

'Four kids is a handful.'

'Yeah, but what a problem to have.' She smiled, big

and deep, and touched something inside him. Then her expression became wistful, probably thinking of the kids she might've had if her marriage hadn't gone off the rails.

'Not for me.' An image of Madison holding her own baby, smiling softly, rocking gently, her face full of love, wove through his mind, wouldn't let go. It was a beautiful picture that he needed to burn. His hand jerked, his knuckles banging against his glass and upending it. Water pooled on the counter and dripped over the edge. Snatching up a cloth to mop up the mess, he was reeling, his head spinning. Damn but Madison tripped him up too easily just by being normal.

Madison was wiping her fatigues where water had soaked the fabric. 'You don't want four kids?' Her dazzling smile faded as she looked directly at him. She knew something wasn't right.

'Hard to imagine when I'm here.' Which reminded him—where was their food? As good an excuse as any to escape while he got his brain back under control. 'I'll see what's cooking in the kitchen.'

So Madison adored children and from the look that had come over her when talking about them would be quite happy to have a brood of her own. She'd make a great mum. Probably be quite strict but soft as butter on the inside.

After ordering fries and chicken, he plonked an elbow on the counter and leaned back to study Madison. She was chatting to the barman, no longer wary of his questions and what she might reveal about herself. He'd swear she'd told him more than she'd intended to. But, then, his usual reticence had taken a hike, too. It showed Maddy was capable of tipping his world sideways. What it didn't show was why. Why her? How had she been able to sneak under his radar even a tiny bit when that had been iron cast?

Look at her. There was part of his answer. Guys were gathering around Maddy, eager to tell her about themselves, to claim her attention, drawn in by that face that could launch a thousand ships, the body that promised heaven, and the smile that would not let them look away. He completely understood their reaction; she'd captivated him within minutes of turning up on his patch.

Crossing over to the group, he reached around one officer for his drink and was astonished to hear Madison say, 'Make way for Sam. That's his spot.'

Pleasure oozed through him like he'd been handed a present to unwrap. His fingers curled around the icy bottle of water she nodded to, and he nudged a guy off his stool. 'Thanks, mate.'

Madison's lips were pressing down hard on a burgeoning smile as she tapped her bottle against his. 'To Kiwis in out-of-the-way places.'

He tapped back. 'To unusual places.' Playing it safe? Damn right.

'What do we do around here on our days off?' Maddy asked no one in particular.

'Go into town to check out the stalls at the markets.'

Her face lit up. 'Markets? Bring them on. I can't think of a better way to spend a morning.'

'Happy to show you around any time,' one of the guys told her.

I'll drive you into town whenever you ask. Sam swallowed hard. *Down, boy. Be the mature man you pride yourself on being.*

'Here you go, Captains.' Two plates of steaming food were banged down on the counter between Sam and Maddy.

'Thanks, Bud.' His mouth watered as the wonderful smell of fried chicken reached his nostrils. 'Get stuck into that.' He pushed a plate closer to Madison and glared around at the crowd. 'Give us some space, guys.' *I want to talk to Captain Hunter—alone.*

Surprisingly the officers did back off, heading to the snooker table.

'This is yum.' Madison munched on a drumstick.

'Unhealthy and delicious,' he agreed as he reached for some fries. 'For someone who wasn't hungry, you're making short work of this.'

'I never turn down a good offer.'

His chicken went down his throat only half-chewed as his mind came up with more than one good offer. At least he managed to keep them to himself. Just. 'What was all that about the dust yesterday?'

Her plate hit the counter with a thud, quickly followed by fierce colour staining her cheeks. Her breasts rose on a long breath. She was pulling on a shield. 'I told you. I thought it was smoke,' she ground out in a don't-ask-me-any-more tone, bringing his focus back to where it should be.

'What happened, Maddy?' Why the fear of smoke? Or was it the fire that had caused the smoke that had given her grief? Had she lost her possessions or a place she frequented because of fire?

Madison slid off the stool she'd been sitting on. Her

eyelids were blinking rapidly, as if he was shining a torch in her eyes to see beyond her reticence. She was keeping tears at bay, or hiding them from him.

Neither made him happy. 'Talk to me, Maddy. Please.' Though it was none of his business, he wanted to know everything, had to wipe away that despair, that agony darkening, dulling her eyes to the colour of burned wood.

She'd turned for the exit but came back. Her hands were fists at her sides, her feet wide apart, her chin pushed forward. But she wasn't fooling him. Regret had replaced the pain in her eyes. 'I don't know you well enough, Sam.' She spoke softly, carefully, and her words wrapped around him, tugged him in.

Would she biff him around the head if he enveloped her in a hug? He shrugged. If that's what it took to banish whatever was bugging her, tying her into knots so tight she might take a week to loosen up, it would be worth it. But— 'Try me.'

'I don't think so.'

'Tell me why.'

This protectiveness had started yesterday almost immediately after that dust had got to her. Then on patrol in the morning he'd been constantly alert, watching out for her—and keeping his attention hidden. Madison was beating at his long-held barricades that kept people exactly where he wanted them. He should be the one rushing out of here, not Madison. But he couldn't, wouldn't. 'You're not trusting me?'

'Bang on, Sam.' Blink, blink.

'Why not?' Her response didn't hurt. He understood

from his own perspective. But he would like different from her.

Sadness mingled with despair as her eyes locked on him. 'Would telling you it's none of your business work?'

He shrugged deliberately. The next move was hers.

'Okay, then how's this? I don't talk to anyone about what happened to me. Get it? I trust no one not to hurt me.' Her hand fluttered over her stomach. It didn't touch down, just hovered in a protective way. Or was that as a reminder of something she needed to fear? 'I'm sorry.' She turned on her heel and left him.

'Maybe you should,' Sam whispered to her fleeing back. The muscles in his legs corded, his knuckles on the hand holding his drumstick whitened as he struggled to remain on his stool. He had to let her walk away, drop whatever was upsetting her, because she'd asked him to. Because he wasn't the right person to share her pain.

Clink. The water bottle banged his bottom teeth as he took a swig. The cool liquid wetted his parched tongue and slowly the tension eased. *I've missed something important.* It was staring him in the face and yet he could not grasp it.

Madison didn't laugh freely often, and when she had moments ago that sound had been full of everything but happiness and amusement. She didn't rush to get onside with everyone around her. That lack of trust had a lot to answer for, but what had brought it on? What had gone down to make her so wary? There was a broken marriage in her background. Was that the root of her problems? But the way she subconsciously touched her midriff when upset suggested the question might be what had hurt her, not who.

Smoke. Fire. That touching movement she made. She'd been in a fire. Was that the complete answer? No way of knowing, but there had to be more. Sam stared sightlessly in front of him as the questions nagged. This guessing game was a waste of time with no substantive answers available.

CHAPTER SEVEN

'HOW'RE YOU FEELING this morning, Reece?' Madison read the chart from overnight. 'Everything's looking good.'

'Fighting fit, Captain.' It was said with a chuckle. 'Captain Lowe says I can go on patrol this morning.'

Sam was here already? And she'd thought she was early, skipping breakfast in the hope of avoiding him for a little longer. Last night's revelations on her part had been a little too close for comfort and she wasn't ready to see that understanding in his eyes again. 'Is that so?'

'Just kidding, Captain.'

'I believe Captain Lowe is taking a patrol out to that old police building again. I'll see that you're fixed to join them.'

The private's face dropped. 'If you say so, Captain.'

Madison laughed. 'Just kidding, Private. Have you had breakfast?'

'Yes. Though not enough. Could do with some more bacon and eggs.'

'I bet you could.' She headed for the door, calling over her shoulder, 'That's a no from me.'

'What are you saying no to?' Sam stood in front of

her, hands in pockets, a smile tugging at the corners of his mouth.

'Reece wants a second breakfast.' The way the top of Sam's fatigues moulded to his chest, defining that amazing shape, had her nipples in tingling peaks. He looked good enough to eat. She was hungry after all. But suddenly not for toast.

'You look like you could eat two as well.'

Rolling her head from side to side, she tried to negate the cravings swamping her. 'I'm fine,' she muttered.

Let me out of here before I touch him, run my hands over that divine body.

'You haven't eaten.'

Didn't say I had, but I want to.

Sam hadn't finished. 'You finished your run at six hundred hours, less than thirty minutes ago. Time only for a shower and to tidy your room, wouldn't you agree, Captain?'

More than enough time to try out that body, Captain. Voices came from behind her, snapping her out of her wishful thinking. 'You had nothing better to do than see who was out on the track this morning?'

'I was finishing my run as you began yours.'

Which meant he'd been outside some time around four a.m. 'Trouble sleeping, Sam?'

'About as much as you. If I'm not mistaken, your lights were on at that hour.'

He wasn't mistaken. But he might not know they'd been on for hours before that. 'I was messaging home.' And beating up the pillow, guzzling water, pacing the ten strides from wall to wall over and over. And thinking about Sam. Mostly thinking about him. She might've left him in the mess last night but his questions had followed her into her room and right into the short sleep she'd managed before waking up completely around two. Those blasted questions had still been there, coated in the husky tones of Sam's voice. Rough, sexy, annoying, caring. Yeah, that about summed him up.

'Go to breakfast, Madison. You're not putting in a full day without eating properly. The heat is debilitating without starving yourself.'

She huffed at him. 'You're not my keeper. If I'm not hungry then I'm not hungry.' Even to her that sounded petulant. But the thought of food had nausea rising up to the back of her throat, while the lack of sleep made her feel like something the dog had chewed and left on the side of the road. 'I don't always have breakfast, okay?' she added for good measure, because she knew she was wrong to go without food.

It didn't work. 'Out here you do. We never know what's going down from one hour to the next and we have to be prepared. That means having regular meals.' His hands were on his hips now, his fingers pressing deep as he leaned towards her. *'Comprendo?'*

Very nice hips. Shaped the perfect body outline. His torso was all muscle. Basically he was a lean machine. The youthful softness she vaguely remembered had gone from his face, replaced with lines and knowledge. A fighting man, prepared for battle, as all the soldiers on base were. As she was. And if she had to go into battle—please make that a skirmish—she needed to be fully ready. Which meant breakfast. 'You win.' She turned away, intent on getting back here as quickly as possible.

'Madison,' Sam called after her.

Ignore him. She paused, faced him. 'Sam.' Her heart went wild, beating a rhythm all of its own, not one she recognised. But, then, she wasn't at all familiar with the reactions that pelted her body whenever Sam was around. Phew, but it was hot in here.

He stood in the doorway, his hands back in his pockets in that, oh, so nonchalant manner of his. Which meant he was about to say something she mightn't like. 'I wasn't trying to score points off you, merely looking out for you.'

Knock me over. Did I hear that right? Did she like that? Oh, yeah. She did. Lots. She melted, a slow sensation of warmth trickling through her belly, over her skin, encompassing her heart. With this man at her back she didn't have to worry about a thing. But the days were running out and soon she'd be back to looking out for herself. Dipping her chin, she acknowledged, 'See you in a bit.' He didn't need to know how his statement made her feel, but she could enjoy the warmth that molten sensation brought.

'Don't take too long. I hear there's already a queue forming to see the new doctor.' He flicked her a grin before heading away. He'd got the last word in. Again.

She didn't care. Especially when he grinned in a sexy way that stirred up all sorts of sensations in places she really should keep under lock and key. The man was almost too good to be true. But she was never going to find out how good he was. Hot as— Yeah, so was the air around here. And her blood. Phew. The back of her hand slid across her forehead. How had she not noticed all this before?

There was only one way to control herself. Remember Jason and how he'd switched off from her the moment he'd seen her scars. Sure, he'd hung around for six months before asking for a divorce, but during that time he'd slept in the spare room—so as not to disturb her sleep apparently—and he'd never held her close or kissed her, or said he loved her. It had taken one look at her body for him to leave her mentally.

Madison chewed toast thoughtfully. She could not afford to forget that lesson. Not even for an hour of bliss.

'Eggs sunny side up.' The cook slid a plate in front of her.

'Ta muchly,' she said. Her stomach was in turmoil now. Could it handle eggs on top of that little shock she'd given it? But she did need to eat. Sam had been right about that.

Sam. Sam this, Sam that. Her second full day here had barely started and already he was taking over every thought process.

Hurrying through her eggs and coffee—which did stay in place—she returned to the medical block. A few hours working alongside the man would soon have her brain back in sync. He'd annoy her to bits and she'd be thinking what a pain in the butt he was. *Not what a gorgeous sexy man he was, one she'd like to take to her bed and learn more about?*

Shut up, brain.

Wasn't your brain talking, it was your hormones.

Thank goodness for long queues of bored soldiers needing vaccination updates. The hours flew past without Sam getting under Madison's feet too often. 'What's on after lunch?' she asked him as they wrapped up the morning.

'The commander's letting some of the locals in for us to treat. They'll be brought across in batches of four or five, depending on who the patient is and who's with them.'

'As in children and their parents?' Woo-hoo, she was going to see people who needed more from her than all the morning's soldiers put together had. 'What can we expect?'

'I'll tell you after you've eaten lunch.' She couldn't tell from his poker face if he was joking or warning that the afternoon wasn't going to be pleasant.

She'd go for the joke, and hope she was right. 'That good, huh?'

'You're not always easy to wind up.' Sam laughed.

A deep-bellied sound that curled her toes, and had her trying to think up things to say just to evoke more laughter. Nothing came to mind. 'I used to be. Guess I've changed.'

The laughter died in his eyes. 'People do, Maddy.' Somehow he'd moved right up to her without appearing to shift. And now his hand was on her chin, his thumb softly caressing her jawline, back and forth, oh, so gently. *Don't stop.* 'I think it's called life.'

He didn't know the half of it. Couldn't. Not unless he'd emailed someone back home, and that was unlikely. From what she'd learned these past few days, if Sam wanted to know something he asked outright. Anyway, who would he ask about her? He hadn't kept in touch with anyone she knew.

'So I've heard,' she choked around a huge dollop of

lust. That, unusually, was the stronger of the emotions roiling through her. Sam's thumb was magic, eliciting all sorts of sensations to spread out from her chin. She was leaning towards him, against his hand, afraid he'd stop.

Maddy took a big step backwards, disappointment rising as Sam's hand slid away. If he had her in such a twist from a mere thumb rub, what would…? *Don't go there. You're never going to find out. Understand?* Oh, yeah, she understood all right. One look in the mirror at her abdomen would give her all the brakes she needed and more. Unless she made a blindfold for him. A sharp laugh huffed across her lips, bitter in its taste. Sam really had got to her if she was coming up with such ridiculous ideas. 'Right, lunch.' She strode away without looking at him, for fear of melting on the spot.

'I want to kiss Maddy.' Sam could not drag his eyes away from her as she crossed the parade ground, heading for the mess. That butt was doing manoeuvres in her fatigues that had nothing to do with soldiering. Moves that had his hormones in a spin.

'I'd wait until lights are out,' Jock drawled from somewhere behind him.

Sam swore. *Did I speak aloud?* Take that as yes. 'Shut up, Jock.'

'Just saying.' He nodded. 'You going to tell Maddy what you just told the whole medic unit?'

'What?' Sam scanned the room. They were alone.

'You're running out of days to make good on your wish.'

'That's got to be a plus.' Kissing Maddy would not

be wise. Getting all wound up in knots of need would only make for a very uncomfortable flight back home. Not that there'd be any kissing. She wasn't going to allow him close enough. Besides, he wouldn't be able to stop at that. And he had to. No. He had to stop this daydreaming before acting on it. Not after.

Jock rubbed his belly. 'Let's go eat, man. We've got a fair whack of patients this afternoon and you know how frustrating that's going to be.'

Wrong word, buddy. I'm frustrated already, and it has nothing to do with patients.

'What made the boss agree to letting more people in today? It's not like we haven't fulfilled our quota for the week.'

The commander stuck to the rules when it came to allowing locals onto the base, even those with serious medical conditions. Something both Sam and Jock disagreed with. Helping those in need was integral with being doctors, but try explaining that to the commander and they'd find themselves doing more patrols than usual. The commander was the guy who'd take the fallout if anything went wrong, though.

'No idea, and I'm not asking. He's just as likely to change his mind.'

'True.' Sam sure as hell didn't want those cute little kids missing out on treatment because he'd said something out of order. 'Wonder how Maddy will cope with the clinic?'

'You really have to ask that?'

'No.' Just making conversation. Of course her name had popped up unbidden. It seemed nothing he did banished her from his mind. She hadn't crept in. She'd bashed her way into his mind, his dreams, his body. A groan escaped him. 'Four days to go.' And counting. Could he get beyond them without following through on the driving need turning him in an ever-decreasing circle? Without dealing to the almost overwhelming need to kiss her?

Only time would answer that one. Four days and counting.

'They don't cry when I touch their broken arms or in-fected sores.' Madison was in shock. She'd seen chil-dren as young as two this afternoon and their stoic little faces had cut into her heart, making her want to wrap them up and take them home.

'It has you wondering what else they've endured, doesn't it?' Sam held up an X-ray taken of a six-year-old boy's arm Madison had handed him. 'Both the ulna and radius are broken. Looks like blunt force trauma to me.'

'His mother said he fell off the roof of their dwelling.'

'His mother? Or the interpreter?' Sam shrugged. 'Remember, what's most important is getting those bones set and on their way to mending. It's all we can do.'

'You're right.' But she didn't have to like it. 'You want a hand putting a cast on?'

'Come and work your charm while I try not to hurt the poor little blighter.' Sam nodded. 'We'll give him something for the pain first. Can't stand to inflict any more than he's already dealing with.'

Straightening those bones before applying a cast was going to be awful for the lad. And for them. 'I think he's underweight for his age, but I'm not sure what's normal here.'

'He very well could be. Any fever, cough, breathlessness?'

'Not that I've noticed.' And she would've. She'd done all the obs, and more. The boy had barely stirred as she'd poked and prodded as gently as possible. The only sign he was in distress was his big black eyes getting larger.

'Let's get this over so the wee guy can go home with his mum.'

'How did they get here?' She hadn't seen any vehicles outside the camp since she'd arrived.

'They walked.' Sam held up his hand in a stop sign. 'Don't even say it. We are not allowed to give them a lift back to town, but sometimes it so happens a truck needs to go for some supplies just as people are trudging away from seeing us.'

'Cool.' Madison picked up the equipment to make a cast and followed Sam over to their patient, who lay curled up beside his mum. 'We have to give Khalid an injection,' she told the interpreter.

When the boy heard that from the interpreter he pushed harder against his mother but didn't utter a sound. 'I'll try not to hurt you,' Madison said in as soothing a voice as she could manage. Rubbing Khalid's arm with her palm, she felt him tense, so continued to rub until he slowly relaxed. When she finally slid the needle into his muscle he didn't blink, but who knew if that was because he hadn't felt the prick or not.

Sam opened the top drawer of a cabinet by the bed. 'Here you go, young man. A lollipop for being so brave.'

The small mouth slowly expanded into a smile as Khalid snatched his treasure from Sam's fingers. His mother said something and the boy nodded at Sam.

'I'm picking that's thank you in Khalid-speak.' Sam grinned briefly before working quickly to align the radius at the break.

'Right, now for the messy bit.' Madison spread a plastic cover over the bed and began to apply the cast. She wanted to work fast so Khalid would soon be out of his misery, but she also didn't want to make the cast too tight or too loose, so he'd have to come back for a second attempt. 'I can't remember the last time I did one of these.'

'Back to basics, isn't it?'

'Yes, and you know what? I'm enjoying it.' Sometimes it was easy to forget the simple stuff, hand it over to a nurse and move on to the next surgery.

Sam said, 'I've been watching you. You've enjoyed helping these people.'

'I have.'

'Don't get too involved, Maddy. They're not why we're here. You've got to remember that. If you don't you could find yourself in a dangerous position one day. Not everyone is as they seem out here.'

Go and spoil the moment, why don't you? Even if you are right.

For a moment there she'd forgotten the military side of being here, had become lost in the medical world that was her first love. Swallowing the flare of annoyance his words had caused, she acquiesced. 'You warned me of that the day I arrived.'

'Think of Porky and his foot. That's why we're here.

Not to get blown up but to defend the innocent. As an aside, we do what we can for the locals if time and safety permit.' Serious Sam was as mesmerising as the other versions. Then his face softened and he totally had her attention. 'I don't ever want to hear that you've been injured while here, Maddy.'

Moisture filled her eyes. That had to be the nicest, kindest thing anyone had said to her in a long time. Her family had learned to keep those thoughts to themselves after she'd broken down one day saying they were undermining her efforts to be strong and capable alone. That had hurt them but since then they'd all tried hard to follow her wishes. Now, after a simple comment from Sam, nearly a stranger, she understood she'd been wrong. 'I'll be doing my damnedest to keep anyone, especially my family, from hearing any such news.' Suddenly she missed her mum and dad, her sister and those nieces so much her arms ached to hold them and her heart slowed with sadness.

'You'd better.' Sam's voice had become gruff, deeper and darker, full of an emotion she didn't recognise. Maybe he cared more about what happened to people than he'd admit.

'Sam?'

'Better get on with the last patient.' He quickly turned to snatch up a piece of paper from the nearest desk and headed to a man and his son, waiting quietly.

Sam was in a right old pickle. That page he'd grabbed was the score sheet from last night's medics' snooker contest, not notes about any patient. Maddy chuckled. Sam in a stew was like a small boy trying to decide which flavour ice cream he was going to have.

* * *

Downing his water, Sam nodded to the sergeant behind the bar. 'Another thanks, Randy.' No such thing as drinking too much water out here.

At long last the day was over, and unless, touch wood, there were any incidents during the night, he was free to do as he pleased. That did not include kissing Maddy, something that was becoming a bit of an obsession since the idea had first struck. No, he needed to find another way of letting his hair down and eliminating the pent-up needs keeping him on tenterhooks since he'd gone and told Madison he'd be worrying about her.

'Up to some rock?' Jock leaned a hip against the bar.

'Exactly what I need.' An hour getting lost in the guitar with the band would knock him into mental shape. 'Boyse and Carter around somewhere?' The drummer and xylophonist were integral to their band.

Jock, the voice and other guitarist, nodded. 'They're on their way over.'

'Show time, then.' Sam stood up. Friday nights in the officers' mess were his favourite. He'd play his guitar and try to get lost in the music, something not always possible since the quality of music depended on who was stationed on base at the time. There'd been some clangers in the past all right but tonight he'd have no trouble getting immersed in the music.

As he settled on a stool and picked at the guitar strings, tightening two, he glanced across to the corner of the room where a group had gathered with Madison in the centre. Of course. Not that she looked overly comfortable, wasn't putting on the charm or being too friendly with any of the men. When she glanced his

way and met his gaze she nodded and gave him a knowing smile.

Knowing what? Racking his brain didn't toss up any
ideas of what that had been about.

'You joining us?' Jock nudged him.

'Try and stop me.' For the next half-hour Sam played
whatever tune the other band members started, letting
himself go in the rhythms of rock music. His mind
was blank apart from the keys he played, the strings
he strummed and picked. The music flowed over him,
eased the tension he'd been carrying since Madison's
arrival on base.

Ah, Madison. Snap. The tension was back. He
scanned the room. There. Parked on a stool, a soda in
one hand, her feet tapping in time to the music, and a
smile of pure happiness lightening her face. For the first
time she appeared to have no worries in the world. Then
she looked his way and stood up with a determined expression and placed her drink on the counter.

Now he remembered. 'Hide the microphones.' Last
year at school. The senior's social, Maddy and her pals
on stage.

'She can't sing?' Jock asked into the silence that
came with the end of their current song.

Her voice had been strong, alluring, sweet, but having her up here beside him…? Not happening.

'She doesn't know a C scale from a fish scale.'

Don't drop a bomb on me tomorrow for lying. If
Maddy picked up a microphone he was leaving. One
guitar down wouldn't matter, the other guys could make
great music without his input, while having her standing beside him, belting out words in a voice made for

an angel, would stir him up even more. Wouldn't matter if she was in tune or not.

'Let's do something heavier,' Jock said, and started banging out another rock song.

Maddy's face lit up some more, and that smile would now blind a city with its intensity. Her feet were done with tapping; now she was moving on the spot, her hips swaying and her arms moving above her head in time to the music.

Sam needed a drink—fast. His tongue was stuck to the roof of his mouth, his throat so dry he couldn't even squawk along with Boyse's singing. Just as well. The guys would fire him on the spot.

'Get that down your throat.' A can appeared in his line of vision.

He nodded thanks to Jock. Still couldn't talk. How was it his mate seemed to know what was going on in his head almost as soon as he did? Damn but that cold liquid was good. Wet in the right places, cooled the heat in his throat, even tasted wonderful. Did absolutely nothing to chill down the heat tightening his groin.

'Can I join in?' Madison stood in front of him, that supple body the only thing his eyes could see.

Of course he nodded agreement; of course he did. Damn it.

Boyse called out the next song, and began the beat. Not a tune Sam had been expecting, but with a bit of luck it would be beyond Maddy. She'd sung the light girl band music that got everyone up dancing. He began playing his guitar, refusing to watch as she stepped between the guys to stand legs wide, head back and a microphone to her mouth. He did not see her lips almost swallow the mouthpiece. He did not feel apprehension and awe alternatively cool and heat his skin. No, not at all.

And then the first words came out of her mouth and Sam forgot to play, forgot where he was, forgot everything but Madison.

So much for thinking she couldn't sing rock. She *was* rock. She owned the song, took it from ordinary to sensational. She moved with it, became it, striding, swaying, dancing from one edge of the band to the other and back again, her head tipped so far back it seemed impossible she wouldn't crash into something or someone. Where was her long hair when he needed it to be hanging behind her?

He knew his mouth had fallen open and his eyes were wide, felt his lungs stall, his stomach sit still in shock, and the beat of his heart was so out of whack with the song it was awful.

What happened to sweet? What was spilling out of Maddy's mouth was raw emotion. Deep, husky notes that played his senses like a bow on violin strings, that lifted goose bumps on his skin and sent prickles of heat down his spine. This was nothing like her speaking voice. She'd stepped into the song as though she'd experienced what was behind the words. Maybe she had. Maybe they'd hit on the one song she could relate to so deeply.

And then— And then she took it up a level. Sam's gut tightened. Where did that come from? The drama behind the words filled the air, stopped everyone except the band in their tracks, drinks frozen in hands on tables or halfway to mouths. Sam's guitar rested on his

thighs, his fingers slack against the strings. He was beyond playing, had lost the ability to pick a tune. This
was not a one off—Madison would sing every song as
though she'd lived it.

As she proved again and again over the next thirty
minutes. She had the room mesmerised. The guy behind the counter was out of a job while she sang. Sam
reckoned every male fell in love with her during those
loud, emotional, magical minutes.

But not him. Of course not. Somehow he finally
managed to play his guitar, keep in tune and not look
like a three-year-old with a plastic toy. Somehow he
didn't give Jock an elbow when he cocked a knowing
eye at him and said, 'If that's not knowing her scales,
what is it?'

Sam didn't have an answer. What could he say that
wouldn't dig a bigger hole for him to fall into?

Four days and counting.

CHAPTER EIGHT

MADDY WAS BUZZING. Joining the guys for a few songs had been a blast. She hadn't sung as though there was nothing else in the world but the message in the song for a long time.

Come on. That's not how she'd sung at all. Neither had she ever before. Tonight she'd poured every painful emotion possessing her into each word and note. The fire that had destroyed everything good about her life had strangled her with deeper, harsher emotions. Tonight she hadn't been able to stop them expanding through her. But at least she'd faced them, hadn't run away.

And she was buzzing. How did that work? Because she still carried the agony of losing her granddad, the anger at Jason's rejection, still bore the sadness of not knowing if she'd have a child one day. The big unknown.

Like she was drugged or something, the buzz did not fade as she recalled the infections that had run rampant through most of her body as her burns had seemed to take for ever to heal. Chest infections, kidney issues and stomach problems from the endless antibiotics she'd swallowed. But the worst by far—a tubal infection that had refused to clear up for months. No one had been able to state categorically whether infertility would be a result. According to the gynaecologist there was only one way she'd find out for certain, and the woman hadn't sounded very positive. Another mark against her already uncertain future. Something else she couldn't ask a man to accept.

Madison refused to let the familiar desolation shove her high away. Tonight had been good for her. She'd let a lot of pain go during that short span of time where she'd poured everything into the songs and forgotten where she was. Right now she was on top of the world. She would probably crash tomorrow but tonight she'd enjoy the ride. It was the first in a very long time.

Reaching for her water bottle, she glanced around the noisy room. Laughter and jokes were coming in every direction from the officers she was starting to get to know. No sign of Sam, though.

The band had set their instruments aside to take a few drinks on board and he'd been the first to the barman to grab a water bottle, but now he was nowhere in sight.

The buzz faded a little. She wanted to share it with Sam, not these people who didn't understand her. Sam understood her? Since when? Yes, she thought he did, at least a little bit, because of the grief she'd noted in his eyes when he'd let his guard down.

'He went outside.' Jock stood beside her.

She looked into the understanding gaze locked on her and whispered, 'Thanks.' But what if Sam didn't want to talk to her? Why should he? 'Maybe I'll wait and see if he returns.'

Jock tilted his head at her. 'Yellow doesn't suit you.' He said it quietly, calmly, not menacingly or cheekily. Just a nudge in the right direction according to Jock.

She slid off her stool, tightened her grip on her soda bottle and said, 'Thanks again.'

Her skin squeezed tight in the cooler outdoor air, and for a moment she couldn't see beyond the line of light thrown from the open door. As her sight returned to normal she looked around. No sign of Sam. But he'd be out there. It was where he went when he wanted to be alone. *So go hunt him down.*

He was walking, head down, hands stuffed in pockets, covering the track that followed the perimeter with a slowness that seemed foreign to the man she was getting to know. So far she'd only seen a guy who tackled things without looking over his shoulder.

Madison hesitated, familiar doubts nodding at her. 'Yellow doesn't suit you.'

Yes, thanks, Jock, got that message, but what if Sam tells me to go to hell, to get out of his face? She'd do as he demanded. But she didn't want that. They had started something over the last few days; a friendship based on next to nothing but one she was grabbing with both hands. A friendship with someone who was unaware of her history, had no compunction about asking the hard questions because he didn't understand the ground he was treading on. It had been a long time since anyone had treated her without first pulling on kid gloves. Other than the army, of course. The military didn't care about things like that, only demanded loyalty, hard work, and obedience. A balm for her prickly nature. And now Sam seemed to be approaching her from a different perspective to either of those. An approach she liked, appreciated, wanted more of. She felt there might be a cure for her in there.

So, take a deep breath and go talk to the man. Or walk in silence with him. Whatever. But do something. He won't mind. He'll walk away. He'll… She stepped after him.

'Maddy, thought you'd be lapping up the crowd's attention for a while yet.'

If he thought that'd turn her around he was wrong. She kept walking towards him. 'It was fun.'

'But?'

I'd like to be with you. 'Why aren't you inside with your band buddies?' When his mouth tightened, she swore under her breath. She'd just flipped the question back at him. 'Let me start again. It was more than fun. Singing with you and the guys was incredible, and I loved every moment. I'd forgotten what it's like to let rip without thought of anything else.'

'How many years since you last sang to an audience?'

Madison got the feeling he was really asking what had made her stop. 'Too many.' Had he seen through her usual façade?

She had thrown herself into the music, put everything out there for the first time ever. Could be because she was so far from home, from where her nightmare had begun. Whatever the reason, it had been liberating, and she yearned to be able to tell someone—Sam?—about her insecurities. *I'm trapped until I do.* Madison gasped. That was true. Until tonight she hadn't seen that. Already, coming to the Peninsula was proving to be good for her.

But standing here with Sam, already the shutters were closing. When he said, 'Tell me more,' she swayed on her feet, like she rocked on the edge of a precipice, tightening her muscles around the pain and anger, wishing the words would escape across her tongue.

She took the easy option in answering his question; the tried-and-true one, the safe one. The only one she trusted. 'You know what it was like. When I was studying and doing long shifts as part of my training, there wasn't any time for much else.' Only Jason, and he'd put the kibosh on her singing, saying it belonged in the shower, if at all. She gasped. He *had* been a bit of a control freak, come to think of it. 'Guess I just forgot to sing.'

'That's a waste.'

'Thanks. I wouldn't win one of those TV singing shows.' She didn't hit every note perfectly, lost her way in the tune sometimes.

'Maybe not, but you'd get a standing ovation. When did you start singing rock? I mean—' he was shaking his head with something resembling disbelief '—your voice is ideally suited for that genre. It's so expressive. Unbelievable.'

Her lungs swelled up, her heart stretched to almost bursting at his compliment. That it was genuine she was in no doubt. A step closer to him. There was wonder in those sunny eyes. Wonder for her. And somewhere deep, deep inside her, another knot of pain, of anger and confusion, slipped loose and began to unwind. One coil at a time the tightness that had held her upright for two long years was slackening off and she wasn't falling down. There just might be a future for her that held some of the hopes she'd had when growing up. She might be able to dream again.

'Maddy.' Sam reached for her and tucked her against his chest, his arms wrapped around her.

Against her cheek she felt his lungs rising and falling faster than normal, matching her quickened rate. Under her palms, resting against his waist, muscles were tightening. Breathing deep, she savoured the mix of aftershave, sweat, man. Sam. Clutching at his shirt, she leaned back to peer up at his face, seeing the lines carved out by grief, by the determination that must've been behind him becoming a surgeon, the humour that hid his feelings, and the loyalty he had for those he cared about.

If she dropped all her defences and let him in then what? They didn't have a future together. She didn't know him well enough to trust him with everything. He could still wreck her. But…

Sam held Madison tight against his hungry body and absorbed her into him. Her heat, softness and those curves, the surprise that had sparked at him when he'd told her what he thought of her voice, her hair tickling his chin. *This is Maddy.*

Desire rolled through him, tightened him. This is what he wanted. Now. With no thought to the consequences. Shock stunned him. He followed a rigid line when it came to friendship and relationships, never deviated, and yet here, tonight, he wasn't; couldn't haul up the usual defence mechanisms. His body was afire with need.

To hold her wasn't enough.

It was too much.

Turmoil churned his gut, fear chilled his blood. This hug had to be enough. They couldn't have a relationship, not even for one night, because he suspected that once he let his guard down with Maddy he'd never be able to pull it back in place. And he had to.

He wasn't free to fall in love and marry, not when the guilt kept him hogtied. How could he be happy when he'd taken that from William the day he'd talked him into a final tour with the army before he married his fiancée? William hadn't been keen to delay marrying Ally for another six months, but he'd given in to Sam's plea to go to Afghanistan with him. Now Sam could not move forward, could not be happy and take enjoyment from life when William and Ally couldn't. There were many obstacles to him settling down, and they were all in his head. Didn't mean they were any less real.

Gently setting Maddy aside, he worked hard to ignore the disappointment that dulled her eyes and drooped her shoulders, mimicking what was pouring through him. He re-ran the band through his head, playing those songs that Madison had blown out of the water. That voice. It had stroked him, rasped his skin, evoked all sorts of fantasies. What if he did follow through and hauled her back against him? Oh, and kissed her? And…

'Let's walk.' Then he surprised himself. He caught up her free hand and slipped his fingers between hers.

A jolt reminiscent of an electric current he'd once

copped when he'd tried to change a power switch for his mother pinged where their palms touched. *Let go of her now.* Just like when he'd been zapped for real, he couldn't. Beggar for punishment that he was, he wound his fingers tighter around Maddy's. And she reciprocated. Which meant what?

Stretching his steps into strides, he took them out to the perimeter and beyond the mess and bar, away from prying eyes. Unable to drop her hand, he enjoyed the sheer delight of holding hands with a woman. *This woman.* Warmth worked its way up his arm and down into his chest, softening his breathing, turning his fears and guilt into a puddle of wonder. And worry. This was not how things were meant to be for him now. Madison. Stick to Madison and this whole wanting her thing might evaporate in a cloud of reality. *If only.*

So what now?

Letting go of her hand wasn't an option.

Maddy couldn't believe it. Holding hands with Sam was so—so out there. It wasn't even high-powered, hot, sexy stuff. It was gentle and caring and nice—she hated that word but it was true. All right, try wonderful. Unbelievable, more like. Perfect. Yes.

She squeezed his hand to make sure she wasn't making this up. His fingers tightened briefly around hers. Definitely for real.

Had to be the heat and the foreign location and that music and… Madison sighed, long and slow. Had to be something in the drinking water because holding hands was nothing like what she'd expect with this man. He gave the impression of being more the let's-get-in-the-sack-fast kind of guy. Exactly what she felt around him when she admitted her feelings. Don't go there. Enjoy the moment. Because it would only be a moment, a few minutes at most, then Sam would realise what he was doing and drop her hand like a hot potato. And one of them needed to be sensible.

If she talked, would that burst the bubble? But her blood was fizzing, her whole body buzzing from earlier and now topped up with a dose of Sam. Holding hands was nowhere near enough. His mouth on hers would go a lot further towards improving the situation.

Madison gasped. Again kissing was on her mind. What would he do if she turned to him and placed her lips on his? Would he kiss her back? Soft and gentle? Hard and demanding, giving as much as he took, she'd bet.

'You okay?' her biggest distraction asked.

'Fine.' If wanting to kiss him was fine. If needing to get closer was fine.

'Damn.'

'What's wrong?'

'You and me. That's what.' Was that longing making his voice lower and huskier than usual?

She was probably imagining it because of the need clawing through her. 'How are we wrong?'

'As in for each other, Maddy.' There. The way he dragged out her name, turned it into a caress, turned her insides into that molten mess of need she was learning to live with on an hourly basis.

'Maybe it's our time.' Gulp. She'd given herself away with that desire-laden comment. A beggar on her knees couldn't be more obvious.

Sam extricated his hand.

She'd gone too far. But he was here, for real, and every stop sign had disappeared.

'I'll tell you something for nothing, Madison. When you were singing that first song the emotion that poured out of you, I've never heard anything like it. You had me in the palm of your hand. You could've done anything to me at that moment.'

She'd sing it again—now. Definitely begging. 'If only I'd known.' She tried for a laugh, came out with a squeak.

Sam managed better with a chuckle that didn't sound strangled. 'I'm glad you didn't. I could've ended up looking foolish in front of the guys.'

'And that matters?'

He turned to her and with one finger lifted her chin so there was no avoiding his eyes. 'You've got to live and work with them.' There was no grin for her now. Just complete seriousness. 'We can't forget we're on different tracks. I don't do relationships, long term or otherwise, while I think that's what you're looking for.'

'Wrong. I won't be marrying again, or getting into a permanent relationship of any kind.'

'You will get over your broken marriage, Maddy. You must.'

If only it were that simple. She stumbled sideways, putting a gap between them, away from those eyes boring into her in case he saw the truth. That she wanted him despite everything. She could not let him near, would not undress in front of him, or let his hands explore her body. He'd unwittingly given her the wake-up call she needed. While she'd been leaning in for more of Sam, desperate to get close in a sexual way, yearning for his touch, to touch him, she'd completely forgotten the truth. She was not going to let him see her body. Not going to see that look of horror when it filled his eyes, twisted his mouth. It would break her completely.

She couldn't trust herself to accept someone might want her as she was. Didn't believe it possible. Not when her husband, who'd declared his undying love for her only two days before the fire, hadn't been able to accept the new her.

Sam watched the argument going on in Madison's head. It leapt through her eyes, marked her face, flattened those kiss-worthy lips. She wanted him as much as he did her. But fear had her fighting her desire all the way. Something he understood completely.

But… One kiss. What harm could that do? It wouldn't mean there was more to come, but it would satisfy an ache.

Or create a bigger one.

There was that.

One kiss would definitely crank up the heat into an inferno.

But he had to taste her. Had to know those lips, had to satisfy a quest he'd begun unknowingly only days ago. At the same time it was as though all the barriers he'd erected were tightening, warning him not to do it. But the clawing need for affection and sharing was stronger.

'I think I'll head inside.' Madison stood before him, looking sad and lost.

He did what he shouldn't. He ignored those damned warnings. 'Don't go yet.' Reaching out, he took Maddy's shaky fists into his hands and wrapped her arms around his waist. She fitted like she was an extension of him. And that scent—he drew a long breath and savoured that summer fruit memory, rearranged his memories from a four-year-old's to a man's. Nothing set his senses tripping the tango like the smell of Maddy.

Dropping his head, he found her mouth, covered those enticing lips with his, and knew her softness. Her sharp indrawn breath made him pause until she relaxed into him. Then he went back to kissing her. One hand reached up to push through the silk that was her hair. The other cupped her chin as he continued to taste her, and an all-consuming need burst alight inside him, making everything he'd known before redundant.

When her body melted into his those glorious breasts pushed against the hard muscle of his chest, her hips pressed his, while the apex of her body touched his hardness.

Sam groaned. This was hell on earth. This was wonderful.

Maddy tensed. Her hands left his waist, flattened on his chest. Slowly she lifted her mouth away from his, tipped her head back to lock those eyes on him. 'Sam?'

'Yes, Maddy, it's me.' He recaptured her mouth before she could deny him another kiss. One had not been enough. Two wasn't going to be either.

She sank back into him, causing him to relax, except where it mattered. His tongue stroked her lips, her mouth. It wasn't enough. He tasted the skin on her jawline, and below her ear.

Under his hands he felt the change in her posture,

the slow tightening of her arms before she began to pull away.

His first reaction was to haul her closer, tighten his hold, kiss her deeper. But Madison was withdrawing, and he had to allow that.

And being Madison, if he took too long to let her go, stole another kiss first, she'd probably want to kill him.

And I want to live. Really want that more than anything. Sam jolted backwards, his arms dropping to his sides while he rocked on his feet as though slammed by a runaway truck. *I'm starting to feel alive for the first time in years. I want to love, and laugh, and make a home, and settle down, instead of wandering wherever the army sends me.*

This was what happened when those protective ties around his soul began unwinding.

This was what happened when Madison Hunter had stepped into his life.

This was dangerous.

There was too much flotsam to deal with before he could even begin to undertake a relationship. He had to walk away from Madison, let her get on with her life without him, because he wasn't able to become a part of it. She'd been badly hurt. He could not add to her anguish. He had to hold onto that raw emotion she'd poured into her singing so as he didn't add to it.

But he was damned if he'd ever forget that kiss.

CHAPTER NINE

'WE'RE WANTED AT the hospital in town,' Sam told Madison the moment she stepped inside the unit.

So much for last night's kiss. The way he was looking at her, it might well have been a figment of her imagination. Only problem there was that her brain wasn't that imaginative. Hadn't known that a kiss could transport her to places out of this world, or turn her inside out with desire. If that's what Sam's kisses did to her, she hated to think what his lovemaking might do. A very good reason not to go there, since this morning she was struggling to cope with acting like nothing had happened. As for sleep after she'd crawled between the sheets around midnight—forget it. Sam had ruled. In her head; had even tickled her heart.

Yet here he was, looking relaxed and cool, like nothing had occurred between them.

Her blood began to boil. Sam did that to her. *Don't let him. Be as blasé as he appears to be.* Maddy appraised him harder, finally saw the telltale twitch of that amazing mouth. Not so cool after all. *Yeah. Got you.* She wanted to punch the air, but refrained by folding her arms across her breasts. 'Why are we headed to the hospital and not out on patrol, as we're supposed to be?'

He tossed some packets of swabs at a bag. His casualness didn't fool her this time. The packets missed their destination. 'There's been an accident…' he flicked fingers in the air '…involving a school bus.'

'Can't the local doctors cope?'

'We're under orders, Madison. This is what we do, follow orders.' He snatched the swabs up from where they'd landed on the floor and shoved them inside the bag. 'We'll travel in convoy with armoured vehicles as there're reports of trouble at a village along the way.'

Her heart thumped against her chest. *Reality check. This is what I was sent here for, not for sensational kisses.* She was about to go out into danger. Or the possibility of it, which amounted to the same thing, according to her heart, which was now beating a sharp and rapid tattoo. 'What do you want me to do? Do we take supplies with us?'

'The truck's being loaded as we speak. You're in charge of making sure nothing important is left behind.'

In other words, she was superfluous to requirements but he was stuck with her. Digging deep, she found a smile and refused to utter anything antagonistic. Two could play at being nice. Except she meant it. 'On to it.' She reached for the check sheets that hung on a clip by the phone and drew calming breaths to quieten her heart before it threw itself into a fit. That patrol she'd gone on had only been a taster for bigger and scarier things to come.

'There are injured children, Maddy.' Sam was beside her.

Children. The innocent victims. She looked up at him, her eyes seeking his, looking for reassurance that she'd cope, that she'd do her job without breaking down. That he'd be there for her, with her, helping, encouraging. Why she needed him for that she had no idea, but if that's what it took to cope then that's how it was.

A light grip on her shoulder surprised her and told her Sam had read her concerns. 'It's hard, but we'll manage. Go check the supplies, Maddy.' This time his voice was like a caress, gentle and warm and comforting. A man of many facets.

'Will do.' She headed outside to the truck and Cassy, who was ordering soldiers to be careful as they loaded boxes of equipment. 'How are we going?'

'You'll need your weapon,' Sam told her.

'I knew that.' But in her hurry to see they had everything they required for their patients, she'd forgotten she was a soldier before she was a doctor. She would be a liability to the others if she wasn't armed and ready as they made their way into town.

Squashed into the cab of the truck between Sam and the driver, she stared around as they rolled out through the gate and along the dusty road, heading in the opposite direction from where she'd been before. Heat shimmered on the horizon, dust spewed from the vehicle in front to engulf their truck. 'So inhospitable.'

'Nothing like the green of home, is it?' Sam agreed.

'It hadn't occurred to me how lucky we are in NZ until I saw this.'

'Homesick?'

'Not at all.' She wasn't about to cry for home the moment things got rough.

'Too soon, I guess, but it will get you.' When she rolled her eyes at him, Sam shrugged. 'Find me a soldier who hasn't had periods of wanting to be back home with family when the heat's got to him or something's gone horribly wrong on patrol. Me included.' He was still surprising her with the things he came out with.

She told him, 'My sister emails every day, giving me snippets of what her kids are up to, how Mum and Dad are.' She wasn't admitting to missing them last night.

'That's good. Hopefully she'll keep the homesickness at bay for you.' Doubt darkened his voice.

'Might make it worse. Who knows? But I'll not go looking for trouble. Right now I've got something more important to concentrate on.'

The hospital was rundown on the outside, but inside it gleamed. Medical personnel ran back and forth, looking harried, while children cried and mothers screamed for help. Police and armed personnel were making a show of being there. Utter chaos. But as Madison looked around she realised it was organised chaos. The staff knew what they were doing, which made it easy to slip into her role and ignore everything else.

'This way.' Sam took the lead after receiving directions from a gun-toting policeman. Was it only in New Zealand that cops didn't carry weapons as a norm? 'The men will bring our supplies through for us.'

Her first patient was a wee girl with the biggest brown eyes she'd encountered. Eyes filled with pain and resignation. 'Hello, sweetheart.' Madison knelt on the floor beside the mat the child lay on with a woman looking frantic with worry, presumably the girl's mother.

Watching over an injured child, depending on strangers to tend the wounds, had to be any mother's nightmare. Terrifying and bewildering. Madison's hand slipped across her stomach. Children. What were her chances of having any? Despite what she was dealing with here, she'd give anything to raise her own.

Through an interpreter she introduced herself and learned the child's name was Nubia and that she'd been trampled when teachers had rushed off the bus.

Fortunately Nubia's head had not suffered any injury, but she had five broken ribs and the cartilage holding them had been torn. With gentle probing Madison discovered the spleen was ruptured. One arm was fractured and there were numerous abrasions on most of the girl's body.

Her heart breaking for the child, Madison explained to her mother about the surgery she'd need to remove the spleen. When tears rocked the woman Madison slipped her arms around her and held her until the storm passed. Then she went to see when and where she'd be operating.

'Join the queue,' she was told by a harassed doctor.

Sam came across. 'I've got a theatre lined up. We'll share.'

When she rocked back on her heels at the outlandish suggestion he added, 'It's how it is, Madison. Cassy and the others will work with us.' Then he took pity on her. 'It's not easy, I know, but you'll be fine.'

'Grow a backbone, huh?'

His finger brushed her cheek. 'You've got one, just needs a little straightening at the moment.'

Somehow she chuckled. Not a very strong or mirthful one, but better than a grumpy retort. 'Love your support.' And a few other things she wasn't mentioning any time soon. 'Let's go.'

Nubia's surgery was straightforward and she was soon being watched over by Cassy as she came round.

'No complications?' Sam glanced up as Madison joined him at his table.

'Not a one.' She watched Sam at work and admired his skill. No wasted movements, or any unnecessary use of the scalpel.

'This is Ra,' Sam told her. 'He was thrown through a window off the bus. Both femurs are fractured, and there's damage to his lower bowel that I'm about to repair.'

'Do you need me, or shall I find another patient?'

'I'd like a second opinion on the colon.'

After scrubbing up again and pulling on fresh gloves, she went to help Sam.

Many hours and procedures later they sat slumped around a metal table with the other members of their crew, drinking coffee and picking at sandwiches they'd brought with them from camp.

Madison sipped the coffee, not really enjoying the strong brew, which was unlike anything she'd had before. But she needed something to fire up her sluggish cells after working in the hot and cramped conditions. 'Glad that's over,' she muttered to anyone within hearing.

'You're not feeling up to singing with the band tonight, then?' Sam asked as he picked up a sandwich and opened it to scrutinise the contents.

'Haven't got the energy.' She wasn't going to sing

again while Sam was still on base. Last night's gig had led to complications that she couldn't afford to repeat.

'You might not get off that easily,' Cassy said. 'The whole camp was talking about you this morning.'

That explained a few looks and nudges between soldiers she'd noted that morning in the dining mess. 'They'll get over it,' she sighed. 'Jock and Sam will be gone in a couple of days anyway.'

'All the more reason for a repeat performance tonight, only this time you're wanted out on the parade ground so we can all listen, not just the officers.'

'Thanks for nothing, Cassy.' Seemed everyone was deaf when it came to her saying she wasn't doing it. All she could hope was for the trucks to be late getting them back to base so that by the time they'd had showers and dinner everyone would've gone to their barracks. Hopefully.

But it seemed she had no say in the matter. By ten o'clock that night she was lounging in the bar with a water bottle in her hand when Jock and the gang started dragging the gear outside. 'Give us a hand, Maddy,' Jock called out.

'I'm not singing.'

'You're one of the band now. You have to help.'

'That's a yes,' Sam said from behind her.

She dropped her head and stared at her feet. It had been hard today, working with those beautiful, trusting children. Last night, pouring her soul into the songs had been cathartic. Kissing Sam afterwards hadn't been. Simple. Don't kiss the guy. Sing then leave. Looking up, she found Sam watching her with amusement written all over his gorgeous face. 'What?' she growled.

'You love it.'

A sigh whispered across her lips. 'Yeah, I do.'

'Come on, take an end of this table, will you? We can put our gear on it.'

'We haven't got any gear.' She hoisted her end up.

'We? Looks like we've got ourselves a singer, guys.'

The cheers were embarrassing. 'I'll need lots of soda.' It was hot work singing and leaping around in the tight space amongst the band. *And afterwards I will leave on my own, will not walk the perimeter. Will not kiss Sam. Will get some sleep.*

Sounded very boring. But playing safe often was.

'Did someone put out a bulletin about a party?' Sam asked Jock as he looked around the parade ground. Every soldier except those on duty had to be out there.

'Looks like it.'

Most of the guys were waiting for Madison, Sam would wager. Who could blame them? When she opened her mouth and let rip with the vocals she was something else.

Not just in the singing department either. Those kisses had stayed with him all night, kept him awake and hard. They hadn't gone away during the day while he'd operated. And they were there now, reminding him of what he would soon be walking away from. 'Let's make it our farewell bash,' he suggested to Jock.

Leaving the base was part of the deal when he'd signed up. It came with relief from getting through working in a hostile territory, and then there was the regret of leaving men he'd become friendly with. Some would go with him, heading for the same place, others would remain here for another six months. That's how the system worked. But this time he'd be leaving Madison just when they were getting to know each other. So why wasn't he pleased he was being saved from facing up to his guilt and denying himself the opportunity for happiness? Hanging around, pretending to push her away, all the time falling into confusion, was a recipe for disaster.

'You haven't heard a thing I've been saying, have you?' Jock sounded more than a little peeved with him.

'Tell me again.'

'You going to listen?'

'If you hurry up.' Sam tipped fluid down his parched throat and waited, almost patiently.

'Your eyes are already misting over with lust for Maddy. What are you going to do about her? I hope you've got her contact details stored in your phone.' Jock picked up his guitar and strummed a few chords, underlining his comments. 'I'd hate for you to let her go.'

'You're overstepping the buddy line,' Sam growled.

Jock rolled his eyes expressively. 'Don't go before you've told her why you're so cautious. I reckon you'll end up regretting it if you do.'

'Relationship counselling your thing, is it?' Regret was guaranteed. So was relief for what he'd save Maddy from.

'Hey, guys, what's our first song?' Maddy stepped into his line of sight, looking happy at the prospect of singing to those soldiers hanging around waiting for the music to begin.

Boyse called, 'I've written a list. Come take a look, Maddy. Let me know if there's any song you don't know.'

She gave Sam a wink. 'Now, there's a man who gets things done.' When she sauntered away she gave a wee wiggle of her butt.

And sent his hormones into overdrive. 'Someone dim the bloody lights.'

Jock's roar of laughter was the only reply he got.

Sam took one last slug of his water and set the bottle aside. Time to get rocking. And if he couldn't ignore Maddy strutting her stuff in front of him, he'd enjoy every last movement she made, absorb each note she sang, and store up a load of memories to take away with him.

His pick slid across the guitar strings effortlessly and the guys immediately joined in. They had themselves a show.

Then Maddy raised her microphone to that sexy mouth and the notes began to pour out, stunning the soldiers into silence. Then some clown let rip a wolf whistle and the silence was over, with people swaying to the beat and joining in the chorus.

Sam played hard, barely letting one song finish before starting the next. He let the music filter into his soul and went with the energy being created out in front of them. And he watched Maddy as she moved from one side of their stand to the other, almost swallowing the mic as she belted out the emotion-filled words.

Words that scorched him. Words that tugged at his heart. Words she'd given new meaning to, and had him yet again wondering where all that pain and anger came from.

'I need a break,' Maddy called after nearly an hour.

'A cold drink wouldn't go amiss. My throat's drier than the desert out there.'

'Get that into you.' Sam passed over her favourite soda and savoured the moment her fingers touched his. Warm, soft temptation. He bit down on a groan, and shifted out of the way to avoid any more accidental touching. Despite sixty-odd personnel hanging around in front of them, his ability to control the need for her was hanging by a thread. Another touch of that satin-like skin and he'd have to haul her close, kiss that erotic mouth. Make himself some more images to carry home.

'You going to miss this?' Maddy followed him.

'The band? Yes.' Another step backwards. Then another, and he was tipping off the edge of their stand. As his arms windmilled and his feet hit the ground he heard Jock's annoying laugh.

'Good one, man.'

Thanks, buddy.

'Sam, are you okay?' Maddy was standing where he'd been, her eyes twinkling with laughter and that mouth twitching. 'You should look where you're going.'

You should back off and give me more space. He leapt back onto the stand and brushed past her. Even that felt excruciating—so close and yet so far. 'Boyse, where's that song list?'

'Yes, Captain.' She flicked a salute in his direction, but the amusement had died, as he'd intended.

What he hadn't meant to happen was for the hurt turning her chocolate eyes to bog. He hated that bog colour. 'I deserve that.'

'Forget it. Let's get the band cranked up again.' She

turned a shoulder to him, looked around for the other guys. 'Ready?'

'Madison,' Sam growled, and moved close so he could talk without being overheard. 'I did tell you how your voice affected me.' Had he really said she was screwing with his head? His hand slammed across his skull as frustration of every kind alternated between turning him hot and cold.

'I see.' Her mouth tipped ever so slightly upward. 'Then let's get the music cranked up again. I want to see more of you out of control.' Her forefingers made parentheses between them.

She was toying with him. 'Easy, Maddy. You have no idea what you're starting here.' Neither did he, when he thought about it. And he owed it to himself, if not Maddy, to give his thoughts and feelings due consideration. Wanting her and having her—two different outcomes. Outcome? It would be a conflagration if he followed through on the heat burning him up. Where was the next wave of cold coming from? He needed it. 'Guys, Madison's ready to start rocking again.'

Maddy leaned close and whispered, 'Are you sure you want this? I'm going to sing like you've never heard so you'll always remember these few days we've shared.'

He should've quit while he'd been running parallel with her.

CHAPTER TEN

POUNDING ON THE door of her room dragged Madison from a rare deep sleep.

'Maddy, you in there?' Sam called.

'Go away. It's my day off,' she muttered as she tugged on cotton track pants and a long T-shirt. Opening the door, she said, 'This had better be good.'

It was. Sam was. Dressed in navy shorts and an open-necked cream shirt that contrasted perfectly with his tanned skin, here were all her forbidden dreams wrapped up in one stunning package. Her shoulder bumped against the doorframe and she kept it there to keep from dropping to the floor. To think she'd thought he was good looking. She'd been so far off the mark it was hilarious. If this was a laughing matter.

Sam was waving keys in front of her. 'We're going to the market.'

'We are?' Her eyes followed those keys. Off to the market. Off to the market.

'I've the loan of a car and you said you enjoyed shopping at stalls so here's your chance. I need to get a few knick-knacks to take home.' He grinned. 'If you need further convincing, this is my last day here. You won't get another offer like it.'

'What sort of knick-knacks?' she stalled.

'A couple of souvenirs for Ma and Pa Creighton. I am going to see them when I get home,' he added lamely.

'I'm glad. They'll be thrilled.'

'You think? After I've been avoiding them?' He winced. 'I've never been good at getting too close to people,' he admitted in a rush.

'That's sad. You're missing out on a lot,' said she who hadn't done any better in the previous couple of years.

Sam's fingers combed through his hair. 'Right from the day Ma and Pa Creighton took me in I worked hard at making them like me and at living up to their expectations with good results at school, but I always kept a bit of me back.'

The bit that was unconditional love and acceptance, she'd bet. 'Why?' Though she'd guessed the reason, she wanted to hear him tell her as a start to admitting what held him back. Not that she'd be following her own example any time soon.

'I tend to lose those who are important to me.'

Strange conversation to be having at her door but she wasn't about to stop it. 'Was there someone you got close to after your mother died?' He'd been very young when his father had left. The incomprehension of that act would've hurt a small boy deeply, and to be followed a few years later by the death of his mother must've been catastrophic for a teenager trying to make his mark on the world. But if he'd suffered another bereavement as an adult, that would be tough to accept, might make him feel like a pariah.

His eyes darkened as he stared blankly along the barracks corridor. His voice was a monotone as he recited the facts. 'My best mate. We met in the army and after I rescued him on day two from a pounding he was receiving from three thugs who had issues with soldiers we got on famously. Were always posted on the same tours of duty, or at the same base back home. He was a great guy.'

'Where is this friend now?' Something in his expression told her this mate hadn't just decided not to be friends any more. Another loss for Sam to take on board and cope with. But talking about his friend might ease some of the tension tightening his shoulders, his hands.

A shudder ripped through him. 'Gone.' Sam turned to stare through the outside door, his mind not with her.

Madison waited quietly, giving him space, feeling for him and knowing there were no words to lighten his grief.

Finally he glanced over at her, hope warring with regret in his face. 'So, you up to helping me buy souvenirs?'

'Give me thirty minutes.' There was no way she wasn't going with him now.

'Too easy, Maddy.' That grin was back, lopsided and uneasy but back. 'Meet me over at the gate.' And he was gone.

She wasted precious minutes watching him stride across the parade ground. In coming to the Peninsula she'd met a man she could relate to. A man who was sad and lonely, and yet brave and determined to carry on despite the burden he carried. He was good at disguise, hid his true self behind a cheeky grin and cocky attitude.

Inside her room, Madison looked over at her skimpy collection of mufti clothes and quickly decided on the knee-length blue shorts and white T-shirt. Then she remembered the warnings about what to wear when going out amongst the locals. Cotton pants replaced the shorts, a long-sleeved shirt the T. Snatching up a towel, she raced to the shower stalls.

As cool water blasted her from the shower head another thought slammed her. Sam had effectively told her they were never going to get close. As if that was likely anyway, with her hang-ups about her body and being left by the man who'd professed to love her, and with Sam's fear of people leaving him. What a great mix that'd make for any relationship.

She'd barely discussed her feelings for Sam with herself, wasn't sure about anything except keeping herself safe, and now, if it all got too much and she did try to explain to Sam—well, now she had the perfect excuse to keep quiet. There'd be no happy endings for them.

Sudden panic filled Madison. Sam was leaving tomorrow. They'd barely got started on getting to know each other. But it was best that way. There was no future in spending more time with him and falling a little bit in love with him.

Shampoo stung her eyes. Sluicing it away, she came to a decision. She'd spend the day with Sam, enjoy his company and have some fun. Tomorrow she'd say goodbye and accept that none of this mattered.

She'd worked with him over the previous few days, now she'd play with him. Then they'd get on with their lives and maybe, since their career paths were similar, bump into each other occasionally over the years and swap notes on what they were up to.

Her body slumped. So not what she wanted, but all she could face since she didn't have the courage to expose herself to him, or ask him to take a chance on not having a family. Besides, minutes ago he'd warned her off getting involved, and if showing him the result of that fire wasn't getting involved, nothing was.

'Try this.' Sam held out the kebab that he'd bought from the street stall in the bustling town they'd arrived in twenty minutes ago. 'It makes a good breakfast.'

Madison shook her head at him as she chewed on a mouthful of beef shawarma. The pita bread and its fillings were delectable, putting her in food heaven. Swallowing, she said, 'No, thanks. I'm not sharing this.'

'Typical.' He laughed before taking her elbow to lead them along the street towards a long, low building where a constant stream of people, locals and tourists, was coming and going. 'This is the market,' he said unnecessarily.

'The noise level's off the scale,' she muttered five minutes later, and had to shout it again when Sam stared blankly at her.

'It sure is. Try to stick with me, okay? It's too easy to lose each other in here.'

'I reckon.' She didn't want to find herself alone, facing some the men who were eying her up and down. Tossing her sandwich wrapper in a bin, she slipped her arm through Sam's and held on. For safety reasons, of course, nothing to do with enjoying the warmth of his skin under her fingers or the sensation of belonging that enveloped her. Where that came from she wasn't sure and had no intention of exploring the answers that were popping up in her head. Not now, at least. Today was purely for fun, nothing else.

'What do you want to look at?' Sam asked.

'Those scarves look pretty.' She nodded at the stall they were approaching. 'They'd be great gifts for Mum and Maggie.' She wouldn't mind a couple for herself either.

'Ma Creighton might like one, too.' Sam choked back a laugh after some harsh bargaining had gone down between her and the stallholder. 'Do you really need nine? How many sisters have you got?' Sam's laughter faded. 'It's strange. I feel I should know more about you than I actually do.'

'I've only got one.'

'I thought that's what you said, but seeing all those scarves I figured I'd misheard.'

'They're vibrant and colourful. My sister's going to love them, whether she wants to or not,' she retorted. 'She's four years older than me, which she believes makes her wiser, something I disagree on.'

'Sounds like I've got something in common with your sister. Disagreeing with you.' That laugh was back, nudging aside the tightness that had started creeping into her system when he'd turned it off.

'There are some similarities when I think about it. She's driven, always right, and never slows down for anyone else.' Maddy said it all with a smile and sighed with relief when Sam didn't get uptight.

'A top-notch character, then. What does she do?' His hand was back on her elbow, holding her close to his body as he navigated them through the throngs of people too busy peering at all the merchandise to look where they were going.

'She has a double degree in business studies and clothing design, which I have to admit she's exceptional at. Her fashion label is building a reputation for quality and style so fast I only hope she can keep up, considering those four gorgeous girls who keep her busy, too.'

'Bet they miss their aunt.'

'Their aunt misses them heaps.' Madison looked along the stalls for something to send home to them. 'What are you going to get Pa Creighton?' she asked next. 'We could go back for more scarves later.'

The hours disappeared in a haze of shopping, teasing, and laughter. It was the fun she'd hoped for, and more. They got along with no hiccups, like this was something they did often. The heat had built up all morning, the sun beating down on the street and the rooves of the buildings they entered.

Finally Madison said, 'I could kill for a cold drink.' She wouldn't acknowledge the heat from a different source that also drained her of energy. Heat she'd like to do something about, but then she'd spoil the day. Sam would have them back at base quick smart if he thought she wanted to get closer, get beyond kissing and clothes.

Beyond clothes? her brain screeched. *Seriously?* Of course not.

'I know just the place.' Sam swung some of her shopping bags in front of her. 'It's near the car so we can dump these first.'

Going back to base might be wise. With his hand on her arm for most of the morning, Sam had cranked up her desire level to a simmer. If this was what one hand could do then she couldn't imagine what it would be like to have Sam's total concentration. Boiling wouldn't begin to describe it.

'Here's the car.'

'I'd never have found it again,' she admitted as she stepped around him, putting a gap between them as she placed her shopping in the boot.

'We'll cut through that alley by the barber's. There's a café at the other end that's primarily used by Westerners, and serves hot and cold drinks.'

Sam's arm was draped over her shoulder, drawing her along with him. All she had to do was stop, tell him she wanted to go back, and that would be it. Easy. End a perfect day. But a little devil zipped her mouth shut and lifted her feet one after the other so she was moving with Sam.

The alley was dark and cold after the sun. She shivered, peered around, shivered again. 'This is creepy.'

'We'll be fine. It's not in the tourists' brochures as a place to visit or shop in, that's all.'

She upped her pace, and was glad Sam followed suit. 'Everyone's staring at us,' she murmured. The few stallholders had stopped talking and were standing watching as she and Sam headed for the far end. Two men ducked into a doorway. 'I'm not liking this.'

Sam's hand tightened on her shoulder, and she was tucked closer to his hard body. 'We're fine, I promise.'

Great. Her strides lengthened and Sam went with the flow, heading for the splash of sunlight at the far end of the alley. Then they were out in the glaring light and her heart rate started slowing back to normal.

'In here.' Sam pushed open the door and she stepped into a cool room filled with small tables and chairs. A man lounged against a counter, talking to the waiter or possibly the cook, who was rubbing the countertop with a cloth as though he had all day to do it.

There was nothing uncomfortable about the place. It was so normal Madison had to pinch herself to make sure she hadn't imagined the previous minute outside. 'Did that happen? Was I wrong to think there was something bad out there?'

'You're not used to being an object of intrigue by strangers in a foreign setting.' He placed money on the counter. 'Two sodas, thanks, Bix. Okay if we have a booth at the back?'

'Go for it.' The barman answered in a light American twang.

'Why do we want a booth?' Maddy asked. 'I'm quite happy sitting in here.' She liked the sense of space and being able to see what, if anything, was going on. That alley had spooked her more than it should have.

'Sure. No problem. Want something to eat as well?' Sam asked. 'Falafels? A kofta?'

Until then she hadn't thought she was hungry again, but the thought of those delicacies made her mouth water. 'I'm glad you haven't run out of good ideas yet.'

When the cook headed out to the kitchen to start preparing their order, the other customer downed his drink and stood up. 'See ya,' he called, and headed for the door.

Madison raised her glass and tapped it against Sam's. 'Thanks for a great day. I'm glad you brought me. I'm not sure how I'd feel about coming into town on my own.'

'Best you don't, being female and—'

Boom. An explosion ripped through the building, followed by another. One moment Maddy was sitting on a chair, the next she was sprawled on the floor, being rained on by ceiling tiles and cups and glasses from where the counter used to be. 'Sam,' she screeched, but heard nothing above the throbbing in her ears. 'Where are you? Sam,' she yelled as fear spread through her.

Knew there was something evil out in that alley. We shouldn't have come in here.

Then she heard timber creaking, followed by a loud thud, and the floor shook. More debris poured down over her. The fear intensified, tightened her stomach, chest, mouth. Not again. Please, no. She screamed. 'Sam.'

Peering through the thick dust, she couldn't find him. Her heart was blocking her throat, making breathing impossible. 'Sam. Where are you? Don't do this to me.' Was that squeaky sound really her voice? The power for the lights must've been taken out because it was semi-dark in here, making everything feel close and looming. What just happened? 'Sam, please.'

You'd better be all right. I can't deal with something happening to you on top of all this. I don't want another Granddad scenario.

A chill settled over her.

'Maddy.' A hand gripped her ankle. 'I'm here. Got you covered. Are you all right?'

Yes, apart from a racing heart and nauseous stomach, and the crippling fear keeping her sprawled on the floor. 'Y-yes.' She tried to clear her throat of some of the dust. 'What about you?'

'Everything seems in working order.'

'What happened? Tell me it wasn't those men in the alley.'

'No idea, but I doubt it.' His hand moved up her leg, reached her knee.

Her hand shook continuously as she reached for Sam's. She needed to feel those fingers gripping hers, to feel his strength and tenderness and warmth. She was frozen. Her teeth chattered. 'Wh-which way is out?'

'Wait there. I'll take a look. Be right back.'

'No.' Her grip tightened around his hand. 'Don't leave me,' she gasped. *Suck it up, Madison. You're a soldier, not a wimp.* It made sense if only one of them did a recon of the situation. Though sense didn't come into it if it meant being on her own, even for a very short time.

An arm wound around her, pulled her against a strong, steady torso. 'You're okay, Maddy. We're okay.'

He was so calm, comforting, at ease. 'Take your time, get your breathing back to normal.' His neck was twisting left then right as he looked around, probably sizing up their position. 'The dust is settling, allowing daylight in. From what I can see, it looks like the roof came down on top of us.'

'That's a lucky break.' The beams might hold the weight of the roof off them. Beams? The fear was back, winding up tighter than ever. 'Fire. There were explosions. There must be fire.'

'Sniff the air, Maddy. I can't smell smoke. Neither

can I hear the sound of crackling flames.' His words were measured, calming in their ordinary delivery.

'We don't know for sure.' Fire moved fast, devoured everything in its path. 'The building could be burning further away from us.'

'I'm going to take a look, see how far I can get. Hopefully there's a way out. Wait here. I'll be right back.'

Around the thudding of her heart she implored, 'Sam, be very careful. I don't want anything to happen to you.' She'd go nuts with fear if he didn't return. Suddenly it was impossible to imagine a world without Sam in it.

He cupped her face between both hands and leaned in to touch his nose to hers. 'It won't. I promise.'

'Don't make promises you have no control over.' Then she pushed forward to cover his lips with hers, felt his mouth open under hers, took a quick dip with her tongue to taste him. What if she'd lost him when that explosion blew the bar apart? *You don't have him.* But he was there, under her skin, waking her up, taunting her with possibilities.

His lips returned the kiss, soft and slow and full of something she didn't recognise, not from Sam. It felt like concern and care, almost like love, but she was wrong about that. She didn't know love, had got it badly wrong with her ex. And Sam had clearly told her he didn't get close to people, had indicated he didn't do love.

Sam pulled away, leaving her feeling bereft. 'Don't move,' he told her as he crawled along what used to be a gap between tables and was now full of twisted, broken stools.

Rubbing her hands up and down her arms, she made up her mind to do some exploring of her own, be proactive instead of reactive. Sitting here, waiting for Sam, only led to her mind conjuring up all sorts of nasty ideas about what had happened.

'Looks to me like we're stuck in here,' Sam told her when she bumped into him under a flattened door.

'How stuck?'

'As in the roof is on top of the tables, saving us from being flattened. The walls appear to have fallen inwards. I can't find a way out. Not even a small opening for you to squeeze through.'

No, no, no. They couldn't stay in here, waiting for someone to reach them. She sniffed the air, sneezed when she got a lungful of dust. But no smoke. One bit of luck anyway. A huge bit. 'I'm going to check this out.'

'I'm telling you we're stuck.' He tugged his phone from his pocket. 'I'll text someone on the base.'

Sam was right. She'd known he would be but, desperate for a way out, was driven to check. This was one time she'd love to prove him wrong.

Her hands shook as she felt her way around the edge of their cell. It took less than a minute to concede. Frustration and worry built up inside her, creating waves of nausea. Being confined in a small place would never have bothered her once. 'We could be here for days. No one knows where we are,' she cried.

'They do now.' Sam waved his phone in her direction.

'You're kidding. You got coverage in here?'

'Yep. I've texted Jock and the commander. One of them will get guys here with gear to haul us out.'

She swallowed the fear in the back of her throat. Tried to, any rate. Focused on something else. 'What about the barman? He went to the kitchen. Did you hear anything from him? He might be worse off.' Her heart was in overdrive, beating like that of a wild bird. She couldn't do this. She'd go mad thinking about the last time she'd been stuck, unable to move to save her grandfather.

There is no smoke. There is no smoke. You're going to be all right. You're with Sam. He won't let anything bad happen to you.

Both hands were on her stomach, her fingers digging in, warding off any blows that might come her way.

Sam was texting and reaching for her hands at the same time. 'Stop this, Maddy. You can do better than wind yourself up into a ball of nerves. You're strong.'

Worry was only half of it. But, 'You're right. It's just…' Stop. Don't tell him. He was going tomorrow, and whatever was going on between them would be over. 'This isn't the first time a roof has come down on me. Part of one, any rate.'

Sam stuffed his phone back in his pocket and reached for her other hand. 'Tell me.'

She nibbled her bottom lip until it hurt. 'There was a fire.' Nibble, nibble. 'My granddad lit a candle and set it by his bed.' Her hands gripped Sam's. 'He had early dementia and I was there for the night to give Mum and Dad a much-needed break. The fire investigators believe Granddad knocked the candle over in his sleep.'

Then it became impossible to stop the torrent of words.

'A crashing noise woke me. I rushed to get Granddad out, but there was smoke everywhere and I couldn't find my way around the house I'd lived in most of my life. It freaked me out.'

Sam's hands squeezed hers, his thumbs rubbing her skin softly, encouragingly.

'His room was ablaze. And his bed. I managed to drag him out the door, along the hall to the lounge...'

Her voice trailed away so that her next words were a whisper. She'd never talked about this to anyone. People knew, but putting any of it into words had been beyond her—until today.

'A ceiling beam dropped on us, and that's where we were found not long afterwards.'

Strong arms wound around her. Sam lifted her onto his thighs and held her close, stroking her shoulder. 'We're safe in here, Maddy. There's no smoke or the sound of approaching flames.'

'I've been sniffing the air non-stop,' she admitted against his chest.

'I saw. Now I understand why you freaked out when you saw your first dust whirl.'

'Yeah, that was a bit of a giveaway.'

'But you've done well since. No flinching on patrol where there was dust and smoke for Africa.'

'I work hard at hiding it.' Had to if she wasn't going to be treated with disdain—by this man and the troops.

'Then there's that stomach rub thing you do when you're upset.' His head might be above hers, but the increased tension in his body told Madison he was waiting for a strong reaction from her.

Damn him for being too observant. She quickly slid off those thighs, muttering, 'Just an old habit,' as she tried to make herself comfortable on the floor beside him, averting her face from his prying eyes in case she let slip some emotions best kept hidden.

'Right.' Sam's disappointment fell between them.

She was damned if she was going to explain so he'd feel happier, because she sure wouldn't.

A phone beeped, and Sam dug into his pocket.

Saved by the bell.

'The men are on their way.'

Relief loosened her muscles. 'They know where to come?'

'Everyone knows this place.' He tapped out a text and pushed 'Send'. 'Might as well make ourselves comfortable. They'll be a while putting some gear together and we have no idea what it's like outside our cocoon. They'll have to take it carefully, working through to us. Don't want any more timber coming down.'

'As long as there are no more explosions I can handle that.' *As long as you're with me.* 'Would've loved those koftas, though.'

'I wonder.' Sam tapped his finger against his chin. 'Bix went out to the kitchen to heat up the oil for our order. Then everything blew up.'

'You think the gas might've been leaking? Wouldn't there be fire?' Bang, bang. Her heart rate shot through the roof again.

'No, Maddy. We'd know by now if there was a fire.' Sam leaned back against what was their temporary wall and tugged her against him. 'So, probably not the gas. Guess we're going to have to wait to find out what happened.'

It was warm in the small space, yet snuggling into

Sam gave her a different kind of warmth, finally obliterating the chill she'd been fighting since finding herself face down on the floor. He gave her hope they'd be all right. Couldn't ask more of him than that. 'So, got any cards in your pocket?'

He laughed. 'We could try finding a game app on the phone.'

'You'd hate me winning.'

Another laugh. 'Not at all.' Then, 'Okay, maybe a little bit.'

Madison glanced around. For a prison it was quite snug in here. Nothing wrong with the company she was keeping either. 'When I thought we'd spend a day having fun together I never envisaged this.' She'd wanted to make new memories to take into the future as she learned to live without the man she might be falling for, but she'd got more than she'd bargained for.

Seemed her future was going to be all about memories—good and bad. The best she could hope for was the good ones outweighing the bad.

CHAPTER ELEVEN

'"We're outside the pub".' Sam read Jock's text out loud. '"Give us a clue where you might be".'
In the centre of the café, he tapped back.

'Told you they wouldn't waste any time getting here,' he said to Maddy.

'I'm glad.' There was a quiver in her voice, belying her resolute face.

'It's nearly over, and you'll be back on base before you know it. I'll be able to take a look at that cut on your head then.'

'What cut?' Her fingers tripped around her skull until she found a sticky patch. 'Ouch. Never felt a thing but now it's throbbing.'

'You're relaxing at last.' Stretching his legs out in front of him, Sam tipped his head back against the boards behind them, stared around their tight space. They were incredibly lucky that the roof had fallen onto chairs and tables, creating a safe haven. Three feet either way they'd have been hit and badly injured for sure. Or worse.

He suppressed a shudder, knowing the woman tucked into him would recognise it for the stab of horror it was, and probably freak out a lot more. Maddy had struggled to keep her terror at bay, but it had been there in her eyes, zipping across her face and twisting his gut. He hated that she was frightened, and yet admired her for not going screaming mad. Now that he knew about the fire he marvelled that she was holding it together at all.

It was kind of cosy in here, even if they were trapped. While he should be worrying about getting them out safely, it was the scent that he'd been noticing since Madison's arrival on the Peninsula getting him worked up. Again summer enveloped him. Not any old summer but Christchurch in February when the temperature could be thirty or fifteen in the same hour, where the sky ranged from blue to grey, and the wind had its own agenda. But it was always summer. The trees were green, the farms brown from lack of water, and the locals were at the beach or the parks. Homesickness floored him. 'I've missed home.'

Maddy sat up. 'Lucky for you Burnham's your next posting then. You'll be able to catch up with lots of people in Christchurch, as well as Mr and Mrs Creighton.'

'I suspect I'll be busy. The army has a way of filling our time.' There weren't any others to call on as he hadn't bothered staying in touch much after he'd finished school. *Got Dad's genes there?* Shock blasted him, dried his mouth, curdled his gut. No damned way. But he had walked away from his mates without looking back. What about the guys he'd befriended while training to become a doctor? He knew where most of them were, occasionally emailed to see what they were up to. Not often, and not involved enough to call being friendly.

Maddy's gaze met his. 'Sounds like an excuse to me.'

'That's because it is,' he admitted as he assimilated the truth. He had always walked away from people, had been the one to set the bar. Except for William, who'd become closer than any other friend he'd had, and had been impossible to ignore. Then William had done the leaving.

'How long are you going to stay in the military?' Maddy asked, unaware of his shock.

'I've not decided. It's my career so as long as they'll have me, I guess.' He'd joined to get away from his life, to do something for his country. Now he saw he'd been avoiding the intimacy of a practice in a town with a steady stream of locals and had gone for the broader picture of helping his country and strangers in out-of-the-way places. There'd been no excitement, only a hard slog that had done nothing to make him happy, only sadder that soldiers were even needed in this world. For a while after William died he'd almost had a death wish, had certainly pushed the boundaries when there had been danger in the zone. That was slowly ebbing away. Since Maddy had turned up? Or as a result of too much time away from home, doing as ordered without thought or concern?

She was talking again. Needing to override the sounds of creaking timbers as the soldiers uncovered them. 'You're not interested in getting into surgical practice full-time? It seems a shame when you've done all that training and obviously like the work.'

Glad to be drawn away from where his own thoughts had been headed, he said, 'None of it's wasted, Maddy.' He realised now that the idea of getting into surgery on a full-time basis had been simmering in a corner of his mind. As if he had stopped looking back and was instead now looking ahead for a future to immerse himself in. He instantly put up the usual barriers. 'I'm getting the best of two worlds.'

There had been a time in med school when he'd imagined his own rooms back in Christchurch, a partnership with other specialists to cover a range of medical fields. But the nervous energy that kept him from settling or getting close to people, from creating his own comfort zone, had thrown up the fear he might become bored with being tied to one place and career that would stretch out until he retired many years down the track. Now hauling heavy packs and weapons around a desert no longer held any appeal either.

'I'm hoping to figure out my next moves while I'm here.' Maddy smiled ruefully. 'Can't see me making the army my life. I'll do all I can as a soldier while here and then I'll make some decisions.'

Did she realise her hands were on his thighs? Heat sizzled from her palms into his upper legs. How was he supposed to ignore her? Turn her away? He was no saint. And right this minute he had to fight with everything he had not to place his hands on her body and feel her, know her, have her. So much so that he daren't even push her hands away as that meant touching her.

Shouts and voices were coming closer, audible over the crashing and banging of timber and who knew what else being moved aside. 'Sam? Madison? Can you hear us?'

'They'll be hearing you back at base,' he called out, relieved at the interruption. Disappointed he wouldn't have the chance to follow through on those heart-stopping sensations Maddy caused him.

'Okay, you two, time you stopped lazing around and got back to camp.' Jock pushed through a gap behind them.

'What took you so long?' Sam growled, despite being grateful for the time he'd had with Maddy. A time of discovery—about Madison and himself. Though he wasn't so grateful for what he'd learned about himself.

'Anyone would think we had nothing better to do than come hauling you out of here.' Jock grinned. 'Next time you're going to town, take a hard hat and an axe.'

Maddy pushed up onto her knees. 'There isn't going to be a next time.'

Somehow that felt like a stab to Sam's heart. As though she was talking to him and not to Jock about where he'd found them.

'Want one of the boys to drive you back to base?' Jock asked.

No, he didn't. 'You heading back?'

'Orders are to look around, see if we can learn what caused the explosion.' Jock eyeballed him. 'Take Madison and fix that bang on her head. Leave this to us.'

Sounded much like an order to him. Sam nodded. 'Sure.' Though he would probably be safer staying here with the troops than spending more time alone with Maddy, he did want to snatch whatever hours he could with her.

'Glad you see things my way.' Jock backed out. 'Follow me, Madison. Keep low or you'll be banging your noggin again.'

* * *

The medical unit was empty of all personnel when Madison and Sam pushed through the door. 'Where's everyone?' she asked, looking around. She'd never seen it so empty, so quiet.

'Back in town, cleaning up after us.' Sam dropped his bag of shopping on a desk. 'Let me look at that cut.'

'It'll be fine.' It didn't hurt, though when she had a shower the water would sting a little.

A firm grip on her elbow had her heading towards the treatment room, regardless of any protests she uttered.

'I've gone deaf,' Sam said as he pushed her onto a chair by the bed. 'Now, this might be a little uncomfortable.' His fingers probed her skull, gentle with their touch. 'Not bad. I'll clean it up and put some tape on to keep the dust out.'

Succumbing, Madison sat still and let the fear and fright of the last few hours wash out of her. Unbelievable that she'd been in another disastrous situation. Unbelievable she'd come out virtually unscathed. 'I wonder what happened to Bix.'

'The guys are searching for him,' Sam muttered. 'Try not to think about him.'

'Easily said.' She drew air into her lungs, breathed in Sam, aftershave and man and sweat. There was comfort in that scent, in the quiet of this room with its walls and roof in their right place, in being safe.

'There.' He snapped off the gloves he'd tugged on moments earlier. His finger lifted her chin so she looked into his eyes. 'You're all good to go.'

'Thank you for being there for me,' she managed around a thick tongue.

'You wouldn't have been there if not because I took you to town.'

'Don't come the guilty party. You didn't blow that café up. It was bad timing, that's all.'

His head was closer to hers now, that mouth so near she only had to lean a bit further upwards and her lips were skimming Sam's.

His hands fell to her shoulders, his fingers splayed and pressing into her.

And all the brakes came off. Not slowly, not one by one, but instantly, freeing her from the restraints she kept wound tight.

She pushed up for a kiss, a deep, bone-melting one that sent shockwaves through her body and aimed for her centre. Heat pooled at her apex as days of withheld desire overwhelmed her. Her hands shoved under his shirt, found his skin, spread across his chest, touched his nipples. It wasn't enough. Tearing at his buttons, she ripped the shirt open and took a nipple between her lips, teased, licked, and ran her teeth lightly across the peak.

Above her Sam groaned. Then he was lifting her, placing her on the bed. Two fast strides and the door was locked. Two strides back and he was lying down beside her, reaching for her.

His erection pressed against her thigh, bringing a moan to her lips. She flipped over, straddled him, felt his sex against her core. Knew she had to have him. Then his hands were under her shirt, gliding over her breasts, satisfying her need to be touched yet rocking her to the core with the intensity of sensations his urgent caresses released.

She was going to make love with Sam. Even as that heat-hazed thought spilled through her mind he was moving his hands downwards, away from her smooth breasts towards her stomach.

'Stop,' she cried, jerking upright.

No. I can't do it. I won't do it. He'll touch me and that look of horror will fill his eyes. I'd rather have been flattened in the explosion.

She climbed off his body to sit on the chair with her knees drawn up and her arms wrapped tight around them. 'Sorry,' she muttered. 'I should never have started that.'

Sam was breathing hard as he sat upright and looked at her with nothing but puzzlement in his expression. No censure at all. But he didn't know, hadn't seen. 'Talk to me, Maddy.'

She shook her head. 'No.' What was the point? Been there, and couldn't face a rerun. Especially not with Sam. From the moment she'd seen him across the parade ground the day she'd arrived there'd been some connection between them, and for him to see the scars that distorted her body would destroy that. Even if it was never going anywhere, she couldn't cope with their relationship being reduced to sympathy on his part and agony on hers.

He reached down, took her hands in his, gently lifted her arms away from her knees, opened her to him again. A tremor ran through his body, reaching her through his fingers. She had cut him off in mid-stride when he'd been hard, tight and in need of release.

'That touching your midriff you do? You were injured when that beam came down on you and your grandfather, right?'

Sam's voice was so compelling it coaxed her to look at him, even when she was afraid of what she'd find in his eyes. She gasped. Nothing but care blinked out at her. 'Yes,' she whispered.

'You received burns?' He tightened his grip on her hands as she made to pull free.

Her head dropped downwards in answer to his question. *Now you know, you'll leave me alone. Please.*

'I should've figured that out. It's why you always wear long shirts, isn't it?'

Another nod. 'Are we done?' He didn't need to know anything else.

'Not by a long way. We're only getting started. Look at me, Maddy.'

When she finally did, Sam smiled at her, a long, slow smile that reached his eyes and touched her in places she didn't want touched. Her heart was meant to be unavailable due to fear and vulnerability.

But his smile was continuing the thaw he'd started days ago. She had to stop it before she messed up and let him in. 'No, Sam. I made a mistake kissing you, by taking it further.' He still didn't look upset. 'I am not making love with you. We're not getting close.'

'How long were you in hospital?'

Surprised at his question she answered instantly. 'More than three months while the burns healed and I fought endless infections. Afterwards I took a year convalescing before returning to work at the hospital.'

'That would've put your training behind schedule.'

'It did, but I got there in the end.'

'No side effects?'

She looked away. Her hand covered her tummy where her uterus lay.

Sam's fingers shifted through her short hair. 'Tell me, Maddy. We've come this far you might as well share the whole story.'

She fidgeted with the hem of her shirt. What did it matter if he knew? They weren't going to get together so there wouldn't be any talk of having babies. 'I might be infertile. The worst part of that is I won't know until I try to get pregnant—if I try.' What man was going to accept her on those terms? 'That's the conundrum. Do I ask someone to risk trying with me and watch him walk away when I fail to become pregnant? Or do I accept it's unlikely to happen and work at making my career into something bigger than I'd intended so I won't waste time regretting what I haven't got?'

'That's an agonising decision to have to make.'

Not if she had someone at her side. But she didn't.

'You are amazing, Maddy. So strong to deal with all this.' Sam leaned down for another kiss; a long, slow, burning one.

Maddy fought the incoming waves of need that instantly fired up and began shoving her anguish aside. That anguish was meant to keep her out of trouble. Pulling her head away, she managed, 'Stop.'

He was still holding her hands, and when she tried to withdraw he only tightened his grip. 'Don't.'

'Why? There's nothing to be gained.' Except more hurt.

A sigh escaped Sam. 'I touched your breasts, felt

their weight in my hands. For days I've been aware of them pushing out the front of your shirts. They're beautiful, Madison.'

'I got lucky there.'

'Not only there. You're a striking woman who's intelligent, a wonderful doctor, and can sing me into a lather in an instant.' His mouth tipped up into one of those smiles she was coming to recognise as her addiction. Smiles that made her feel special, as though he only gave them to her. 'Don't hide from me. Or anyone. Or life. You're missing out on so much by doing this to yourself.'

'Easy for you to say. Think I should chuck my clothes aside and let a man get an eyeful? See horror or worse fill his gaze just before he turns away from me for ever? I don't think so.'

'Who did that to you?' His arms were cradling her, but he still managed to watch her with fierce intensity.

'Jason,' she whispered.

Of course Sam swore. She'd expect nothing less. While it felt good knowing he was on her side it changed nothing. He asked, 'Is that why your marriage failed?'

'Yes.' So much for the wonderful relationship she'd believed she'd had with her husband if he could leave so effortlessly.

Sam placed the softest of soft kisses on her forehead. Then one on the tip of her nose. 'Don't cry.'

She wasn't aware she was.

Then Sam's mouth covered hers and there was nothing tame about the kiss he gave her. It was deep, intense, and his rising passion told her she hadn't put him off at all. He wanted her.

She wanted him.

Her body arched under his hands as longing pulsed through her veins and moisture pooled at her centre. She wanted Sam.

Could she have him? As in take her clothes off? If she was going to do this then she wasn't going to hide anything. Gulp. Her heart slowed its mad beating. *I can't do it.*

Sam's hands on her shirt-covered waist told her differently. Their tenderness told her she had to, needed to. *Wanted* to.

Her breath hitched in her throat as she began to ease her top up. Her hands shook, her toes curled tight. There was no moisture in her mouth. Get it over with. Drawing in a deep breath, she grabbed the hem of her shirt and tugged it over her head. She didn't want to look at Sam but knew she had to. Words could never tell her the truth as clearly as his eyes would.

In silence Sam regarded her hideous scars, and no disgust or horror darkened his eyes. Only sadness and acceptance. When his fingers traced some of the marks left by that burning beam she held her breath, unable to comprehend what was happening. He should be running for the hills, or at least saying something condescending. But no. His eyes held only tenderness. Tenderness that changed to awe as he lifted his gaze to her breasts. When his tongue lapped his lips the tension began receding, making her feel light and dizzy.

Sam still wanted her.

Her fingers splayed across his chest. Under one palm his fast heartbeat replicated hers.

Sam wanted her.

With one smooth move Madison stood up to shuck her trousers and panties, tossed her bra to join her shirt. Then she went to work undressing Sam.

'Condom,' he said through clenched teeth.

'You come prepared?' Her heart rate wavered.

'In the top drawer of the desk. For the guys who forget to buy them.'

'How—?'

'Maddy, shut up.' He was kissing her thigh, moving ever upward to where she throbbed with need.

Gripping his head, she held him against her. 'Don't stop, whatever you do.'

His reply was to use his tongue to send shockwaves rolling through her.

She gasped. Her fingers dug harder at his skull. When he did it again she clung to him, not wanting to move for fear of putting air between them.

'I want you,' she croaked. 'I want to touch you, hold you in my hand.'

Slowly he withdrew, lifted her up over his body as he sprawled across the bed. 'You're on top. I want to watch you come.'

Reaching between them, she sought and found his shaft, wound her hand around him. Down, up. He strained against her, pushing up into her hand.

'Let me put the condom on,' he groaned through clenched teeth.

She shook her head. 'That's for me to do.' And she proceeded to, slowly, delighting in the feel of his throbbing manhood. When she couldn't wait any longer she raised herself over him and slowly slid down his length. Sam pressed upward, filling her and still pushing inside. When he withdrew she knew a moment of panic before he filled her again. And again. Pleasure spilled across her lips in a roar, filled the air with acknowledgement of her release.

Sam, oh, Sam. She lay curled, *naked*, in his arms, her head on his still rapidly rising and falling chest. Unafraid of being seen without clothes to cover her scars.

CHAPTER TWELVE

'DID YOU FIND BIX?' Madison asked Jock the next morning as he packed up his last bits and pieces from the medical unit. Sam was conspicuous by his absence. As he had been since he'd returned to town to help search for the café owner after they'd made love.

'Not in any condition we could take the guy back home.' Jock snapped the latches on his bag. 'Must've taken the full force of the explosion.'

'Was it the gas mains?'

'The verdict is still out and, knowing this place, likely to stay out.' He looked directly at her, said, 'Take care out here, Madison. The dangers aren't always those that you're looking at.'

Don't I know it?

If that was commiseration in his face she was going to hit him. She didn't want sympathy for having been an idiot yesterday. She'd take the rap on her chin and get on with soldiering and doctoring. Sleeping with Sam was just another thing to pretend hadn't happened. There was no one to blame bar herself. Sam had given her full warning there'd be no future with him. Knowing those snatched hours would be the end of anything between them before she laid her soul on the line was one thing. *Knowing* it afterwards was…agony. This was knowing with all the emotions she'd promised herself never to suffer again, only now deeper, sharper. Knowing did not soften the blow. She'd fallen for Sam in a bigger way than she'd ever have believed possible. While she wouldn't have to allow for shock and injuries and grief, she wasn't going to wake up tomorrow morning feeling like she had everything under control either.

Jock cleared his throat. 'Madison?'

'Have a safe trip home,' she snapped, and spun away to walk slap bang into the man she'd have sworn had been avoiding her. Of course he had, otherwise he'd have joined her on her run that morning.

'Hey,' he said.

'Hey, yourself,' she retorted, and tried to walk around him.

Sam stepped into her path. 'Maddy, can I have a minute?'

'There's nothing to say, Sam.' He'd kept away from her. Regretting having made love with her? Unable to accept her body after all? Her skin was cold, her heart heavy. She'd known what would happen if she exposed herself and yet she'd gone ahead, thought it was all okay. More fool her. Now she had to move on, go back to protecting herself, and take this as a lesson not to be forgotten.

Desolation stared at her out of those bleak eyes. Desolation that filled her heart, too. 'I think there is.'

'Like what? You're sorry about yesterday? Don't say it, Sam. I don't want to hear you verbalise that.'

'I wasn't going to. I want to explain myself to you.'

'You could've dropped by when you got back last night.' After waiting for him out by the perimeter until late, she'd finally crawled under her sheet to stare into the dark until the sun came up. A fast run first thing had not altered the growing sense of abandonment that had been gathering since he'd headed back to town and left her to face up to having let him in under her guard.

'We were very late. Took some effort finding Bix's body under all the debris.'

'You didn't need to go and help. There were more than enough troops to clear the mess.' Anger vied with sorrow and kept her talking when she really wanted to shut up and see him out of the centre. She was aware of Jock leaving, quietly closing the door behind him, shutting them in together, away from prying eyes. Too late. They were finished yesterday. 'I'll say what I said to Jock. Have a safe trip.'

'Maddy.' Her name was sweet and sad on his lips, pulling at her heartstrings. 'I'm sorry.'

'Sorry because we made love? Or because you can't accept me as I am?'

'No,' he almost shouted. 'Not that. I promise.' He stared at her, shaking his head in disbelief. 'I promise,' he repeated quietly. Was he struggling with that now? He'd denied it but she wouldn't be surprised if he'd found the sight of her daunting despite everything he'd said. She wasn't going to ask. Would rather not know than find out it was true. She'd be crippled.

'Why did you do it if you already knew you were going to walk away? And don't even think of blaming your commitment to non-commitment.' She was trembling. That was solvable if they seriously wanted to have a relationship.

'I could turn that back on you, Maddy. It's not as though I didn't warn you. Why did you have sex with me?'

Sex. Not making love. The coils holding her together that had been slowly unwinding over the past days began tightening again. But she couldn't hold back the truth. 'I couldn't help myself.'

'I wanted you so bad.' Honest, if nothing else.

The anger stepped back, leaving her shaken. 'Once I'd exposed myself I didn't want to hold back,' she whispered.

Sam shook his head. 'But I still shouldn't have gone ahead. I don't deserve you, or the happiness you might bring me.'

'Sugar-coating the situation?'

'Maddy.' His finger was under her chin, lifting her head so she had to look at him. 'Don't go there. I meant it when I said you are beautiful, inside and out. Promise me you won't forget that.'

'Yeah, right.' Somehow his words hurt more than anything else could have. He didn't want a bar of her. She'd read the lack of horror in his eyes, on his face to mean he cared enough to take her as she was. Wrong again, Madison. He'd accepted her enough to have sex, and now he'd had time to think about it he was giving her the heave-ho. Seemed her second attempt at showing a man what had become of her had been little better than the first. At least there were no lies this time. Neither could she deny his warning that he wasn't interested in a relationship, something she might've accepted more easily if she hadn't been expecting his rejection even before they'd become intimate.

Impatient honking from outside the medical unit broke through the tension. Sam's transport had arrived.

'I have to go, Madison.'

Madison, not Maddy. Back to square one. He'd pulled up the barricade. He wasn't just saying he had to get on that truck. She knew it deep down. Had always known Sam would return to New Zealand and she would not feature in the life he made there, or anywhere. She'd known this outcome was coming and had still enjoyed time in his arms, had all but precipitated it. This was the price she'd known all along would come due. But… Did it have to be so hard? Once again everything she wanted, hoped for was being undermined, stolen from her. Because for a few crazed minutes she'd dared to hope. 'Why?' When he said nothing, she asked in a tighter, louder voice, 'You don't even want to stay in touch?'

He looked up at the ceiling, gulped some air, and dropped his head to lock his eyes with hers. Emotion she struggled to recognise had darkened that sky blue to near navy. 'No.'

Ouch. He didn't mince his words. She turned away, unable to look at him any longer as pain saturated her.

'You deserve better. I could take a risk and ask you to join me in life, for life, and I might learn to love you unconditionally. But others I know are missing their chance of happiness because of me. The guilt I carry is too strong to thrust aside. It destroys everything around me. That's all I can say.'

When she turned around he was staring at her as

though storing memories, which made no sense when he wanted to leave her, forget her. He should be fighting that guilt, not taking mental pictures of her.

'Goodbye, Sam,' she choked out. She hadn't missed the 'I might learn to love you' bit either. This was the end. The shortest relationship in history. In hers anyway. Until this moment she hadn't realised how much she'd come to care for him. Love him? Absolutely. That's why it was hurting so badly to hear him say what deep down she'd already known.

His finger traced a line from her chin to her mouth, outlined her lips. 'Madison.' Then he turned and walked away.

She watched every step he took across the room to the door, hunger for him gnawing at her. 'Sam, wait.' And she ran to throw her arms around him. Her heart was breaking as she kissed him, a kiss full of the love she could not tell him about. Then before he could say a word she ran for the office and slammed the door shut.

She would not watch him leave the room. Or climb aboard the waiting truck. In her heart he'd already gone, she didn't need to underline his defection.

She'd get busy going through files and checking stock in the drugs cupboard. She'd quash the anger unfurling in her stomach before it became too big to hold in. Because she was angry—with Sam, but more particularly with herself for letting him close, for falling for him.

Slap. A pile of files hit the desk. Then another, and another. There. Plenty to keep her busy and her mind off anything that wasn't army related. Dropping into the chair, she propped her elbows on the desk and got down to business. She would not acknowledge Sam was gone, wouldn't admit he'd even been here. She'd been a fool to think anything would be different just because she'd laid herself on the line. Now she'd bury the whole episode in work.

But an hour later she raised her head when a plane flew over the base. 'Goodbye, Sam Lowe.'

'That was a boring patrol,' Cassy quipped as she unloaded the medical kit from her backpack in the medical unit.

'Like you want exciting,' Madison retorted. She was more than happy to return to base with no casualties and no bullets fired. 'Or do you?'

'Not if I'm in serious danger,' Cassy admitted. 'Life is for grabbing with both hands, but I might add not if it's at risk of being cut short.'

'I understand.' But did she? The fire had shut her down in every way possible. She'd studied hard to gain her qualifications, and appreciated being able to give back hope to people who were despairing because of a medical condition playing havoc with their lives. But she hadn't moved forward an inch if the heaviness of her heart was an indicator.

Instead she'd repeated her mistakes. Talk about a slow learner. It had to have been hope that had seen her opening up to Sam. It certainly hadn't been common sense. That would've said, *Don't go there because there'll only be one outcome.* An outcome she was now struggling to cope with. Despite everything, her dreams were full of Sam every night. It had been better when she couldn't sleep, had tossed and turned for hours.

Madison made herself a bitterly strong coffee in an attempt to crank up her cells and squash the tiredness dragging her down. She took it out into the sun.

Life is for grabbing with both hands.

Funny how most people didn't get that until something big threatened or overwhelmed them. As for her, she'd got it but had determinedly ignored the message, afraid of what waited out there for her. Her one, brief foray over the line had bitten back hard. Sam was not, would never be, a part of her future. He'd made that very clear.

She'd fought hard to get beyond the results of the fire, and physically she'd made it. But the hurt dealt to her heart had remained, had made her scared to risk opening up to anyone. Then along came Sam. His reaction to her messed-up body had been little short of amazing, and she'd been quick to let her desire take over.

But in the harsh light of reality fear still lurked in the shadows of her mind. Because if everything had been fine with him then where was he? Why wasn't she receiving texts and emails from him, telling her what he was up to? Telling her his plans and where he might next be sent with the army?

It seemed he'd been better at covering up his reactions than her ex.

Pulling her knees up, Madison dropped her chin on them and hugged herself tight. Sam had said and done the right things but he didn't want her. Whether that was because of her scars or because he didn't love her, it didn't matter. He didn't want her.

And she'd known it before they'd made love.

Known he didn't love her.

Her own feelings had been hazy until they'd made love.

There'd been sparks between them from the get-go. Sparks. She shuddered. How had she overlooked that? Sparks were dangerous, they burned people with the fire they created. Yet she'd put her heart out there to be consumed.

During the ten days Sam had been gone she'd filled her time and mind with work, and then more work. There were patrols most days, and troops requiring basic medical consults after returning to base. When time was dragging with nothing to distract her she'd go into town to help at the hospital. Most nights she fell into bed without pulling her shirt off, she was that tired. Somehow Sam still raged in her head, never left her in peace.

It didn't seem to matter how hard she tried to banish him, he would not go away. She had let him in because she hadn't been able to keep him out. Extricating him was proving to be beyond her. She needed to get on with finding a different kind of happiness than she'd grown up thinking was her right. It's why she'd come here in the first place, yet in a matter of days she'd lost her way, forgotten everything she'd learned over the past two years. All she had to do now was get back on track, put down plans for the future that wouldn't trip her up.

Sounded absolutely wonderful, if impossible.

Well, what else was she supposed to do?

Grab life with both hands.

'Captain, got a minute?' Cassy asked from the doorway.

Her body ached as she unwound from the top step and tipped the revolting coffee into the dirt. 'Sure.'

Got twenty-four hours' worth of them.

CHAPTER THIRTEEN

SAM STEPPED OUT of the Auckland taxi into the drizzle outside the downtown restaurant William's fiancée had recommended for this catch-up.

'Hey, Sam, looking good. The army always agreed with you.' Ally was running towards him from further along the pavement where another taxi was pulling away from the kerb. She leapt at him, threw her arms around his shoulders and plopped a sisterly kiss on his cheek.

Sam struggled to grapple with this welcome after expecting Ally to be quiet and sad. *And* still blaming him. 'Hey, you're looking pretty swish yourself. Being a barrister suits you.'

She slipped out of his arms and smoothed her jacket. 'Isn't that so? It's been a steep learning curve, though.' Now she was quieter, less relaxed with him. More like the Ally he'd been expecting. 'Let's get out of the weather and order some wine. There's a lot to catch up on.'

Oh, he bet there was. Nothing he wanted to talk about but he'd contacted her for a purpose so backing out now wasn't an option. Not if he wanted to start living life to the full again. And he did. If nothing else had come out of his encounter with Maddy it was that he'd discovered how much he'd been missing out on since William's death. Of course that had been deliberate, his punishment. But even jail sentences came to an end, and he sensed his was coming.

Seated in the restaurant's lounge area, wine on the table between them, Sam studied the woman whose life had been tossed upside down by William's death. Where was that crippling sadness that had kept her in bed for weeks afterwards? 'Tell me about the law firm you've joined.' He'd start with the easy stuff, and hopefully Ally would relax again.

Her eyes brightened and her mouth tipped up into a generous smile, though probably not for him. 'I have been so fortunate. All because I studied with the son of one of the partners of Auckland's top litigation firms. He put my name forward to his dad and before I knew it I had an interview and a job. I'm a very small player in the scheme of things but loving every minute of it.'

'You won't stay on the bottom rung for long, if I know anything about you.' She had a sharp mind and had often talked about the excitement of a courtroom in the middle of a trial.

'I agree.' Her laughter tinkled in the air between them.

Once he'd have given everything to hear her laugh again after William had been taken from her, but now he struggled to understand how she could be so happy. Of course he was pleased for her, but also a little confused. 'I'm glad you've got your mojo back.'

'Oh, Sam, it's so exciting some days I keep thinking I'll wake up and find this job—all of this—was only a dream.' Her smile faded, and the shine of her eyes dimmed.

'So how are you really?' he asked quickly.

'While my career is catapulting me ever upwards, it's not what I'd wished for, planned on. This is a new life for me, very different from what William and I had been looking forward to.' Ally took a gulp of wine and set her glass carefully on the table.

When she raised her eyes to his Sam felt a frisson of concern slither down his spine. 'I totally understand, and admire you for what you've done.'

'There are days, weeks even, when I'm crippled with missing him.' No need to say his name. They both understood.

'You and me both.' He stared into his glass, then back to her. 'It never leaves me.'

She nodded slowly. 'I wish…' Her sigh was loud between them, filled with all the things she'd once shouted at him—the blame, the anger and pain, the tears.

Sam reached for her hand, covered it with his. 'Don't, Ally. We can't change what happened.' But he'd give his life to do exactly that.

'No, neither of us can,' she whispered through tears.

His heart tore apart for her—again. And for himself. Pain speared him, took his breath away. He shouldn't have come, shouldn't have called her. But he'd had to, this time for his own sanity. He had to get out of the hole he'd dug himself into, and talking to Ally was the first step. His chest rose. 'I'm sorry, Ally.' When her forlorn eyes met his the anguish and guilt threatened to bury him again. But no. It was time. Time to live Sam

Lowe's life, not hover in the dark because of what he'd done to this woman. 'I'll always be sorry for my role in what happened, but I won't say it again. I can't.'

She stared at him, making him squirm, but he didn't back down. He had no idea where this strength had come from but knew it for the truth it was. He'd started living again. The guilt was huge, but it had to be exorcised so he could be free to get close to people he cared about, to love them. But he needed Ally's forgiveness. So help him, he needed that badly.

If it wasn't forthcoming he would be stuck in a holding pattern, going round and round, the army one week, a hospital the next, New Zealand one month, some inhospitable location the next, alone with his thoughts and needs. That was no longer feasible. Maddy had made him start feeling again.

'I'd like another glass of wine.' Ally stood up, empty glass in her shaking hand. 'What about you?'

He had barely touched his. 'Let me get you one.'

A waiter appeared before either of them moved. 'Ma'am? Another?'

With a nod Ally sank back onto her chair, her back rigid, her hands locked together.

What was going on? Yes, he was guilty for William signing on for that fateful tour and thereby destroying this lovely woman's happiness and future, but there was something else in her gaze, her stance. 'Ally?'

'I've booked the table for three people. There's someone I want you to meet. He'll be joining us shortly.'

Sam sank back in his chair. This woman had been all but comatose at William's funeral and for months after. Now she'd found someone else? No, he'd got that wrong. Surely?

'You're shocked.'

'Yes. No.' He dredged up a half-smile. 'I'm not sure what I'm thinking.'

'You're thinking it's too soon, that William's only been gone two years, that I'm not ready. Right?'

'Possibly. But if you're happy then so am I. William wouldn't have wanted you mourning him for ever, missing out on a family, a loving man, a home.'

'You're right. He wasn't a selfish man.' Abby took the wine the waiter placed before her, sipped the liquid, all the while watching him. 'Dave. The guy joining us is Dave, and he's special. We are planning to move in together shortly.'

'I see.'

'No, you don't. You're thinking this is too soon, that I haven't mourned long enough.'

Am I? He didn't know. 'How'd you meet?'

'We shared an umbrella one day when it began to rain at the cemetery where we were both putting flowers on our respective partner's graves. Then we had coffee and talked, and slowly over the last few months we've become close.

'I love William, Sam.' Ally's voice was low but firm. 'I still love him and probably always will in a way.' She swallowed, looked around the room before returning her shaky gaze to him. 'But he's gone and I can't remain unhappy for ever. It's not natural. I want to move on, have those children I'd believed I'd have with a man who's got my back, who will love me always.'

'And has this guy got your back?'

'Yes, Sam, he has. He's quieter and more serious than William, but maybe that's why I fell for him. He's not a rerun. This is a new relationship and I'm not comparing anything.'

Where did this leave him? Guilty as ever? Yep, nothing had changed there. Ally was right: William was gone, couldn't be the father to those children she mentioned or watch her grow old. All because he'd listened to Sam, had been talked into going abroad for another stint in the army.

Now her hand covered his. 'It's okay to start again. It really is. Hanging onto my grief and spending the rest of my life mourning William isn't right.' Her fingers squeezed gently. 'Nor is it for you.'

You think? But I've left Maddy for that grief and the guilt. I've thrown away the greatest opportunity of my life.

He cleared his throat and tried to speak, but words failed him.

'Stop blaming yourself. William didn't have to sign on for that last tour. He'd received his discharge papers. It was his choice not to sign them. He had a wild streak, contained by the army's restrictions, sure, but he liked to get out amongst it. You didn't force him to do anything he didn't want to do.'

'He was worried he wouldn't handle settling down completely.' His pal could be a little crazy at times. Sam had forgotten that.

'I was wrong to blame you, but I didn't know how to cope, could hardly open my eyes every day to face William not coming home to me. It was so unfair. I had to lash out and you were the easy target. In the end I realised William made his own mind up about going, about postponing our wedding, about staying in the army, even though I begged him not to. It's my turn to apologise for the way I treated you.'

The weight didn't leap off his heart, the bands holding him together didn't break free, but there was a loosening deep inside. The start of his future? No, that was too easy. But, 'Thanks.'

'You're not getting off that lightly. Let him go, Sam. You can't hold onto him any more than I can. It's not wrong to start living life to the full again.' Her fingers curled around his hand and squeezed. 'Please.'

'Now you're rushing me.' This time his grin was wide and genuine. 'I'm a bloke, remember? We don't do the emotional stuff easily.'

After an awkward dinner with Ally and her new man Sam walked along the quay at the edge of Auckland Harbour, ignoring the drizzle dampening him. His hands filled his pockets, and his shoulders were hunched as he wandered aimlessly towards the Viaduct.

Memories of Maddy fighting her fears swamped him. She was so vulnerable and yet tough. She'd told him everything that had happened, had exposed herself to him in a way that must've taken every drop of courage she could dig up and then some. But, then, she was strong. That strength had got her through a devastating time when the man who should've been glued to her side had let her down. The pain of that alone must've devastated her.

Which was why he had to keep away, couldn't

change his mind about a relationship with her. He'd hurt her. Somehow, some time, he would let her down.

'It wasn't your fault William died,' Ally had said when she'd kissed him goodbye. 'If he hadn't gone to Afghanistan he'd have found some other dangerous occupation or hobby. It was his nature to push the boundaries way beyond possibility.'

True. So if he wasn't at fault for William's death then what next? Had Ally just freed him to chase life, grab what he wanted and hold on tight?

No, it couldn't be that simple.

Why not? Ally believed he should, he could.

Sam shivered. He might be able to let go of the guilt but getting close to anyone had never been easy. Too many risks.

Water splashed up as he stepped into a puddle. Bring back the desert. A sudden wind brought heavier rain driving at him, chilling him down fast. Time to head for his hotel. He could continue thinking inside the dry warmth with a bourbon in his hand.

The drink warmed him all right, but it didn't solve his dilemma. Madison… Maddy…the woman he'd left behind after she'd given him her heart on a plate. She hadn't voiced the sentiment but that had been love in her eyes when they'd made love. But not when she'd lifted her shirt. No, fear and dread had pulsed out of her then. Had that love given her the courage to open herself up to him? And then he'd walked away because he'd been afraid.

Afraid of hurting her more than she already was. Those scars were harsh, yes, but did they make Maddy less of a sexy, attractive woman? No way. She was still

Maddy, the same woman who'd put Porky's foot back together, who'd poured her heart and soul into her singing, who'd become a doctor to help others.

The woman I've fallen in love with. Suddenly and abruptly. Frightening, yet exciting, if he accepted the truth.

Was he ready to take the risk? To lay it all out for her to see? What if she left him? There was more than one way to go, and however it happened he'd be devastated, broken.

'Another drink?' the barman interrupted.

'Sure, why not?' He wasn't on duty for the next three weeks. Draining the last centimetre from his glass, he handed it over.

His father had walked away from him and his mother without a backward glance, showing what little importance they'd had in his life. For a wee guy that had been beyond his comprehension. As an adult he still didn't get it, but, then, he'd never seen or spoken to his father since that day so had no knowledge of what had been behind his actions. If his mother had known, she'd never shared it. And then she'd left him, too, when he'd woken up one morning and found her cold in her bed.

'Here you go.' The replenished glass slid into view. 'Cheers.'

Sam glugged down the bourbon. Banged the empty glass back on the counter and nodded to the barman.

Waiting for his refill, he glanced around the nearly empty bar. Was this what his life had come to? Drinking alone in an impersonal hotel downtown in a large city? Tomorrow he'd fly back to Christchurch and Burnham base, and fill in the weeks waiting for orders for his next move. Except he didn't want to do that any more. Had had enough of moving from camp to barracks to off-the-beaten-track towns.

Maddy had given him a taste of what life could be, a taste of the love he'd craved all his life. He wanted more, wanted it—with her. But most of all he wanted to give love back to her, to show she was cherished, adored by him. To make her feel safe again, to help her find the missing links in her make-up, to love her as she deserved to be loved.

And if something went wrong? If he found himself alone again?

Then he'd have to deal with it. But until then he'd have a life worth having.

CHAPTER FOURTEEN

CAUTIOUSLY LIFTING HER helmet-protected head above the mound of dirt, Madison scanned the land ahead of her troops. Empty buildings baked in the relentless sun, too far away to hold a threat yet. Between those and the patrol nothing moved. Eventually satisfied they were alone, she called in a low voice, 'All clear.'

Around her soldiers rose to their feet, keeping low as they moved forward, guns at the ready in case their captain was wrong and the sniper who'd attacked a vanload of locals returning to the town after visiting family at a village further away was still out here.

Along with the latest doctor to arrive on base, Madison had spent most of the night in Theatre, putting people back together by sewing up gunshot injuries. She should be exhausted but right now she was revved, running on adrenalin and lots of caffeine. The sniper had to be found and locked up before he hurt anyone else.

'Down,' the leading sergeant called, his hand flicking a signal at them to hit the ground fast. 'Three o'clock, behind the rocks.'

After assessing the layout, Madison led the men out.

'Circle him, and be careful. I do not want to be sewing any of you back together after this.'

'Who needs Captain Lowe when we've got you?' The sergeant grinned.

'Get on with it, Sergeant,' she growled as she swallowed a bitter laugh. *I'm like Sam?* Now, there was a joke. One that would have him in stitches. Sam. What was he up to? Had he managed to wangle another posting overseas yet?

Running low to the ground, she kept beside the sergeant until they reached their target—a filthy, middle-aged man screaming at them in a language she couldn't understand.

Two soldiers caught him, held him still.

'Who have we got?' she demanded of the interpreter.

After five minutes of shouting back and forth the interpreter informed her, 'He's denying it but I'd say we've got our man. He has no explanation about that gun he was burying.'

Madison shivered. The man must've run out of ammo or he'd have used it on them. 'Call the situation in,' she told their comms technician.

'Just in time,' the private told her minutes later. 'You're wanted back on base.'

'I'm not the only doctor they've got.' Yet she had been acting as if she was, grabbing every case she could, working all hours to fill in the empty days that threatened to knock her down. 'Tell them we're on our way.'

'You enjoy the army, Captain?' her sergeant asked as they bounced and rocked in the truck heading back to base.

'Most of the time.' She was hardly going to say no to someone under her orders. 'Don't like the abrupt way life can go from safe to dangerous in a flash.' Like when that corporal had been hit last week. It had made her wonder if she'd return home in one piece at the end of her stint here, or if there was a bullet with her name on it waiting out in the desert. Thoughts she shoved aside as quickly as they rose. Negative notions were a hindrance to even the sharpest minds and played havoc during the dead of the night.

'Know what you mean,' muttered the sergeant, and that had her wondering what tragedies he'd witnessed. Everyone came with baggage. Everyone.

She knew hers. But she didn't know all Sam's. In the midst of a conversation he'd often gone places she'd been unable to follow. She loved him without restrictions, but there were a lot of gaps in what she knew about him. Making love with Sam had temporarily blown away the last of her barriers. Now he knew everything, had seen everything. But he'd gone without a backward glance, without returning her final kiss. Without showing her the real, deep-down Sam. Had he been protecting her, as he'd said? Or himself?

Madison held the water bottle to her mouth and poured the wonderful icy liquid down her dry, dusty throat as she elbowed the door to the medical unit open. 'Wow, that's good,' she spluttered, and slapped her mouth with the back of her hand.

Cassy followed her in. 'I always drink more when I've been out on patrol. I say it's the dust and heat, but I think fear has a lot to do with it.'

Madison spun around and caught at the nurse's arm. 'Don't let that fear get to you or it'll destroy you.' Hadn't she given herself the same speech on the drive in? And she was going to be fearless from now on? Ha! *Good point, Captain.*

'I know all that, been to the lectures, learned how to cope,' Cassy drawled. 'But…'

'There's always a "but".'

Why were Cassy's eyes widening in confusion? Madison glanced in the direction the nurse was gaping and felt the floor heave up under her feet. Her arms shot out, fumbling for something to hold onto while she retrieved her balance. Finding nothing but air, she tottered forward a step.

'Sam?' He was in Christchurch. Wasn't he? She snapped her eyes shut, flicked them open again. Definitely Sam. 'Ah, hi. We've been on patrol, think the heat got to us.'

He was sitting in her chair, his feet up on her desk, those hands that had done marvellous things to her body behind his head. And, yes, he wore that blasted grin that undid all her good—and not so good—intentions. A steady blue gaze bored into her, so direct, so compelling she could feel her insides melting in an instant what little resistance she'd hurriedly mustered. He was seeing everything she kept hidden. Everything. Surely not? Not that she loved him. She stared back, tightened her spine, tried to hide that L word from her posture, her face, her eyes. *That* he did not need to know.

But something flicked through his eyes. If she hadn't known better she might've thought it was passion. 'Hello, Maddy.' The grin slipped, quickly recovered.

At the sound of that gravelly, deep voice she tipped forward, bending at the waist. So much for standing up to him. Two words and she was lost.

His feet hit the floor and he strode to her, catching her arms and hauling her close. 'I've missed you.'

As her cheek was pressed against his chest, his hand firm in the centre of her back, she drew in his life scent, pure male, full of warnings—and melting the last of her resistance. She'd make a fool of herself if that meant being held by him. Meant being told—

'You missed me?' She jerked back, away from everything she craved. 'Ever heard of email? Your phone gone on the blink?'

Another step back to put more space between them because she couldn't trust herself not to reach for him, to splay her hands over his chest and feel his heartbeat under her palms.

'I prefer using a plane.' The grin had softened into a lopsided smile filled with uncertainty.

'Why?' she asked.

'I need to see you as we communicate, to watch for innuendo and hear the laughter or annoyance in your voice. Email doesn't allow that, and phones can make interpretation difficult.' His eye twitched. 'I only know you well when I'm standing in front of you, reading you as we speak to each other.'

He'd better not have read that L word. 'You've come back to the Sinai to talk to me?' She shook her head in an attempt to clear the dross. 'No one mentioned you being posted back here.'

'I'm on leave. I'm here to see you. Nothing else.

I've also taken a discharge from the army, effective next month.'

Her fingers dug into her hips as she tried to remain upright. 'I don't understand.' What did any of this have to do with her? 'The commander knows you're here?'

'He's given me a room in the barracks for the next couple of days, then I'm moving into town to work at the hospital until you're sent home at the end of your tour.'

'I still don't get it. Why would you do that? You hated the desert and heat.'

Sam wanted to chuckle at the stunned expression on Maddy's wonderful face, but he daren't. There was too much at stake. If only she knew how hard it had been not to leap up and grab her to him the moment he'd seen her come into the medical unit. Maddy was not ready for that. She was not ready for him at all. But she was quickly getting over the shock of finding him here, was wrapping herself in confidence, pulling on the feisty armour she was so good at producing. All false, every last piece.

Softness extended through his heart. The woman he loved stood in front of him, holding him at bay with nothing but refusal in her eyes, not ready to trust him. He wanted her ready for everything he had to tell her. Hell, he wanted *her*. So much it debilitated him. That need had driven him to clear the obstacles so he could come to her a free man, but there was a way to go yet. 'I've had a change of heart,' he said, knowing she wouldn't understand. Not until he told her everything and first he needed her to relax. 'I admit to missing home, such as it is. Christchurch is where I grew up, where Ma and Pa Creighton are. Where you'll return to at the end of your time in the army. I want to be there when you do.' Maddy wasn't usually slow on the up-take, but he wondered if she'd realise he'd wound her and home into the same package, that he needed both to become one for him to make her happy.

'Sam.' Her fingers were white as they dug deeper into her flesh. 'It's great to see you but I'll have to catch up later. I'm needed elsewhere.'

'If you're referring to the message sent through comms, that was from me. I had them send it.'

'You couldn't just wait for me to get back?'

'I hate thinking of you out on patrol, looking for snip-ers. It was my way of saying come back safe.' It was true. From the moment he'd walked in here and learned Maddy was with a group hunting out a sniper, he'd been gripped with fear. So much so that when she'd walked in as though back from a stroll to the shops he'd alter-nately wanted to kiss her and shout at her.

'It's the job, Sam.' The bite had gone from her voice.

'Yeah.' He glanced around, only now aware of ev-eryone watching them. 'Let's go somewhere private.'

'On an army base?' Her eyebrow lifted in a cute fashion, sending ripples of longing through him. 'You haven't been gone that long to forget what it's like.'

The office had been very private the afternoon they'd made love. 'Want to walk the perimeter?'

'I'm done with the sun for today.' She whistled si-lently. 'We could grab a water and find a corner no one else is interested in.'

At least she hadn't kicked him into touch. 'Let's.'

'Where will you live when you're working in town?'

Maddy asked as they settled on outdoor chairs in a private spot behind the barracks block.

'There's a small hotel on the same street.'

The plastic bottle spun back and forth in her hands. Her eyes seemed to be focused on a lone blade of grass at her feet. Then her head came up and she said, 'Okay, what's this about?'

Should he leap in? Or lead up to the crux of his visit? He leapt. 'You and me. I love you, Maddy. That week we worked here together pulled me up short, brought me to my knees.'

If he'd expected her to leap into his arms he was out of luck. Her widening eyes were the only indication that she'd heard him. 'Yet you went away without telling me. What's changed?'

'Me.'

Maddy stared at him, her lips parted and her eyes wide. 'Go on.' She wasn't making it easy for him but, then, she had a lot at stake. She wouldn't be wanting to risk having her heart smashed again.

If she loved him. Cold fear slid over him. What if she didn't? She wouldn't have made love that day if she didn't, surely? Not Maddy. Not with her insecurities.

'I know I told you I'd never let you close, that my heart wasn't available. I did that because I was afraid. I've fought becoming too close to anyone because I couldn't face being left again.' He'd told her that before, but needed to remind her before going on. 'When William was killed in Afghanistan I blamed myself for talking him into going with me. I believed I didn't deserve love and happiness.'

'And now?'

'We each are responsible for our choices in life. William could've stayed home and got married, as was planned.'

Maddy nodded abruptly. 'Go on.'

She was tough. 'That first day I saw you walking across the parade ground? That's when I fell for you.' Just hadn't recognised the emotions rolling through him at the time.

She swallowed hard, but remained silent.

'I've never stopped loving you from then on, Madison.'

She leapt to her feet, stormed over to the fence and stared out across the sand. Her hands were gripping her hips, her legs spread wide.

He waited, and waited. The next move was hers.

His water was gone by the time she turned and walked back to him. His heart rate was off the scale.

'Is this when you head away again?' she asked in a strangled tone. Then she began shaking, her hands, her legs and shoulders, her teeth chattering.

'No. Never.' Sam leapt up, pulled her into his arms. That soft body was home for his starved one, warming him where he'd been cold for years. Her scent his beacon. 'I want to marry you, have you at my side for ever.'

She jerked and his arms were empty. 'No,' she cried.

'Maddy.' Another chill overrode the warmth. 'Is that so bad?'

She spun away, spun back to stare at him. Tears poured down her cheeks. 'You love me?'

'With all my heart.'

She slumped, pain removing all the colour from her cheeks. Her hands gripped her midriff. 'Have you thought this through?' she gasped through those tears he desperately wanted to wipe away. 'Considered everything? Like possibly never having a family?'

'Maddy, it's you I want, I love. If we have children I'll love them, too, but if we find we can't then I won't stop loving you because of it.'

Longing warred with denial in her face. 'You're talking for ever here. Have you really thought what that means? I couldn't cope if you changed your mind.' Her breasts rose on a breath. 'Go back to wherever you've decided is home, Sam.' Her tears had become a torrent, and she stumbled as she started to run—away from him.

'No way, Maddy. No damned way. You and I belong together.' He caught her up in his arms, lifted her feet off the ground, held her against his body.

She writhed and wriggled, trying to get away from him. Her sniffs were muffled against his shirt.

'I love you, Maddy. I love you. As in now. I always will. I love you, Maddy.' Over and over the words spilled between them. 'I love you.' His hands soothed, his body sheltered her from herself, and slowly, oh, so slowly, she calmed. He eased his embrace enough to let her stand against him, but he did not drop his arms from his woman.

Finally a shudder rippled through her length and she pulled back to rub her arm across her swollen face. Then she looked up at him. Hope swam in those wet eyes. And something else.

Sam held his breath.

Finally she spoke so quietly he had to lower his head to hear her. 'I love you, too, Sam.'

All the air in his lungs rushed across his lips. *She*

loves me. That was all he needed. All he'd ever wanted. Pulling her back into his arms, Sam kissed those swollen lips.

When he stopped to draw breath she told him, 'There must've been something in the air the day I arrived here. Not only dust. I think I started to feel hope for the future when you didn't laugh at my meltdown. I'm ready now, ready for whatever we might face. With you beside me I can cope with anything.'

Putting his finger on her lips, he managed, 'Shh…'

As he leaned close to reclaim those lips his own tears splashed on her face. She tasted of love and hunger and the future. And of a home together, a life together.

She was his life.

EPILOGUE

Five months later...

MADISON TAPPED HER foot impatiently as the Christchurch immigration officer studied her arrivals card. All around her people seemed free to go, while she was stuck with this annoying man.

'Whereabouts in the Middle East have you been?'

'The Sinai Peninsula. With the army,' she added for good measure, hoping that'd hurry him along.

'I see you're not with your contingent today.'

'They're coming next week. I'm getting married in seven days and was given an earlier flight.' One with seats and food and cabin crew. Yahoo.

Tick, tick. He finally smiled. 'There you go, Captain. Have a great wedding.'

'Oh, I intend to.' Her pack bounced on her back as she ran for the exit and charged out into the wide space. 'Sam,' she shrieked. 'Sam.'

'Over here.' And there he was. That smile she'd been craving since he'd headed home to finalise details for their wedding and to pick up the deeds to the house they'd bought last month on the net after her family had checked it out for them.

'Sam.' She dropped the pack and leapt at him, wrapped her arms and legs around him tight. She was never going to let go of him again.

He staggered but didn't drop her. 'Maddy, babe, what took you so long? I've been waiting twenty minutes.' That smile widened into a grin, and his hands splayed across her waist, firm, warm and demanding. 'I've missed you every second of every day.'

'I've missed you more,' she teased, before plastering her lips back on his, and forgetting everything but the man holding her. Her fiancé, the man she'd fallen in love with as quickly as a lightning flash could cut through the sky. Finally she removed her mouth enough to whisper, 'Take me home'. To the house they were going to have so much fun making into a home. Their home.

They weren't having a decadent honeymoon on an island beach in the Pacific or at a swanky hotel in Australia. Nope, they were staying at home, buying furniture and linen and kitchen utensils, and all the things necessary and not so necessary to fill their home and make it comfortable. And finding rooms to set up their joint surgical practice in.

Sam held her away from him to lock those gorgeous blue eyes on her. 'Hate to spoil the fun but we are not alone.'

'Really? Who's here?' She stared over his shoulder and right into the amused gaze that she'd known all her life. 'Dad.' She leapt from Sam to her father, wrapping her arms around him. 'I've missed you.'

'And me you, sweetheart. Glad you're back safe and sound.'

Then she was being swarmed by the rest of her family, and the tears streamed down her face. Who would've believed six months ago she'd be coming home to all this? 'Sam?'

'Right here, Maddy.' He leaned close and whispered, 'It's all real, right down to that chocolate stain on little Midge's brand-new shirt she wore specially for Auntie Madison.'

'And how did she come by chocolate?' Her sister wouldn't have let Midge have it.

'Seems there was a lot of it hanging around on the shelves in the book store over there and, well, we just couldn't walk past without helping the shopkeeper out by buying some.' Sam was grinning down at her nieces.

Maddy's heart swelled. That grin had a lot to answer for. It had snagged her right from the get-go, and still made it hard for her to ignore Sam. But now it had changed. There was no hidden agenda behind Sam's grin, no challenge, nothing to suggest anything other than he was happy.

Stretching onto her toes, Madison kissed her man. 'I love you so much it's scary.'

'I know what you mean but let's not be afraid. We've got too much good going on to be sidetracked by what might be out there waiting for us.' With another kiss he set her on her feet again. 'There are two people here who are busting to meet you.'

Of course. She should've gone to them immediately. 'Ma and Pa Creighton. I am thrilled to finally meet you.' It was easy to hug this woman who'd been so kind to Sam and his mother, easy to accept a return hug.

'It's us who are thrilled.' Ma Creighton stepped back to swipe at her cheeks where small tears tracked a line through her make-up. 'Sam's so happy. We've never seen him like this. Thank you.'

'Don't thank me. We're in love. That tends to make even grey days look sunny.'

'What my wife isn't saying is that you've brought Sam home to us. As in he drops by all the time, has meals with us, talks as though he's got to make up for all the years we've known him.'

'I'm glad. Really glad. He adores you both.'

'Right.' Sam started rounding everyone up. 'Time we headed home.' He was looking at Maddy and when he said 'home' his eyes lit up with excitement. 'Maddy hasn't seen her house yet and I can't wait any longer to show her.'

There was a general groan from everyone. 'Guess that means we should take our time getting there.' Maggie laughed.

Definitely, thought Madison.

'Definitely,' muttered Sam. 'Take about three days.'

Madison skidded to a halt in front of the terminal doors now sliding open. 'We haven't got a chance of being alone until this lot have had dinner.'

'I figured.'

She grabbed his hand. 'Come on. I need you to myself for five minutes.'

'A quickie on the way home?' Sam wiggled one eye-brow at her.

Her elbow jabbed him in the side. 'I have a present for you.'

'What is it?'

'Patience, man. Where's our car? What colour is it?'

'Aren't you supposed to ask what make it is first?'

She kissed the back of his hand that held hers. 'How many seats has it got?'

'Four.' He dragged out his answer, confusion darkening his eyes.

'Has it got a large boot?'

'Ye-es. Maddy…?'

'It's just that we're going to need all of that. There's going to be a third member of this family arriving in seven months' time.'

'Maddy!' Sam said as he dropped her bag and swung her up into his arms. 'Seriously? We're going to be parents?'

A tidal wave of happiness rolled through her and she clung to the man who had helped her get her life back on track. 'I love you, Sam Lowe. Always will. And, yes, we're going to have a baby!'

* * * * *

A MONTH TO MARRY
THE MIDWIFE

BY
FIONA McARTHUR

MILLS
BOON

Published in Great Britain 2017
By Mills & Boon, an imprint of HarperCollins*Publishers*
1 London Bridge Street, London, SE1 9GF

© 2017 Fiona McArthur

ISBN: 978-0-263-92638-5

Our policy is to use papers that are natural, renewable and recyclable
products and made from wood grown in sustainable forests. The logging
and manufacturing processes conform to the legal environmental
regulations of the country of origin.

Printed and bound in Spain
by CPI, Barcelona

Dear Reader,

Lighthouse Bay is the best place to find caring and spirited midwives, fabulous townspeople, and the most gorgeous docs around. I love lighthouses, I adore mums and babies, and I thrive on strong women and men who make me laugh.

In this first of three books set in Lighthouse Bay, midwife Ellie Swift has been told the ultimate lie and has now vowed to dedicate herself to her love of midwifery and the nurturing of her friends. She won't be trusting a young man any time soon.

Obstetrician Sam Southwell, a man dealing with the loss of his wife and babies, doesn't plan on staying in Lighthouse Bay—he's just doing his dad a favour. But then he meets Ellie…

The Midwives of Lighthouse Bay series is the place to come when your heart needs healing and your soul needs restoring. You just might find true love.

I wish you, dear reader, as much emotion and fun reading about Ellie and Sam as I had writing their story. Then you can look forward to Trina and Faith's stories, too. We have some hot twin brother Italian docs who have no idea what these feisty Aussie midwives have in store for them under the guiding beam of the lighthouse.

I can't wait to share those stories with you and would love to hear from you as we celebrate love in Lighthouse Bay.

Fi McArthur xx

FionaMcArthurAuthor.com

Dedicated to Rosie, who sprinted with me on this one,
Trish, who walked the beach with me, and Flo,
who rode the new wave and kept me afloat.
What a fab journey with awesome friends.

Books by Fiona McArthur

Mills & Boon Medical Romance

Christmas in Lyrebird Lake

Midwife's Christmas Proposal
Midwife's Mistletoe Baby

A Doctor, A Fling & A Wedding Ring
The Prince Who Charmed Her
Gold Coast Angels: Two Tiny Heartbeats
Christmas with Her Ex

Visit the Author Profile page
at millsandboon.co.uk for more titles.

**Praise for
Fiona McArthur**

'You do not want to miss this poignant love story.
I have read it twice in twenty-four hours and it is
fantastic!'

—*Goodreads* on
Midwife's Mistletoe Baby

PROLOGUE

THE WHITE SAND curved away in a crescent as Ellie Swift descended to Lighthouse Bay Beach and turned towards the bluff. When she stepped onto the beach the luscious crush of cool, fine sand under her toes made her suck in her breath with a grin and the ocean breeze tasted salty against her lips. Ellie set off at a brisk pace towards the edge of the waves to walk the bay to the headland and back before she needed to dress for work.

'Ellie!'

She spun, startled, away from the creamy waves now washing her feet, and saw a man limping towards her. He waved again. Jeff, from the surf club. Ellie knew Jeff, the local prawn-trawler captain and chief lifesaver. She'd delivered his second son. Jeff had fainted and Ellie tried not to remind him of that every time she saw him.

She waved back but already suspected the call wasn't social. She turned and sped up to meet him.

'We've got an old guy down on the rocks under the lighthouse, a surfer, says he's your doctor from the hospital. We think he's busted his arm, and maybe a leg.'

Ellie turned her head to look towards the headland Jeff had come from.

Jeff waved his hand towards the huddle of people in the distance. 'He won't let anybody touch him until you come. The ambulance is on the way but I reckon we might have to chopper him out from here.'

Ellie worked all over the hospital so it wasn't unusual that she was who people asked for. An old guy and a surfer. That was Dr Southwell. She sighed.

Ten minutes later Ellie was kneeling beside the good doctor, guarding his wrinkled neck in a brace as she watched the two ambulance women and two burly life-savers carefully shift him onto the rescue frame. Then it was done. Just a small groan escaped his gritted teeth as he closed his eyes and let the pain from the movement slowly subside.

Ellie glanced at the ocean, lying aqua and innocent, as if to say, *it wasn't my fault*, and suspected Dr South-well would doggedly heal and return to surfing with renewed vigour as soon as he could. The tide was on the way out and the waves weren't reaching the sloping plateau at the base of the cliffs any more where the life-savers had secured their casualty. The spot was popular with intrepid surfers to climb on and off their boards and paddle into the warm swell and out to the waves.

'Thanks for coming, Ellie.' Dr Southwell was look-ing much more comfortable and a trifle sheepish. 'Sorry to leave you in the lurch on the ward.'

She smiled at him. He'd always been sweet. 'Don't you worry about us. Look after you. They'll get you sorted once you've landed. Get well soon.'

The older man closed his eyes briefly. Then he winked at Ellie. 'I'll be back. As soon as I can.'

Ellie smiled and shook her head. He'd gone surfing every morning before his clinic, the athletic spring to his step contradicting his white hair and weathered face, a tall, thin gentleman who must have been a real catch fifty years ago. They'd splinted his arm against his body, didn't think the leg was broken, but they were treating it as such and had administered morphine, having cleared it with the helicopter flight nurse on route via mobile phone.

In the distance the *thwump-thwump* of the helicopter rotor could be heard approaching. Ellie knew how efficient the rescue team was. He'd be on his way very shortly.

Ellie glanced at the sweeping bay on the other side from where they crouched—the white sand that curved like a new moon around the bay, the rushing of the tide through the fish-filled creek back into the sea—and could understand why he'd want to return.

This place had stopped her wandering too. She lifted her chin. Lighthouse Bay held her future and she had plans for the hospital.

She looked down at the man, a gentle man in the true sense of the word, who had fitted so beautifully into the calm pace of the bay. 'We'll look forward to you coming back. As soon as you're well.' She glanced at the enormous Malibu surfboard the lifesavers had propped up against the cliff face. 'I'll get one of the guys to drop your board at my house and it will be there waiting for you.'

Ellie tried very hard not to think about the next few

days. *Damn*. Now they didn't have an on-call doctor and the labouring women would have to be transferred to the base hospital until another locum arrived. She needed to move quickly on those plans to make her maternity ward a midwifery group practice.

CHAPTER ONE

FOUR DAYS LATER, outside Ellie's office at the maternity ward at Lighthouse Bay Hospital, a frog croaked. It was very close outside her window. She shuddered as she assembled the emergency locum-doctor's welcome pack. Head down, she concentrated on continuing the task and pretended not to see the tremor in her fingers as she gathered the papers. She was a professional in charge of a hospital, for goodness' sake. Her ears strained for a repeat of the dreaded noise and hoped like heck she wouldn't hear it. She strained...but thankfully silence ensued.

'Concentrate on the task,' she muttered. She included a local map, which after the first day they wouldn't need because the town was so small, but it covered everywhere they could eat.

A list of the hours they were required to man the tiny doctor's clinic—just two in total on the other side of the hospital on each day of the week they were here. Then, in a month, hand over to the other local doctor who had threatened to leave if he didn't get holidays.

She couldn't blame him or his wife—they deserved a life! It was getting busier. Dr Rodgers, an elderly bachelor, had done the call-outs before he'd become ill. She hummed loudly to drown out the sound of the little voice that suggested she should have a life too, and of course to drown out the frogs. Ellie concentrated as she printed out the remuneration package.

The idea that any low-risk woman who went into labour would have to be transferred to the large hospital an hour away from her family just because no locum doctor could come was wrong. Especially when she'd had all her antenatal care with Ellie over the last few months. So the locum doctors were a necessary evil. It wasn't an onerous workload for them, in fact, because the midwives did all the maternity work, and the main hospital was run as a triage station with a nurse practitioner, as they did in the Outback, so actually the locums only covered the hospital for emergencies and recovering inpatient needs.

Ellie dreamed of the day their maternity unit was fully self-sufficient. She quite happily played with the idea that she could devote her whole life to the project, get a nurse manager and finally step away from general nursing.

She could employ more midwives like her friend and neighbour Trina, who lived in one of the cliff houses. The young widowed midwife from the perfect marriage who preferred night duty so she didn't lie awake at night alone in her bed.

She was the complete opposite to Ellie, who'd had the marriage from hell that hadn't turned out to be a marriage at all.

Then there was Faith who did the evening shifts, the young mum who lived with her aunt and her three-year-old son. Faith was their eternal optimist. She hadn't found a man to practise heartbreak on yet. Just had an unfortunate one-night stand with a charismatic drifter. Ellie sighed. Three diverse women with a mutual dream. Lighthouse Bay Mothers and Babies. A gentle place for families to discover birth with midwives.

Back to the real world. For the moment they needed the championship of at least one GP/OB.

Most new mums stayed between one and three nights and, as they always had, women post-caesarean birth transferred back from the base hospital to recover. So a ward round in maternity and the general part of the hospital each morning by the VMO was asked to keep the doors open.

The tense set of her shoulders gradually relaxed as she distracted herself with the chore she'd previously completed six times since old Dr Rodgers had had his stroke.

The first two locums had been young and bored, patently here for the surf, and had both tried to make advances towards Ellie, as if she were part of the locum package. She'd had no problem freezing them both back into line but now the agency took on board her preferences for mature medical practitioners.

Most replacements had been well into retirement age since then, though there had also been some disadvantages with their advanced age. The semi-bald doctor definitely had been grumpy, which had been a bit of a disappointment, because Dr Rodgers had always had a kind word for everyone.

The next had been terrified that a woman would give birth and he'd have to do something about it because he hadn't been near a baby's delivery for twenty years. Ellie hadn't been able to promise one wouldn't happen so he'd declined to come back.

Lighthouse Bay was a service for low-risk pregnant women so Ellie couldn't see what the concern was. Birth was a perfectly normal, natural event and the women weren't sick. But there would always be those occasional precipitous and out-of-the-ordinary labours that seemed to happen more since Ellie had arrived. She'd proven well equal to the task of catching impatient babies but a decent back-up made sense. So, obstetric confidence was a second factor she requested now from the locums.

The next three locums had been either difficult to contact when she'd needed them or had driven her mad by sitting and talking all day so she hadn't been able to get anything done, so she hadn't asked them back. But the last locum had finally proved a golden one.

Dr Southwell, the elderly widower and retired GP with his obstetric diploma and years of gentle experience, had been a real card.

The postnatal women had loved him, as had every other marriageable woman above forty in town.

Especially Myra, Ellie's other neighbour, a retired chef who donated two hours a day to the hospital café between morning tea and lunch, and used to run a patisserie in Double Bay in Sydney. Myra and Old Dr Southwell had often been found laughing together.

Ellie had thought the hospital had struck the jackpot when he'd enquired about a more permanent position and had stayed full-time for an extra month when the last local GP had asked for an extended holiday. Ellie

had really appreciated the break from trying to understand each new doctor's little pet hates.

Not that Dr Southwell seemed to have any foible
Ellie had had to grow accustomed to at all. Except his
love of surfing. She sighed.

They'd already sent one woman away in the last two
days because she'd come to the hospital having gone
into early labour. Ellie had had to say they had no locum
coverage and she should drive to the base hospital.

Croak... There it was again. A long-drawn-out, gut-
tural echo promising buckets of slime... She sucked in
air through her nose and forced herself to breathe the
constricted air out. She had to fight the resistance because her lungs seemed to have shrunk back onto her
ribcage.

Croak... And then the *cruk-cruk* of the mate. She
glanced at the clock and estimated she had an hour
at least before the new doctor arrived so she reached
over, turned on the CD player and allowed her favourite country singer to protect her from the noise as he
belted out a southern ballad that drowned out the neigh-
bours. Thankfully, today, her only maternity patient had
brought her the latest CD from the large town an hour
away where she'd gone for her repeat Caesarean birth.

It was only rarely, after prolonged rain, that the frogs
gave her such a hard time. They'd had a week of down-
pours. Of course frogs were about. They'd stop soon.
The rain had probably washed away the solution of salt
water she'd sprayed around the outside of the ward window, so she'd do it again this afternoon.

One of the bonuses of her tiny croft cottage on top
of the cliff was that, up there, the salt-laden spray from

waves crashing against the rocks below drove the amphibians away.

She knew it was ridiculous to have a phobia about frogs, but she had suffered with it since she was little. It was inextricably connected to the time not long after her mother had died. She knew perfectly well it was irrational.

She had listened to the tapes, seen the psychologist, had even been transported by hypnosis to the causative events in an attempt to reprogram her response. That had actually made it worse, because now she had the childhood nightmares back that hadn't plagued her for years.

Basically slimy, web-footed frogs with fat throats that ballooned hideously when they croaked made her palms sweat and her heart beat like a drum in her chest. And the nightmares made her weep with grief in her sleep.

Unfortunately, down in the hollow where the old hospital nestled among well-grown shrubs and an enticing tinge of dampness after rain, the frogs were very happy to congregate. Her only snake in Eden. Actually, she could do with a big, quiet carpet snake that enjoyed green entrées. That could be the answer. She had no phobia of snakes.

But those frogs that slipped insidiously into the hand basin in the ladies' rest room—no way! Or those that croaked outside the door so that when she arrived as she had this morning, running a little late, a little incautiously intent on getting to work, a green tree frog had jumped at her as she'd stepped through the door. Thank goodness he'd missed his aim.

She still hadn't recovered from that traumatic start to her day. Now they were outside her window... Her hero sang on and she determined to stop thinking about it. She did not have time for this.

Samuel Southwell parked his now dusty Lexus outside the cottage hospital. His immaculate silver machine had never been off the bitumen before, and he frowned at the rim of dust that clung to the base of the windscreen.

He noted with a feeling of unreality, the single *Reserved for Doctor* spot in the car park, and his hand hovered as he hesitated to stop the engine. *Doctor*. Not plural. Just one spot for the one doctor. He couldn't remember the last time he'd been without a cloud of registrars, residents and med students trailing behind him.

What if they wanted him to look at a toenail or someone had a heart attack? He was a consultant obstetrician and medical researcher, for heaven's sake.

At that thought his mouth finally quirked. Surely his knowledge of general medicine was buried miraculously in his brain underneath the uteruses? He sincerely hoped so or he'd have to refresh his knowledge of whatever ailment stumped him. Online medical journals could be accessed. According to his father it shouldn't be a problem—he was 'supposed to be smart'!

Maybe the old man was right and it would do him good. Either way, he'd agreed, mainly because his dad never asked him to do anything and he'd been strangely persistent about this favour. This little place had less than sixty low-risk births a year. And he was only here for the next four weeks. He would manage.

It would be vastly different from the peaks of drama

skimmed from thousands of women and babies passing through the doors of Brisbane Mothers and Babies Hospital. Different being away from his research work that drove him at nights and weekends. He'd probably get more sleep as well. He admired his father but at the moment he was a little impatient with him for this assignment.

'It'll be a good-will mission,' Dr Reginald Southwell had decreed, with a twinkle in his eye that his son had supposedly inherited but that his father had insisted he'd lost. 'See how the other half live. Step out of your world of work, work, work for a month, for goodness' sake. You can take off a month for the first time in who knows how long. I promised the matron I'd return and don't want to leave them in the lurch.'

He'd grinned at that. *Poor old Dad.* It dated him well in the past, calling her a matron. The senior nurses were all 'managers' now.

Unfortunate Dad, the poor fellow laid back with his broken arm and his twisted knee. It had been an accident waiting to happen for his father, a man of his advanced age taking random locum destinations while he surfed. But Sam understood perfectly well why he did it.

Sam sighed and turned off the ignition. Too late to back out. He was here now. He climbed out and stretched the kinks from his shoulders. The blue expanse of ocean reminded him how far from home he really was.

Above him towered a lonely white lighthouse silhouetted against the sapphire-blue sky on the big hill behind the hospital. He listened for traffic noise but all he could hear was the crash of the waves on the cliff below and faint beats from a song. *Edge of Nowhere*. Not surprising someone was playing country music somewhere. They should be playing the theme song from *Deliverance*.

He'd told his colleagues he had to help his dad out with his arm and knee. Everyone assumed Sam was living with him while he recuperated. That had felt easier than explaining this.

Lighthouse Bay, a small hamlet on the north coast of New South Wales at the end of a bad road. The locum do-everything doctor. Good grief.

Ellie jumped at the rap on her door frame and turned her face to the noise. She reached out and switched her heroic balladeer off mid-song. The silence seemed to hum as she stared at the face of a stranger.

'Sorry, didn't mean to startle you.' A deep, even voice, quite in keeping with the broad shoulders and impeccable suit jacket, but not in keeping with the tiny, casual seaside hospital he'd dropped into.

Drug reps didn't usually get out this far. That deeply masculine resonance in his cultured voice vibrated against her skin in an unfamiliar way. It made her face prickle with a warmth she wasn't used to and unconsciously her hand lifted and she checked the top button of her shirt. Phew. Force field secure.

Then her confidence rushed back. 'Can I help you?' She stood up, thinking there was something faintly familiar… But after she'd examined him thoroughly she thought, no, he wasn't recognisable. She hadn't seen this man before and she was sure she'd have remembered him.

The man took one step through the doorway but couldn't go any further. Her office drew the line at two chairs and two people. It had always been small but somehow the space seemed to have shrunk to ridiculous tininess in the last few seconds. There was a hint of humour about his silver-blue eyes that almost penetrated the barrier she'd erected but stopped at the gate. Ellie was a good gatekeeper. She didn't want any complications.

Ellie, who had always thought herself tall for a woman, unexpectedly felt a little overshadowed and the hairs on the back of her neck rose gently—in a languorous way, not in fright—which was ridiculous. Really, she was very busy for the next hour until the elderly locum consultant arrived.

'Are you the matron?' He rolled his eyes, as if a private thought piqued him, then corrected himself. 'Director of Nursing?' Smooth as silk with a thread of command.

'Acting. Yes. Ellie Swift. I'm afraid you have the advantage of me.'

The tall man raised his eyebrows. 'I'm Samuel Southwell.' She heard the slight mocking note in his voice. 'The locum medical officer here for the next month.' He glanced at his watch as if he couldn't believe she'd forgotten he was coming. 'Am I early?'

'Ah…'

Ellie winced. Not a drug rep. The doctor. *Oops.*

'Sorry. Time zones. No Daylight Saving for you northerners from Brisbane. Of course. You're only early on our side of the border. I was clearing the decks for your arrival.' She muttered more to herself,

'Or *someone*'s arrival...' then looked up. 'The agency had said they'd filled the temporary position with a Queenslander. I should have picked up the time difference.'

Then the name sank in. 'Southwell?' A pleasant surprise. She smiled with real warmth. 'Are you related to Dr Southwell who had the accident?' At the man's quick nod, Ellie asked, 'How is he?' She'd been worried.

'My father,' he said dryly, 'is as well as can be expected for a man too old to be surfing.' He spoke as if his parent were a recalcitrant child and Ellie felt a little spurt of protectiveness for the absent octogenarian. Then she remembered she had to work with this man for the next month. She also remembered Dr Southwell had two children, and his only son was a consultant obstetrician at Brisbane Mothers and Babies. A workaholic, apparently.

Well, she certainly had someone with obstetric experience for a month. It would be just her luck that they wouldn't have a baby the whole time he was here. Ellie took a breath and plastered on a smile.

First the green frog jumping at her from the door, then the ones croaking outside the window and now the Frog Prince, city-slicker locum who wasn't almost retired, like locums were supposed to be.

'Welcome. Perhaps you'd like to sit down.' She gestured at the only other chair jammed between the storage cupboard and the door frame. She wasn't really sure his legs would fit if he tried to fold into the space.

He didn't attempt to sit and it was probably a good choice.

There was still something about his behaviour that

was a little…odd. Did he feel they didn't want him?
'Dr Southwell, your presence here is very much appreciated.'

It took him a couple of seconds to answer and she
used them to centre herself. This was her world. No
need to be nervous. 'We were very relieved when someone accepted the locum position for the month.'

He didn't look flattered—too flash just to be referred
to as 'someone', perhaps?

Ellie stepped forward. Bit back the sigh and the
grumbles to herself about how much she liked the old
ones. 'Anyway, welcome to Lighthouse Bay. Most people call me Swift, because it's my name and I move fast.
I'm the DON, the midwife, emergency resource person
and mediator between the medical staff and the nursing
staff.' She held out her hand. He looked at her blankly.
What? Perhaps a sense of humour was too much to
hope for.

His expression slowly changed to one of polite query.
'Do they need mediation?' He didn't take her hand and
she lowered it slowly. Strange, strange man. Ellie stifled
another sigh. Being on the back foot already like this
was not a good sign.

'It was a joke, sorry.' She didn't say, *'J. O. K. E.,'*
though she was beginning to think he might need it
spelled out for him. She switched to her best professional mode. The experience of fitting in at out-of-the-
way little hospitals had dispatched any pretensions she
might have had that a matron was anyone but the person who did all the things other people didn't want to
do. It had also taught her to be all things to all people.

Ellie usually enjoyed meeting new staff. It wasn't

something that happened too often at their small hospital until Dr Rodgers had retired.

Lighthouse Bay was a place more suited to farming on the hills and in the ocean, where the inhabitants retreated from society, though there were some very trendy boutique industries popping up. Little coffee plantations. Lavender farms. Online boutiques run by corporate women retreating from the cities looking for a sea change.

Which was where Ellie's new clientele for Maternity rose from. Women with considered ideas on how and where they wanted to have their babies. But the town's reliable weekend doctor had needed to move indefinitely for medical treatment and Ellie was trying to hold it all together.

The local farming families and small niche businesses were salt-of-the-earth friendly. She was renovating her tiny one-roomed cottage that perched with two other similar crofts like a flock of seabirds on the cliff overlooking the bay. She'd found the perfect place to forget what a fool she'd been and perfect also for avoiding such a disaster again.

Ellie dreamed of dispensing with the need for doctors at all. But at the moment she needed one supporting GP obstetrician at least to call on for emergencies. Maybe she could pick this guy's brains for ways to circumvent that.

She glanced at the man in front of her—experience in a suit. But not big on conversation. Still, she was tenacious when there was something she wanted, and she'd drag it out of him. Eventually.

In the scheme of things Lighthouse Bay Maternity

needed a shake up and maybe she could use him. He'd be totally abreast of the latest best-practice trends, a leader in safe maternity care. He should be a golden opportunity to sway the sticklers to listen to the mothers instead of the easy fix of sending women away.

But, if he wasn't going to sit down then she would deal with him outside the confines of her office. She stood and slipped determinedly past him. It was a squeeze and required body contact. She'd just have to deal with it. 'Would you like a tour?'

Lemon verbena. He knew the scent because at the last conference he'd presented at, all the wives had been raving about the free hotel amenities and they'd made him smell it. It hadn't resonated with him then as it did now. Sam Southwell breathed it in and his visceral response set off rampant alarm bells. He was floundering to find his brain. There was something about the way her buttoned-to-the-neck, long-sleeved white shirt had launched a missile straight to the core of him and exploded, and now the scent of her knocked him sideways as she brushed past.

The way her chin lifted and her cool, grey eyes assessed him and found him wanting, giving him the ultimate hands-off warning when he hadn't even thought about hands on—hadn't for a long time until now—impressed him. Obviously a woman who made up her own mind. She wasn't overawed by him in the least and that was a good thing.

He stared at the wall where 'Swift' had stood a second ago and used all of his concentration to ram the feelings of sheer confusion and lust back down into the cave he used for later thought, and tried to sound at least present for the conversation. She must be thinking he was an arrogant sod, but his brain was gasping, struggling, stumped by the reaction he was having to her.

She was right. Being jammed in this shoebox of an office wasn't helping. What an ironic joke that his father had thought this isolated community would help him return to normal when in fact he'd just fallen off a Lighthouse Bay cliff. His stomach lurched.

He turned slowly to face her as she waited, not quite tapping her foot. He began to feel better. Impatience wasn't a turn-on.

'Yes. A tour would be excellent,' he said evenly. She must think he was the most complete idiot but he was working to find headspace to fit it all in. And he could work fast.

The place he could handle. Heck, he could do it in his sleep. He had no idea why he was so het up about it. But this woman? His reaction to her? A damnably different kettle of fish. Disturbing. As in, deeply and diabolically disturbing.

'How many beds do you have here?' A sudden picture of Ellie Swift on a bed popped into his head and arrested him. She'd have him arrested, more likely, he thought wryly. He was actually having a breakdown. His dad was right. He did need to learn to breathe.

CHAPTER TWO

SAM HADN'T SLEPT with a woman for years. Not since his wife had died. He hadn't wanted to and in fact, since he'd used work to bury grief and guilt, with all the extra input, his career had actually taken off. Hence, he hadn't had the time to think about sex, let alone act on it.

Now his brain had dropped to somewhere past his waistline, a nether region that had been asleep for years and had just inconveniently roared into life like an express train, totally inappropriate and unwelcome. Good grief. He closed his eyes tightly to try and clear the pictures filling his head. He was an adolescent schoolboy again.

'Are you okay?' Her voice intruded and he snapped his lids open.

'Sorry.' What could he say? He only knew what he couldn't say. *Please don't look down at my trousers!* Instead he managed, 'I think I need coffee.'

She stopped. Dropped her guard. And as if by magic he felt the midwife morph from her as she switched to nurture mode in an instant. No other profession he knew did it as comprehensively as midwives.

'You poor thing. Of course. Follow me. We'll start

in the coffee shop. Though Myra isn't here yet. Didn't you stop on the way? You probably rushed to get here.' She shook her head disapprovingly and didn't wait for an answer but bustled him into a small side room that blossomed out into an empty coffee shop with a huge bay window overlooking the gardens.

She nudged him into a seat. Patted his shoulder. 'Tea or coffee?' It had all happened very fast and now his head really was spinning.

'Coffee—double-shot espresso, hot milk on the side,' he said automatically, and she stopped and looked at him.

Then she laughed. Her face opened like a sunburst, her eyes sparkled and her beautiful mouth curved with huge amusement. She laughed and snorted, and he was smitten. Just like that. A goner.

She pulled herself together, mouth still twitching. 'Sorry. Myra could fix that but not me. But I'll see what I can do.'

Sam stared after her. She was at least twelve feet away now and he gave himself a stern talking-to. *Have coffee, and then be* normal. He would try. No—he would succeed.

Poor man. Ellie glanced at the silent, mysterious coffee machine that Myra worked like a maestro and tried to work out how much instant coffee from the jar under the sink, where it had been pushed in disgrace, would equate to a double shot of coffee. She didn't drink instant coffee. Just the weak, milky ones Myra made for her from the machine under protest. Maybe three teaspoons?

He'd looked so cosmopolitan and handsome as he'd

said it—something he said every day. She bit back another snuffle of laughter. Classic. *Welcome to Lighthouse Bay.* Boy, were they gonna have fun.

She glanced back and decided he wasn't too worthy of sympathy because it was unfair for a man to have shoulders like that, not to mention a decidedly sinful mouth. And she hadn't thought about sinful for a while. In fact she couldn't quite believe she was thinking about it now. She'd thought the whole devastation of the cruelty of men had completely cured her of that foolishness.

She was going to have to spend the next month with this man reappearing on the ward. Day and night if they were both called out. The idea was more unsettling than she'd bargained for and was nothing to do with the way the ward was run.

The jug boiled and she mixed the potent brew. Best not to think of that now. She needed him awake. She scooped up two Anzac biscuits from the jar with a napkin.

'Here you go.' Ellie put the black liquid down in front of him and a small glass of hot milk she'd heated in the microwave.

He looked at it. Then at her. She watched fascinated as he poured a little hot milk into the mug with an inch of black coffee at the bottom.

He sipped, threw down the lot and then set it down. No expression. No clues. She was trying really hard not to stare. It must be an acquired taste.

His voice was conversational. 'Probably the most horrible coffee I've ever had.' He looked up at her. 'But I do appreciate the effort. I wasn't thinking.' He pushed the cup away. Grimaced dramatically. Shook his whole upper body like a dog shedding water. 'Thank God I brought my machine.'

She wasn't sure what she could say to that. 'Wow. Guess it's going to be a change for you here, away from the big city.'

'Hmm…' he murmured noncommittally. 'But I do feel better after the shock of that.'

She grinned. Couldn't help herself. 'So you're ready for the walk around now?'

He stood up, picked up the biscuits in the napkin, folded them carefully and slipped them into his pocket. 'Let's do it.'

Ellie decided it was the first time he'd looked normal since he'd arrived. She'd remember that coffee trick for next time.

'So this is the ward. We have five beds. One single room and two doubles, though usually we'd only have one woman in each room, even if it's really busy.'

Really busy with five beds? Sam glanced around. Empty rooms. Now they were in with the one woman in the single room and her two-day-old infant. Why wasn't she going home?

'This is Renee Jones.'

'Hello, Renee.' He smiled at the mother and then at the infant. 'Congratulations. I'm Dr Southwell. Everything okay?'

'Yes, thank you, doctor. I'm hoping to stay until Friday, if that's okay. There's four others at home and I'm in no rush.'

He blinked. Four more days staying in hospital after a caesarean delivery? Why? He glanced at Matron Swift, who apparently was unworried. She smiled and nodded at the woman.

'That's fine, Renee, you deserve the rest.'

'Only rest I get,' Renee agreed. 'Though, if you don't mind, could you do the new-born check today, doc, just in case my husband has a crisis and I have to go at short notice?'

New-born check? Examine a baby…himself? He glanced at the midwife. Who did that? A paediatrician, he would have thought. She met his eyes and didn't dispute it so he smiled and nodded. 'We'll sort that.'

Hopefully. His father would be chortling. He could feel Ellie's presence behind him as they left the room and he walked down to the little nurses' alcove and leaned against the desk. It had been too many years since he'd checked a new-born's hips and heart. Not that he couldn't—he imagined. But even his registrars didn't do that. They left it to Paediatrics while the O&G guys did the pregnancy and labour things.

'Is there someone else to do the new-born checks on babies?'

'Sorry.' She shook her head. 'You're it.'

He might have a quick read before he did it, then. He narrowed his eyes at the suspicious quirk of her lips. 'What about you?'

Her hair swished from side to side. He'd never really had a thing for pony tails but it sat well on her. Pretty. Made him smile when it swayed. He'd faded out again.

'I said,' she repeated, 'I did the online course for well-baby examination but have never been signed off on it. One of those things I've been meaning to do and never got around to.'

Ha. She thought she was safe. 'Excellent. Then perhaps we'd better do the examinations together, and at
least by the time I leave we'll both be good at them.
Then I can sign you off.'

She didn't appear concerned. She even laughed. He
could get used to the way she laughed. It was really
more of a chortle. Smile-inducing.

The sound of a car pulling up outside made them
both pause. After a searching appraisal of the couple
climbing out, she said, 'The charts are in that filing
cabinet if the ladies have booked in. Can you grab Josie
Mills, please?'

When he looked back from the filing cabinet to the
door he could hear the groans but Swift was already
there with her smile.

He hadn't seen her move and glanced to where she'd
stood a minute ago to check there weren't two of her.
Nope. She was disappearing up the hallway with the
pregnant woman and her male support as if they were
all on one of those airport travellators and he guessed
he'd better find the chart.

Which he did, and followed them up the hall.

Josie hadn't made it onto the bed. She was standing
beside it and from her efforts it was plain that, apart
from him, there'd be an extra person in the room in
seconds.

Swift must have grabbed a towel and a pair of gloves
as she came through the door, both of which were still
lying on the bed, because she was distracted as she tried
to help the frantic young woman remove her shorts.

In Sam's opinion the baby seemed to be trying to escape into his mother's underwear but Swift was equal

to the task. She deftly encouraged one of the mother's legs out and whipped the towel off the bed and put it between the mother's legs, where the baby seemed to unfold into it in a swan dive and was pushed between the mother's knees into Swift's waiting hands. The baby spluttered his displeasure on the end of the purple cord after his rapid ejection into a towel.

'Good extrication,' Sam murmured with a little fillip of unexpected excitement as he pulled on a pair of gloves from the dispenser at the door. Could that be the first ghost of emotion he'd felt at a birth for a long while? With a sinking dismay it dawned on him that he hadn't even noticed it had been missing.

He crossed the room to assess the infant, who'd stopped crying and was slowly turning purple, which nobody seemed to notice as they all laughed and crowed at the rapid birth and helped the woman up on the bed to lie down.

'Would you like me to attend to third stage or the baby?' he enquired quietly.

He saw Swift glance at the baby, adjust the towel and rub the infant briskly. 'Need you to cut the cord now, John,' she said to the husband. 'Your little rocket is a bit stunned.'

The parents disentangled their locked gazes and Sam heard their indrawn breaths. The father jerked up the scissors Ellie had put instantly into his hand and she directed him between the two clamps as she went on calmly. 'It happens when they fly out.' A few nervous sawing snips from Dad with the big scissors and the cord was cut. Done.

'Dr Southwell will sort you, Josie, while we sort the

baby.' Swift said it prosaically and they swapped places as the baby was bundled and she carried him to the re-suscitation trolley. 'Come on, John.' She gestured for the father to follow her. 'Talk to your daughter.'

The compressed air hissed as she turned it on and Sam could hear her talking to the dad behind him as automatically he smiled at the mother. 'Well done. Con-gratulations.'

The baby cried and they both smiled. 'It all happened very fast,' the mother said as she craned her neck toward the baby and, reassured that Swift and her husband were smiling, she settled back. 'A bit too fast.'

He nodded as a small gush of blood signalled the third stage was about to arrive. Seconds later it was done, the bleeding settled, and he tidied the sheet under her and dropped it in the linen bag behind him. He couldn't help a smile to himself at having done a tidy-ing job he'd watched countless times but couldn't ac-tually remember doing himself. 'Always nice to have your underwear off first, I imagine.'

The mother laughed as she craned her neck again and by her smile he guessed they were coming back. 'Easier.'

'Here we go.' Swift lifted the mother's T-shirt and crop top and nestled the baby skin-to-skin between her bare breasts. She turned the baby's head sideways so his cheek was against his mother. 'Just watch her co-lour, especially the lips. Her being against your skin will warm her like toast.'

Sam stood back and watched. He saw the adjust-ments Ellie made, calmly ensuring mother and baby were comfortable—including the dad, with a word here and there, even asking for the father's mobile phone to take a few pictures of the brand new baby and parents. She glanced at the clock. He hadn't thought of looking at the clock once. She had it all under control.

Sam stepped back further and peeled off his gloves. He went to the basin to wash his hands and his mind kept replaying the scene. He realised why it was different. The lack of people milling around.

Swift pushed the silver trolley with the equipment and scissors towards the door. He stopped her. 'Do you always do this on your own?'

She pointed to a green call button. 'Usually I ring and one of the nurses comes from the main hospital to be on hand if needed until the GP arrives. But it happened fast today and you were here.' She flashed him a smile. 'Back in a minute. Watch her, will you? Physiological third stage.' Then she sailed away.

He hadn't thought about the injection they usually gave to reduce risk of bleeding after the birth. He'd somehow assumed it had already been given, but realised there weren't enough hands to have done it, although he could have done it if someone had mentioned it. Someone.

As far as he knew all women were given the injection at his hospital unless they'd expressly requested not to have it. Research backed that up. It reduced postpartum haemorrhage. He'd mention it.

His eyes fell on Josie's notes, which were lying on the table top where he'd dropped them, and he snicked the little wheeled stool out from under the bench with his foot and sat there to read through the medical records. The last month's antenatal care had been shared between his father and 'E Swift'. He glanced up every minute or so to check that both mother and baby were well but nothing happened before 'E Swift' returned.

An hour later Sam had been escorted around the hospital by a nurse who'd been summoned by phone and found himself deposited back in the little maternity wing. The five-minute cottage hospital tour had taken an hour because the infected great toenail he'd been fearing had found him and he'd had to deal with it, and the pain the poor sufferer was in.

Apparently he still remembered how to treat phalanges and the patient had seemed satisfied. He assumed Ellie would be still with the new maternity patient, but he was wrong.

Ellie sat, staring at the nurses' station window in a strangely rigid hunch, her hand clutching her pen six inches above the medical records, and he paused and turned his head to see what had attracted her attention.

He couldn't see anything. When he listened, all he could hear were frogs and the distant sound of the sea.

'You okay?' He'd thought his voice was quiet when he asked but she jumped as though he'd fired a gun past her ear. The pen dropped as her hand went to her chest, as if to push her heart back in with her lungs. His own pulse rate sped up. Good grief! He'd thought it was too good to be true that this place would be relaxing.

'You're back?' she said, stating the obvious with a blank look on her face.

He picked up the underlying stutter in her voice. Something had really upset her and he glanced around again, expecting to see a masked intruder at least. She glanced at him and then the window. 'Can you do me a favour?'

'Sure.' She looked like she could do with a favour.

'There's a green tree frog behind that plant in front of the window.' He could hear the effort she was putting in to enunciate clearly and began to suspect this was an issue of mammoth proportions.

'Yes?'

'Take it away!'

'Ranidaphobia?'

She looked at him and, as he studied her, a little of the colour crept back into her face. She even laughed shakily. 'How many people know that word?'

He smiled at her, trying to install some normality in the fraught atmosphere. 'I'm guessing everyone who's frightened of frogs.' He glanced up the hallway. 'I imagine Josie is in one of the ward rooms. Why don't you go check on her while I sort out the uninvited guest?'

She stood up so fast it would have been funny if he didn't think she'd kill him for laughing. He maintained a poker face as she walked hurriedly away and then his smile couldn't be restrained. He walked over to the pot plant, shifted it from the wall and saw the small green frog, almost a froglet, clinging by his tiny round pads to the wall.

Sam bent down and scooped the little creature into his palm carefully and felt the coldness of the clammy body flutter as he put his other hand over the top to keep it from jumping. A quick detour to the automatic door and he stepped out, tossing the invader into the garden.

Sam shook his head and walked back inside to the wall sink to wash his hands. A precipitous human baby jammed in a bikini bottom didn't faze her but a tiny green frog did? It was a crazy world.

He heard her come back as he dried his hands.

'Thank you,' she said to his back. He turned. She looked as composed and competent as she had when he'd first met her. As if he'd imagined the wild-eyed woman of three minutes ago.

He probably thought she was mad but there wasn't a lot she could do about that now. Ellie really just wanted him to go so she could put her head in her hands and scream with frustration. And then check every other blasted plant pot that she'd now ask to be removed.

Instead she said, 'So you've seen the hospital and your rooms. Did they explain the doctor's routine?'

He shook his head so she went on. 'I have a welcome pack in my office. I'll get it.'

She turned to get it but as she walked away something made her suspect he was staring after her. He probably wasn't used to dealing with officious nursing staff or mad ones. They probably swarmed all over him in Brisbane—the big consultant. She glanced back. He was watching her and he was smiling. She narrowed her eyes.

Then she was back and diving in where she'd left off. 'The plan is you come to the clinic two hours in the morning during the week, starting at eight after your ward round here at seven forty-five. Then you're on call if we need you for emergencies, but most things we handle ourselves. It's a window of access to a doctor for locals. We only call you out for emergencies.'

'So do you do on-call when you're off duty?' He glanced at her. 'You do have off-duty time?'

Ellie blinked, her train of thought interrupted. 'I share the workload with the two other midwives, Trina and Faith. I do the days, Faith does the afternoons and Trina does the nights. We cover each other for on-call, and two midwives from the base hospital come in and relieve us for forty-eight hours on the weekends. We have a little flexibility between us for special occasions.'

'And what do you do on your days off?' She had the feeling he was trying to help her relax but asking about her private life wasn't the way to do that.

She deliberately kept it brief. Hopefully he'd take the hint. 'I enjoy my solitary life.'

She saw him accept the rebuke and fleetingly felt mean. He was just trying to be friendly. It wasn't his fault she didn't trust any man under sixty, but that was the way it was.

She saw his focus shift and his brows draw together, as if he'd just remembered something. 'Syntocinon after birth—isn't giving that normal practice in all hospitals?'

It was a conversation she had with most locums when they arrived—especially the obstetricians like him. 'It's not routine here. We're low risk. Surprisingly, here we're assuming the mother's body has bleeding under control if we leave her well enough alone. Our haemorrhage rate per birth is less than two percent.'

His brows went up again. 'One in fifty. Ours is one in fifteen with active management. Interesting.' He nodded. 'Before I go we'd better check this baby in case your patient wants to go home. I borrowed the computer in the emergency ward and read over the new-born baby check. Don't worry. It all came back to me as I read it.'

He put his hand in his pocket and she heard keys jingle and wondered if it was a habit or he was keen to leave. Maybe he was one of those locums who tried to do as little as possible. It was disconcerting how disappointed she felt. Why would that be? Abruptly she wanted him to go. 'I can do it if you like.'

'No.' He smiled brilliantly at her and she almost stumbled, certainly feeling like reaching for her sunnies. That was some wattage.

Then he said blithely, 'We will practise together.' He picked up a stethoscope and indicated she should get one too.

Ellie could do nothing but follow his brisk pace down the corridor to Renee's room. So he was going to make her copy him. Served her right for telling him she'd done the course.

In Renee's room when he lifted back the sheet, baby Jones lay like a plump, rosy-cheeked sleeping princess all dressed in pink down to her fluffy bloomers. Ellie suppressed a smile. 'Mum's first girl after four boys.'

'What fun,' he murmured.

He started with the baby's chest, listening to both sides of her chest and then her heart. Ellie remembered the advice from the course to start there, because once your examination woke the baby up she might not lie so quietly.

Dr Southwell stepped back and indicated she do the same. Ellie listened to the *lub-dub, lub-dub* of a normal organ, the in-and-out breaths that were equal in both lungs, nodded and stood back.

He was right. She'd been putting off asking some-one to sign her off on this. Before Wayne, she would have been gung-ho about adding neonatal checks to her repertoire. A silly lack of confidence meant she'd been waiting around for someone else to do it when she should really just have done this instead. After all, when she had the independent midwifery service this would be one of her roles.

By the time they'd run their hands over the little girl, checked her hips didn't click or clunk when tested, that her hand creases, toes and ears were all fine, Ellie was quite pleased with herself.

As they walked away she had the feeling that Dr Southwell knew exactly what she was feeling.

'Easy,' he said and grinned at her, and she grinned back. He wasn't so bad after all. In fact, he was de-lightful.

Then it hit her. It had been an action-packed two hours since he'd walked in the door. This physically at-tractive male had gone from being a stranger standing in her office, to coffee victim, to birth assistant, to frog remover, to midwife's best friend in a couple of hours and she was grinning back at him like a smitten fool. As if she'd found a friend and was happy that he liked her.

Just as Wayne had bowled her over when they'd first met. She'd been a goner in less than an evening. He'd twisted her around his finger and she'd followed him blindly until he'd begun his campaign of breaking her. She'd never suspected the lies.

Oh, yes. Next came the friendly sharing of history, all the warm and fuzzy excitement of mutual attraction, pleasant sex and then *bam*! She'd be hooked. The smile fell off her face.

Not this little black duck.

Ellie dragged the stethoscope from around her neck and fiercely wiped it over with a disposable cleaning cloth. Without looking at Sam, she held out her hand for his stethoscope. She felt it land and glanced at him. 'Thank you. I'll see you tomorrow, then, Dr Southwell.'

She watched his smile fade. Hers had completely disappeared as she'd looked up at him with the same expression she'd met him with this morning. Polite enquiry. He straightened his shoulders and jammed his hand back in his pocket to jingle his keys again.

'Right,' he said evenly. 'I'll go check into my guesthouse.' Without another word, he strode away to the front door and she sagged with relief.

Lucky she'd noticed what she'd been doing before it had gone too far. But at this precise moment she didn't feel lucky. She felt disheartened that she couldn't just enjoy a smile from a good-looking man without getting all bitter, twisted and suspicious about it. Wayne had a lot to answer for.

She did what she always did when her thoughts turned to her horrific marriage that really hadn't been a marriage—she needed to find work to do and maybe Josie or her baby could give it to her.

CHAPTER THREE

THREE NIGHTS LATER, alone in her big oak bed on top of the cliff, Ellie twisted the sheets under her fingers as the dream dragged her back in time. Dragged her all the way back to primary school.

Her respirations deepened with the beginning of panic. The older Ellie knew what the dream Ellie didn't. Her skin dampened.

Then she was back.

To the last day of compulsory swimming lessons she'd used to love. Now school and swimming lessons made her heart hurt. Mummy had loved helping at swimming lessons, had even taught Ellie's class the first two years, but now all they did was remind young Ellie how much she'd lost, because Mummy wasn't there anymore. Daddy had said Mummy would be sad that Ellie didn't like swimming now, but it made her heart ache.

And some of the big boys in primary school were mean to her. They laughed when she cried.

But today was the last day, the last afternoon she'd see the grey toilet block at the swimming pool for this year, and she pushed off her wet swimming costume with relief and it plopped to the floor. When she reached

*for her towel she thought for a minute that it moved.
Silly. She shook her head and grabbed for it again so
she could dry and get dressed quickly, or she'd be last
in line again and those boys would tease her.*

*Something moved out of the corner of her eye
and then she felt the cold shock as a big, green frog
leaped towards her and landed on her bare chest. She
screamed, grabbed the clammy bulk of it off her slimy
skin and threw it off her chest in mindless revulsion,
then fought with the lock on the change-room door to
escape.*

*The lock jammed halfway. Ellie kept screaming,
then somehow her fingers opened the catch and she
ran out of the cubicle, through the washroom and outside through the door—into a long line of stunned primary school boys who stared and then laughed at the
crying, naked young Ellie until she was swooped on by
a scolding teacher and bundled into a towel.*

*She wanted her mummy. Why couldn't she have her
mummy? It should be her mummy holding her tight and
soothing her sobs. She cried harder, and her racking
sobs seemed to come from her belly, even silencing the
laughing boys...*

Ellie sat bolt upright in bed, the sob still caught in
her throat, and shuddered. She didn't know why frogs
were so linked with her mother's death. Maybe it was
something she'd heard about her mother's car accident,
coupled with her childhood's overwhelming sense of
loss and grief—and of course that incident at the swimming baths hadn't helped—but she couldn't hear a frog
without having that loneliness well back up in her again.
It had become the spectre of grief. All through her

childhood, whenever she'd been lonely and missed her mother, she'd had the frog nightmare. She'd eventually grown out of it. But, after Wayne, it had started again.

She hadn't had the dream for a while. Not once since she'd moved here a year ago—and she hoped like heck she wasn't going to start having it repeatedly again.

She glanced at the window. It was almost light. She'd have time for a quick walk on the beach before she'd have to come back and shower for work. Find inner peace before the day.

Then she remembered the new doctor. Sam. Day four. One more day and then she'd have the weekend off and wouldn't have to see him. Was that why she'd had the dream? The problem was she liked him. And every day she liked him more. He was lovely to the women. Great with the staff. Sweet to her. And Myra thought the sun shone out of him.

Ellie didn't want to like Sam. Because she'd liked the look of Wayne too, and look where that had ended up.

Of course when she went down to the beach the first person she saw was Dr Sam. Funny how she knew it was him—even from the spectacular rear. Thankfully he didn't see her because he was doing what his father had done—watching the ocean. Sam's broad back faced her as he watched the swells and decided on where to swim. Then he strode into the water.

She walked swiftly along the beach, her flip flops in her hand, waves washing over her toes while she tried not to look as his strong arms paddled out to catch the long run of waves into the shore that delighted the surfers.

She couldn't even find peace on 'her' beach. She stomped up the curve of sand and back again faster than usual, deliberately staring directly in front of her. If she hadn't been so stubborn she would have seen that he was coming in on a wave and would intercept her before she could escape.

He hopped up from the last wave right in front of her. 'Good morning, Ellie Swift.'

She jumped. She glared at his face, then in fairness accepted it wasn't his fault she was feeling crabby. 'Morning, Sam.' Then despite herself her gaze dropped to the dripping magnificence of his chest, his flat, muscled abdomen, strong thighs and long legs, and her breath caught in her throat. Even his feet were masculine and sexy. *My goodness!* Her face flamed and she didn't know where to look.

Sam said, 'The water's a nice temperature,' and she hoped he hadn't noticed her ears were burning.

'Um…isn't it warmer in Queensland?' Her brain was too slow to produce exciting conversation.

He shrugged and disobediently her eyes followed the movement of his splendid shoulders despite her brain telling her to look away. He said, 'Don't know. I haven't swum in the ocean for years.'

That made her pause. Gave her a chance to settle down a little, even wonder why he hadn't been to the beach back home. She needed to get out of here. Create some space. Finally she said, 'Then it's good that you're doing it here. I have your father's surfboard up at my house. I'll arrange to get it to you. I'm late. See you soon.'

* * *

Sam stood there and watched her leave. He couldn't help himself and he gave up the fight to enjoy the sight. She had a determined little walk, as if she were on a mission, and trying hard to disguise the feminine wiggle, but he could see it. A smile stretched across his face. Yep. The receding figure didn't look back. He hadn't expected her to. But still, it was a nice way to start the day. Ellie Swift. She was still doing his head in. He had to admit it felt novel to be excited about seeing a woman again. Could it be that after only these few days here he was finding his way to coming back to life?

He hadn't made any progress as far as breaking through her barriers went. Maybe he was just out of practice. But the tantalising thing was that, despite coming from different directions, he sensed the rapport, their commonalities, the fact that inherently they believed in the same values. And he was so damnably attracted to her. He loved watching her at work and would have liked to have seen the woman outside work hours. He didn't understand her aversion to having a friendly relationship with him, but that was her right and he respected it. Thank goodness for work. He'd see her in an hour. He grinned.

Ellie disappeared from sight and Sam strode up the beach to scoop up his towel from the sand. He rubbed his hair exuberantly and stopped. Breathed in deeply. Felt the early sun on his skin, the soft sea breeze, and he glanced back at the water. The sun shone off the pristine white sand and the ocean glittered. He'd needed this break badly. He hadn't enjoyed the world so much as he had since he'd come here. Life had been grey and closed off to him since Bree's death.

The only light in his long days had been the progression of his patients' pregnancies to viable gestation—so that, even if the babies were born prematurely, it was later in the pregnancy and, unlike his and Bree's children, they had a fighting chance. Other people's surviving children had helped to fill the gaping hole of not having his own family.

Now this place was reminding him there was a whole world outside Brisbane Mothers and Babies. He really should phone his dad and thank him for pushing him to come here.

Thursday night, the nightmare came back again and Ellie woke, breathless and tear-stained, to the phone ringing.

That was a good thing. She climbed out of bed and wiped the sweat from her brow. She grabbed for the phone, relieved to have something else to drive the remnants of the nightmare away. 'Hello?' Her voice was thick and wavered a little.

'Sorry, Ellie. Need you for a maternity transfer. Prem labour.'

Her brain cleared rapidly. 'Be there in five.' That sounded much more decisive. She was in no fit state to walk in the dark but she'd have to. Hopefully a frog wouldn't do her in. Ellie dragged off her high-necked nightdress and pulled on a bra and trousers. Her shirt was in the bathroom and she stumbled through to get it, glancing at her face in the mirror. Almost composed.

But her hands shook as she buttoned her shirt all the way up. Damn nightmares.

She dragged her thoughts away from the dream. 'Who's in prem labour?' Ellie muttered as she ran the comb through her hair. The fringe was sweaty and she grimaced. It wasn't a fashion show and she'd find out who soon enough.

When she reached the hospital, swinging her big torch, she saw the Lexus. Dr Southwell. Trina had called him in as well.

If she thought of him like that, instead of as Sam, there was more distance between them and she was keeping that distance at a premium. That was what she liked about midwifery—nothing was about her. She could concentrate on others, and some 'other' must be well established in labour for Trina to call the doctor as well as Ellie.

She made a speedy pass of the utility vehicle parked at an angle in front of the doors as if abandoned in a hurry. Her stomach sank.

She recognised that car from last year because it had the decals from the fruit market on it.

Marni and Bob had lost their first little girl when she'd been born in a rush, too early. It had all happened too fast for transfer to the hospital for higher level of care, too tragically, and at almost twenty-three weeks just a week too early for the baby to have a hope to survive. Marni had held the shiny little pink body on her skin, stroking her gently, talking through her tears, saying as many of the things she wanted to say to her daughter as she could before the little spirit in such a tiny angel's body gently slipped away.

There had been nothing Ellie could do to help before it was too late except offer comfort. All she'd been able to do was help create memories and mementoes for the parents to take home because they wouldn't be taking home their baby.

Ellie had seen Marni last week. They'd agreed about the fact that she needed to get through the next two weeks and reach twenty-four weeks, how she had to try not to fear that she was coming up to twenty-three weeks pregnant again. That a tertiary hospital couldn't take her that early if she did go into labour. This was too heartbreaking. When Ellie walked into the little birth room her patient's eyes were filled with understandable fear that it was all happening again.

She glanced at Bob chewing his bottom lip, his long hair tousled, his big, tattooed hand gripping one of Marni's while the other hand dug into the bed as if he could stop the world if only it would listen. Old Dr Rodgers would have rubbed their shoulders and said he was so sorry, there was nothing they could do. So what *could* they do?

Marni moaned as another contraction rolled over her.

Sam looked up and saw Ellie, his face unreadable. He nodded at the papers. 'We're transferring. Marni's had nephedipine to stop the contractions and they've slowed a little. I've given IV antibiotics, and prescribed the new treatment we've just started at our hospital for extreme prematurity with some success, but we need to move her out soon before it hots up again. Are you happy to go with her?' There was something darkly intense about the way he said it. As if daring her to stand in his way.

'Of course.' What did he mean? If he was willing to try to save this baby and fight for admission elsewhere, she'd fly to the moon with Marni. But he knew as well as she did that most of the time other hospitals didn't have the capacity to accept extremely premature labour because they wouldn't be able to do anything differently when the baby was born. Too young to live was too young to live. 'They've accepted Marni?'

His face looked grim for a moment. 'Yes,' was all he said, but the look he gave was almost savage, and she blinked, wondering what had happened to him to make him so fierce.

'Ambulance should be here soon,' Trina said. She'd been quietly moving around Marni, checking her drip was secure, removing the used injection trays. She kept flicking sideways glances at Sam, as if he was going to ask her to do something she didn't know how to do, and Ellie narrowed her eyes. Had he done something to undermine her friend's confidence? She'd ask later.

Her gaze fell on the admission notes and she gathered them up to make sure she had the transfer forms filled out. She heard the ambulance pull up outside and didn't have the heart to ask Bob to move his car. They'd manage to work around it with the stretcher.

She rapidly filled in the forms with Trina's notes, added the times the medications were given and waved to the two female paramedics as they entered.

'Hello, ladies. This is Marni. Prem labour at twenty-three weeks. We need a quick run to the base hospital. I'm coming as midwife escort.'

One of the paramedics nodded at Marni. 'Hello.

Twenty-three?' Then a glance at Sam that quickly shifted on. 'Okey-dokey.' She said no more.

Ellie finished the transfer forms and disappeared quickly to pluck the small emergency delivery pack from behind the treatment room door just in case Marni's baby decided otherwise. She sincerely hoped not.

Four hours later Sam watched Ellie for a moment as she filled in paperwork at the desk. He had slipped in the back door from the main hospital and she hadn't seen him arrive, which gave him a chance to study her. Her swanlike neck was bent like the stalk of a tired gerbera. His matron looked weary already and the day had only just started. *His* matron? *Whoa, there.*

But he couldn't help himself asking, 'What time did you get back?' He knew the answer, but it was a conversation opener.

He watched the mask fall across her face. Noted he was far too curious about the cause of that wall around her and kept telling himself to stop wondering. Dark shadows lay beneath her eyes and her skin seemed pale.

She said steadily, 'Five-thirty. It was a lovely sunrise.'

Sam had thought so too—a splash of pink that had blossomed to a deep rose, and then a bright yellow beam soaring out of the cluster of clouds on the horizon over the ocean. The bay itself had already captured him, though he preferred to walk down on the pristine sand of the beach rather than along the cliff tops.

He hadn't been able to sleep after the ambulance had left so he'd sat well back from the edge on the small balcony that looked over the road and across to the headland. He'd spent time on the creakingly slow Internet catching up on his email.

By the time the ambulance had returned past his boarding house to drop Ellie back at the hospital, the sky had been pinking at the edges. She still had an hour before she started work and he'd wondered if she'd go in or if someone else would replace her after a call-out.

Now he knew. He was ridiculously pleased to see her and yet vaguely annoyed that she didn't have backup.

'How was Marni after the trip?'

Her face softened and he leant against the desk. Watched the expressions chase across her face whenever she let the wall down. He decided she had one of the most expressive faces he'd seen when she wasn't being officious. No surprises as to what she was thinking about because it was all out there for him to see.

'Of course, she was upset it was happening again. But the contractions slowed right off.' Concern filled her eyes and he wondered who worried about her while she worried about everyone else. He doubted many people were allowed to worry about her.

Her voice brought him back. 'How do you think she'll go?' She looked at him as if he could pull a miracle out of his hat. It was harder doing it long distance but he'd damn well try. Marni would have the benefit of every medical advance in extreme premature labour from his resources he could muster, every advance he'd worked on for the last four years, or he'd die trying. He wouldn't let *her* down.

'My registrar will arrange for the new drug to be forwarded to Marni and they'll start her on that. The

OG at the base hospital will put a cervical suture in tomorrow if she's settled. And she'll stay there in the hospital until she gets to twenty-four weeks, and then after a couple of weeks if everything stays settled she can come home and wait. I'll phone today and confirm that plan with the consultant, and will keep checking until she's settled and sorted.'

'What if she comes in again then? After she comes home?'

Then they would act as necessary. 'We transfer again. By then the baby will be at an age where he or she can fight when we get a bed in a NICU.'

'We didn't get to twenty-four weeks last time.' Worry clouded her eyes.

He resisted the urge to put his hand on her shoulder and tell her to stop worrying. He knew she'd push him away. But the really strange thing was that he even wanted to reach out—this need for connection was new in itself.

He had this! He'd never worried about a response from a woman he was trying to reassure before and wasn't sure how to address it. Or even if he wanted to. Instead he jammed his hand into his pocket and jiggled his keys while he kept his conversation on the subject she was interested in. 'With treatment and persistence, we will this time.'

'Then they're lucky you're here.' Now she looked at him in the way he'd wanted her to since he'd met her. But this time he didn't feel worthy.

But he forced a smile. 'Finally—praise. And now I'm going.' The sooner he did the clinic, the sooner he could come back and check on her.

* * *

Ellie watched him walk away. Marni was lucky. She didn't feel so lucky, because a nice guy was the last thing she needed. Why was he being so friendly? She couldn't trust him no matter how nice he was. He'd be here in her face for another three weeks, that was all. Then he'd never come back. Why had his father had to break his arm and send the son?

She closed the file with a snap. Life was out to get her.

She heard the plaintive thought even though she didn't say it out loud and screwed her face up. *Stop whining*, she scolded herself and stood up. *We are lucky to have him. Very lucky.*

But she couldn't help the murky thoughts that were left over from the nightmare. The next day was always a struggle when she'd had the dream. And sometimes it meant she'd get some form of contact from Wayne, as if he was cosmically connected to her dream state so that she was off-balance when he did contact her.

'Hello, my lovely.' Myra's cheerful voice broke into her thoughts and thankfully scattered them like little black clouds blown away by a fresh breeze. Then the smell of freshly brewed coffee wafted towards her from the stylish china mug Myra was holding out for her.

'I hear you had a call-out so I've brought you a kick-start. Though it's not much of a kick.' She grimaced with distaste at the sacrilege of good coffee. 'Half-strength latte.'

Ellie stood up and took the mug. The milky decoration on top looked like a rose this morning. Ellie blew a kiss to the silver-haired lady who always looked quietly elegant in her perfectly co-ordinated vintage outfits. She reminded Ellie of the heroine from a nineteen-twenties detective show, except with silver hair. Myra had said that the only things she'd missed when she'd moved to Lighthouse Bay from Sydney were the vintage clothes shops.

Ellie sipped. 'Oh, yum.' She could hug her friend and not just for the coffee. Myra always made her feel better. 'Just what I need. Thank you. How are you?'

'Fine. Of course.' Myra seated herself gracefully in the nurse's chair beside Ellie. 'I'm going away for the weekend, this afternoon—' she looked away and then back '—and I wondered if you'd feed Millicent.'

'Of course.' Myra's black cat drifted between both crofts anyway and if Myra was away Millicent would miaow at Ellie's front door for attention. 'Easily done. I still have tinned food from last time.'

'Thank you.' Myra changed the subject. 'And how are you going with our new doctor?'

Ellie took another sip. Perfect. 'He seems as popular with the women as old Dr Southwell.'

Myra looked away again and, despite her general vagueness due to lack of sleep from the night before, Ellie felt the first stirrings of suspicion. 'I know you like him.'

'Sam and I have coffee together every morning. A lovely young man. Very like his father. What do *you* think of him?' There was definitely emphasis on the 'you'.

Myra was not usually so blunt. Ellie's hand stilled as she lifted it to have another sip. 'He seems nice.'

'Nice.' Myra rolled her eyes and repeated, 'Nice,'

under her breath. 'He's been here for nearly a week.
The man is positively gorgeous and he has a lovely
speaking voice.'

Ellie pulled a face. Really! 'So?'

For once Myra appeared almost impatient. 'He's perfect.'

Ellie was genuinely confused. The cup halted halfway to her mouth. 'For what?' Maybe she was just slow
today.

Myra's eyes opened wide, staring at her as if she
couldn't believe Ellie could be so dense. 'For you to
start thinking about young men as other than just partners of the women whose babies you catch.'

'As a male friend, you mean? You seem awfully invested in this doctor.' A horrible thought intruded into
her coffee-filled senses. Surely not? 'Did you have anything to do with him coming here?'

Her friend raised one perfectly drawn eyebrow. 'And
what influence could I possibly have had?'

It had been a silly thought. Ellie rubbed her brow.
She tried to narrow her eyes to show suspicion but suspected she just looked ludicrous. The glint of humour
in Myra's eyes made her give up the wordless attempt.
So she said instead, 'You seemed pretty cosy with his
father last time I saw you.'

Myra ignored that. 'And what have you got against
young Dr Sam?' She produced a serviette, and un-
wrapped a dainty purple-tinted macaroon and placed
it precisely on the desk in front of Ellie. She must have
retrieved it from the safety of her apron pocket. The
sneaky woman knew Ellie couldn't resist them.

'Ooh, lavender macaroon.' Briefly diverted, Ellie put down her cup and picked up the macaroon.

Myra was watching her. She said again, 'He seems a conscientious young man.'

Ellie dragged her eyes from her prize. 'Think I said he was nice.' She looked at the macaroon again. She'd had no breakfast but was planning on morning tea. 'He's too nice.' She picked it up and took a small but almost vicious bite. Sweetness filled her mouth and reminded her how she could be seduced by pretty packages. Wayne had been a pretty package... Her appetite deserted her and she put the remainder of the biscuit back on the plate with distaste.

'Poor macaroon.' There was affectionate humour in Myra's voice. 'Not all men are rotten, you know.'

Ellie nodded. Myra always seemed to know what she was thinking. Like her mother used to know when she'd been a child. Ellie didn't want to risk thinking she was a part of Myra's one-person family. Myra would move on, or Ellie would, and there was no sense in becoming too attached. But she suspected she might be already. It was so precarious. Ellie could manage on her own very well. But back to the real danger—thinking a man could recreate that feeling of belonging. 'I've met many delightful men. Fathers. And grandfathers. The other sort of relationship is just not for me.'

'It's been two years.'

This was persistent, even for Myra. 'Are you matchmaking? You?' She had another even more horrific thought. 'Did you and old Dr Southwell cook this up between you?'

'I hardly think Reginald—whom I would prefer you

didn't call *old* Dr Southwell—would break his arm just to matchmake his son with the midwife at the hospital.'

Ellie narrowed her eyes. 'So neither of you discussed how poor Ellie and poor Sam could be good for each other?'

Myra threw up her hands in a flamboyant gesture that was a little too enthusiastic to be normal. 'For goodness' sake, Ellie. Where do you get this paranoia?'

She hadn't answered the question, Ellie thought warily, but she couldn't see why the pair of them would even think about her that way. She was being silly. Still, she fervently hoped Dr Southwell Senior hadn't mentioned her as a charity case to his son. That would be too embarrassing and might just explain his friendliness. A charity case...please, no.

Myra left soon after and Ellie watched her depart with a frown. Thankfully, she was diverted from her uncomfortable suspicions when a pregnant woman presented for her routine antenatal visit, so the next hour was filled. Ellie liked to add an antenatal education component if the women had time. She was finding it helped the women by reducing their apprehension of labour and the first week with the baby after birth.

Then a woman on a first visit arrived to ask about birthing at Lighthouse Bay instead of the base hospital where she'd had her last baby and Ellie settled down with her to explain their services. Word was getting out, she thought with satisfied enthusiasm.

The next time Ellie turned around it was lunchtime and she rubbed her brow where a vague headache had settled. She decided lack of sleep was why she felt a little nauseated and tried not to worry that it could be one of the twelve-hour migraines that floored her coming on.

Renee's husband arrived, armed with a bunch of flowers, and with their children hopping and wriggling like a box full of field mice, to visit Mum. The way his eyes darted over the children and the worried crease in his forehead hinted that Renee might decide to leave her safe cocoon early and return to running the family.

Ellie suspected the new mum was becoming bored with her room anyway and could quite easily incorporate her new princess into the wild household and still manage some rest.

It proved so when a relieved father came back to the desk to ask what they needed to do before discharge.

'It's all done. Renee has a script for contraception, baby's been checked by the doctor, and she's right to go.'

The relief in his face made Ellie smile at him despite the pain now throbbing in her head. 'Did you have fun with the kids, Ned?'

He grimaced. 'Not so much on my own. They've been good, but...'

Ned carried the smallest, a little carrot-topped boy, and an armful of gift bags out of the ward doorway with a new purpose and possibly less weight on his shoulders. Two more toddlers and a school-aged boy carrying flowers appeared from down the ward, with Renee bringing up the rear with her little princess in her arms, a wide smile on her face.

The foyer in front of the work station clamoured with young voices, so Ellie missed Sam as he returned from clinic and stood at the side of the room.

'Thank you, both,' Renee said. 'It was a lovely holiday.' She was looking past Ellie to the man behind her.

Ellie turned in time to see her new nemesis grin back. She didn't have the fortitude to deal with the 'charity' overtones left from Myra, so she turned quickly back again.

'I think you may be busy for a while,' Sam said to the mother.

Renee nodded calmly and then winked at Ellie. Lowering her voice, she confided, 'It does Ned good to have them for a day or two—lets him see what it's like to be home all day with the darlings in case he's forgotten.'

CHAPTER FOUR

THE AUTOMATIC DOORS closed behind the big family and they both watched them disappear. Sam turned and Ellie saw that flashing smile again. 'Imagine juggling that mob! It wouldn't be dull.'

There was a pause but she didn't say anything. She couldn't think of anything to say, which was peculiar for her, and had a lot to do with the fact that her vision had begun to play up. Small flashes of light were exploding behind her eyes. Migraine.

He filled the silence. 'Do you enjoy watching the women go home with their new babies?'

'Of course. That's a silly question!' He was looking at her with a strange, thoughtful intensity but she was too tired to work it out. She really wasn't in the mood for games. 'Don't you?'

'It isn't about me.' He paused, as if something was not right. 'I'm wondering why a young, caring woman is running a little two-bit operation like this in a town that's mostly populated with retirees and young families.'

Go. Leave me so I can will this headache away. Her patience stretched nearly to breaking point. 'Me?' She needed to sit and have a cup of tea and maybe a couple of headache tablets. 'Our centre is just as efficient as any other centre of care. What's the difference between here and the city? Are you a "tertiary hospital or nothing" snob?'

'No.' He looked at her. '"Tertiary hospital" snob?'

'Size isn't everything, you know.'

He raised his brows at her. 'I'm very aware of that. Sorry. I was just wondering when you were going to be one of these women coming in to have your perfect little family.'

That stung because she knew it wasn't a part of any future waiting for her on the horizon. Though it should have been. 'There is no perfect little family.'

She looked at him coldly, because abruptly the anger bubbled and flared and her head hurt too much to pretend it wasn't there. 'Where's your perfect little family? Where are your children?'

Lordy, that had sounded terrible. She felt like clapping her hand over her mouth but something about his probing was getting right up her nose.

He winced but his voice was calm. 'Not everyone is lucky enough to have children. I probably won't have any, much to my father's disgust. You're a midwife with empathy pouring out of every inch of you, just watching other women become mothers.'

Easily said. She closed her eyes wearily. 'There's no difference between you and me.'

He didn't say anything and when she opened her eyes he shook his head slowly. 'I saw the way you looked at Renee's baby. And Josie's. As if each one is a miracle that still amazes you.'

'And you?' She waved a listless hand. 'There's nothing there that spells "misogynist and loner".'

He physically stepped back. 'I really shouldn't have started this conversation, should I?'

'No.' She stood up and advanced on him. She even felt the temptation to poke him in the chest. She didn't. She never poked anyone in the chest. But the pressure in her head combined with the emotion, stresses, and fear from the last few days—fear for Marni's baby, her horrible fear of frogs and this man who was disrupting her little world—and she knew she had a reason to be running scared. Add lack of sleep and it wasn't surprising she had a migraine coming on like a fist behind her eyes.

Stop it, she told herself. She closed her eyes again and then looked down. She said with weary resignation, because she knew she was being unreasonable, 'Sorry. Can you just go?'

She didn't know how she could tell he was looking at her despite the fact she was considering his shoes. His voice floated to her. 'I'm sorry. My fault for being personal.'

That made her look up. He actually did look apologetic when it was she who was pouring abuse like a shrew and had lost it. Her head pounded. She felt like she was going to burst into tears. Actually, she felt sick.

She bolted for the nearest ladies' room and hoped like hell there wasn't a frog in the sink.

Afterwards, when she'd washed her face and didn't feel much better, she dragged herself to the door, hoping he had gone. Of course, he hadn't; he had waited for her outside in the corridor.

'You okay?'

'Fine.' The lights behind her eyes flickered and then disappeared into a pinpoint of light. She swayed and everything went dim and then black.

Sam saw the colour drain from Ellie's face, the skin tone leeching from pink to white in seconds. His brain noted the drama of the phenomenon while his hands automatically reached out and caught her.

'Whoa there,' he muttered, and scooped her up. She was lighter than he expected, like a child in his arms, though she wasn't a tiny woman with her long arms and neck that looked almost broken, like a swan's, as she lay limp in his embrace.

Unfortunately there was no denying the surge of protective instinct that flooded him as he rested her gently on the immaculate cover of the nearest bed. He'd really have to watch that. He was already thinking about her too much when he wasn't here, when in fact it was unusual for him to feel anything for anybody at all.

Her damn collar was buttoned to the neck again— how on earth did she stand it?—and he undid the first and second buttons and placed his finger gently against her warm skin to feel the beating of her carotid artery.

Her skin was like silk and warmer than he expected. She must be brewing something. Sudden onset, pallor, faint… He didn't know her but she hadn't struck him as the fainting type… Before he could decide what to do she groaned and her eyelids fluttered. Then she was staring up at him. Her blue eyes were almost violet. Quite beautiful.

'Where am I?'

He glanced at the sign on the door. 'Room one.'

She drew her dark brows together impatiently. 'How did I get here?'

'You fainted.'

The brows went up. 'You carried me?' He quite liked her brows. Amusing little blighters. Her words penetrated and he realised he was going mad again. She was the only one who did that to him.

He repeated. 'You fainted. I caught you. Can't have you hitting your head.' She struggled to sit up and he helped her. 'Slowly does it.'

'I never faint.'

He bit back the smile. 'I'm afraid you can't say that any more.'

She actually sagged a little at that and he bit back another smile. Behind her now not-so-tightly buttoned collar, which she hadn't noticed he'd unbuttoned, she wasn't the tough matron she pretended to be. She was cute, though he'd die rather than tell her that. He could just imagine the explosion. 'Stay there. I'll get you some water.' He paused at the door. 'Did you eat breakfast this morning?'

She passed a hand over her face. 'I can't remember.'

'I'll get you water and then I'll get you something to eat.' He could already tell she was going to protest. 'You made me coffee on Monday. I can do this for you. It'd be too embarrassing to fall into my arms again, right?'

She subsided. The fact she stayed put actually gave him a sense of wicked satisfaction that made his lips curve. *Tough luck. My rules this time.*

With a stab of painful guilt that washed away any amusement, he remembered he hadn't looked after Bree

enough, hadn't been able to save her, or his own premature children. But maybe he could look after Ellie—at
least for the month he was here.

He heard her talking to herself as he left. 'I'll have
to get a relief midwife to come in.'

He walked out for the water but didn't know where
to get the glass from. He'd have to ask her, so was back
a few seconds later.

She was still mumbling. 'I'll be out for at least twelve
hours.'

He stopped beside the bed. 'Does your head hurt?'

She glared at him. 'Like the blazes. I thought you
were getting water.'

'Cups?'

'Oh. Paper ones on the wall beside the tap.'

Ellie closed her eyes as Sam left the room. How embarrassing! She hadn't fainted in her life and now she'd
done it in front of a man she'd particularly wanted to
maintain professional barriers with. She'd never fainted
with a migraine before. Oh, goody, something new to
add to the repertoire.

Where was Myra when she needed her? She wished
Sam would just leave. Though when he returned with
the water she gulped it thirstily.

'Go easy. I don't have a bowl or know where they
live.'

Ellie pulled the paper cup away from her lips. He
was right. She was still feeling sensitive but her throat
was dry and raw. She sank back against the pillows.
She'd have to strip this bed because she'd crumpled it.

Maybe the weekend midwife could come early. This
afternoon. She'd meant to go shopping for food and now

she knew she didn't have the energy. She'd just hole up until tomorrow, when she'd be fine. The thoughts rolled around in her head, darting from one half-considered worry to another.

'Stop it.'

She blinked. 'Stop what?'

'Trying to solve all the logistical problems you can see because you do everything around here.'

'How do you know I'm thinking that?' It came out more plaintively than she'd expected. How did he know she did do most things?

He looked disgustingly pleased with himself. 'Because the expressions on your face mirror your every thought. Like reading a book.'

Great. Not! 'Well, stop reading my book.'

'Yes, ma'am.' But his eyes said, *I quite like it*.

She reached down into her fast fading resources. 'If you would like to help, could you please ask Myra to come around from the coffee shop?'

'Myra has left for the weekend. Going away somewhere. There's a young woman holding the fort, if you would like a sandwich.'

Her heart sank. Clarise… Clarise could make toast, which might help, but she'd have to do everything else herself. 'Already? Damn.'

'Can I do something for you?' He spread his hands. 'I've done all my homework.'

Ellie looked at him. Tall, too handsome, and relaxed with one hand in his pocket. Leaning on the door jamb as if he had all the time in the world. She had a sudden picture of him in his usual habitat surrounded by a deferential crowd of students, the man with all the answers, dealing with medical emergencies with swift decision and effectiveness. She had no right to give this man a hard time. Her head throbbed and the light was hurting her eyes. Now she felt like crying again. Stupid weakness.

His voice intruded on her thoughts and there was understanding in his eyes, almost as if he knew how much she hated this. 'You look sad. Is it so bad to have to ask me for help?'

My word, it is. 'Yes.'

Of course he smiled at that. 'Pretend I'm someone you hired.'

'I don't have to pretend. I did hire you.'

He laughed at that. 'Technically the administration officer hired me.'

'That would be me.'

'So what would you like me to do?'

She sat up carefully and swung her legs over the bed. He came in closer as if to catch her if she fell. It was lucky, because her head swam and she didn't want to smack the linoleum with her face.

'Just make sure I make it to the desk and the phone and the rest I can manage. Maybe you could stay in case anyone else comes in while we wait for my replacement. Even I can see there's no use me being here if I can't be trusted not to fall on my face.'

'Especially when it's far too pretty a face to fall on.'

She looked at him. Narrowed her eyes. 'Don't even go there.'

He held up his hands but she suspected he was laughing at her again. Together they made their way over to the desk and with relief she sank into her usual chair.

She reached into her handbag, pulled out her sunglasses and put them on. The pain from the glare eased.

It only took an hour for her replacement to arrive but it felt like six. She just wanted to lie down. In fact her replacement's arrival had been arranged faster than expected, and was only possible because the midwife had decided to spend an extra day at Lighthouse Beach, on the bay, before work.

Ellie had sipped half a cup of tea. She'd taken two strong headache tablets and really wanted to sink into her bed. Standing at the door with her bag over her arm, she wasn't sure how she was going to get up the hill to her croft.

'I'll drive you.'

He was back. And he'd read her mind again. She wished he'd stop doing that. He'd left for an outpatient in the other part of the hospital after Ellie had assured him she'd be fine until the relief midwife arrived and she had been hoping to sneak away.

She'd have loved to say no. 'If you don't mind, I'll have to take you up on that offer.'

'So graciously accepted,' he gently mocked.

He was right. But she didn't care. All she could think about was getting her head down and sinking into a deep sleep.

He ushered her to his car, and made sure she was safely tucked in before he shut the door.

'Do you always walk to work?'

'It's only at the top of the hill.' She rested her head back against the soft leather headrests and breathed in the aroma of money. Not something she'd sniffed a lot of in her time. 'I always walk except in the rain. It's a little slippery on the road when it's wet.'

'Did you come down in the dark, last night?'

She didn't bother opening her eyes. 'I have a torch.'

'You should drive down at night.'

Spare me. 'It's two hundred and fifty metres.'

He put the car into gear, turned up the steep hill and then turned a sharp left away from the lighthouse, onto the road with three cottages spaced privately along the headland. 'Who owns the other ones?'

'I'm in the first, Myra is the end one and the middle one is Trina, so try not to rev your engine because she's probably sleeping.'

'I'll try not to.' Irony lay thick in his voice. He parked outside the first cottage and turned the car off. She'd hoped she could just slip out and he'd drive away.

They sat for a moment with the engine ticking down. Ellie's headache had reached the stage where she didn't want to move and she could feel his glance on her. She didn't check to see if she was imagining it. Then she heard his door open and the car shifted as he got out.

When her door opened the cool salt air and the crash from the waves on the cliffs below rushed in and she revived a little.

Sam spoke slowly and quietly as if to a frightened child. 'If you give me the key, I could open the door for you?'

'It's not locked.'

'You're kidding me?' The words hung in disbelief above her. Apparently that concept wasn't greeted with approval. He said in a flat voice, 'Tonight it should be.'

She held her head stiffly, trying not to jar it, and

turned in the seat. She locked it at night but the day-time was a test for herself. She would not let her life be run by fear. 'Thank you for the lift.'

He put out his hand and Ellie wearily decided it was easier just to take it and use his strength to achieve a vertical position. Her legs wobbled a bit. He hissed out a breath and picked her up.

'Hey.'

'Hey, what?' A tinge of impatience shone through.

'You'll fall down if you try to walk by yourself.'

And then she was cradled tight against his solid warm chest and carried carefully towards her door. He leant her against the solid wood and turned the handle, then they were both inside.

Sam had expected the inside to be made up of smaller compartments but it was a big room that held every-thing. There was a tiny kitchen at the back with a chim-ney over the big, old wood-burner stove. A shiny gas stove and refrigerator stood next to it and a scrubbed wooden table and four chairs.

A faded but beautiful Turkish rug drew the sections of the home together in the middle where it held a soft cushioned sofa with a coffee table in front that faced the full-length glass doors out to sea. Bookshelves lined the rear walls and a couple of dark lighthouse paintings were discernible in the corners. There was a fireplace. A big red-and-white Malibu surfboard leant against the wall. His father's. He looked at it for a moment then away.

A patchwork-quilted wooden bed sat half-hidden behind a floral screen, pastel sheets and towels were stacked neatly in open shelves and across the room was a closed door which he presumed was the bathroom. Nothing like the sterile apartment he'd moved into after Bree's death and where he'd never unpacked properly.

The bed, he decided, and carried her across and placed her gently on the high bed's quilt.

'Come in,' she said with an exhausted edge to her voice as he put her down. Talk about ungrateful.

He stepped back and looked at her. She looked limp, with flushed spots in her pale face. Still so pale. Pale and interesting. She was too interesting and she was sick. He told himself she was a big girl. But that didn't mean he liked leaving her. 'Can I make you a cup of tea before I go?'

'No, thank you.'

He sighed and glanced at the room behind him again, as if seeking inspiration. He saw his dad's surfboard again. He'd said the midwife was minding it for him and that Sam should try it out. Maybe he would one day. But not today. It would be a good reason to come back.

He glanced through the double-glazed doors facing the ocean and he could imagine it would be a fabulous sight on wild weather days. But it was also too high up and exposed for him to feel totally comfortable. And she lived here alone.

He thought about the other two crofts and their occupants. It was a shame Myra was away.

'How about I leave a note for Trina and ask her if she'll check on you later?' *Before she goes to work for the night and leaves you up here all alone*, he added silently.

'No, thank you.' Her eyes were shut and he knew she was wishing him gone.

She was so stubborn. Why did he care? But he did. 'It's that or I'll come back.'

She opened her eyes. 'Fine. Leave a note for Trina. Ask if she'll drop in just before dark. I'll probably be fine by then.'

Sounded reasonable. Then she could lock the door.

That was all he could do. He saw her fight to raise her head and tilt it meaningfully at the door and he couldn't think of any other reason to stay.

He walked to the sink. Took a rinsed glass from the dish rack and filled it with water. Carried it back without a word and put it beside her. Then he felt in his pocket, retrieved his wallet and took out a business card. 'That's my mobile number. Ring me if you become seriously ill. Or if you need medication. I'll come. No problem.'

Then he tore himself away and shut the door carefully behind him, grimacing to himself that he couldn't lock it. Anybody could come up here and just waltz in while she was sleeping. Surely she locked it at night?

When he went next door and wrote on another of his business cards, he decided he should at least see if he could hear if Trina was awake. He walked all the way around the little house. Because he could. It was just like Ellie's, though there was a hedge separating them from each other and the cliff path that ran in front of the houses.

Anybody could walk all the way around these houses. The view was impressively dramatic, except he didn't enjoy it. The little crofts clung to the edge of the cliff like fat turtles and the narrow walkway against the cliff made his mouth dry.

At least the dwellings looked like they wouldn't blow off into the sea. They were thick-walled, with shutters tied back until needed for the really wild weather. Daring the ocean winds to try and shift them.

He was back at the front door again. No sounds from Trina's. She could sleep right through until tonight. He'd have to come back himself. Before dark, like Ellie had said.

Sam drove back down the hill to his guesthouse. He let himself in the quaint side entrance with his key and up the stairs to his balcony room. He threw the keys from his pocket onto the dresser, opened the little fridge, took out a bottle of orange juice and sipped it thoughtfully as he walked towards the windows.

She'd sleep for a while. He wished she'd let him stay but of course she'd sleep better without him prowling around. He knew it was selfish because if he'd been there he wouldn't have had to worry about her. Being away from her like this, he couldn't settle.

He felt a sudden tinge of remorse that made him grimace, an admission of unfaithfulness to Bree's memory. It hung like a mist damning him, because he was so fixated on Ellie, but also underneath was a little touch of relief that he was still capable of finally feeling something other than guilt and devastation.

His father would be pleased. He'd say it was time to let go of the millstone of his guilt over Bree, that it was holding him back and not doing the memory of their relationship justice. Was it time finally to allow himself the freedom to feel something for someone else?

His heartbeat accelerated at the thought but he told himself it would all be fine. He was only here for another few weeks, after all, and he'd be heading home after that. Strangely, the time limit helped to make him feel more comfortable with his strange urge to look after Ellie.

The sun shone and turned the blue of the ocean to a brilliant sapphire and he decided he'd go for another swim. No wonder his dad had raved about this place. Then he'd go back and check on Ellie after he'd showered.

CHAPTER FIVE

ELLIE HEARD SAM close the door when he left. She pulled
the blanket up higher to calm the shudders that wracked
her body. He'd been very good, and she should have said
thank you, but the headache had built steadily again. It
was easier to breathe in and out deeply, to make it go
away and wait for sleep to claim her, and then maybe
she'd wake up and all this would just have been a bad
dream. Her hair was heavy on her forehead and she
brushed it away. She was too disinclined to move to
take a sip of the water he'd put there. Mercifully, everything faded.

When she fell asleep she had the nightmare.

She moaned because her head hurt as well.

Slowly the afternoon passed. As evening closed in
the nightmares swirled around her, mixed themselves
with imagined and remembered events.

But while she slept her troubled sleep there were
moments when she felt safe. Moments when she felt a
damp, refreshing washcloth on her brow. She dreamt
she sipped fluid and it was cool and soothing on her
throat. Even swallowed some tablets.

The bad dream returned. Incidents from her time

with Wayne mixed in with it. Incidents from their spiral downhill flashed through her mind: cameos of her hurt and bewilderment when he'd barely spoken to her, mocked and ridiculed her...her phobia, her need for nurturing. Screaming he never wanted a family that time she'd thought she was pregnant. *All* she wanted was a family.

The dream flashed to the afternoon at the swimming pool again and she moaned in the bed. Twisted the sheets in her hand.

She fought the change room door. Ran into the boys outside...

She sobbed. She sobbed and sobbed.

'It's okay, sweetheart. Stop. My God. It's okay.'

The words were seeping through the horror and the mists of sweat and anguish. Sam's voice. His arms were around her. Her head was tucked into his chest, her hair was being stroked.

'Ellie. Wake up. It's a dream. Wake up!'

Ellie opened her eyes and a shirt button was pressing into her nose. A man's shirt.

'It's okay.' It was Sam's voice, Sam's big hands rubbing her back. A man's scent. So it must be Sam's shirt. Sam?

She was still foggy but clearing fast. What was he doing here? She pushed him away.

His hands moved back and his body shifted to the edge of the bed from where he'd reached for her. 'That's some nightmare.'

She brushed her damp hair out of her face, muttered, 'Why are you here?'

'Because Trina is at work, Myra's away and I wasn't sure you wouldn't get worse.'

He raised his brows and shook his head. 'You did get worse. It's almost midnight and you've been mumbling and tossing most of the evening. If you didn't get better soon I was going to admit you and put up a drip.'

Dimly she realised her head didn't hurt any more but it felt dense like a bowling ball, and just as heavy. It would clear soon, she knew that, but she couldn't just lie here crumpled and teary. The tendrils of the nightmare retreated and she wiped her face and shifted herself back up the bed away from him, pushing the last disquieting memories back into their dark place in her brain at the same time.

As she wriggled, he reached and flipped the pillows over and rearranged them so she could sit up.

Then he rose. She wasn't sure if that was better because now he towered over her, and it must have shown on her face, because he moved back and then turned away to walk to the kitchen alcove.

He switched on the jug, turned his head towards her and said quietly, 'Would you like a drink? Something hot?'

Her mouth tasted like some dusty desert cavern. She'd kill for a cup of tea. Maybe it wasn't so bad he was here. 'Yes, please. Tea?' She sounded like a scared kitten. She cleared her throat, mumbled, 'Thank you,' in a slightly stronger voice. She glanced down at her crumpled uniform but it was gone and she was in her bra and pants. Her face flushed as she yanked the covers up to her neck.

'You took off my shirt and trousers?'

'You were tangled in them. Sweating. I asked you and you said yes.'

She narrowed her eyes at him. 'I don't remember that.'

He came back with the mug of tea. 'I'm not surprised. You've been barely coherent. If that's a migraine, I hope I don't get one. Nasty.'

'I can't believe you undressed me.'

He waggled his brows. 'I left the essentials on.'

Her face grew even hotter. *Cheeky blighter.*

He put the tea down beside her. 'Do you have a dressing gown or something I can get you?'

'In the bathroom, hanging behind the door.' She took a sip and it tasted wonderful. Black. Not too hot. He must have put cold water in it so she didn't burn her tongue. That was thoughtful. While she sipped she poked his head into the little bathroom and returned with her gown.

Speaking of the bathroom… She needed to go, and imagined taking a shower. Oh, yes…that wouldn't go astray either if she could stay standing long enough to have it. The idea of feeling fresh and clean again grew overpoweringly attractive.

'Um… If you turn around, I'd like to get up.'

He considered her and must have decided she had more stamina than she thought she had because he nodded.

'Sure.' He crossed his arms and turned around, presenting his broad back to her. She shifted herself to the edge of the bed and swung her legs out. For a moment the room tilted and then it righted.

'You okay?' His voice came but he didn't turn. At least he played fair.

'Fine.' She took another breath, reached down and snatched clean underwear and a nightgown from the drawer beside her bed and stood up on wobbly legs. By the time she shut the door behind her in the bathroom, she was feeling better than she expected. *Good tea.*

By the time she showered and donned her night-dress and dressing gown again, she was feeling almost human.

When she opened the door the steam billowed into the room and for a moment she thought the cottage was empty. But he was sitting on the sofa with his head resting back and she remembered he'd been here all evening.

Guilt swamped her and she padded silently towards him to see if he'd fallen asleep. His eyes were definitely open as she tipped her head down to peer at him. There was a black cat at his feet. She'd forgotten Myra's cat.

'Did you feed Millicent?'

He patted the sofa seat beside him. 'Yes. She had sardines. You look better. I'll go soon, but first tell me about your dream.'

Instinctively she shook her head but she saw there were two cups and her teapot on the low table in front of him. She could do another civilised cup of tea after he'd been so good.

She remembered his arms, comforting her, making her feel safe, as though she were finding refuge from the mental storm she'd created from her past, and her cheeks heated.

She pulled her dressing gown neckline closer and

sat gingerly a safe distance along the sofa from him. 'Thank you for looking after me,' she said, and even to her own ears it sounded prim and stilted.

'You. Are. Very. Welcome.' He enunciated slowly as if to a child, and she glanced at him to see if he was making fun of her. There was a twinkle, but mostly there was genuine kindness without any dramatics.

She glanced back at the bed. It was suspiciously tidy. And a different colour. 'Did you change the sheets?'

'I did. The damp ones are on the kitchen chair. Where is your laundry in your little hobbit house?'

She had to smile at that. 'Does that make me a hobbit?'

'If so, you're a pretty little hobbit.'

'That's a bit personal between a doctor and a patient, isn't it?'

He waggled his finger, making the point. 'You are my friend. Definitely not my patient. I'm glad I didn't have to admit you.'

She wasn't quite sure how to take that and then he said very quietly, 'But listening to you suffer through those dreams was pretty personal. You nearly broke my heart.'

She moved to rise but he touched her arm. 'As your non-doctor friend, can I say I think now is a really good time for you to share your nightmares. Stop the power they have over you.'

She shivered but she subsided and glanced around the room. Anywhere but at him. The dish rack was empty. No dirty dishes. Distractions would be good. 'Have you eaten?'

He patted his flat belly. 'I ate early, before I came.

In case I needed to stay. But I've helped myself to your tea.'

His arm came out and quite naturally he slid it around her waist. Bizarrely her body remembered that feeling, although her memory didn't, as he pulled her snug up against his firm hip. 'Tell me. Was it frogs?'

She shuddered. 'It's a long story.'

She felt him shrug under her. 'We have many hours until morning.'

She looked at him. 'It's not that long a story.'

He chuckled quietly, and it was an 'everything is normal even though we are sitting like this in the dark' sound, and despite the unconventional situation she felt herself relax against him.

'I'm all ears,' he said.

She turned her head and looked at him. 'They're big but I wouldn't say you are *all* ears.'

'Stop procrastinating.'

So she told him about the frog in the change room at school and the boys and, hearing it out loud for the second time since the therapist, she felt some of the power of it drain away. It was a little girl's story. Dramatic at the time but so long ago it shouldn't affect her now. In the cool quiet of the morning, with waves crashing distantly, she could accept that the frog was long dead and the little boys were all probably daddies with their own children now. That quite possibly Sam's idea of repeating it now could have merit because it seemed to have muted its power.

He said thoughtfully, 'If you could go back in time, to the morning before that, if you could prepare that little girl in some way, how could you help that young Ellie? What would you tell her?'

She thought about that. Wondered about what the misty memory of her mother might have said to her as a little girl if she had known it was going to happen.

'The frog is more frightened than you are?' The words came from some distant place she couldn't recognise but with them came a gentle wave of comfort. Relief, even. She thought of the child that she had been all those years ago. Sad eyes under the pony tail, freckles, scuffed knees from climbing tress to get away from teasing boys.

'If I had the chance. That might help her,' she said, and looked at Sam.

Sam nodded and squeezed her shoulder. 'So it was the same dream. Over and over?'

She looked at the floor. 'The other one's an even longer story and I don't think I'm up to that tonight.'

He looked at her and she shifted under his scrutiny. 'Okay. So, will you invite me back?'

Why on earth would he want to come back after these last exhausting hours? 'For frog stories?'

He shrugged again. 'There doesn't have to be stories. Can't I come back because I'd like to come back?'

She felt the shift in herself. Felt the weight of his arm, suddenly unbearable. Could almost imagine the bricks all slamming together between them, creating a wall like a scene in a fantasy movie.

Her voice was flat. Different from what it had sounded like only minutes ago. There was no way he could miss the change. 'You live in Brisbane. Your world is different to mine. We'll never be friends.' She tried to shrug off his arm and after a moment he let it fall. He shifted his body away to give her space and she appreciated his acceptance.

He looked at her and suddenly she felt the wall go up from him as well. Contrarily, she immediately wanted the openness that had been there before. Served her right.

But his voice was calm. It hadn't changed like hers had. 'I disagree. Friends can be made on short acquaintance. I'd like to come back later today and just check you're okay.'

Was he thick? Or just stubborn? How did she say no after he'd sat up here and minded her? Made her tea? After all, he would be gone in a few weeks. 'Did you give me water and wipe my face?'

He nodded. 'I didn't think you'd remember that. You weren't awake.'

'There were parts of the dream that weren't all bad.' She looked at him. 'It gets cool here in the night. Were you warm enough?'

He gestured to the throw folded at the end of the sofa. 'If somebody had visited, they would have found a very strange man wearing a blanket.'

She digested that and said simply, 'Thank you.' She shook her head because she couldn't understand the mystery of his actions. 'Why did you stay?'

He shrugged. As if it was nothing special. No mystery for him. Lucky him. 'Because I didn't know if you would actually ring me if you needed help. You might have needed someone and I couldn't see anyone else coming.'

He'd stayed out of pity. The thought sat like dirty oil

in the bottom of her stomach. She shouldn't have been surprised, because she was alone. No family. No husband. 'So you felt sorry for me.'

Sam compressed his lips as if being very careful about what came out of his mouth. She could live with the truth as long as it *was* the truth.

'I had sympathy for you, yes. You were unwell. I hope you would have done it for me if the roles had been reversed.'

She thought about that. Narrowed her eyes. 'Maybe. That's a sneaky way of wriggling out of the "pity" accusation.'

He sighed. Stood up. 'I'm tired. And I might yet get called out. I'm going home. I'll drop back before lunch and see how you are.'

'You could just call me on the phone to check on me.'

He studied her. 'I'll drop back after I do a round at the hospital.'

She stood up, careful to keep distance between them. 'You don't have to do rounds on the weekend. Only if they call you.'

He shrugged. 'Patients are still there. I'll do a round every day unless I can't.' He gestured to the corner of the room. 'You should go back to bed. I think you'll sleep better now.' Then he walked to the door, opened it and quietly closed it after himself. She heard the lock click.

Sam walked away but his thoughts remained focussed on the little cabin on top of the hill. There was something about Ellie, and this place, that connected so strongly with his emotions. He didn't know what it was about her that made him feel so anxious to help. Shame he hadn't been able to break through the barriers to Bree the way he seemed to be able to with Ellie, especially as for the last few years he hadn't really connected to anyone. He glanced out over the bay as he walked down the hill to the hospital. The lighthouse seemed to look down on him with benevolence.

CHAPTER SIX

ELLIE WENT BACK to the bed. Climbed into the clean sheets that a man she'd only known for less than a week had changed for her. She saw the hospital corners and wondered who'd taught him to make a bed like that. It certainly wouldn't have been med school. She looked at the half-full glass of water he'd left her in a fresh glass.

Then she thought of the fact she'd been in her underwear when she'd woken properly, and wondered with pink cheeks when he'd undressed her. Had she helped him, or fought him, or been a limp lump he'd had to struggle with? Had she missed the opportunity of a lifetime?

She frowned at the random and totally inappropriate thought. How on earth would she face him? Then stopped herself. *It's done. You're not eight years old now.*

She considered the result of holding in the swimming pool incident for all those years and even now the tragedy was fading. When Sam returned to Brisbane she'd be able to thank him for that, too.

Her eyes closed and it didn't happen immediately but eventually she drifted off and, strangely, she didn't dream at all.

* * *

The next morning was Saturday. Ellie woke after the sun was well and truly up and lay with her eyes open for several minutes as she went over the recent events, both hazy and clear, and how a man who was almost a stranger had taken control of her world, if only for a few hours.

Even a few days ago the idea of that happening would have been ludicrous but in the cold light of day she could be grateful if a little wary. He'd been circumspect, really. Except for taking off her uniform but then she would have done the same if she'd been nursing someone in the throes of sweaty delirium. She tried not to think of stripping off Sam's shirt and trousers if he was sick—but the option to expand her imagination was tantalising her. *No!*

She glanced at the clock. Almost ten. He said he'd drop in after his weekend round.

When she put her feet on the ground her head didn't hurt. The headache had gone. It had disabled her but now her step was steady as she made her way into the bathroom with an armful of clothes.

By the time she came out, hair piled into a towel, teeth cleaned and mouth washed, she was starting to feel the emptiness in her belly and a hankering for fresh air.

As she opened the door to let the world in, Sam was standing outside with his phone in his hand.

That would be Sam who had seen her frogs and all. Sam who looked ridiculously handsome. Sam who'd carried her into her bed. 'Oh. Hello. Have you been here long?'

'Just a few minutes. I knocked and when you didn't answer I was going to ring you.'

She opened her eyes wide. 'Do you have my number?'

'The relief midwife gave it to me when I said I might check on you again.'

Confidentiality clauses and all that obviously didn't hold much water when it was Sam asking. Nice of her, she thought sourly. But sensible too. 'I'm much better, thank you.'

She examined him in the bright morning light. Tall. Smiling like he was glad to see her. She shied away from that thought. Not too many shadows under his eyes, considering his onerous midnight duties. 'How are you after spending the evening with a raving woman?'

'Starving.' He gestured to the plastic shopping bag that hung from his hand. 'Any chance of a table and chairs where I can lay this out?'

'Food?' Her stomach grumbled and heat ran up her cheeks. She peeked at him from under her eyelashes to see if he'd heard and saw he was biting his lip. She could see the dimple at the side where he was holding it in.

He'd heard her stomach. Not much mystery left about her for this guy. 'Okay. I'm hungry. So in that case you are very welcome.' Although as she said it she remembered she hadn't made her bed yet, then mentally shrugged.

He'd changed the blinking sheets. He'd survive an unmade bed. 'We'll take it through to the front deck. We can open the doors from the inside.'

Sam followed her and she was very conscious that the collar on her long-sleeved top wasn't as high as normal and there was some cleavage showing. Maybe she should put on a scarf? Again she reminded herself that he'd seen her in her bra and pants so any more than that was not a concern.

She sighed. He had the advantage of more knowledge of her than she had of him and she didn't like it. In fact she wasn't sure how she'd ended up with a guy who knew so much stuff about her and was walking around in her house like he owned it.

Before he followed her out onto the little veranda, he paused. 'Can I put my milk and cold things in your fridge? I came straight here from the supermarket, but have a few supplies for my flat as well.'

'Sure. There's plenty of room in the fridge.' Ellie winced a little at the hollow emptiness of the food supplies in her kitchen. She needed to shop and restock the cupboards herself.

When he'd done that he followed her to the balcony that overlooked the ocean. She noticed he hesitated at the door.

As he stood there he said quietly, 'Who built these cottages? The view is incredible.'

She stopped and looked in the direction he was looking, sweeping her gaze over the little cliff top that held the three tiny homes, the expanse of the sea out in front of them with the wheeling gulls and fluffy white clouds, the majesty of the tall, white lighthouse on the opposite ridge, which drew visitors on Sundays for lighthouse tours, its tiny top deck enclosed by a white handrail for the visitors as they examined the internal workings of the light through the windows.

'The cottages were built for three spinster sisters in

the middle of the last century. They were all nurses at the hospital down the hill.'

She laughed. 'Myra said that the three of us who live here now are modern day reincarnations. Their father ran the lighthouse and when they were in their mid-twenties the eldest came into some money and had the cottages built. There's only one of them alive now. I visit her sometimes in the nursing home. She's ninety and sharp as a tack. Just frail and happy to have other people make her meals now.'

'So they lived here, unmarried, until they were too old and then they moved out?'

'Yep. Fabulous, isn't it?' There were privacy hedges between the three dwellings. In the past the sisters had kept the hedge levels down below waist height but since she'd moved in they'd grown and it was their own little private promontory over the ocean. She loved it. She moved to the edge and peered out at a ship that was far away on the horizon.

When she turned back she could see that Sam was looking uncomfortable and she glanced around to see why. 'You okay?'

'Not a fan of being at the edge of heights.'

'Oh.' The last thing she'd do was make someone with a phobia uncomfortable. 'We'll go back inside, then.'

'No. Just sit me on this side of the table and I'll be fine.' He lifted the bags up and placed them on the little outdoor table. 'It's perfect here.'

She smiled at him. 'As we dwell in Phobia Central.'

For some silly reason she felt closer to him because he'd admitted to having a weakness for heights. It made her feel not so stupid with her phobia of frogs. She had a sudden horrid thought that perhaps he'd made that up, just to get into her good graces, and then pushed the thought away.

Wayne had done that.

But Sam was not like Wayne. She pushed harder on the thought and it bobbed around in her mind like a cork in a bathtub. She couldn't make it stay down. Sam was not like Wayne, she repeated to herself. Sam told the truth. She hoped.

As if he could read her thoughts, Sam said, 'My aversion to heights is not quite a phobia but I might not be particularly keen to fix the aerial on the roof.'

Somehow, that helped. 'And I'll never be a plumber because of the frogs. You're a good doctor. That's enough.'

'I'm a doctor but not your doctor.' He grinned at her. 'That said, I'm pretty impressed with your recovery mechanism.'

She shrugged. 'I don't get many migraines but when I do get one it's bad.' She didn't add that they usually came after she had the nightmare, or had forced contact with Wayne, and that she'd had fewer nightmares and migraines since she'd shaken him off her trail.

'I can see they wipe you out. If it happens again, you could call me.'

Yeah, right. 'All the way from Brisbane?' She raised her brows at him. At least she knew he was joking. 'Good to know.'

She began laying out the fresh rolls and ham as she reminded herself he'd be gone in a few weeks. Maybe she could just enjoy his company while she had it. It was the first time she'd had a man in her house to share lunch since she'd moved in. Not that she could take any credit for him being here. The only reason it had happened was because he'd invited himself.

It was strange but pleasant. Mostly because she knew it was just a window of opportunity that would close soon when he went back to where he'd come from. Back to his busy trendy life with its 'double shot espresso and milk on the side' lifestyle.

Sam paused as if to say something but didn't. Instead he opened a tray of strawberries and blueberries and produced a tub of Greek yoghurt. 'I'll grab the plates and spoons.' He headed back inside and Ellie looked after him.

'I guess you know where they are,' she murmured more to herself. Then she lifted her voice. 'And grab the butter out of the fridge, please.'

This was all very domestic. Apparently there was nothing like being undressed when semi-delirious for breaking down barriers. But what was she supposed to say? *No. That's my kitchen! Stay out!*

Sam was back while she was still staring after him and mulling over the phenomenon of his intrusion into her world.

He looked so at ease. 'You're very domesticated. Why aren't you married?'

His face stilled. 'My wife died four years ago. It's unlikely I'll marry again.' Then he looked down at the food in his hands.

Oh, heck. 'I'm sorry.' Then added almost to herself, 'Don't you hate that?' The last words fell out as if she hadn't already put her foot in her mouth enough.

He looked up. 'Hate what? When wives die?' He was

looking at her quizzically, when really she deserved disapproval. But underneath the lightness of tone was another wall. She could see it as plain as the sun on the ocean below. She knew about walls.

She'd done it again. Talk about lacking tact. She'd said what she thought without thinking. She wasn't usually so socially inept but there was something about this fledgling relationship… She paused at that thought and shied away, slightly horrified.

Anyway… 'I'm making it worse. Of course it's terrible your wife died, but I meant when you ask a question and the worst possible scenario comes back at you and you wished you'd never opened your mouth.'

'I know what you mean. Forget it. A *Monty Python* moment.'

His eyes were shadowed and she hesitated. His wife must have been young. She couldn't help herself.

'How did your wife die?'

He looked up, studied her and then glanced away. 'I'll tell you some time.' Then without looking at her, 'Why do people ask that?'

Now she felt even more inept. Crass. He had answered her and deserved an answer himself. 'I don't know. Curiosity. Because they're afraid of their own mortality?'

That made him look up. 'Are you afraid of your own mortality?'

She shrugged. 'That's a heavy question for eleven in the morning.'

'Heavy question any time of the day,' he said quietly.

The silence lay thick between them. He straightened and looked like he'd wait all day until she answered.

So she did. 'No. I'm not afraid to die. I'm not that special that the world will weep when I'm gone.'

A flash of what looked like pain crossed his face. 'Don't say that. Don't ever say that. Everyone is special and the world will always weep when someone leaves it.'

A breeze tickled her neck from the ocean and she shivered. This conversation was the pits. 'Can we just talk about the weather?'

He stopped. He looked at her and then slowly he smiled, mocking them both. 'Sure. There's a very nice ocean breeze sitting out here.'

She smiled at him primly. Relief rolled over her like one of those swells away down below running in towards the cliffs. A hump. They'd managed to get over a hump. One that she'd caused. 'I like the way the clouds make shadow patterns on the ocean.'

He glanced at the blue expanse a long way below, then away. 'Yes, very nice.'

She looked at the food spread out. Okay. Now it was awkward. 'Eat.'

So they ate. Conversation was minimal and that kept them away from such topics as death and dying, which was fine by Ellie, and gradually their rapport returned and desultory conversation became easy again.

Sam said, 'Josie went home.'

She looked up. 'Did you do the new-born check?'

'Of course.' A pained look. 'Very efficiently.'

That made her smile. 'I have no doubt.' She took a bite of her roll and chewed thoughtfully. She swallowed, then said, 'When you return to your real world in your hospital will you make sure all of your registrars are proficient at checking new-born babies prior to discharge?'

He shrugged. 'There's a little less time for leisurely learning than there is here but I will be asking the question.' He pretended to growl, 'And they'd better be able to answer it.'

Which made her remember that he was a very distinguished and learned man, one many people looked up to, and she was eating rolls with him and treating him like a barely tolerated servant. *Oops.*

She put her roll down. 'Speaking of questions I've been meaning to ask… Do you know anything about midwifery-led birthing units? Do you think it would work here?'

He paused eating his own meal. 'I don't know. Work how?'

She shrugged, looking around for inspiration, how to explain her dream. 'It would be wonderful if we could provide a publicly funded service for pregnant women that didn't need locums.'

'Gee, thanks.' He pretended to be offended.

'Nothing personal. But cover isn't consistent.' She grinned at him. 'I'd like to see a proper centre for planned low-risk births here without having to rely on locum doctors to ensure we can have babies here.' She was gabbling. But she half-expected him to mock her and tell her she was dreaming, that big centres were more financially viable—although she already knew that. But he didn't mock her. She should have had more faith.

'There are models like that springing up all over New South Wales and Victoria.' He said it slowly, as if he was searching around in his mind for what he knew. Ellie could feel herself relax. He wasn't going to tell her she was mad.

He went on. 'Not so many in Queensland yet, but I'm hearing that mothers and midwives are keen. But you'd need more staff.' He gestured to the isolation around them. 'You're a bit of a one-man band here.'

She'd get help. She'd already had two nibbles from the weekend midwives to work here permanently. And why not? A fulfilling job right on the ocean and the chance to become a respected part of a smaller community wasn't to be sniffed at. Trina and Faith were also in.

'We may be a small band at the moment. Or possibly five women, anyway—Trina, Faith, and I and the weekend midwives from the base. If we changed our model of care we could attract more midwives. We would certainly attract more women to birth here if we offered caseload. Most women would love to have the option to have their own midwife throughout the whole pregnancy and birth. Then get followed by them for the next six weeks after the baby is born. It's a wonderful service.'

He studied her for a moment as if weighing up what he was going to say. 'It would be a great service.'

She sagged with relief.

Then he went on, 'Though it does sound demanding for the midwives, seeing as babies come when they want and pregnant women have issues on and off for most of the forty weeks. If one person was responsible for all that—and I imagine you'd have a caseload of about twenty women a year—it seems a huge commitment and would almost certainly affect your private life. Are you prepared for that?'

Private life? What private life. She was a Monday-to-Friday, love-my-job romantic. Not the other sort. But she didn't say any of that.

Instead she said, 'We are. And, paperwork wise, I have a friend who has just set up a service like that on the south coast. She said she'd come up and help me in the early stages. And Myra was a legal secretary before she bought her restaurant. She said she'd give me one day a week.'

'So you have gone into it a bit.' He nodded. Paused. 'And how are you going to deal with emergencies?'

'The same way we deal with them now—stabilise and transfer if needed. But the women will be healthy and the care will be excellent.'

'I have no doubt about that,' he said, and the genuine smile that accompanied the statement warmed her with his faith when he barely knew her.

This wasn't about her as a woman. This was about her as a midwife and she could take compliments about that. 'It's women's choice to decide how and where they want to meet their baby, and women here have been asking for that choice.'

It was so satisfying to have this conversation with somebody who at least understood the questions and the reasons behind them. So she didn't expect the turn when it came.

'Very ideological. So you're going to submerge yourself even deeper in these new families—be available for more times when you're needed—because in my experience babies tend to come in waves. Slow and then all at once. You'll be working sixty hours a week. Be the auntie to hundreds of new babies over the next thirty years.'

What was he getting at?'

Her smile faltered. 'I hope so.'

His brows were up. She didn't like the expression on his face.

'And wake up at sixty and say "Where has my life gone?"?'

'No.' She shook her head vehemently. 'I'll wake up at sixty and feel like I'm having a life that enriches others.'

The mood plunged with her disappointment. She'd thought he'd seen the vision but now he was looking at her like she needed psychiatric help. Like Wayne used to look at her. That was sad and it was stupid of her to have thought he would be different.

Ooh… Ellie could feel the rage build. Somewhere inside she knew it was out of proportion to what he'd said. That if she chose that path it didn't mean she'd never have a family of her own. But him saying that seemed to ignite her anger.

She leaned towards him. 'How is that different from your life? You said yourself you're probably not going to marry again or have children. Will you spend the next thirty years working? How is that different to me?'

He shrugged. 'I'm a man. It's my job to work till I'm sixty-five or seventy, so it should be rewarding.'

'You're a chauvinist. My working life deserves reward too. How about you stay barefoot and pregnant and make my dinner while I go to work? Is that okay?'

* * *

Sam had no idea how the conversation had become so heated. One minute it had been warm and friendly— she'd been gradually relaxing with him—and then she'd waxed on about giving the rest of her life to strangers like some first world saint and he'd found himself getting angry.

He needed to remind himself that he was a man who respected women's choices, and of course he respected her choice. She was right. He should recognise that what she wanted to do was parallel to his own ambition of single-minded dedication. And look how useless that had been for getting over Bree's death. Maybe it was because he did recognise himself in what she said that he'd reacted so stupidly to seeing it through her eyes.

He took one look at her face and concluded he needed to redeem himself fast or he'd be out on his ear with his blueberries in his lap.

He held up both hands in surrender. 'I'm sorry. I have no right to judge your life decisions. You should choose your path and do whatever fulfils you. Truce.'

Her open mouth shut with a click and he knew he'd just averted Armageddon. Wow.

She was a feisty little thing when she didn't like what he said. And, come to think of it, what the heck had come over him? If she wanted to grow old in this eyrie of a house, alone every night just living for her work, then that was her choice. A small voice asked if that wasn't his choice too. He might not live on top of a cliff, but it wasn't so different from his trendy city flat overlooking the Brisbane River that he barely saw and the twenty-four-seven availability he gave his own hospital.

He'd known her for less than a week and already he was sticking his nose in. Normally he didn't even see other people and what they were doing with their lives but the idea of Ellie's future life made him go cold. It sounded very like his and he wanted more for her. He shivered.

She sat stonily staring out over the ocean and he could discern the slow breaths she was taking to calm down. Typical midwife—deep breathing experts. His mouth twitched and he struggled to keep it under control. Imagine if she saw him laughing at her.

They were both being silly. Fighting about the next thirty years when they should be enjoying the present moment. He was here with a gorgeously interesting woman. He wasn't sure when she'd changed from pretty to gorgeous, but the word definitely fit her better. The sun was drying her dark hair, bringing out red highlights, and the ocean stretched away behind her. He liked the way her hair fell heavily on her neck when she didn't have it in the pony tail. He could remember the weighty silkiness of it in his hand as he'd held it off her face as he'd soothed her during her nightmare.

He remembered unbuttoning her shirt when she'd lifted her hand to her buttons as if the neckline and collar were choking her. He'd slipped the whole shirt off her shoulders, and she'd pushed at her buttoned work trousers, so he'd helped her with those too. She'd relaxed back into the cool sheets with relief and he'd covered her up, trying to blot out the delectable picture of her golden skin in lacy bra and briefs. Feeling a little apprehensive about what she'd say to him when she woke.

'You.' She turned towards him and his little flight

of fantasy crashed and burned. Apparently the deep breathing hadn't worked.

'Tell me how your wife died!' There was nothing warm and fuzzy about the request.

That snapped him out of his rosy fantasies and the guilt he mostly kept at bay from his failure to save Bree swamped him. He didn't know why he answered her.

'She killed herself.'

CHAPTER SEVEN

'IT LOOKED LIKE a parachute accident. Except she left a note.' He kept staring at his clenched fingers. Didn't look at her. He couldn't believe he'd said that to a stranger and opened himself up to the inevitable questions.

Ellie's voice was a whisper. 'Oh, heck.' Closer than before. 'Why would she do that?'

He figured he might as well get the rest out. Be done with it. 'Because we lost our third baby at twenty weeks' gestation and she said she couldn't go on.' His voice was flat because if he let the emotion in it would demolish him. His inability to help his own family had destroyed Bree. 'I was next to useless, and using work to bury my own grief, and she refused to talk about it together. We drifted apart. Each suffering in our own way but unable to connect. Then it was too late.'

Her voice was different now. Compassionate. 'Is that why you were so determined Marni be transferred?'

He jerked back to the present with the question. Her thought processes were way different to his. He took a deep breath of his own. Was that the only satisfaction he'd had in the last four years?

Sam thought about what she'd asked. It had kept him sane, having a mission. 'Probably. Since Bree died I've been working on a regime for women who have repeat extreme premature labours, and the results have been promising with the new treatments.'

When he looked up from his hands he saw she was beside him. Her voice was soft. 'Your way of managing the grief?'

'Or the guilt.' Why was he talking about this? He never spoke about Bree. Her hand touched his shoulder as she bent over him. It was feather-light but he felt the pressure as if it was burning into him like a hot coal through ice. Melting him.

'What was she like? What did she do? Your dad must have been upset as well.'

'Before the babies Bree was happy. A great paediatrician, wonderful with kids. Afterwards…' he paused and shook his head, speaking so quietly it was as if he'd forgotten she was there. 'She hid her depression using work too. We both did. She said she wanted more space. When she died my dad felt almost as bad as I did that we hadn't seen it coming. So it was tough for him as well.'

She leant her head down and put her face against his hair. 'I'm sorry for your loss.' Her lemony freshness surrounded him like angel dust as she reached down and hugged him.

Nobody had hugged him since Bree had died. His dad was more of handshake kind of guy and he didn't have any women friends. Then she slid her hands around his shoulders, pulled his head onto her chest and stroked his hair. Her hands were warm whispers of comfort, infused with empathy. 'I'm so sorry. But it's not your fault.'

He twisted his head and looked at her, saying very slowly and deliberately, his voice harsh and thick, 'You've got as much right to say that as I had to say you can't waste your life the way you're planning to.'

He thought she'd draw away at that. He hoped she would because the scent was fogging his brain and the emotions of the last few minutes were far too volatile for bodily contact. All those fantasies he'd been battling with since he'd arrived in this damn place were rising like mist off the ocean. She was holding him close. Pulling him in like a siren on a rock. Drowning him.

She pressed her face against his. 'I should never have asked. We're both too nosy.' She kissed his cheek as if she couldn't help herself. 'I'm sorry.'

If he'd thought her enticing while he watched her from a distance, up close she was irresistible. The scent of her, the feel of her, the warmth of her, was intoxicating, and when she leaned in to say something else he lifted his mouth and captured hers as it passed. She stilled—she tasted like the first day of spring.

She'd made it happen. The kiss had been an apology. A dangerous one. Kissing Sam was a mistake because when he kissed her back driving him away was the last thing on her mind.

Somehow she was on his lap, both her arms were around his hard shoulders, and he was holding her mouth against him with a firm palm to the back of her head.

Inhaling his scent, his taste, his maleness was glorious. The kiss seemed to go on and on even though it was only a minute. His mouth was a whole subterranean world of wonder. In heated waves he kissed her and she kissed him back in time to the crash of the ocean below—rising and falling, sometimes peaking in a crest and then drawing Ellie down into a swirling world she was lost in…one she hadn't visited before. Until the phone rang.

It took a few moments for the sound to penetrate and then she felt his hand ease back.

He pulled away but his eyes were dark and hot as he watched her blink. She raised her trembling fingers to her lips.

His voice was deep, too damn sexy, and he smiled at her in a way that made her blush. 'Your phone is ringing.'

She blinked. Scrambled off his lap. 'Right.' She blinked again and then bolted for the phone while all the time her mind was screaming, *what the heck made you start that?*

It was the weekend midwife, Roz. 'Can you come, Ellie? One of the holidaymakers from the caravan park is in labour. Just walked in. Thirty-five weeks. Twins. Feeling pushy. I'll ring the doctor next.'

'Twins! Sam's here. I'll bring him. We'll be there in three minutes. Get help from the hospital to make some calls. Get them to ring the ambulance to come ASAP.'

Ellie strode to the door where Sam was collecting dishes away from the edge from his side of the table. 'Let's go, Sam. Thirty-five-week twins. Second stage.' Ellie was pulling on her sneakers. She could put a surgical gown over her clothes.

Sam matched Ellie's calm professional face. 'My car's outside.'

They were there in less than two minutes. Just before they arrived, Sam said, 'Ellie?'

She looked at him. She was still off-balance but immensely glad her mind could be on a hundred things other than what position she'd been in and where that could have led only five minutes ago.

This was an emergency. She'd had two sets of twins when she'd been working with a midwife in the centre of Australia. She'd need to watch out for so many things in the coming hour. They had very little equipment for prems. They'd either have a birth of two premature babies here or a harrowing trip to the base hospital. Twin births could be tricky.

'Ellie?'

'What?'

Sam's voice was so calm. 'This is what I do. Thirty-five-week twins are fine. Not like pre-viable twins. Everything will be fine.'

Ellie felt the tension ease to a more useful alertness. He was asking for a little faith in the team. She smiled at him. 'Okay. You're right.'

A dusty campervan with flowers and a slogan painted on it sat haphazardly in the car park. There was no sign of anyone as they hurried through the doors to the maternity unit but sounds coming from the birthing rooms indicated action.

'We'll just use the one neo-natal resuscitation trolley. The other's too slow to heat up and warmth will be the issue.' Ellie was thinking of the babies. The twins could stay together if they needed help. They'd been closer than that inside their mum and might even comfort each other if kept together.

The obstetric part, Sam could handle. Thank goodness. The mother might not feel lucky at the moment but she was.

They entered the room one after the other and the relief on Roz's face would have been comical if the situation hadn't been so serious. 'Her waters just broke. Nine centimetres. At least it's clear and not meconium-stained.'

Then Roz collected herself. Glancing apologetically at the mother and father, she explained, 'Dr Southwell's an obstetrician from Brisbane Mothers and Babies, and this is the midwife in charge here, Ellie. This is Annette and Paul Keen.'

Everyone tried hard to smile at each other. Sam succeeded and Ellie gave them a wave on her way to sort out the required equipment in case they needed to resuscitate either baby or, heaven forbid, both.

Roz was reciting, 'Annette's twins were due in five weeks. They were packing up from the park to go home today. Labour started an hour ago but she thought she had a tummy bug because Paul had one a few days ago.'

Annette opened her mouth to say hello and changed it to a groan as the next wave of contraction hit her. She ground out, 'I feel like pushing.'

Sam stepped closer to the bed. He looked into the terrified woman's face as she sat high in the bed with lines of strain creasing her face and touched her arm. 'I'm Sam. It's okay, Annette, we've got this. You just listen to your body and your babies, let go of the fear and we'll do the rest. It's their birthday.'

Ellie's hands paused on the suction as she heard his voice and in that moment realised what she was missing in her life. A safe harbour. It would never be Sam, but just maybe someone somewhere might be out there for her, someone like this man who could invest so much comfort in words and took the time to offer them. Such a man would be worth coming home to. She wondered if he had always been such a calming influence. Whether he'd grown to understand a parent's fears since his own loss.

'It's my fault,' Paul mumbled from the corner of the room as he twisted his hands. 'I should never have pushed for this holiday before the babies were born. It's my fault.' Ellie glanced his way but it looked like nobody else had heard him.

Roz bent down and placed the little Doppler on Annette's stomach. First one and then, after she shifted to the other side of Annette's magnificent belly, another heartbeat echoed around the room.

Sam nodded, patted Annette's arm, turned, walked to the sink and washed his hands.

Ellie checked the oxygen and air cylinders were full and then moved to Paul's side. She spoke very quietly so no one else could hear. 'You heard the doctor, Paul. The time for worrying is gone. Now is the time to be the rock Annette needs you to be. Hold her hand. Share the moment. You're about to be a father.'

Paul's eyes locked on hers and he nodded jerkily. 'Right. Rock.' He looked at his hand and scurried over to his wife. He took up her fingers and kissed them. 'Sorry. Lost it for a minute.'

Annette squeezed his hand and Ellie saw the man's

fingers go white. Saw Paul wince as the pressure increased and with a smile her eyes were drawn to Sam as he stood quietly at the side of the bed with his gloved fingers intertwined, waiting. As if they had all the time in the world and this was a normal day. She felt the calm settle in the room and smiled quietly to herself.

Roz folded back the sheets to above Annette's thighs.

The first twin came quickly, a fine scattering of hair on her head, a thick coating of white vernix covering her back, and then she slipped into Sam's waiting hands. Not as small as they'd feared, probably over two thousand, five hundred grams, which was good for a twin.

The little girl feebly protested at the brush of air on her skin until Ellie wiped her quickly with a towel and settled her against her mother with a warmed bunny rug over her back. Annette's hands came down to greet her as she shifted the sticky little body so she could see her. The mother's face was round with wonder.

'Oh, my. Hello, little Rosebud.'

Ellie smiled to herself at the name, actually appropriate for the pink pursed mouth, and positioned the tiny girl strategically to make room for the next baby, making sure her chin was angled to breathe easily.

Ellie slipped a pink knitted beanie on the downy head. The soft cap was too big but would do the job of keeping her little head warm and slow the loss of heat. When she glanced at Paul, tears were sliding down his cheeks as he gazed in awe at his wife and new daughter.

Annette's brows drew together but this time she was confident. 'I need to push again.'

Paul started, and Ellie grabbed another towel and

blanket from the stack Roz had collected under the warmer. They all waited.

'This one's breech,' Sam said quietly.

The contraction passed and they all waited for the next.

Annette breathed out heavily and Ellie looked down and saw the little bottom and scrotum inching out, the cord falling down as the belly and back eased up in a long sweep. First one leg sprang free and then, finally, the other leg. It was happening so fast. The contraction finished and they all waited.

'Going beautifully,' Sam murmured two minutes later as the pale shoulders rotated and birthed one by one, followed by the arms, in a slow dance of angles and rotations that magically happened the way nature intended thanks to the curves of his mother's pelvis.

Ellie stood awed at how quickly the baby was delivering by himself.

Sam hadn't touched the torso. His gloved fingers hovered just above in case baby took a wrong turn as it went through the normal mechanisms and she remembered the mantra 'hands off the breech'. He was certainly doing that.

Then, unexpectedly, the rapid progress stopped. Annette pushed again. Just the head to come, Ellie thought. *Come on.* Annette was still pushing.

'Deflexed head,' Sam muttered and glanced at Ellie. He slipped his arm under the baby's body to support it and gently felt for the face with his lower hand. With the hand she could see he placed his second and fourth fingers on each side of the baby's nape at the back.

'Annette. We need to flex the baby's head for birth.

I'm going to get Ellie to push on your tummy just above the pelvic bone.'

Annette hissed an assent as she concentrated.

Sam went on. 'Ellie, palpate just above the pelvic brim. You'll feel the head. Lean on that ball firmly while I tip baby's chin down from here.' He glanced at Annette. 'Don't be surprised if baby needs to go to the resus trolley for a bit to wake up, okay?'

Paul's eyes widened. Annette nodded as she concentrated. Ellie could feel the solid trust in the room and marvelled how Sam had achieved that in so short a time. It was worth its weight in gold when full co-operation was needed.

Sam's firm voice. 'Okay, push, Annette. Lean, Ellie.'

Ellie did as she was asked and suddenly the head released. Baby's chin must have shifted towards his chest, allowing the smaller diameters of the head under the pubic arch and through the pelvis, and in a steady progression the whole head was born. Sam expelled a breath and Ellie began to breathe again too.

The little boy was limp in Sam's hands.

Paul swayed and Roz pushed the chair under him. 'Sit.' The dad collapsed back into the chair with his hand over his mouth.

Sam quickly clamped and cut the cord and Ellie reached in, wiped the new-born with the warm towel and bundled him up to transfer to the resuscitation trolley. 'Come over when you're up to it, Paul,' she said over her shoulder as she went.

Sam spoke to Roz. 'Can you take over here, Roz? Call out if you need me.' He followed Ellie.

Ellie hit the timer on to measure how long since

birth, and dried the new-born with another warm towel to stimulate him, but he remained limp.

Sam positioned the baby's head in a sniffing position and applied the tiny mask over his chin and nose. The little chest rose and fell with Sam's inflation of the lungs through the mask.

Ellie listened to the baby's chest. 'Heart rate eighty.' She applied the little pulse oximeter to the baby's wrist which would allow them to see how much oxygen from their lung inflations was circulating in the baby's body.

'Thirty seconds since birth,' Ellie said, and leant down to listen to his heart rate again, even though the oximeter had picked it up now. 'Seventy.' If the rate fell below sixty they would have to do cardiac massage.

'Okay,' Sam said and continued watching the steady rise and fall of the small chest. They both knew it wasn't great but it also wasn't dire yet. Babies were designed to breathe. Unlike adults, new-born babies needed inflation of their lungs to start, were respiratory driven, and even more important than cardiac massage was the initiation of breathing and the expulsion of the fluid from the untried lungs.

Ellie reminded herself she had great faith in the way babies had recovered from much more dramatic births than this one.

Sam continued with his inflations for another thirty seconds, Ellie wrote down the observations and finally the baby wriggled a tiny bit. Ellie felt the tension ease. 'Come on, junior.'

'His name is Thorn.' Paul was there and he wasn't swaying. He seemed to have pulled himself together.

'Come on, Thorn,' he said sternly, staring down at his son. 'This is your dad speaking. Wake up.'

Ellie decided it was just coincidence but Thorn's blue eyes opened at the command. The baby blinked and struggled and began to cry. The pulse oximeter rate flew from eighty to a hundred and thirty in the blink of an eye and Sam eased back on the mask.

'Well, that worked,' she said and smiled at Paul. A sudden exuberance was bubbling inside her and she looked across at Sam, who grinned back at her. She guessed he was feeling it too.

'Good work, Thorn,' Roz's relieved voice called across and Ellie heard Annette's shaky relief as she laughed.

Thorn was roaring now and, after a glance at Sam and catching his nod, Ellie scooped the baby up and carried him back to his mother. He was soon nestled in beside his sister on his mother's chest.

There was a knock on the door and one of the young ambulance officers poked her head in. 'Did you guys call us?'

Sam said, 'Thanks for coming. Transfer to the base hospital, thirty-five-week twins, but we'd like to wait half an hour—check the bleeding is settled and babies stable—if you want to come back.'

'We'll have coffee. Haven't had lunch. Ring us when you're ready.' She looked to the bed. 'Congratulations.' Then she disappeared.

Ellie decided that was eminently sensible. The impact of an urgent emergency transfer of all concerned would have ruined the moment when everyone was settled. More brownie points for Sam.

She wouldn't have taken the responsibility for delaying transfer but having an obstetrician on site made all the difference. It was fabulous for Annette and Paul to have a chance to collect themselves before they had to leave.

Roz was standing beside Annette, helping her sort the babies, and Sam and Ellie went over to the sink to strip off their gloves and apply new ones.

'Rosebud and Thorn,' Sam said in an undertone, and his eyes were alight with humour.

The names clicked. 'Cute,' she whispered back, grinning, and realised this was a moment she wasn't used to—savouring the feeling of camaraderie and a sudden urge to throw her arms around Sam and dance a little.

She whispered, 'That was very exciting and dramatic. Thank goodness everything is great.'

'Ditto.' Sam grinned at her.

Normally the nurse from the hospital disappeared as soon as the birth was safely complete, and most of the locums were burnt out and uninterested, so as soon as the excitement was over Ellie didn't usually have a third person to talk over the birth with. 'I'll remember that hint with the after-coming head if I have another unexpected breech delivery,' she said now, thinking back over Thorn's birth. The two breeches she'd been present at before had progressed to birth easily.

Sam nodded sagely. 'He was star-gazing. Silly boy. You have to keep your chin tucked in if you want your head to pop out.'

Ellie bit her lip to stop the laugh. Stargazing... A funny way to say it, but clear as a bell to her. She smiled up at him as the last of the tension inside her released.

She stayed with Roz in birthing until the ambulance officers returned. Thorn and Rosebud were positioned twin style at each breast and did an excellent job with their first breastfeeding lesson in life. Besotted parents marvelled, wept and kept thanking the three staff, so much so that Sam escaped from the room to write up the transfer papers.

Just under an hour after the twins were born, Ellie and Sam stood watching as they were loaded into the back of the ambulance.

'Come back and visit us next year when you come on your holiday. We'd love to see you all.' Ellie said.

She'd offered to go in the ambulance but Roz had laughed and said she should take the easy job and stay with the empty ward. Hopefully nobody would come in. Surely they'd had their quota for the week?

Which left Ellie and Sam standing at the door, waving off the ambulance.

As the vehicle turned out of the driveway Ellie told herself to keep her mind on what needed to be done but she could feel Sam's gaze. She kept her own on the spot where the ambulance disappeared and then suddenly turned away. Over her shoulder she said, 'Thank you. You were great. I'll be fine now.'

Sam didn't move. 'So I should go?' His voice was quiet, neutral, so she had to stop or it would have been rude. But her feet itched to scoot away as fast as she could because this man was the one she had kissed. On whose lap she had squirmed and wanted more. *Oh, my*—where was she supposed to look?

She didn't decide on flight quickly enough.

Still quietly, he said, 'You don't need me any more—

that right? And we both pretend this morning didn't happen? Is that what you want, Ellie?' She didn't say anything so he added, 'Just checking.' There was definite sardonic tinge to that last statement.

She forced herself to look at him. Maybe she could tell him the truth about Wayne. Because she wasn't going to pursue any crumbs of attention he wanted to give her for the next three weeks and it was all her fault this morning had got out of hand. Maybe she owed him that—telling him how she'd been made a fool of. Lied to. Ridiculed. Abused. She shuddered at the thought. Or perhaps she owed him an apology. She could do that at least.

'I'm sorry, Sam. I don't know what happened. It's all my fault, and I apologise. Can't we just blame the aftermath of my migraine for the strange behaviour on my part and forget it?'

He was studying her thoughtfully, and for so long that Ellie felt like an insect under a magnifying glass. Finally he said, 'What if I don't want to forget it? What if I want to hear the rest of your stories?'

Why would he want to do that? She couldn't do that. Should never have started it. 'You'll have to do without. Because there'll be no repeat.' She heard the finality in her voice and hoped he did too. 'I'd like you to go now, please.'

Sam looked at the woman in front of him and felt the frustration of the impenetrable wall between them yet again. The really disturbing thing was an inexplicable certainty that Ellie Swift wasn't supposed to be like this. It made no sense. He could very clearly see that underneath the prickly exterior and gazetted loner lay a warm and passionate woman he wanted to know more about. Wanted to lose himself in kissing again. And more.

That she'd had a disastrous relationship was of course the most likely reason she was like this. Underneath her armour lay something or someone who had scarred her and she wasn't risking that kind of pain again. He got that. Boy, did he get that. But it wasn't all about the frog phobia. There had to be something else.

But whether or not he'd get the opportunity to explore that conundrum and the tantalising glimpses of the woman who had reached down and kissed him with such sweetness was a very moot point.

Maybe he should just cut and run. Do what he always did when he felt things were getting too personal or emotional. But, for the first time since Bree had died, he wanted to explore the way he was feeling. Wanted to find out if this glimpse he'd had of a better life was real, or if he was just suffering from some unexpected aberration he'd forget about when he went back to the real world.

Maybe he'd better research his own reasons for pursuing Ellie first before he caused any more damage to this vulnerable woman in front of him, and it was only that overriding consideration which finally made him agree to leave. Since Bree's death he'd lost his confidence in his own emotional stability.

CHAPTER EIGHT

ELLIE WATCHED HIM go and, after having asked him to leave, now, conversely, wanted him to stay. It was the kiss that stopped her asking him to come back. Ellie had never tried to hurt anyone in her life before—so why had she hurt Sam by asking him so baldly about his wife? He was already punishing himself and didn't need her input. He'd been mortally wounded by his love—she knew how that felt—and she'd broken open his unhealed wound with her harsh request. He'd deserved none of it.

So she'd kissed him better—and to make herself feel better. Although 'better' wasn't really the right word for what she'd felt.

Ellie had an epiphany. She'd wanted to hurt him because that way she'd drive him away for her own safety—she'd had no kind thought for him.

And then they'd kissed and everything had changed. And she was running scared. It had all been pushed back by the birth of the twins but the reality was—things had changed.

Ellie sighed. It would have been good to talk more

about the birth. He could have stayed for that. And that was the only reason, she told herself.

She looked around the empty ward, disorientated for a moment. Then she busied herself pushing books across the desk.

It was Sunday tomorrow and she probably needed the space from this man. He was taking up too much room in her head. Luckily she had a whole day to get her head sorted by Monday.

She slowly turned towards the birthing unit and walked in to strip the bed. What a morning. Premature twins. That was a first for her since she'd arrived last year. Thank goodness everything had progressed smoothly.

She thought about Sam's expertise with Thorn's birth in the breech position. Sam's calmness. She wanted to cry, which was stupid. It was Sam's quiet confidence that had made them all seamless in their care and his rock-solid capability that made it so positive and not fraught as it could have been for Paul and Annette with a less experienced practitioner. How lucky they'd been that it had been Sam. She dragged her mind away from where it wanted to go.

She had to stay away from Sam's hands holding her, his lips on hers, their breaths mingled. No. If she let Sam in and he let her down like Wayne had, she suspected she'd never, ever recover.

She took herself into the small staff change room and opened her locker where she kept a spare clean uniform. She'd been stuck here before out of uniform and didn't like it.

She told herself that was the reason she needed more

armour. She took off her loose trousers and blouse and pulled on the fitted blue work trousers and her white-collared shirt and buttoned it to the top. Funny how she felt protected by the uniform. Professional and capable. Not an emotional idiot throwing out accusations and making stupid moves on men who were just being kind.

What an emotional roller coaster the last few days had been. And action packed on the ward.

By rights they should have no babies for a week or more because the ward had been too crazy since Sam had arrived. Maybe he drew the excitement to him like a magnet. She grimaced. He certainly did that in more ways than one and she needed to put that demon to sleep.

By the time Roz returned Ellie had the ward returned to its pristine orderliness, and the paper work sorted and filed. Ellie stood up to leave but Roz put her hand on her arm.

Looking a little worse for wear, Roz said, 'Please stay for a bit. Have a cup of tea with me. I'm bursting to talk about it. Not often you get to see twins born without any intervention. Wasn't Dr Sam awesome?' Roz's eyes were shining and she was obviously still on a high from the birth.

Ellie didn't have the heart to leave. She put the plastic bag with her bundled civilian clothes down.

'Sure. Of course. The jug's just boiled. I'll make a pot while you freshen up if you want?'

Roz nodded and Ellie had to smile at the bouncy excitement that exuded from her.

Roz was right. This was an opportunity to think about how they'd handled the situation, what they'd done well and what they could possibly have done better. All future planning for a unit she wanted to see become one of the best of its kind.

She couldn't believe Sam had driven all her normal thought processes into such confusion. *See?* She needed to stay on track and not be diverted by good-looking doctors who had the capacity to derail all her plans.

As Ellie made a pot of tea and brought two cups to the desk she knew with a pang of discomfort that a week ago Roz wouldn't have been able to drag her away from talking about the birth and the outcomes. Maybe it was just that she'd been sick. Maybe it had nothing to do with the fact that she was running scared because a certain man had disturbed her force field and anything to do with talking about him made her want to run a mile.

'I can't get over the breech birth.' Roz was back. Her hair was brushed, lipstick reapplied and she looked as animated as Ellie had ever seen her. She could feel the energy and excitement and welcomed the uncomplicated joy Roz exuded, because joy was dearly bought.

Yes. They should be celebrating. Every midwife loved the unexpected birth that progressed fast and complication-free with a great outcome. And when it was twins it was twice as exciting.

'I just feel so lucky I was here.' Roz's eyes were glowing and Ellie felt the tension slipping away. She was glad Roz asked her to stay.

Roz went on. 'But I was super-glad when you two walked in together. Especially since, the last time I saw you, you looked like death warmed up.'

Roz stopped and thought about that. 'Did you say on the phone you were together when I called?'

Ellie fought to keep the colour out of her cheeks. 'Dr Southwell had dropped in to ask if I needed anything. But I'm usually good when the migraine goes. It just takes about twelve hours. I'm feeling normal now.' Or as normal as she could, considering the emotional upheavals of the last few days.

Roz studied her. 'You're still a bit pale. And I shouldn't be keeping you here on your day off. Sorry.'

'No. It's good to talk about it. You're right. You did really well getting us here, and everything was ready. You must have got a shock when they walked in and you realised you were actually going to have the babies.'

Roz nodded enthusiastically, totally diverted from the how Ellie and Sam had walked in together. Thank goodness. Ellie returned her attention to Roz, cross with herself, as her brain kept wandering off topic.

'Paul was almost incoherent, Annette was still in the car and I didn't get that it was twins until she was in here and I saw how big she was. Then he said they were premature and she was booked in to have them at the tertiary hospital and I nearly had a heart attack. All I could think about was ringing you, and I was hoping like heck you'd be able to come.'

'I'm fine. But I guess we need to plan that a bit better for the future too. Maybe make a list to work down if one of the call-ins can't make it, rather than ringing around at the time when you have much better things to do than make phone calls.'

Roz nodded agreement. She said thoughtfully, 'I did get the nurse over from the main hospital, and she could have phoned around if needed.'

How it should be. 'That's great. And the babies came out well, which is always a relief.'

Roz frowned as she remembered. 'The boy was a bit stunned. Annette and Paul weren't the only ones worried.'

Ellie thought about Thorn as he'd lain unmoving under their hands, of Sam's presence beside her as they'd worked in unison, both wordlessly supporting the other as they'd efficiently managed the resuscitation. Her stomach clenched as she remembered. At the time it had been all action with no time to be emotionally involved. It was afterwards they thanked their lucky stars everything had worked out well.

That was why debriefing became important, because clearing stark pictures by talking about them and explaining the reasons let her release mental stresses.

Ellie said, 'He wasn't responding for a bit. We gave him an Apgar of three at one minute but by five minutes he was an eight out of ten. I've only been at a few breech births and they often do seem to take a little longer than cephalic births to get going.'

Roz nodded as she thought about it. 'I guess it could be that the cord is out and it has to be compressed against the body coming through. Or the rapid descent of the head afterwards might stun them too. But he came good by two minutes.'

The door opened and they both looked up. Sam was back. Ellie felt her heart give a little leap but it was followed by a frown as all her indecision and tangled emotions flooded back with full force. Damn. She'd been engrossed in this discussion and should have made her escape.

Her face must have shown her displeasure because he raised his brows. 'Sorry for interrupting.'

'No. Come in. Welcome!' Roz jumped up. 'Have a cup of tea with us. It's great you're here.' She turned to Ellie. 'Isn't it, Ellie? We were just talking about the birth.'

Sam looked at her. 'I'll come back.' Then he turned to Roz. 'I thought Ellie had gone and I wondered if you had any questions, Roz. It was a big morning.'

Ellie heard his words and felt ashamed. She reached down inside and retrieved the normal Ellie from the layers of confusion. Found her equilibrium. There she was—the one who'd greeted him, had it been only six days ago?

She smiled almost naturally. 'Please stay. I was going but you're both right. It's really good to talk over things while they are fresh in our minds. We were talking about breech babies that take a while to respond after birth.'

The conversation that followed was all Ellie hoped it would be. Sam shared his fierce intellect and grasp of the intricacies of breech birth from a consultant's perspective—they even covered a spirited discussion on the pros and cons of breech birth for first-time mums— and by the time she was ready to leave Ellie was comfortable again in Sam's company.

Or perhaps it would be fairer to say in Dr Southwell's company, because she was every inch the woman behind the uniform in charge of the ward and her feet were very firmly planted in the real world of the hospital that she loved.

'I'll leave you two to talk more. I'm going home.'

Sam stood up. 'I'll come with you. I need to grab the milk I left in your fridge.'

They both stood and as Ellie walked to the door with him she heard Roz murmur after them, 'Better than checking out her collection of stamps.' Ellie winced and pretended she didn't hear.

'The breech was great,' Ellie said to change the subject. They went out into the sunlight and Ellie was thankfully aware of the cool ocean breeze brushing her face—helping calm the blush that heated her cheeks.

'So, was it easy to find the hard baby's head through the abdomen when you leant down on it?' Sam asked her with a smile on his face. They had shared something special.

Ellie thought back to the moment when little Thorn's birth progress had stalled. The sudden increase in tension in the room. The mother pushing and nothing happening. The clock ticking. The baby's body turning pale. Then the calm voice of Sam instructing her to help with downward pressure just above the mother's pubic bone.

'Yes. A solid little ball that just pushed away, and then he was born.' She pictured the baby's position in her mind. 'So his chin must have lifted and changed the diameters of the presenting part which made him jam up. It certainly made a difference to re-tuck his chin in, and then he was born. All great learning experiences that make sense when you think about it.'

'Something simple like that can change the outcome so dramatically. The days of pulling down on a breech baby, which of course made the chin obstruct further, thankfully have gone.'

'I've seen two other normal breech births, the rest

have been caesareans, so it was a great learning experience for me.'

'You have good instincts. Listen to them and you'll be fine.'

It was a nice thing to say, but she didn't know what to do with the compliment because it was midwifery-orientated but also personal. So she changed the subject. The crashing of the waves from beyond the headland seemed louder than normal. Instead of turning up the hill to her house Ellie turned her head towards the ocean. 'The sea's rough today! I'm up for a walk out to the lighthouse before I go home. If you'd like to have a look, you could come. I need to lose some excess energy.'

'So, excitement makes you energetic?'

She shrugged. 'I'm energetic most of the time.' Except when she had nightmares, but she was well over that now. Luckily they didn't leave her listless for long. 'So what have you been doing on your time off? Have you looked around the bay? Met anybody interesting?'

Sam nodded mock-solemnly. 'My friend with the ingrown toenail is my new best bud. He dropped off a dozen prawns yesterday at lunchtime and offered me a trip on his trawler but I said I needed to be on call.'

She'd never been interested in offshore fishing but she was happy to hop on board a small tin dinghy and putt-putt around the creek.

'Would you like to go out on a prawn trawler?'

'It'd be interesting. Different way of spending your life than in a hospital seven days a week.'

She threw a look at him. 'Seven days a week is not healthy.'

He raised his brows. His long stride shortened to match her shorter one. 'I thought we'd agreed to disagree on how the other person spends their life.'

Oops. 'That's true. Let's talk about lighthouses. Lighthouse keepers worked seven days a week and only had one holiday a year.'

There was a pause while he digested that. 'Lighthouses. Yes. Let's talk about lighthouses.' The smile he gave her was so sweet she had a sudden vision of Sam as a very young boy with the innate kindness she could see in him now. She couldn't say why, but she knew without a doubt he would never tease a heartbroken little girl who missed her mummy. He would more likely scold anyone who did. She really liked that little boy.

She blinked away the silly fantasy and brought herself back to the hillside path they were on now. The grassy path wound along the edge of the cliff edge, a pristine white fence separated them from the drop and tufts of grass hid the crumbly edge. It was maintained by the present custodian of the lighthouse who lived off site. Glancing at Sam she manoeuvred herself to the side of the path nearest the cliff.

'The lighthouse was built in the eighteen hundreds and is part of a network that was built right along the eastern seaboard after ships were floundering on the underwater rocks.'

He was smiling at something then paused, turned and looked at her.

'Are you listening to me being your guide?'

He grinned. 'Sorry. I was thinking I could see you as a lighthouse keeper.'

She thought about that. Yes, she could have been

a lighthouse keeper. 'Except the position was only open to men—though they did prefer married men with families.'

He smiled at that. 'I imagine they would have big families if stuck in a lighthouse together.'

She grinned at him. 'The first couple who lived here had eleven children. He'd been a widower and he fell in love with a local girl—said the bay and the woman he found here healed him. They ended up with a big family. All natural births and all survived.'

'What an amazing woman. And did they live here happily-ever-after?'

'They moved to a lighthouse with bigger family quarters. Once in the lighthouse business, you tended to stay in the lighthouse business.'

'She should have been a midwife.' He laughed at that. 'The children would have had a wonderful childhood.'

'Some families were very isolated but at least here, at the bay, the children went to school and played with other children.'

They arrived at the top of the hill. The base of the lighthouse and the tall tower were painted pristine white with concrete walls that were a third of a metre thick, which gave a hint at how solid the lighthouse was. They both looked up to the wrought-iron rail away at the top where the windows and the light were.

'They have a tour tomorrow. You can go up the stairs inside and come out onto the walkway. It's a great view.'

Sam patted the solid walls. 'Is this how thick the walls of your cottage are?'

'Yep. It wasn't usual for lighthouses to be built of

concrete but there's a couple on the north coast like that. I think the sisters liked it and that's why they copied it.'

Sam watched her glance across the bay in the direction of the three cliff-top dwellings.

She went on. 'I love knowing my cottage is strong. I know the big bad wolf can't blow my house down.'

He'd suspected that was a reason she was holed away here in her house with thick walls. 'Do you want to tell me about your big bad wolf?'

'Nope.' She glanced his way but her eyes skidded past his without meeting them. 'Why spoil the afternoon?'

She pushed past the lighthouse into the little forecourt that looked over the ocean. The thick walls bounded the scrubby cliff face and they could see right out to where the blue ocean met the horizon. An oil tanker was away in the distance and closer to the shore two small sailboats were ballooning across the waves. The wind blew her hair across her face and he wanted to lean in and move it, maybe trace her cheek.

'I'm glad you're enjoying present company.'

She stared out over the ocean. He could feel the wall between them again. She was very good at erecting it. An absolute expert. Darn it.

She said, 'I enjoy the company of most people.'

That showed him. 'I won't get over myself, then.' He smiled down at his hands as he stroked the round concrete cap on top of the wall. She was good for his ego. He wouldn't have one at all by the time he left here.

The stone was warm from the sun, like Ellie had been warm. Sam remembered big hands cupping her firmly, stroking. Enjoying the feel of her under his fingers too.

He could feel his body stir. She had him on the ropes just by being there. He tried to distract himself with the structure of the building. 'It's been designed well.'

'What?' She looked startled for a minute and he guessed it was too much to hope that she'd been thinking the same thing he'd been thinking. She worried at her lip and he wanted to reach out and tell her not to. He felt his fingers itch to touch that soft skin of her mouth. Gentle it. But he didn't. He kept his hands where they were because of the damn wall. Not the wall under his hands. He patted that one. He guessed he had a few walls himself.

'Yes.' She turned away from him, sent him a distracted smile still without meeting his eyes. 'I've had enough. It's getting cool. Think I'll go home and catch up on my Saturday chores. Maybe even light a fire for tonight.'

Those were his marching orders. Get your milk and go. And he was learning that, when she said enough, it meant enough. He'd love to know what the guy in her past had done to her. And maybe take him out into a dark alley and make him regret it.

Sam didn't see Ellie at all on Sunday. He thought about going up and asking for his dad's surfboard as an excuse but that was lame.

Monday and Tuesday there were no inpatients in Maternity and no births, so apart from a sociable few minutes he didn't see Ellie, who was busy with antenatal women. He was called in to a birth Trina had overnight but the woman went home as soon as the four hours were up.

By Friday he was going stir crazy. Maybe it was the wind. There were storm warnings and the ocean had been too rough to swim in this morning. He thought of her up there, with the wind howling, all by herself. Tomorrow he wouldn't even have the excuse of work to see her.

At the end of Friday's work day, late that afternoon before he left as they stood outside in the warm sunshine, he searched his brain for ideas to meet up with Ellie. She had her bag and he was jingling his keys in his pocket even though he hadn't brought his car.

He needed inspiration for an invite. 'That cyclone far north is staying nearer the coast than they thought it would.'

'So it'll be a windy night up in my cottage.' She looked higher towards her house. Clouds were building. 'I love nights when the wind creaks against the windows and you can hear the ocean smashing against the rocks below.'

'It could turn nasty.'

She looked at him as if he were crazy. Maybe he should have suggested picking up the board. He tried again. Time was running out. 'This one might be more wind than you bargain for.'

She shrugged and began walking out to the road. The intersection loomed where she'd head up to her house and he'd head down to his guesthouse. It had been a forlorn hope she'd invite him up.

Obviously that wasn't on Ellie's mind. 'The warnings come all the time. Cyclones usually veer away at the last minute. Either way, I'll be fine.'

Sam wasn't sure what had gone wrong. He'd thought they were getting along well, not too many pitfalls, but it seemed there always were pitfalls with Ellie Swift. And he kept falling into them. But there was nothing he could do except wave her goodbye. There was something about the set of her chin that warned him this wasn't a good time to ask what she was doing tomorrow. He doubted he'd be lucky enough for another set of twins to call her out.

CHAPTER NINE

OVER THE NEXT few hours the wind blew more force-fully, the trees bent and swayed under it, and branches and twigs were flying down the street in front of the hospital. Sam dropped in to see if there were any medical needs but the wards remained quiet. Maternity sat empty. Empty without Ellie.

As he battled his way back to his guesthouse he glared up towards Ellie's house. Trina had gone away for the weekend and Myra had left as well. Again. Ellie was up there completely alone.

He kept telling himself to stop it. She'd managed perfectly well without him worrying about her before. Her house was built to withstand anything the cliff tops could throw at it, and most likely she'd be offended if he asked if she wanted company. He wasn't silly enough to think she'd want to move anywhere else to take refuge.

He kept checking to see when the cyclone would veer out to the ocean and take the wind with it, but it hadn't died down at all. If anything it blew even stronger.

He drove down to the boat shed to chat to his friend, the prawn-trawler captain, and the seafarer shook his head sagely and said they were in for a 'right good blow'.

On the way back to the guesthouse, the weather warning over the radio finally clinched it.

'Cyclone Athena will hit land just north of Lighthouse Bay in less than an hour.'

That did it.

He turned the car around, drove slowly up the cliff road to Ellie's house and parked outside. He sat for a minute and looked at the other two houses, dark and deserted. He stared at Ellie's. The light behind Ellie's blinds bled into the late-afternoon gloom and the little flowering shrubs outside her door were bending in the wind.

When he opened his car door it was a struggle to climb out. The wind pushed hard and he manhandled his door open and almost lost his grip when the wind slammed into him in a gust that would have broken his arm if he'd been caught between the car and the door.

Now that would be embarrassing—coming up to help and having to be saved by Ellie. The wind pushed him towards Ellie's door like a big hand in the small of his back and he realised that it really was too dangerous to be outside in this.

Ellie only heard the knock at the door because it fell just as there was a pause in the commercial break.

Funny how she knew who it was. When she opened the door, Sam would have loomed over her in his big coat if he wasn't down one decent-sized step from her. As it was their noses were level. 'Didn't you see the weather warning?'

Nice greeting. She had no idea how but she had the feeling he'd been stewing over something. 'No. I'm watching a movie. It's very peaceful inside!'

'The cyclone is heading this way. You can't sleep up here tonight.'

Was he for real? As he finished speaking, a sudden gust buffeted the little house and the windows creaked.

Ellie glared at Sam and narrowed her eyes. Just then a squall of rain swept sideways into Sam's back and Ellie instinctively stepped aside. 'Quickly. You'll get drenched. Come in.'

Sam bent down to take off his shoes and she dragged his arm impatiently. 'Do that in here.' As soon as he was across the threshold, she closed the door on the splattering raindrops that were making their way around his large body and onto the floor.

Sam stood on one leg and pulled his loafers off. She caught the smell of damp leather, the expensive suede mottled in places, with grass stuck to the edges from where she'd furiously cut the lawn even shorter as she'd tried to exorcise her demons earlier this afternoon.

'You've probably wrecked your shoes coming up here in them.'

His face was strangely impassive. 'Normal people don't live on cliff tops.'

What was his problem? 'Normal people leave other people alone when they've been asked to.' They were both speaking in the polite tones of people with patience tried by another's stupidity.

At that moment a fist of wind slammed solidly against the glass double doors facing the sea. The panes rattled. Then the wind sucked back fiercely before it slammed into the window again.

Ellie stopped and stared. The windows creaked and Sam placed his second loafer onto the little tray of seashells Ellie used for lining up inside shoes off the floor and he wiped the water droplets from his hair with a handkerchief.

'That's strong,' she said lamely in a normal voice.

'Really?' She could hear the exasperation in his voice. 'I couldn't leave you up here by yourself.' Sam was still speaking quietly.

'I wasn't by myself.' She indicated Myra's cat. Millicent appeared absorbed in the television and the antics of a well-dressed woman feeding cat food to a white Persian feline.

'Perfect reasoning,' he said mildly. It was infuriating he had regained equilibrium faster than she had. She'd just have to try harder.

'Would you like a cup of tea?' Politeness was good. The wind slammed against the windows again. No doubt it was slamming against her solid thick walls as well but nobody could tell that. 'My croft won't blow down, you know.'

Sam looked at the walls thoughtfully. 'I can imagine that you are correct. But it has weaknesses.' His voice lowered to an almost undistinguishable mumble. 'And obviously so do I.'

She heard him sigh as he straightened. 'I just want to make sure you...' He glanced at Millicent and corrected himself. 'You're both okay.'

He pointed to the windows. 'I seem to remember there are shutters that close from the outside—is that right?'

Ellie had forgotten the shutters. Too late. Next time. She didn't fancy the idea of going out in that maelstrom to shut them. 'Yes, but it might be too windy to shut them now.'

Sam looked at her as if she'd grown two heads. What was his problem? 'A woman's logic.'

'Excuse me?'

As if to a child, he said, 'The shutters are there to use during extreme wind.' He spoke as if she was slow to understand. She was getting sick of his 'silly little Ellie' attitude. 'So the glass doesn't blow in?'

'The glass won't blow in.' She said it confidently. At least, the words came out confidently. Ellie had a sudden vision of glass flying all over the room. Of Millicent splattered with dangerous fragments and the wind and rain belting into the little room. Her calmness wavered. Millicent had to be safe. 'You're sure it's going to be that strong?'

Just then Ellie's feline friend disappeared and the serious voice of the weather forecaster broke into the room.

'This is an SES announcement. Severe wind warning for the north coast of New South Wales has been posted. The tail of Cyclone Athena, which had previously been expected to head out to sea, has swung back into the coast with two-hundred-kilometre winds expected right along the eastern seaboard. Residents are recommended to stay in their homes and cancel all unnecessary travel on the roads until further notice. Flash flooding and wind damage is expected. The State Emergency Service can be reached on this number...'

A six-digit number flashed onto the screen just before the power went out.

The windows rattled menacingly in the sudden silence. Ellie stared at Sam.

He said quietly, 'Now can we close the shutters?'

'Might be a good idea.' The wind slammed again.

Sam was staring at the rain spotting the windows. 'Maybe it is too late for that. I think coming down to the hospital and staying there might be a better idea.'

As if. 'I'm not dragging Millicent through this wind. We'll be fine. But you're right. You should go before the wind gets stronger and you can't make it down the hill.'

He rolled his eyes. 'I'll do the shutters.'

No way! 'I'll do the shutters, because this is my house and I know how they fasten. And you're afraid of heights.'

He sighed, this time with exasperation. 'I'm wary of heights and more afraid that you'll blow off the cliff.'

Her eyes flew to his and the certainty in his face made her stop. He really was worried about her, to the extent he was willing to do something he normally wouldn't consider. Wayne would never have done that. The little voice inside her whispered, *Sam isn't like Wayne.* From the set chin to the determined gaze, he wasn't going to be swayed.

He lowered his voice. 'You need to stay here with Millicent.' He smiled down at the black cat who had crept across and was rubbing against Ellie's leg. He spoke to the animal. 'Can you mind Aunty Ellie while I go out and close the shutters against the wind, please?'

Millicent miaowed and Sam laughed. 'The cat wins.'

Ellie looked around. It was dark without the television.

'Fine. I'll light the lamps that I keep in the cupboard

for when the silly old lights and TV go off.' She added breezily, 'It happens all the time when the wind blows strongly.'

'Do you have candles?'

She thought about Sam and her in her house, cut off from the world, with candles. 'I might.'

Ellie's face heated and she hoped he couldn't see. It was pretty dim in here. She couldn't read his eyes but she suspected they'd darkened.

Instead she went to the cupboard beside the door and took out a huge pair of black gumboots and a man's raincoat. 'These came with the house. You might still be able to salvage your loafers if you leave them to dry.'

Sam stood outside the hastily closed door, the wind buffeting him. He was mad. Obviously he still needed to feel as though he was protecting Ellie. Leftover from not protecting Bree, maybe? The wind tore at the belted raincoat and the splatter of needled rain hit his nose, and he turned his face to protect his eyes. This was dumb. Maybe they should have just let the windows blow in.

A picture of Ellie in her rain-damaged room if that did happen made his feet move and he chose to start with the worst of them first—the windows that backed onto the cliff edge. Here the force of the gale was building and he moved into it out of the lee of the building, where the full force struck him and he staggered against the wall of the building on the little porch overlooking the ocean. Ellie was looking at him from the inside with absolute horror on her face. *Great. Thanks. Very reassuring.* He managed to keep his face calm.

'Continue blowing me against the house,' he muttered. 'Happy with that.' And he kept that picture of Ellie watching him through the window in his mind to keep out the one of him being sucked off the porch and over the cliff to his death.

How had he got here? Right on the edge of a cliff in a cyclone, to be exact. Risking his life for a woman who wouldn't let him close to her. Did he hope being the hero might work when everything else hadn't?

Not that she'd wanted him to be there, and it served him right, because now he was clinging for his life, shutting oil-bereft hinges on shutters that should have been closed hours ago.

When he'd said he was more worried she would do it herself, he'd been one hundred percent telling the truth. It was that thought that drove him like a machine, un-clipping, manhandling and latching each shutter closed until he was back at the side door.

He couldn't quite believe he'd been all the way around the house. It had been a real struggle, and by the end, when the wind had built to almost twice the strength from when he started, he knew Ellie would not have been able to do it.

When he fell into the room and the door was shut, he stopped. He was dripping, gasping for breath, his face stinging from the lash of the rain, back on secure foot-ing and out of the wind into the calm of another world. Now he felt as if…he'd come home.

CHAPTER TEN

THE ROOM WAS lit rosily. The fire Ellie kept mostly for decoration was burning merrily and Millicent was lying in front of it washing her paws. The cat barely glanced at him, she was so intent on her ablutions. *It's okay. I saved you, cat.*

But Ellie stared. Her worried face was pale, deathly pale, and he remembered the time she'd fainted, but then she flew across the room and smashed into him. She was pulling at his coat, helping him get out of his boots and then hugging him. And she buried her beautiful head in his chest. Okay. This was nice.

'That was…was dangerous. Don't do that again. I had no idea it would blow up that strong. I should never have let…' She was whispering and gabbling, Sam couldn't help thinking to himself it had all been very worth it, then, and the only way to stop her seemed perfectly reasonable to him.

He kissed her.

Sam kissed her. It was a short, cold, hard kiss, then another slower one, as if he needed to do it again, in case she'd missed the first one. She hadn't missed it. Then he hugged her. 'It's okay. I'm fine.' He spoke quietly into her hair as if she needed comfort. Darn right she needed comfort.

He tasted like the storm. It was different from the kiss they'd shared at lunch that day. Ellie hugged the wet coldness of his skin close to her. He buried her face in his damp chest, inhaling the strong scent of the sea, his aftershave and the briny tang of a man who had struggled against nature and won. For her.

He could have been blown off the cliff and she wouldn't have been able to do anything to help him. She should have gone with him, watched him, held a rope or something... It hadn't sunk into her how dangerous it was until she'd seen Sam battling to stay upright through the balcony's glass doors. She'd been so frightened for him. She'd never experienced wind like that before and even now her heart thumped at the memory.

In fact, she'd never seen someone so close to death before and that it was lovely Sam, who'd only wanted to help her, seemed ironically tragic. And she was so hard on him.

When he'd safely traversed the more dangerous face of the building she'd run around lighting candles and lighting the old fuel stove that always sat with kindling waiting in the corner of the kitchen alcove in case of blackouts. She'd set the old kettle on to heat water.

He put her away from him. 'You'll get wet. Wait until I dry and then you can cuddle me.'

She half laughed, half sobbed. 'Sorry. I got a bit emotional.' She scurried away, grabbed a towel and handed it to him. 'That was terrifying, watching you out there.'

'Tell me about it,' he said and rubbed his hair. 'It

was a lot worse from where I was.' He dabbed around his neck and handed back the towel. Smiled at her. 'All good. Done now.' He glanced around and she saw the approval. 'This looks nice. Can I stay till the storm blows out?'

She looked at him. Tall. Tousled. Ridiculously handsome, yet reassuring too. The full package. Obviously he cared about her, and she wasn't stupid…she knew he fancied her. Well, heck, she fancied him too, if she was honest with herself, despite all her kicking and screaming. And he was only here for another two weeks so it wouldn't be a long-term commitment.

The wind howled and continued to build outside. 'I suppose I can't throw you out now,' she agreed a little breathlessly, happy to play down the tension of the last few minutes while he'd been outside. That had been horrible.

She remembered his car. 'Though I'm not sure how happy your lovely car will be out there with all the debris flying round.'

'There are probably less branches up here than down in the town. I'm not worried. Plus, it's there if I get called out.'

Despite the fact every birth helped her numbers and the overall viability of her plans for the hospital, she actually preferred the idea that he would not be called out. *Please.*

Ellie looked across at the stove and saw the kettle wasn't even steaming yet. 'Are you cold? I've got the kettle on. The good news is I have pasta already cooked, and can just transfer it to an earthen dish and pop it in the fuel stove to reheat.'

He frowned. 'I've landed myself on you for dinner. I should have brought something.'

'You brought lunch the other day.' *And yourself tonight.* Her turn to look around the softly lit room. At the fire crackling. The candles. She'd pretended to herself she'd only set them because Sam had suggested them. But there was no denying the soft light added to the ambience. 'Even if the power comes on, now that I'm sorted, I like the power off.'

She suddenly felt quite calm that Sam was here. Felt strangely peaceful now she'd accepted she was attracted to him, but somehow because of the wind and the fact they were battened down here like a ship at sea in a storm it was bizarrely safe to allow herself the luxury, because it was done. He was here. She even walked across and turned off the television so it didn't blare at them in a surge when they were reconnected. She remembered the light switch and did the same to that.

It was as if some other Ellie had morphed from her body and evicted the prickly one. 'The refrigerator will make a noise when the power comes back on. That's enough to wake the dead.' The other Ellie sat down on the sofa and patted the seat beside her. 'Sit down. Rest after your efforts. Relax.' Then she thought of something. 'I've got a question.' It was a silly question but it had been bugging her.

He sat down next to her, right next to her, his hip touching hers, and the sofa creaked with his weight. He was warm, so the coat must have worked well or he had a really good reheating system. Her mind took a little wander and she imagined what it would feel like to have a lot more of Sam's skin against hers. She wondered how much heat they could generate together. How his skin would feel? She knew from the solid impact they'd just shared, when she'd thrown herself at him like a maniac when he'd come in, that his body would be rock-solid under her hands. Her face heated and she hurriedly diverted her mad mind. The question. Yes.

After a sideways glance, Ellie decided he looked a little wary and, considering some of the questions she'd asked him, she wasn't surprised.

'I just wanted to know who taught you to make a bed with hospital corners.'

He laughed. His look said, *Is that all?* 'My mother. She was a matron, like you,' he teased. 'Met and married my dad late in life and brought us up to be "useful", as well as doctors. My sister and I were the only ones at med school who made their beds with hospital corners. We had a great childhood.'

Ellie knew his dad was a widower. 'Where is your sister now?'

His answer was easy and affectionate. 'In Italy. Doing a term of obstetrics in Rome.' Ellie could see they were still close. 'She's a workaholic.'

'Imagine. Another person striving for further knowledge.' She thought of his father. 'And your dad doesn't think of retirement? Don't you people have holidays?'

He shrugged. 'Every year when we were kids. My parents always loved the sea, so we spent summer holidays there. Christmas at whatever beach house they'd rented for the New Year. But we always had to make our own beds.' He smiled at the memories. 'Mum and Dad adored each other until she passed away ten years ago.'

The sadness was tinged with wonderful memories.

Ellie wished she had more memories of her mother. 'I'm sorry for your loss. I knew your dad was a widower.'

He smiled gently at her. 'Dad's been surfing ever since. Says it's when he feels happiest.'

Sam's smile wasn't melancholy, so she shouldn't be. 'That makes sense. He always had a smile on his face when he came in after being in the ocean.'

'So, that's my story.' He turned fully to face her. 'You owe me a little about your life, don't you think?'

'Mine's boringly tragic. As you know from my nightmares, Mum died when I was six. My dad brought me up. He never married again, though I had a nice auntie.' She smiled at him. 'A real auntie—Dad's sister. I'd go for holidays with my Aunty Dell. She was an Outback nurse and I visited her in whatever little hospital she was working at. That was when I was happiest. I admired her so much that nursing and midwifery were the natural way for me to go. We've done a few emergency births together. She can do everything.'

He was watching her and she suddenly felt a little shy at being under such scrutiny. Wayne had asked questions about her early in their relationship, but once he'd established nobody was going to rescue her he'd stopped hearing her answers. It was something she'd missed early on and should have realised it was a danger sign.

Sam's voice brought her back and she wanted to shake off the sudden darkness that had come with thoughts of Wayne. Sam wasn't pretending interest. He *was* interested. 'So, no brothers or sisters?'

She shook her head. 'Nope.'

'And where's Aunty Dell now?'

Aunty Dell. For her, Ellie could smile. 'Kununurra.

She's slowly moving around the top of Western Australia in her mobile home.'

His voice had softened. 'So no rowdy family Christmases for you?' Wayne had played on her need for 'jolly family time', and she knew it with a bitterness that stung.

Sam's face was sympathetic but she couldn't help her reaction. It erupted like a little volcano of hurt. 'Don't pity me. I've had lots of lovely Christmases at work. Making it special for people who find themselves away from home.'

Sam's expression didn't change and she took a quick breath to calm herself—remind herself this was Sam, not Wayne—and felt a little ashamed of her outburst.

He said, 'That was empathy, not pity. I can see you have a thing about pity. There's a difference. What I'd really like to know about is the relationship that's made you so bitter and prickly. It obviously didn't work out.'

Wayne hadn't been a relationship. He'd been a debilitating illness that had almost become terminal. The kettle began to sing and she heard it with relief. 'No. My relationship didn't work out.' The old Ellie was back and she stood up. 'I'll make a hot drink. Would you like tea, coffee or hot chocolate?'

He put his hand on her arm. 'Do you know what I'd really like? More than a hot drink?'

The kettle sang louder. 'What?'

Sam seemed oblivious to the noise. 'To hear about that time in your life that still affects you so much now.'

She looked down at him. Nope. She couldn't do that. She knew what would happen. Talking about Wayne and the loss of her innocence, the tearing down of her dreams, the descent into abuse she'd suffered, would spoil what she had here with Sam. Tonight couldn't be the start of a long-term thing but it was special. She wouldn't infect this moment with the past.

This thing with Sam, this fledgling, careful awareness that she was only just allowing into her world along with Sam, was too precious. Too easily damaged. 'How about you talk about your marriage first?'

'Touché.' He grimaced. She read it in his face. He knew analysing his past would harm what they had as well. 'Let's have hot chocolate instead.'

Sam sipped his hot chocolate. The fire flickered, the woman who had attracted him crazily for the first time in years sat beside him, while a big black cat purred against his side. A hell of a lot different from work, work, work. It was probably the most peaceful evening he'd spent since well before Bree's death, which was crazy, considering the tempest outside. But since he'd closed the shutters they were locked in an impervious cave, immune to the elements. There was just the rattle of rain on the roof and the background thrum of the ocean crashing on the cliffs below joining with it to make a symphony rather than a discordant refrain.

The candles flickered and as far as he was concerned Ellie looked like an angel, her cheeks slightly pink as she laughed about the time when Jeff, the lifesaver and prawn-trawler captain, the meanest, toughest guy in town, had fainted at his wife giving birth.

She turned to look at him. 'You must have had funny things happen in your work?'

'Not often.' Or maybe he'd lost his sense of humour

so long ago that he'd missed the occasions. He hadn't smiled as much as he had since he'd arrived here. He wondered if it was the place or the woman beside him. He suspected it was the latter and marvelled that one person could turn his thoughts around so swiftly.

It was almost as if, the first time he'd seen her, she'd magically switched on his party lights.

She nudged him with her shoulder. 'Come on. Something funny must have happened at your work!'

He pretended to sigh. 'Very recently I was called into a birth centre and the husband was stark, staring naked in the shower with his wife and two sons while she pushed the baby out. They were from a nudist colony.'

He could tell she was trying not to laugh but he suspected it was more at his horror than the picture he painted.

She pursed her lips in mock shock. 'What about the midwife?'

He looked sternly at her. 'She was dressed. Thank goodness.'

She let go and laughed. 'You're a prude. I'm guessing if they'd had a home birth the midwife from their colony would have been naked. Birth is such an important event that, if your belief system celebrates the naked body, I can see why they would want to be naked for it.'

He'd started the story to make her smile but she made him think more about the people, not the events. It was something he'd had trouble doing at the time and now he felt slightly ashamed. 'I'm not really complaining. The mother had had a previous caesarean, which ruled out a home birth, and they were "reclaiming her birthing ability".'

She tilted her head and looked at him. 'It's pretty cool you get that.'

He grimaced. 'I didn't get it.' He shook his head. He couldn't take credit when it wasn't due. 'I'm repeating what the midwife told me when she saw my face.'

Her gaze softened. 'But you get it now. I can see that.'

More than that had shifted since he'd come here. 'I think so.'

He tried to explain. 'I've been living a very narrow existence since Bree died. Concentrating on the end goal, which is my research on extreme premature labour. And, although it's too late to save Bree or our babies, maybe I could save other babies and somehow she'd know I was still trying.' He shook his head. 'I don't know. I've been avoiding where possible the more emotive and connecting aspects of my work. My father saw how distanced from people I was becoming so it's not surprising he saw this place as a change of scene for me.' He glanced at her ruefully. 'A chance to try to jolt me out of it.'

'And have we jolted you out of it?'

You have, he thought, but he didn't say it. He let his gaze drift around the candlelit room. Somehow it was easier to talk about it here, now, in the quiet, with just the two of them. 'I feel different. Even that first fast birth in the first half-hour here, with Josie and John. I felt connected. Involved. Not a separate watcher who only stepped in as needed.' He grimaced. 'I even recall their names.' To his shame he hadn't been able to do that for far too long.

He could see she remembered the moment. He wasn't surprised she smiled at the memory. 'You were needed.'

He shook his head. 'Not really. You had it under control. And you loved it all so much. Lived it. It slapped me in the face that I'd lost that in my work.'

She winced at his choice of words. 'Slapped? I'm definitely not a violent person.'

He smiled. 'It was a gentle, metaphorical slap. But I can change that to "nudged me into realising", if you prefer.'

He bumped her shoulder gently with his own. 'Like you nudged me to remember something funny a minute ago.'

'I'm glad you've seen the light.' She said it simply.

'And since then it's been a roller coaster. Lighthouse Bay doesn't win the birth number-count but every patient has had a story, an emotional tag I'm seeing now. That's a good thing. I think.'

She touched his arm. 'It's definitely a good thing.'

That wasn't all he was seeing. He was seeing a beautiful woman, just out of reach. He really wanted to reach. He just hoped she was also feeling the magic that had snared him.

'Come here.' He lifted his arm and to his immense relief she snuggled in under the weight of it. Then it was easy to tilt her chin with his other hand and brush her lips with his. He could feel the tingle of connection all the way down to his toes. He sighed and suddenly felt ten years younger. Now he was alive.

Ellie had known they were going to kiss. Eventually. And surprisingly she was quite calm about it. It wasn't as if they hadn't before and he was very good at it. That other Ellie was stretching inside her and saying, *Yes, please*, as Sam pulled her close. *Hurry up and kiss me some more*, that other Ellie was saying. She was such a hussy.

His mouth touched hers. Mmm... Kissing Sam tasted crazy good. Strangely their bodies were communing like two old lovers—not new ones—and inexplicably she once again found herself in his lap. She kept her eyes closed dreamily as she slid her arms around his strong neck and savoured the virile hardness and warmth of him. The slowness and languorous progression of his mouth from gentle to intense, hard to soft, and back again. It felt so powerful with him holding her face, her cheeks, cradled between his palms as if he held delicate china in his hands. Tasting her and letting her taste him. As though she was precious and special. Breathing in each other's breath as they shared the most intimate connection with their mouths.

Distantly she heard the rain beat on the roof and the spiral of delight just went on, deeper and more poignantly, until she wanted to cry with the beauty of his mouth against hers, his tongue curled around hers, until her whole body seemed to glow from the inside out. Kissing and more kissing. She hadn't realised she could love kissing this much. That kissing was actually the be all and end all. That it could be a whole play and not just an act of the play. She'd never been kissed like this—as if he couldn't get enough of her mouth. His hands roamed, as if gathering her even closer, but always they came back to her face, gently holding her mouth to his as if he couldn't get enough. Yes. She couldn't get enough, either.

Sam was staying the night. Tomorrow was Saturday. They had all night—or even all weekend, if they wanted.

He stayed all weekend. Sunday morning, she woke to the warmth of Sam's big naked body snug up against her and her cheek on Sam's skin. The blond hairs on his body tickled her nose and her hand closed over the wedge-shaped muscle of his chest as her face grew steadily pinker. Oh, my. What they had done since Friday night?

As if he'd heard her thoughts, his voice announced he was awake too. 'I'm wondering if perhaps we could do some of that again...'

Sam's voice was a seductive rumble and she could feel the smile curve across her face. No doubt she looked like Millicent after scoring a treat. She knew now what Trina was missing and why the young widow had chosen to work most nights. Waking to someone warm and loving beside her. A man spoiling her until she begged him to stop. Being held until she fell asleep.

Cheeks still red, she tried to not jump on him. 'Aren't you hungry?'

'Oh, yeah, I'm starving.' He pulled her on top of him and kissed her thoroughly.

An hour later Ellie watched the steam follow Sam out of the bathroom and ran her hands slowly over her tingling body. She'd had no idea such a sensuous world existed, though how on earth she was going to face Sam

at work and not think lurid thoughts defied her imagination. Sam had told her to stay and enjoy the shower
while he made breakfast but what she really wanted to
do was drag the gorgeous person back to bed. She'd
had no idea she was a nymphomaniac. Must be. Surely
other people didn't do it so much as they had in the last
thirty-six hours?

She didn't know how it could work between them.
If it even could work. He was based in Brisbane. She
was here. But they were fabulous together so surely that
meant something? Maybe she could learn to trust a relationship with a man. A long-distance relationship. If
that man was Sam. No. She wasn't in love with him.
Was she? She wasn't going there, but she sure as heck
was in lust with him.

And if it didn't work long-distance, that was okay,
because he would only be here for another two weeks
and she deserved great sex at least once in her life. More
than once. She grimaced over the word. They hadn't
had sex—Sam had made love to her. Gloriously tender
love that healed and nurtured and told her he thought
she was the sexiest woman in the world. Who would
have known? Her cheeks glowed again.

CHAPTER ELEVEN

MONDAY MORNING DAWNED, blustery, and Ellie tweaked her collar tighter to her throat as she closed her front door. She'd slept deeply after Sam had left on Sunday evening. They'd walked for hours hand in hand along Nine Mile Beach, splashing through the waves, coming back after lunch ravenous again. Ellie was convinced that the sun, the exercise and—she grinned to herself—the loving meant she'd slept the best she'd slept for years.

This morning the air felt damp and exhilarating as she trod lightly down the road to work just before seven a.m. She'd skipped her beach walk this morning—strangely, her hips were tender. Must be all the exercise. She blushed sheepishly.

The sea remained wild, white caps out to the horizon, booming swells smashing against the cliff below, and Ellie breathed in the fresh salt with a sigh of pleasure. She loved the coast. Loved the isolation of her croft, though isolation wasn't something she'd savoured over the weekend. She saw Myra's car was back and smiled to herself. She didn't know. *Tee-hee.*

She laughed out loud and conversely had a sudden

desire to share the amusing thought with Sam. There was a little wonky logic in that thought and it was not very loyal to her friend.

On her arrival she saw that Trina had had a slow night. The ward remained empty. Her friend had been bored, hence she had reorganised the whole sterile stockroom—a job Ellie had been putting off until a quiet day—and there was a small pile of out-of-date stock that she needed to reorder from the base hospital. At least she had a chore to start her day with.

Later, if no birthing women came in or needed transfer, Ellie would do the same for the medication cupboard. Spring cleaning suited the feeling of determined efficiency she'd decided she needed to ground herself in. Get her head out of the clouds that her thoughts kept drifting up towards.

The expected arrival of Dr Southwell would not faze her, though seriously she wouldn't be able to look at him without blushing, and she wasn't sure how she was going to manage it.

Maybe, as they had no patients, he could go straight through to the clinic in the main hospital to give her a chance to think of what to say.

Except it wasn't Sam who arrived.

Wayne Donnelly was an undeniable presence. Like everyone's favourite young uncle. You could just imagine him dangling babies on his knees, which was what Ellie had thought when he'd begun to pursue her. Whenever Ellie was around he'd made such a fuss of any child and everyone had smiled at him. He'd made her think of families. Dream families. Christmases, Easter egg hunts. All the things Ellie had ever wanted, and she'd fallen headlong in love with the fantasy.

In truth, he hated kids, and was a narcissist and a sociopath. He had no guilt, no shame, no feeling for other people, and could only see the world through eyes that saw himself first.

But he was like a seasoned politician versed in the art of crowd pleasing. Crinkled laughter lines jumped up at the edges of blue eyes framed by thick, black lashes and high cheekbones. Nothing in his looks gave him away. Except maybe the confident, beaming, too-white smile. He had a small cleft in his strong chin and women instinctively gave him another look.

Later she'd found out there was a pattern. He serenaded his victims, pretended to marry them, created joint bank accounts and then sauntered off after skilfully denigrating the woman so she felt it was all her fault everything had failed. A master of psychological abuse.

When Ellie saw him her stomach lurched with bile. Out of the corner of her eye she saw Trina, about to head home to bed, instinctively pat her hair. Yep. He'd already sucked in Trina.

'What are you doing here?' Ellie watched his smile broaden, the fake smile he used like oil to smooth his way in so he could use someone. She'd been incredibly blind. She wasn't any more.

'Too early in the morning for manners, El? Introduce me to your beautiful friend before we find ourselves bickering.'

'No.' Ellie turned from him to Trina. 'He's a cad and a slime, Trina. I'd leave if I was you.'

Wayne laughed. Trina looked at Ellie and shut her gaping mouth with a click. She blinked a few times as her tired brain tried to work it out. Then she stepped closer to Ellie. 'If you say so, I believe you.'

Ironic choice of words from her friend. One of the people in the room was a huge liar.

Trina frowned. 'But…' She wrinkled her brow. 'If he's a cad shouldn't I stay?'

Ellie shook her head. 'I'd prefer you didn't. He won't be here long. You could ring the security man, though. Ask him to come over and sit at my desk. That would be good in case he won't leave.'

Trina didn't look again at Ellie's acquaintance, just crossed to the desk and picked up the phone. She spoke quietly into it and then picked up her bag. 'If you're sure.'

Ellie nodded again. 'Please. And thanks.'

Trina nodded. 'See you tomorrow morning.'

'Sure.' Ellie Looked back at Wayne. Raised her brows. 'Yes?'

'I need money.'

'Really.' He had taken a great deal of that from her already. Along with her naivety. She looked at the impeccable clothes. 'I've seen people far worse off than you.'

'Thank you.' As if she'd given him a wonderful compliment. 'Nice little caravan park you have here. Think I might stay around for a while. Reacquaint myself with my kin.'

'You have no kin. But I can't stop you. Luckily, it's high season and will cost you an arm and a leg. So you will have to move on eventually.' She wasn't moving on. Not this time.

He spread his hands. 'Gambling debts.'

Nothing new. 'Gamblers tend to get those.'

'This time they threatened to harm my family.'

He'd had three 'wives' that she knew of. 'Which family?'

'All of them. You included. I thought I'd better warn you.'

He didn't give a damn. 'You don't care about anyone but yourself. You'd do better going to the police.'

'I don't think that the police station is a safe place for me to go. Would you look forward to identifying my body?'

'Go away, Wayne. Your disasters have nothing to do with me.' And she could feel the shakes coming on. He'd tried to rape her once. After she'd said she was leaving him. And he'd denied it. Said she'd been playing hard to get.

She'd escaped that night and had begun to plan carefully to get away, because he'd taken all her resources. Her wallet, her licence, her bank accounts… Everything had been unavailable when she'd needed it. She'd stumbled into Myra's coffee shop, distraught, and made a friend for life. Myra had helped her create the wall of protection she needed to be free.

'You've turned all bitter and twisted. Not the sweet Ellie I used to know.'

That wasn't even worth answering. Ellie heard the door from the main hospital open and was glad the security guard was here. She needed to end this. She pretended she didn't know help had arrived. She couldn't keep running.

'Leave the ward, please, Mr Donnelly.'

'You didn't call me "Mr Donnelly" when we were married.'

'We were never married.' Ellie turned away from him to the security guard and her stomach dropped. It wasn't security, it was Sam. No. No. *No*. Her face flushed and she felt dreadfully, horribly sick. She didn't want Sam to know about this. But then maybe it was best. Then he could see she could never truly give a man power over her ever again.

'Good morning, matron,' Sam said.

Ellie saw him glance at Wayne and give him an inscrutable nod. 'We need to discuss the patients.' Sam's voice was surprisingly crisp. Authoritative. No hint of friendliness.

Ellie raised her brows. He knew there were no patients. 'Certainly, Dr Southwell.'

'Fine. When you're ready, please.'

'She's busy. Talking to me.' Wayne squared his shoulders but he was at a disadvantage in both height and muscle. They all knew it. An adolescent part of Ellie secretly revelled in it.

Still politely, Sam said, 'You're a doctor?'

'No. I'm her…'

Before Wayne could complete his sentence, Sam spoke coldly right over the top of him. There was no doubting his authority. 'This is a hospital. If you are not a medical practitioner, matron's attention is mine. There is a waiting room, though, in the main hospital where you can sit, but this could take some time.'

Ellie added helpfully, 'He's leaving.'

'Excellent. Come with me, matron.' Sam indicated with his hand that he expected Ellie to head down the corridor to the empty rooms in front of him.

She looked at Wayne and made the decision to enforce her freedom from dreaded drop-in visits like this. She didn't know why she hadn't done it before but knew it was a fault she needed to remedy immediately. 'If you don't leave town, I'll lodge a restraining order with the police this afternoon. I've kept evidence of our fake marriage certificate. This won't happen again.'

Then she turned to Sam. 'This way, doctor.'

Sam ignored Wayne and followed Ellie. She could feel his large body blocking Wayne's view of her as they turned into an empty room and stood silently in the centre of it out of sight. Ellie clasped her hands together to stop them shaking, unable to look at Sam. They both heard footsteps retreating, and the automatic doors open and close, and Ellie sagged against a wall. Sam watched her but he didn't come any closer, as if he knew she needed space at this moment.

'Your ex-husband, I assume?'

'He was a bigamist. Or trigamist, if there is such a word. So never legally my husband.'

Sam whistled. 'Ouch.'

She said very quietly, 'There were worse things about him than that.'

Sam studied her. 'Would you like me to follow and punch him out?'

He was deadly serious. She could see that.

She could almost smile at that except her heart was broken. Yes, she was beginning to love Sam. That was so dangerous to her peace of mind. It frightened the stuffing out of her. And she loved him even more for the offer, but Wayne had made her see how impossible it all was. She couldn't do this—start again with Sam. She didn't have the trust in her to build a strong relationship and Sam needed a woman to love him wholeheartedly.

Not one who'd locked him out like Bree had. Bree, who had almost destroyed him while she'd destroyed herself. He deserved that trust. She could give him love. She was more than halfway to falling in love with him already. But she couldn't give him trust. She'd thought she could but she couldn't. Trust had died in her for ever. Killed by the man who had just left.

'Thank you for the thought but I wouldn't like to ask you to sink to his level.' She straightened off the wall.

'Now you can see, Sam, why I'm so wary of men. Why I know I'll never let myself get that close to someone again. I'm sorry if I gave you the wrong idea this weekend. It was lovely, what we shared, but it's finished. You'll leave soon and that's good.' She took a step towards the door and it was the hardest step she'd ever taken. 'Let's go back to the desk.'

His fingers lifted to touch her arm, then dropped. 'Ellie.'

'Yes?' She looked at his caring eyes. His beautiful mouth. The kindness that shone on his face. It broke her heart.

'I'm sorry you've been wounded by a pathetic man. We're not all like that.'

She heard him. Saw that he meant it. But that didn't help. She wished she could believe it as deeply as she needed to be fair to Sam. 'I know. I really don't think you are that sort of man, but I don't have the capacity in me to risk a relationship again. A relationship needs to be good for both of us and I wouldn't be good for you.'

'But—'

She cut him off. 'Thank you. I don't want to talk about it any more.'

Sam sighed impatiently. 'I can understand that here. But later, I think we should.'

'No, Sam. We won't.' Then she turned and walked away.

Sam left Ellie soon after. He went out the front door to make sure her ex-bigamist had departed but there was no sign of him. He actually would have liked to slam the sleazy little mongrel up against a wall and warn him never to approach Ellie again, but he might find a place in himself that would do more than that, and he'd taken an oath to not harm.

His fingers clenched by his sides. No wonder she had trust issues and didn't want to ask any man for help. Even himself. He wasn't a violent man but after what they'd shared the last two days the idea of someone abusing Ellie's trust to that extent devastated him. And made him furious. But in the end it wasn't any of his business unless he was looking for something long-term—which wasn't his intention. Or was it? Hell, he didn't know. Did he even have a choice?

Ellie spent the next five days rearranging antenatal schedules and managed to book a different pregnant woman for antenatal appointments for every morning during the time Sam would be around.

They had two normal births, one on Faith's shift and one on Trina's, so Ellie was spared having to call Sam in. She could only be glad the babies were being kind to her. But every afternoon when she went home the house was empty, where before it had been welcoming.

Sam came on Wednesday afternoon for his father's surfboard and she gave it to him, refused to talk and didn't invite him in.

On Thursday Myra cornered her and told her Sam had asked her to see if Ellie would change her mind. Spend some time with him. They had their first ever disagreement when both women were so determined to change the other's mind about what was right.

By Friday Ellie knew she needed to get away or she would make herself sick, so as soon as she finished work she took herself off availability for call-backs and loaded her car.

Ellie felt the need to abandon her cottage and head to a different world. It had everything to do with avoiding a certain visitor who just might drop in again.

She didn't know where to go, so she drove north to the Gold Coast, where she could find a cheap hotel and just hibernate for two nights in a place that nobody knew her.

She stayed in her room all day Saturday and drove back Sunday via the base hospital where two of her patients were still inpatients.

She did her own visiting, with a quiet chat in the big antenatal ward with Marni, who was going home tomorrow. Bob arrived not long after she did, and she was pleased to hear that the young mum's contractions had settled down, and Bob had painted inside their house while Marni was in hospital so she didn't have to be exposed to the smell of new paint.

She showed Ellie the quilt she was making the baby, and there was something about Marni's determined optimism that made her feel ashamed. Marni had explained that when she was bored she sewed another little animal onto the patchwork cot-blanket, pouring love and calmness into it, determined to do everything asked of her to keep her pregnancy on track.

After Marni, Ellie visited the postnatal ward area, where Annette sat happily with her twins, who were being star patients and were almost ready to go home.

'Still perfect?' Ellie grinned at the two sleeping bundles and the relaxed mum sitting with a magazine in her lap.

'They have their moments. Rosebud is the impatient one, so has to be fed first, while Thorn needs a bit of encouragement to keep at it.'

'So they are still how they started out, then.'

'Exactly.' Both women laughed.

'How is that gorgeous Dr Sam?'

'Fine.' Ellie felt her face freeze, as if all the muscles had suddenly stopped working. 'He's here for another week and then he's gone.' Her voice was bright. 'Then I guess we'll have another new locum. Did you know his father was here first? He was a surfer, though I'm not sure how good his surfing will be for a while, because he broke his arm. That's why his son came.'

'So Dr Sam's not coming back?'

'No.' It would be better if Sam never came back. She suspected every time he came it would hurt more to keep saying goodbye to him. 'He has a high-flying

job in Brisbane. He was only doing everyone a favour.'
Including her.

On the drive home she thought about her dilemma.
She'd had sex with a man she'd known for only two
weeks by that point, and who was just passing through.
Maybe she even understood her friend Faith, who had
never said she regretted the man who'd come, disappeared and left her with a baby. She'd never been close
to understanding before.

Sex. She grimaced and reminded herself that that
was all it was. Then her sensible voice returned. That
was okay. She was a grown-up. Afterwards she could go
back to how it had been before and concentrate on work.

On Monday morning when Sam walked in to the maternity ward the Ellie he found was the woman from
three weeks ago. White shirt buttoned to the neck, grey
eyes serene and cool, her manner very businesslike.

'Good morning, doctor.'

His temper was less than sunny after being frustrated all weekend. He'd thought if he just waited until
Saturday morning they could sort it all out. He'd taken
croissants and blueberry yoghurt, as she'd liked that last
time, and then had stood there like an idiot until he'd
realised she'd left. He'd rung Myra each morning and
afternoon all weekend to check in case she'd returned.

Now he stared with narrowed eyes as she stood of-
ficiously in front of him. 'Good morning, Ellie.' He
stressed her first name, disappointed but not surprised
this ice maiden didn't resemble the woman he had held
in his arms all weekend just over a week ago. He was
back to square one, and despite his best efforts there

was no breaking through her barriers. Maybe he should just give up.

They had five days to go. Then he'd be gone. He could lose himself in his work again. Treat it as an interlude that had shown him he could finally care for another woman. But he wasn't so sure he could care for one as much as he'd grown to care for Ellie.

On Friday morning, Sam's last day there, Ellie went back to the beach. She'd been avoiding it all week in case Sam was there in the mornings surfing but she missed the peace she gained from her daily walk. Peace was at a premium at the moment and she needed it before facing today.

It had rained last night, and the ocean was too rough for surfers out there. As she trod down the path even the frogs weren't penetrating the gloom she was wrapped in. At least she had Sam to thank for losing the majority of her phobia. She wasn't going to touch one but the croaking barely bothered her now—there were worse things that could happen than frogs. Such as Sam going and never seeing him again.

She reached the sand, slipped off her footwear and stood for a moment. Gazing out. A new weather pattern was coming in. More high winds and rough seas. She breathed in deeply and let the crash of the waves on the cliffs across the bay penetrate, feeling the cool white sand between her toes, the turbulent, curving waves tumbling onto themselves and running up the sand to kiss her better. The biggest waves made a cracking noise as they slid all the way up to her to foam around her toes then crackle into the sand as it drank in the water and the cries of the gulls overhead. This was why she lived here. Because it made her strong.

Yes, it was sad that Sam was going, more than sad, but it was good as well. It would never have worked and what he'd given her in the two days they'd been together was something she could hold to her heart in the years to come. She wished him happiness with a woman who deserved him. She just wished she could have been that woman.

Ellie lifted her head and breathed in another gulp of sea air past the stinging in her throat and then she set off along the beach. She would get through today, kiss Sam's cheek and say goodbye.

Sam knew she was going to kiss his cheek. He didn't want her platonic guilt. If she wasn't going to kiss him properly then he didn't want her to kiss him at all. He stepped back as she moved forward to say goodbye and saw her blink in confusion as he avoided her.

That's right, Ellie. Feels bad, doesn't it, to be knocked back? He didn't say it but he knew it was there in his eyes. He was still pretty darn angry with her for not fighting for what they might have had.

'Goodbye, Ellie Swift. I wish you a great life with your midwifery centre.' He turned away quickly because if he didn't he'd grab her and kiss her until she begged him to stay. But that wouldn't happen.

He'd driven an hour towards Brisbane when the radio alert of another storm warning jerked him back to sense. Ellie was on the seaboard. Right on the edge of a cliff, to be exact. Her little house would bear the brunt of the storm and he wouldn't be there to make sure she was all right.

Not that she'd want him to be there, but suddenly he asked himself why would he drive away from a woman who'd finally made him want to look at the future again? One he wanted to wake up next to for the rest of his life? He loved Ellie. How many times did real love actually come to a man?

After he'd stepped back from her he'd seen the look of hurt on her face and it came back to haunt him now. What if she was feeling the same pain he was? Wasn't he as bad as she was for not fighting for what they could have?

He'd loved Bree, and it had destroyed him when she'd died. But Ellie was right. It hadn't been his fault. He didn't know she'd been so unstable that she would take her own life. And he'd lost himself in work.

If it wasn't for Lighthouse Bay and Ellie he might be still lost. He could have woken up in thirty years and realised he'd been a shell for decades. He didn't want to be a shell. He wanted to be the man who held Ellie every night. The man who held the babies she was destined to have with him, and might never have if he kept driving away. He loved her. He wanted her. And he would fight for her.

He pulled over and turned around. The storm up ahead was flashing lightning across the hills. Great sheets of white light. Ellie was over there somewhere. Alone.

The thunder crashed outside. The scent of ozone filled the air, lighting up the sky all the way out to sea. This storm was more electrical than the other one. She shied away from those memories of the night Sam came, like Millicent had skidded away from the window.

Myra was gone again and Ellie suspected she had a male friend she was visiting. She even suspected it might be the 'elder' Dr Southwell. Good for her.

But Ellie knew the man she should have fought for was gone. Sam was gone. In her head he was gone. In her heart he was buried under protection so thick she felt like she was walking around inside a big, white cotton-wool ball, adding more layers all week, so that by the time Sam had left this afternoon she could barely hear, she was so distanced from everyone. He'd turned away from her coldly in the end and she deserved that. She'd been a coward and deserved his scorn.

She wished she'd never ever started this painful process of letting someone else in. Because for the first time in a long time she wondered if, if she'd tried a little bit harder to let go of the past, she just might have had a future. With Sam. Was it too late? Could she contact him through his father? Myra would be all over her like a rash if she asked for Sam's phone number. Or his flat address. Maybe she could turn up at his flat. Her heart began to pound and she looked down at Millicent. 'Am I mad to think of it or mad not to do it, cat?'

She had a sudden memory of Marni, determined to fight for her baby. Shoring herself up with positive actions. Stitching her quilt of love so that she would be ready when the good things happened. Ellie had done the opposite, undermined her own confidence with the past every time Sam broke through her barriers.

Stop it. Too late, it's over. She stroked the soft fur between Millicent's pointy ears.

She sat up straight. 'You know what, Milly? It's not over till the fat lady sings. I'll find him tomorrow and see if we can at least spend some time together.' She would try and, if it didn't work out, then she might just have to get a cat of her own. Maybe a kitten so she could have the full experience of being a mother. Yeah, right. Full experience.

The knock came in between two claps of thunder and she frowned at the improbability of visitors.

Then, there was Sam. Standing on the bottom step, his nose level with hers, his dark eyes staring into hers. 'Can I come in?' A flash of lighting illuminated them both and a nearby tree exploded into sparks. The explosion made her ears ring and she put out her hand to drag him in.

'Damn it, Sam. You could get killed standing out in that. You're mad.' Her heart was thumping at the closeness of the strike and the concept that again she could have got Sam killed by keeping him outside her house.

Then he was inside, the door was shut and they both stood there, panting, a few inches of air and a huge chasm between them.

He didn't seem perturbed about what had almost happened. He just said softly, 'You haven't closed the shutters again.'

She couldn't believe he was here. As if she'd conjured him. 'I know. It's not that windy. And you can't do it because it's too dangerous to go out in case the lightning gets you.' She licked her dry lips. 'Why are you here, Sam?'

He was staring down at her. She couldn't read the expression in his eyes but it was nothing like the one he'd left with today. It was warm, gentle and determined. 'Can I share the storm with you?'

Her cheeks were heating. He looked so good. Smelt so good. She knew he would feel so good. 'That would be nice,' she said carefully.

His brows rode up. 'Nice?' He put down his coat. 'It could be more than nice. Because I've decided to fight for you.'

This was all happening way too fast for her to erect the barriers she needed. Hang on—she didn't need barriers. Her brain was fogging. Softening. Revelling in the fact that Sam was here.

Sam said, 'I'm going to wear you down until you say yes.'

He wasn't gone. She hadn't ruined everything. Yet! Then his words sank in. 'Yes to what?'

'Will you marry me, Ellie? Be my wife. We'll work out the logistics—our work, your fears, my baggage. But driving away from you today and knowing I wasn't coming back was the loneliest thing I've ever done in my life, and I don't want to do it again. I love you.'

He loved her. 'Oh, Sam.' She loved him. Lord, she loved him so much. She lifted her head. She loved him too much to push him away for a second time. She would just have to break free from the past and be everything Sam needed. For the sake of both their futures. 'I love you too.'

He closed his eyes. 'It was too close, Ellie. We were too close to losing this.' Then he stepped in and picked her up. Hugged her to him and swung her around. And she laughed out loud. Sam's arms had her. They both were laughing and then he kissed her, and Ellie knew, at last, that she had found her 'for ever' family.

CHAPTER TWELVE

Sam stood waiting, his heart pounding as he watched for the first signs of the bridal car to descend the gravel road to the beach, and he appreciated the grounding effect of the cool sand under his bare feet as he waited for the warmth of the sun. But, more impatiently, he waited for the glowing warmth of the woman he would spend the rest of his life with. Where was Ellie?

The light touch of a hand on his arm broke into his thoughts and he turned with a smile to his father. He saw the old man's eyes were damp and shadowed with that memory of past sadness, yet glowing with pride too. Happy and sad at the same moment. Sam knew all about that. They both glanced at Sam's sister as she stood with her Italian friends, back on sabbatical to her old hospital while she attended her only brother's wedding.

His dad cleared his throat and said quietly, 'Your mother would have been so proud of you, son. So happy for you.'

Sam patted his shoulder. Felt the sinewy strength under his hand and was glad his dad was healed again.

'She'd be happy for you too. We've both been blessed twice with wonderful women.'

'I can see you love your Ellie, Sam.'

Sam felt his face relax, felt his mind expand with just thinking about her. Felt the joy surge up into his chest. Such elation. 'She's turned the world on for me, Dad. Ellie, this place, the future.' He shook his head, still unable to believe his grey life had been hit by a sunburst called Ellie Swift. Soon to be Mrs Southwell. 'I just wish she'd hurry up and arrive.'

The first rays of the sunrise struck the cliff in front of them at the exact moment an old-fashioned black saloon descended the steep slope and finally drew up at the place reserved for the bride in the crowded car park.

The whole town had come out in the dark to wait for the sunrise and for Ellie. The dapper chauffer, not resembling a prawn-trawler captain at all, opened the door onto a long blue roll of carpet that reached all the way across the sand to Sam.

He helped the two golden bridesmaids in their beautiful sheath dresses, Trina and Faith, and the stately Matron of Honour in a vintage gold dress, his dad's fiancée, Myra, and then Sam heard the hushed gasp from a town full of supporters as Ellie stepped out in a vision of white with her father's hand in hers.

Ellie had been shy about a veil, a white dress, the fact that she'd thought she was a bride before and had been mistaken, but Sam had taken her in his arms and told her his dream…of Ellie on the beach dressed as a bride. Sam had spoken quietly of the pureness of their love, the freshness of their commitment and his desire for her to feel the bride of her dreams—because their life together would be that dream.

And there she was, drifting towards him, the veil dancing at the sides of her face in the morning breeze, walking a little too quickly in her bare feet as she always did, her eyes on his, her smile wide and excited as she closed the gap between them. She came first, not after the bridesmaids, almost dragging her dad, and Sam was glad, because he could watch her close the gap between them all the way, and he barely saw the three smiling women behind her. He'd told them he wasn't talking to them anyway—they'd kept his Ellie at Myra's house last night sequestered away from him. They and her Aunty Dell, back from Western Australia for her only niece's wedding.

When Ellie stopped in front of him her eyes were glowing behind the fine material of the veil and he took her hand in his and felt the tension drain from his shoulders like an eddy rushing from a freshly filled rock pool. Ellie's dad released his daughter's hand, smiled wistfully and waved them on.

The sun chose that moment to break free of the ocean and bathed the whole wedding party in golden-pink rays as they rearranged themselves in front of the minister. The crowd drew closer, the waves pounded on the rocks by the cliff, Sam's hand tightened on Ellie's and the ceremony began, accompanied by the sound of the gulls overhead.

Afterwards the wedding breakfast was set out on white-cloth-covered tables on the long veranda of the surf club restaurant that looked out over the bay. The local

Country Women's Association ladies had whipped up a magnificent repast and Ellie's new husband kept catching her eye with such love, such devotion and pride, she constantly fought back happy tears which she refused to let free. Not now. Not today. She had never thought she could be this happy.

She touched the sleeve of his white tuxedo coat. 'Sam, let's take a minute to ourselves. Walk with me on the beach.' She watched his face soften, saw it glow with love and pride, and those blinking tears that had stung her eyes threatened again. She willed them away.

So they turned down the steps of the surf club, away from the revelries, and people parted smilingly and nudged each other. 'Let them go. Young lovers.'

Finally it was just Ellie and Sam walking along the beach, barefoot in the morning sunlight, Ellie's dress hitched over her arm, toes making fresh footprints in virgin sand, and every now and then the froth of the chuckling waves tickled their ankles.

'I love you, Sam.'

'I love you too, my wife.'

She hugged the words to herself and used them to make her brave. She had news and she wanted to share it but they hadn't had a moment together alone all morning.

'This morning…' she began, and felt the nerves well. Hoped desperately he would be glad. 'This morning, I did a test.'

His big, dark brows, those brows she loved and traced at night with her fingers, drew together. He didn't get it. 'And did you pass your test?'

'It was positive.'

She let the words hang suspended with the sound of the sea between them. Squeezed his hand in hers and waited. Felt his fingers still beneath hers.

'Pregnant?' His voice was almost a whisper.

Her heart squeezed and she nodded. 'Our baby. Just weeks in time, but it feels good. The feeling is right. Everything will be fine, Sam.' She stopped and turned to him, took his face in hers instead of the other way around. Felt the skin of his cheeks tense as he realised what she'd been trying to tell him 'My darling, everything will be perfect.'

His face stilled and then slowly, ever so slowly, he smiled. It rose from somewhere so deep inside him that she was blinded by the joy she had been so afraid would be missing, consumed instead by fear that what had happened to Bree would happen to her too.

He smiled, then he grinned, picked her up and swung her around as if she were a feather, and then he hugged her. Fiercely. Put her down. Glanced around and then picked her up again. Laughed out loud. Ellie was giddy with relief, giddy with swinging, giddy with Sam.

The only minor glitch would be the time she spent on maternity leave.

But Lighthouse Bay Mothers and Babies would be fine. Sam had taken the post of Director of Obstetrics at the base hospital an hour away and his father had become the permanent GP for Lighthouse Bay. Soon Ellie would have the midwifery service she dreamed of, because now she had a straight pathway of referral to a higher level of service if needed. She knew the obstetrician in charge—her new husband—very well, and he was extremely supportive. And in the wings was Trina, ready to come off night duty and take over when Ellie stepped down. And after her there was Faith, and then Roz, and other midwives waiting to be a part of the journey travelled by the midwives of Lighthouse Bay.

* * * * *

*If you enjoyed this story,
check out these other great reads
from Fiona McArthur*

*MIDWIFE'S MISTLETOE BABY
MIDWIFE'S CHRISTMAS PROPOSAL
CHRISTMAS WITH HER EX
GOLD COAST ANGELS: TWO TINY HEARTBEATS*

All available now!

MILLS & BOON®

MEDICAL ROMANCE™

THE ULTIMATE IN ROMANTIC MEDICAL DRAMA

A sneak peek at next month's titles...

In stores from 23rd March 2017:

Their One Night Baby – Carol Marinelli *and*
Forbidden to the Playboy Surgeon – Fiona Lowe

A Mother to Make a Family – Emily Forbes *and*
The Nurse's Baby Secret – Janice Lynn

The Boss Who Stole Her Heart – Jennifer Taylor *and*
Reunited by Their Pregnancy Surprise – Louisa Heaton

Just can't wait?
Buy our books online before they hit the shops!
www.millsandboon.co.uk

Also available as eBooks.

MILLS & BOON®

EXCLUSIVE EXTRACT

Dr. Dominic MacBride had no intention of falling in love—yet now he's fighting for paramedic Victoria Christie…and their surprise baby!

Read on for a sneak preview of
THEIR ONE NIGHT BABY

'You got your earring back.'

'They were a gift from my father.'

'That's nice,' Dominic said.

'Not really, it was just a duty gift when I turned eighteen. Had he bothered to get to know me, then he'd have known that I don't like diamonds.'

'Why not?'

'I don't believe in fairytales and I don't believe in for ever.'

There was, to Victoria's mind, no such thing.

She held her breath as his fingers came to her cheek and lightly brushed the lobe as he examined the stone.

If it were anyone else she would have pushed his hand away.

Anyone else.

Yet she provoked.

'It was the other earring that I lost.'

And he turned her face and his hands went to the other.

This was foolish, both knew.

Neither wanted to get close to someone they had to

work alongside but the attraction between them was intense.

Both knew the reason for their rows and terse exchanges; it was physical attraction at its most raw.

'Victoria, I'm in no position to get involved with anyone.'

They were standing looking at each other and his hands were on her cheeks and his fingers were warm on her ears. There was a thrum between them and she knew he was telling her they would go nowhere.

'That's okay.'

And that *was* okay.

'If you don't like diamonds, then what do you like?' he asked. His mouth was so close to hers and though it was cold she could feel the heat in the space between them.

'This.'

Their mouths met and she felt the warm, light pressure and it felt blissful.

Don't miss
THEIR ONE NIGHT BABY
By Carol Marinelli

Available April 2017
www.millsandboon.co.uk

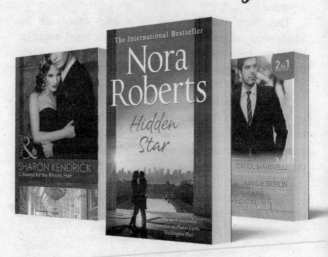